POWERFUL PURPLES

ZADOK SERIES BOOK #3

NIKKI MINTY

The Zadok Series

INDICREATES

ACKNOWLEDGEMENTS

I would like to thank my son RJ for helping form the concept for this novel, and my daughter Lyla and brother Trey, for their creative input.

To my partner Kieran, mother Carrie, grandfather Handel and friend Cheryl, thanks for being my loyal beta readers.

Many thanks to Indiana Maria Acosta Hernandez at Indicreates, for creating such glorious, eye catching covers.

And last but certainly not least, I would like to give a big shout out to my editors Amy Cissell and Christopher Barnes at Cissell Ink, for helping to improve, tighten and smooth out the wrinkles in my story. You have been extremely hands-on and helpful throughout the editing process.

To all my other friends and family members who have given me constant encouragement and support during the writing process, I appreciate the love.

Those of you in the reading/writing community who read, enjoyed, and reviewed Pastel Pink and Ruby Red, thank you, I'm extremely grateful.

IN LOVING MEMORY OF FAU SIAFOLAU

1982-1998

My high school sweetheart who left this world too early. You'll be forever in our hearts

SUMMER

Extremely hot, barren and two thirds desert. The Royals live in a castle protected by guards, while the rest of the Vallons reside as citizens in the kingdom.

Leader of Summer: *Queen Sjaan*

Race: *Vallon (Power of heat and fire)*

Skin colour: *Black/dark chocolate*

Hair and eye colours: *Red, Orange, and Amber (the colour of the irises continually swirl like molten lava)*

Language: *Similar to German*

Facts: *Vallons are the strongest race and have magical, glowing vertic switz tattoos*

AUTUMN

Very windy, but self-sufficient land. Rukes live by a waterfall.

Leader of Autumn: *Chief Waya*

Race: *Rukes (Power of air and wind)*

Skin colour: *Grey and white (marble effect)*

Hair colour: *Black*

Eye colour: *Blue, Aqua, Teal*

Language: *Similar to Iroquoian*

Fact: *Rukes have wings*

WINTER

Extremely cold, and the only land on Zadok with an ocean. Zeeks live inside the ice caves.

Leader of Winter: *Commander Azazel*

Race: *Zeeks (Power of water and ice)*

Skin colour: *White/white chocolate (with a shimmer that matches the Zeek's hair and eye colour)*

Hair and eye colours: *Purple, Magenta, and Pastel Pink*

Language: *Similar to English*

Facts: *Zeeks are the smallest race on Zadok. Pastel Zeeks are weak with poor eyesight and a short life expectancy*

SPRING

A comfortable climate, mostly forest with a crystal-clear lake near the village. Drakes reside in huts and treehouses in the deep of the forest.

Leader of Spring: *Chief Dakari*

Race: *Drakes (Power of the land)*

Skin colour: *Brown/milk chocolate (with a shimmer that matches the Drake's hair and eye colour)*

Hair and eye colours: *Green, Yellow, and Hazel*

Language: *Similar to Afrikaans*

Fact: *Drakes are the tallest race on Zadok.*

WEEKEND MARKETS
-ALEX AS SLATER-

(Saturday morning)

The sun's rays beat down warm on my back as I walk through the crowded markets. I hate the weekend markets; they're hot, congested, and reek of drying animal carcasses hung at the butcher stalls. Raven loves them. Back when we were dating, she'd drive me mental, stopping at every single stall to touch and ask questions about items we had *absolutely* no intention of buying. I quickly got sick of this weekly routine and informed her that the markets were somewhere she should drag her friends to, not her boyfriend.

I'm hoping I don't see her here today, especially as I am here to buy clothes for Ruby. After spending the first few days living in the same outfit she'd arrived in, Ruby finally succumbed to using the t-shirt I'd laid out for her on day two. I'd chuckled when I saw her in it, looking like a mobile tent. Her face turned red, and she folded her arms self-consciously, making me regret my outburst.

"I'm sorry," I'd said, wiping the smile off my face. "I'll grab you some clothes from the markets this weekend."

I would've prebought her a bunch of clothes, only I'd thought she'd be coming packed and ready.

Despite agreeing to wipe the slate clean and start afresh, she's still been frosty towards me. I know I did the wrong thing by taking off on her, but I've apologised a dozen times over. *Why can't she just let it go so we can move forward?*

The name *Jax* springs to mind, and I try desperately to push it aside. Every time I think about the little love letters I found, my blood boils. *That snake.* I can't believe I let him talk me into leaving Ruby with him for a whole month, particularly when I knew full well he had feelings for her. I was a fool to agree to it, and to believe Ruby would stay true to me even though we weren't "technically" together.

For some idiotic reason, I assumed she was still as in love with me as I was with her. She's the one who'd instigated taking our relationship to the next level, and from what I've learnt, most girls don't take sex lightly. I'd imagined she would've been keen to make things work between us, especially after hearing she was pregnant with our children.

My face burns hot with jealousy, and I grit my teeth.

I wish I could push away the image of Ruby lying in Jax's arms for the night—assuming she's telling the truth and that *is* all that happened. It's messing with my head.

You have no right to be jealous, you slept with Raven, my inner voice taunts.

What happened between Raven and me was purely physical and meant nothing, I argue with myself. *Ruby and Jax have connected on an emotional level. That's far worse!*

My heart squeezes painfully. Despite the whole Jax debacle, I'm still in love with her, and I'm terrified that once the month is up, she's going to leave me for him. I've only got a small window of opportunity to win back her heart, and I'm not confident I'll succeed. I get the feeling she hates me. She can't even bring herself to look at me.

A colourful rack of women's dresses catch my eye, and I stop to flick through them. There are a few I like, but they all look way too big for Ruby. Vallon women are tall with accentuated curves and broad shoulders. Ruby might be much curvier than she once was, with a baby bump, but she's still a Zeek, and Zeek women have much smaller builds than Vallon women.

I force myself to step over to the girls' section. I feel like a creep flicking through girls' dresses, but the teen sizes look like they'll be a much better fit.

I pick out a handful of the ones which look as if they'll fit over her baby bump and then head to the underwear section to grab the sexiest panties I can find. I might not get to see her in them, but at least if I know what they look like, I can imagine her in them.

I finish trading for my purchases and leave, only to run—smack bang—into Jacinta and Kenneth.

Damn it! Why? I had a gut feeling something like this would happen, only I'd imagined it'd be Raven who busted me dress shopping.

They eye the colourful clothes in my hands with equally perplexed expressions.

Kenneth's brows shoot downwards, and he clears his throat. "What's with all the dresses, Slate?"

Sweat drips down my temples in stress. Jacinta will know these aren't for Raven, and there's no way I want them finding out the truth. Going with the first thing that pops into my head, I say, "I like to do a little cross-dressing on the weekends. What's it to you?"

He snorts at my reply. "You'd be lucky to fit those tiny dresses on your arms."

I shrug off his comment. "Yeah, well where I like to put them is my business."

"Those look like young girls' dresses," Jacinta points out, her face registering disgust. "Is there something you should be telling us, Slate?"

It sickens me to imagine what's ticking over in their minds right now. I'd much rather they believe I'm a cross dresser than a pervy paedophile, but there's no use in defending myself when I can't admit the truth. *It's too dangerous.*

"Stay out of my business," I growl. "I don't go poking my nose in either of your personal lives, so don't go poking your nose in mine. What I do behind closed doors is my business."

FIRST KICKS

-HARLOW-

*A*lex arrives back from the markets absolutely dripping in sweat. I keep my distance as he kicks the door shut behind him with a grunt. He seems tense and irritable, which is not a good sign. Before leaving, he'd made a point of mentioning how much he hates the markets, but added, he was prepared to go for me, because *that's* how much he loves me. *Talk about a guilt trip.*

A few days ago, he'd asked if we could wipe the slate clean and start afresh, but somehow this must have excluded making small digs about Jax, because he hasn't let up on the topic ever since.

He'd also asked if I would stay here for the rest of my pregnancy to give our relationship a fighting chance. Despite the hurt and anger bubbling between us, I'd agreed to stay. A part of me still cares about Alex, and I'd felt too guilty to abandon him right away, especially while I'm carrying his children. I didn't have the heart to say, "I'm in love with Jax. Please, take me back to the forest."

Alex hasn't put much thought into the reality of our future. I don't think he realises exactly what he's asking me to sacrifice. He's too busy worrying about his own wants and needs to appreciate the bigger picture. He says he loves me and can't imagine his life without me, but I'm beginning to wonder if I'm more of an obsession and possession to him than someone he truly loves with all his heart. After all, he hasn't seemed to notice that I'm lonely and miserable in Summer, or that I feel like a prisoner locked in his chamber.

He dumps a pile of clothing onto the bed. "I tried to go for dresses that will fit over your bump."

"Thank you."

That's the thing about Alex, he gives you whiplash. Sometimes he can be super sweet and considerate, yet other times he'll show no consideration at all. It's like there are two of him, and they're the mirror reverse of each other, Dr Jekyll and Mr Hyde.

He sucks in a breath and wipes the sweat from his brow with the back of his hand. "It's nearing the 50C mark out there today. I'm going to have a quick wash, okay?"

Is he asking my permission? I nod, confused. "Okay."

I'm suffering in this blistering heat too, swimming in one of his oversized t-shirts. I was actually surprised to discover he owned so many t-shirts, considering I've never seen him in one.

As soon as Alex leaves for the washroom, I step over to the bed to pick through the rainbow pile of clothes. I'm guessing Alex is a big fan of bright colours. Beneath the dresses I discover underwear —*or should I say lingerie.* I blush. He definitely didn't buy these little numbers with comfort in mind. *Far out!* If he's planning on seeing me in these, he's up for disappointment. *That's definitely not going to happen!*

I might have agreed to stay with him until the babies are born—out of guilt—but my heart still longs for Jax.

I continue to rummage through the clothes, looking for pyjamas; it seems he forgot about those. *Oh well*, it looks like I'll be wearing his t-shirt to bed. It's probably for the best anyway, better to keep myself fully covered; I can only imagine the types of nighties he would have bought me if he'd thought of it.

After Alex has finished in the washroom, I take my turn. The water feels refreshing and cool on my dry, chafing Zeek skin. I pat myself dry, then squeeze into one of the dresses. It's a lemon-yellow halter neck which stops just above my knees, leaving room around the mid-section.

I take a few moments to glance at my reflection, and my cheeks heat with embarrassment. I'm not used to showing this much skin.

Alex is sitting on the button tufted chesterfield sofa when I step out, and I catch him looking me up and down with delight. A couple of months ago, I would have lapped up his interest, but now I want to beg him to look away.

"You look nice. The dress fits you well." He pats the spot on the sofa next to him, his lips tugging up at the corners in an attempted smile. "Why don't we have a proper catch up. I want to know what's been happening with you these past couple of months."

My thoughts tumble all over themselves as I walk to the sofa. He appears to be trying, and while I'm glad to see him putting in a genuine effort, I'm worried about what comes next. It would be nice if we could get along—but just as friends.

"Do you have any other plans for today?" I ask, praying he does.

I'm afraid of spending the entire weekend with him. It's a lot of time alone together, and a lot can happen; a lot can be said. I don't want to make enemies, but I also don't want to rekindle things, which leaves us in a very precarious position.

"No, no plans. I want to spend proper quality time with you." There's a despondent ache in his eyes. "We said we were going to work on our friendship, but things still feel frosty between us. We barely speak, and when we do, it ends in a squabble. I know you resent me, and you're well within your rights to. I've said and done stupid things, but I mean it this time when I say, I'm going to try to be better. I really want us to be friends again."

"I want that too."

I feel uncomfortable sitting next to him, especially in a skimpy dress, but I force my jittery feelings aside and try to relax into the cushioned backrest.

My body quickly tenses up again, as he fires off a string of questions like—why did Jax take me to the forest and who did I stay with? Did I get to see the Drake village, and if so, what was it like?

He'd asked me about the Drake village once before. I'd flat out told him that I didn't know if I could trust him, and to my relief, the topic was dropped. This time I offer breadcrumbs, tripping over my answers, unsure what to reveal. I'm concerned about sharing too much information with him. If it becomes widely known that the Drakes are allowing a Ruke and a bunch of Zeeks to seek refuge in their village, it could cause an uproar with the other races.

Alex frowns. "What's going on? You're acting weird."

"A lot's changed," I say, fiddling with the hem of my dress. "And I still don't know if I can trust you to keep my secrets."

His spine straightens, and his eyes spark with annoyance, but instead of snapping like he has been, he takes a deep breath and says, "Oh, come on, Rubes, try to have a little faith in me—please. I'm still the same Alex."

Only you're not, I think.

"I'm really not as horrible and untrustworthy as you seem to think I am," he continues. "I know I have a temper, and I've accidentally scared you a few times, but I'm working on it—can't you tell? I've been very calm this morning." His eyes slit. "Even at the mention of Jax's name."

He does appear to be currently keeping his cool, I'll give him that.

I fold and confide extra snippets of information. I'd love to divulge more and tell him that there's another mixed-race baby in the Drake village who our children could have grown up with if I'd stayed, but regardless of whether I honestly trust him or not, I hold my tongue. I don't know what would happen to Stavros, Acacia, and

Atohi if their mixed-race family were discovered by the other races. The Drakes are far more peaceful and accommodating than others, and I don't want war brought to their land.

"I'm surprised the Drakes accepted you, looking like you do." Alex's eyes trace my hair. "You might not be a Vallon, but you are definitely a Red."

"I wouldn't say I was a hundred percent accepted," I admit. "But they tolerated me, unlike my own race. I had to meet with Chief Dakari in the flesh before he would agree to hide me in his village. He made his opinion of the Vallon race known and warned that if I was ever to pose a threat to his tribe, I would be banished."

We speak about the Drakes for a while and Alex tells me how the Vallons have a tenuous alliance with them. He says, besides the fruit pickers, who are allowed to enter the first couple of metres of the Spring border under strict supervision of the Queen's guards, he, Kenneth and the Queen's guards are the only ones permitted to enter deep within the forest, and it must be during the evening hours, when the region is Zeek free.

"Is this why you're a hunter?" I ask.

I had wondered why someone as high up the ladder as a prince would become a hunter. Not that Alex strikes me as your typical Prince type. He's never properly dressed or tied up by obligations. Being the Commander's son, Jax was always in his warrior attire and under the whip with duties, yet somehow, Alex seems to run his own show.

He says that to be a hunter is seen as a royal honour, but I don't see honour in it. I think it's heartbreaking. I could never do it.

As human Ruby, I was always suspicious of people who weren't animal lovers, or people that my dog disliked. This is another red flag I'd ignored when starting up a relationship with Alex. He is a hunter, and animals don't like him.

My thoughts wander to Jax again, and I feel a sharp pinch inside my chest. I love how close he is to Sphinx. Their close bond is beautiful, and I believe it says a lot about his character.

As the morning passes, Alex continues filling me in on the ins and outs of Summer. I learn that they don't have warriors here, only guards, and to be a guard you must be a Red. He says he used to have a few Red friends growing up, but as soon as they became a part of the Queen's guard, he quit talking to them.

"I hate the guards," he continues. "Especially the foot guards. They think they're above the law—and in a way they are. My mother encourages them to be ruthless and allows them to treat the slaves however they please. I've had many brawls with the guards over their treatment of the Pastels. I've even watched as two injected Pastels killed a guard without stepping in to stop them. I told them that 'The piece of shit got what he deserved', then I turned a blind eye while they escaped."

This sparks my curiosity. I wonder if he's talking about Luna and Destiny? Stavros never mentioned anything about a Vallon allowing them to escape.

Alex makes it clear that he detests his brother Kenneth, saying, "He's as cruel and ruthless as the guards."

I find this strange, considering he still really loved Lucas right up until the very end. Talk about setting double standards for his two brothers.

"Your sister Floss is nothing like I'd imagined," he says. "I'm surprised you didn't tell me you two were twins. It would've been useful information a month ago."

"What do you mean?"

He's in the middle of telling me how he'd accidentally mistaken Floss for me, when suddenly, I feel a kick inside and jerk upright.

My hands clutch my tummy. "Alex!"

His eyes flare wide. "What is it? What's wrong?"

Another two kicks follow and this time my hand feels it as well. "They're kicking."

"They are?" His alarmed expression transforms into excitement, and he automatically reaches out for my tummy, but his hand stops short abruptly, and his face falls.

I frown. "What's wrong?"

"You just flinched away from me, like I'm some kind of monster."

Had I? It must've been an instinctive reaction. The hurt and disappointment in his eyes stab at my heart.

"I don't think you're a monster, Alex." I take hold of his hand and close the gap, bringing it to my tummy. I might not want to rekindle a relationship with him, but these babies are his too, and he has a right to share this moment.

Another few kicks follow simultaneously, and tears form in the corners of Alex's eyes. "This is really happening," he says. "I'm going to be a dad."

3

ANTICIPATION

-ZAVIER-

(Saturday morning)

Minty kneels on my mattress, nudges my side softly, and whispers, "What time do you think the linking ceremony will begin? Do you think it's started already?"

I'm snuggling Floss, daydreaming of faraway places, but I leave my blissful fantasy world to roll over and face her. "I have no idea. You should ask Zannah."

Her eyes flick to where Zannah stands, leaning against the back cell wall, wearing her usual resting-bitch-face we've come to know rather well since being locked in this cell these past three weeks.

"She doesn't look like she wants to be disturbed." Minty observes. "It's not overly important, anyway. I'm simply curious how much longer we have to live." Her sarcastic tone has a slight quiver to it.

Our features are rosy, and our physiques remain changed for the better. Minty is around the same size as Floss now, and her sight has improved to the point where she no longer needs glasses—which is a good thing—given the lenses were smashed to smithereens during our torture session. We also seem to have healed much faster than is physically possible. My right shin is mildly sore, and around my ribcage is tender, but I'm no longer in constant agony.

My hand closes over my half of the leather-bound magic rock Harlow had given me as a friendship necklace. How it stayed intact during the torture session, I'll never know. I fiddle with it, watching it sparkle softly under the dim light of the overhead zofts. *I wonder how Harlow is; if she's still alive?*

I know she's already left for Summer, because Jax came down to tell me. It was a decent move on his part, considering we're not exactly friends, and I've never shown him the proper respect he deserves given his commanding title. Not to mention he's saved my life twice without thanks. On the contrary, the first time I had the audacity to throw it back in his face. I grimace with guilt. *I've been a total arse.*

When I'd caught sight of his blood smeared neck, I'd freaked, fearing the worst. "What happened?"

"It wasn't an easy handover." His purple eyes appeared darker than usual, and his head hung heavy with regret. "Things turned violent rather quickly and Harlow agreed to go with Slater to protect me. I tried to persuade her to stay, but she stuck to her decision and wouldn't listen." His Adam's apple bobbed. "She avoided looking at me the entire time and then left for Summer with him, without even saying goodbye."

This struck me as odd, and I'd pushed for more details, but Feeney had wandered over, putting an end to our conversation.

"No conspiring with the prisoners," he'd warned, cutting Jax a hateful glare.

I let go of the rock, allowing it to fall back to my chest. It seems I was wrong about Jax. He is far more honourable than I'd first given him credit for. I've also come to realise that his feelings for Harlow are sincere. She means more to him than a pretty face. It was written in his expression the day he came to see me. He was heart-broken about losing her.

It's easier to accept this now that I'm in a relationship with Floss. While I'll always have a soft spot for Harlow, my feelings for Floss are growing by the day. She can be bratty and downright infuriating, but she also has a sweet, affectionate side that makes me feel loved and desired.

It's past midday, and she's still sound asleep. I don't know how she manages it, especially with one of Nix's cronies watching over us. I struggle to let my guard down.

Floss' bruises have faded completely, but she still bears a few discoloured marks from ice burns, and the cut on her lower lips re-splits whenever she speaks or smiles. None of this detracts from her beauty though, especially when she's sleeping. She looks serene and angelic, a far cry from her true personality.

I slide my arm around her, and I'm about to lower my head onto the pillow alongside hers when two strange whooshing sounds, followed by a cry of pain, startle me upright. I jump up from my mattress, my defences on high alert. Floss and Minty shoot up too, one on each side of me, and we all spin to the back wall.

"What the…!" Floss' legs are wobbly like spaghetti, and her eyes are glazed over from sleep.

My initial thought is, *it's time, we're dead! Austin is shooting shards at us.* But then Austin tumbles backwards, his skull hitting the stone floor with a loud crack, and my momentary confusion is instantly transformed into tremendous satisfaction. Blood spills from his chest onto his shirt, and after two dazed blinks, his eyes roll back into his head. *He's dead.* My gaze shifts from Austin to Zannah. I stare wide-eyed in disbelief. Her arm is raised, glowing bright purple with winter magic. *She killed him.*

If only his death had been prolonged and painful. I would have rather enjoyed watching him squirm in agony.

"The ceremony's starting in twenty minutes, it's time to move," Zannah says matter-of-factly, and then walks over to Austin's fallen body to fish through his pockets.

Before my brain is even able to process what she's said, a familiar voice calls, "Minty."

We turn in surprise and Minty gasps. "Tatum? Tatum…" she says shakily—almost hysterically, as she races to the wall to peek out through one of the larger gaps. "You're here, you're really here. But you shouldn't be, it's too dangerous. Especially today."

There's a jingle as Zannah pulls a set of keys out of Austin's pocket. "We're here to bust you lot out. Now if you could all help me move Austin's body onto the mattress, that would be fantastic."

Thrilled by the prospect of freedom, we eagerly oblige. There's a slight stabbing sensation underneath my ribcage as I help to lift Austin's limp body, but between the four of us taking a limb each, we manage to haul him across to the end mattress without dropping him.

"Cover him up," Zannah orders, as she heads to the cell door. "And make sure there's no blood or purple hair showing."

While I follow orders and grab the blankets, Floss boots into Austin's body with wild aggression.

"Floss, what are you doing?"

Without answering, she drops to her knees and pounds her fists against his chest.

I rush back. "Stop!" I say. "He's dead."

Floss doesn't listen; she keeps smashing into him like a mad woman, causing blood to spray all over her.

I drop the blankets and grab her from behind. "Floss, stop!" My arms wrap tightly around her, drawing her in close. "Stop. He's dead. You're wasting your energy, and we've got a job to do."

Her body shakes violently under my arms. "He had it too easy."

"I know," I agree. "But at least he didn't get away scot-free." I keep hold of her, willing my words to sink in, before adding, "Take a deep breath, forget about him, and look around. Zannah and Tatum are trying to break us out, so let's work with them, okay?" I release my grasp and slip my jumper off. "Here." I hand it to her. "Wipe your face and hands. You've managed to get Austin's blood all over you." I turn to Minty. "Can you please help me with the blankets? I don't want Floss smearing blood on them."

Zannah tries several keys on the cell door until eventually it clicks open with a screech. "Hurry," she says.

Tatum is waiting on the other side, face anxious, and she has a pack resting on each shoulder. Minty eagerly rushes past us to embrace her with a hug and a kiss.

"Save your catch-up time for later," Zannah says sharply, and they promptly pull apart.

Zannah puts her hand out to Tatum, who passes her one of the packs. She unzips it and tosses a jumper and beanie to each of us. "You lot need to cover up." She glances pointedly at Minty and me. "Especially you two. Keep your heads down and your hair and faces hidden. Move fast, don't veer off course, and don't stop to talk to anyone. Just follow Tatum silently all the way to the hunting cavern, got it?"

"What about you?" I ask. "Aren't you coming with us?"

"No." There's a dangerous gleam in her eyes. "My fun is only just beginning."

While we help to get each other's beanies in place by tucking in any loose wisps of hair, another warrior appears. Oscar is the most approachable of Jax's inner circle, as I've come to discover in recent weeks.

He's wheeling a large trolley with an ice sculpture on top. The sculpture is a disturbing depiction of Jax and Electra standing arm in arm.

Floss screws her nose up. "Ewww!"

"Are you ready, Lovely?" Oscar asks, flashing Zannah a mocking grin.

She glares at him. "I can't wait," she bites back. "I've been dreaming about this day, my whole life."

He lifts the lid, and I panic for a second, raising my hand to stop him. I'd pictured the sculpture falling to the floor with a crash, but to my surprise, nothing happens.

Oscar gives a mischievous chuckle. "It's frosted glass, not ice, and it's been glued down for show."

"Huh…" My hand drops back to my side. They've obviously got big plans in place for the ceremony. *I wonder what? If only I could stick around to watch.*

"You lot need to get moving, right now!" Zannah says, and then hops inside the trolley in one fluid movement. "And remember no stopping for anyone, not even family members."

Tatum shoulders one of the packs and hands the other to Minty before heading out into the passage.

Following orders, we keep our heads down and hurry as best we can, while trying not to arouse suspicion. The only Zeeks we pass in the passageways are those wheeling trollies with linking ceremony supplies. Fortunately, they're all too preoccupied with their tasks at hand to notice anything unusual. I sigh a shaky breath with each Zeek we pass. It turns out today is a good day for us to make our escape.

My thrumming heart steadies as we make it inside the hunting cavern without any mishaps. There are huskens hooked up to the hunting sled, and I'm quick to notice one of them is Lucy. As soon as Minty realises this, she calls her name, prompting Lucy to thrash her tail around excitedly.

"There's no time for pats, Minty. Quick." Tatum rushes to the front bench seat and we all hurriedly tumble in after her.

"Do you even know how to drive a hunting sled?" I ask.

"Mush," she calls, and the huskens pull forward. "Yes, Zannah taught me. This plan has been set in place since day one. After Jax agreed to linking with Electra, he fetched me from work, introduced me to Zannah and Oscar, and asked if I was prepared to be a part of your escape plan at the cost of saying goodbye to my family and my life in the caves." She pulls a lever as we pass it, then gazes at Minty adoringly while we wait for the portcullis to rise. "Of course, I said yes."

A chilly, snow filled wind hits our faces as soon as the sled exits the caves. I shiver. It feels weird to be outside. I've only been outside the caves once, back when I was seven. The day of my parents' funeral. To my disappointment, it had been a group funeral. All forty-nine Pastels who'd died in the sewing factory cavern were taken out on the boat together and addressed as a group during the ceremony. It made sense, but I'd resented it. It'd felt cold and impersonal. Harlow hadn't been allowed to come with me either, which was an even bigger blow. Guests were restricted to "family members only" because of numbers.

Floss leans forward, gripping my hand eagerly. "Where are we going?" she asks. Her palm feels sticky with the residue of Austin's blood.

"To the forest," Tatum answers. "Jax has Drakes meeting us there."

"Drakes?" Floss and I repeat, glancing at one another in mirrored astonishment.

"Yes. He says they will take us somewhere safe."

After passing the Spring border and travelling several metres in, Tatum calls for the huskens to halt. The whipping wind and icy snow of Winter has left my cheeks red-raw, but they're slowly thawing with the change of environment. I can't believe the dramatic temperature difference between Winter and Spring. I've never felt this kind of warmth.

I gaze upwards, my mouth forming an O. I've seen drawings of the Spring forest, but I hadn't imagined the trees would be *this* enormous. Even the protruding roots are huge—wider than I am tall! Minty gazes about gape-mouthed too, and when our eyes meet, we grin. Minty's in the same boat as I am. Besides attending her grandmother's funeral, she's spent her whole life locked in the caves. The more I think about it, the more I realise we've been prisoners from the get-go. The caves have been our prison since birth.

I gaze at Floss. She leans against the sled, yawning.

"I can't believe you and Harlow got to come here every weekday to pick fruit," I say, a hint of envy lacing my voice. "It's so—"

"Boring," she supplies, sounding completely unenthused.

"Boring?" I shake my head in disbelief. "How can you say that?"

A nearby crunching sound steals my attention, and I look up to see two extremely tall green Drakes emerging from behind one of the enormous trees. I back up a step at the sheer height of them. I've read Drakes were tall, but again, I'm left flabbergasted by the difference between my imagination verses reality. The man would have to be nearing nine feet.

"I am Sonja, and this is my brother Woody," the Drake woman says—or at least, I'm pretty sure it's what she says.

"Unhook the huskens," Woody tells Tatum and Minty with an accent even thicker than Sonja's. "My father has agreed for them to come."

Does this mean we're staying with them? I wonder if they're who Harlow stayed with? I would ask, but I'm not sure I'll understand the answer, especially if Woody replies.

While Minty and Tatum unhook a husken each, Sonja and Woody give Floss and me an inquisitive look-over. They exchange a few words in their language and then Woody laughs. I can tell Floss is bugged about this, because her hands fly to her hips, and she scowls in their direction. The Drakes can say whatever they want as far as I'm concerned. I'm still counting my lucky stars I'm alive.

The huskens bound over to the Drakes in excitement. "Let's move," Sonja says. "We have a twelve kilometre walk ahead of us."

My high dims a fraction, and I groan internally. I don't know that my shin can take the punishment of a twelve kilometre walk.

I walk hand in hand with Floss for the first part, pointing and gushing at the scenery, only to have her shrug off my amazement, like I'm getting excited over nothing. Deflated by her lack of enthusiasm, I drop back to walk with Minty and the mutts. Floss pouts about being dumped on—even though she deserves it—and Tatum, The Peacemaker, speeds up to join her. Minty is as cheery as I am about being led through the forest to a new location, and it's nice to be able to share this life-changing moment with her. Most of the experiences we've shared of late have been horrendous, to say the least.

"I thought for sure I was going to die today," Minty admits. "But instead, I've got my favourites with me, and we're heading into the glorious unknown. Can you believe it? I've never felt so alive or free."

I smile, feeling the exact same way, only I really wish Harlow were here too. Not as my girlfriend, but as my best friend. She's much easier to bounce off than Floss, and a hell of a lot more enthusiastic.

"I wish Floss would share some of our excitement. She says she's sick of the forest. It reminds her of work."

Minty casts me a sympathetic look. "Well, we all know how much Floss loves going to work. She was quite vocal about it, even to Jax."

We exchange glances and chuckle. "She and I both managed to rile Jax up to the breaking point that day, didn't we?" I say. "I thought for sure he was going to hit me."

"If I wasn't there to mediate, I'm certain he would have. And to be honest, you would have deserved it. You were being an arse."

I wave off her comment. "I know, I know. After all the cheek I've given him these past few months, it's a miracle he went out of his way to save us."

"I think it was done more for Harlow than for us, but whatever the reason, we're out and we're alive."

Floss' attitude perks up further down the track, when according to her, we have entered the danger zone.

I can easily see why this area is classified as the danger zone. It's much darker and denser than the light filtered area we'd just come from. It's pretty though, and I catch sight of several luminous creatures in different shapes, colours and sizes. Some have wings and flutter through the trees while others have scales and lurk behind tree roots.

One of the scaly creatures decides we're not a threat and follows closely, ducking in and out of the trees like it's a game. Woody points it out and laughs, referring to it as a tozik.

It scurries in front of Floss and then freezes, staring up at her with its big reflective eyes. "Zavier," she squeals excitedly, and beckons for me to join her. "Quick, come check this thing out."

I pick up the pace and Minty follows. "Its colours are wild."

While its colouring might be cool, it has a spikey neck and a long-forked tongue, which it flicks in our direction continually, creeping me out.

Floss gets overcurious and reaches to touch it.

"Floss, don't." Minty smacks her hand away just in time. "Are you insane? That thing might bite you, and who knows if it's poisonous or not."

"Relax Minty. You're always such a bossy killjoy."

"I am not! I'm just being protective."

Floss rolls her eyes.

"You know what… FORGET IT! Next time I'll keep my mouth shut and watch as the creature bites you."

I zip my lips, not willing to get on the bad side of either of them. Minty is right, Floss is rash and insane, but Floss has a point too. Minty is, by far, the bossiest Zeek I know.

"Your bossy friend is right," Sonja calls from up the front. "If you're attached to your fingers, you should really keep your hands to yourself."

My shin is burning and about ready to give up on me when a fenced village comes into view. Through the gaps of the pointed fence, I see huts of all shapes and sizes, and overhead, woven between the tree trunks, are hundreds of small wooden houses, connected by a network of suspension bridges which are lit up by natural fairy lights.

Wows and gasps echo from Minty and Tatum.

Floss entwines her fingers with mine, crushing them excitedly. "This is incredible," she says, sounding genuinely impressed. "I certainly wasn't expecting the Drake village to look this magical and inviting." Her smile widens. "This might not be such a bad move after all."

There are two yellow Drakes guarding the front of the village, with two extremely skinny but muscular looking guard-hounds. Sonja and Woody say a few quick words to these men in their language, and then they lead us through the village like a spectacle.

"I can't believe how ridiculously tall all the Drakes are," Floss whispers in my ear as we continue to follow. "Or how little they're all wearing."

The Drakes seem as curious about us as we are about them, and blatantly ogle us as we pass. One of the Hazels points to Floss and mutters something to the Yellow standing beside him. Floss doesn't like this and shoots him a dirty look.

"Ease up, Floss," I say, giving her hand a light squeeze. "Chances are he's comparing you to Harlow. Minus the colour difference, you two look very much alike."

Her face glows red, and I instantly regret my choice of words. "I hate being compared to Harlow! And besides we don't know this for sure because we don't speak their language."

"True… But we are the foreigners here, and we don't want to make enemies, so no more dirty looks, okay?"

Sonja and Woody lead us to a large hut, and we all gasp in amazement yet again, as a Ruke flutters off the deck to greet us.

"WOW, look at her wings. She's absolutely beautiful," Floss gushes in awe.

She is most definitely striking. Her wings are lush and full, and her skin is white and grey veined with a purple shimmer. I wasn't aware Rukes shimmered purple, nor did I know they could have purple eyes. I was taught that their eyes ranged in blues, aquas, and teals. *Weird.*

To think, I've been led to the Drake village by a set of tall Greens, and now I'm meeting a Ruke. A purple Ruke. Today is certainly a big day of firsts for me.

"I'm Acacia," the Ruke says, glancing between the four of us. She has an accent too, although it's not the same, nor is it as strong as the Drakes. Her eyes settle on Floss'. "I take it you're Floss, Harlow's twin."

Surprisingly, Floss seems too awestruck to speak.

"I'm Zavier," I offer, breaking the awkwardness.

Acacia smiles widely. "Yes, I figured. Harlow has told me all about you. It sounds like you were very close."

Floss bristles at her comment.

"And this is Minty and Tatum," I add, gesturing to them both.

Acacia nods, a friendly smile stretching across her lips. "I've heard about you pair too. It's lovely to finally meet you all." She turns to Sonja and Woody. "Thank you for fetching them. That was very kind."

"Enige tyd," Sonja says, and then she and Woody leave.

"You all look hot and thirsty," Acacia says. "Why don't you come inside? I'll fetch some drinks and let you know what's going to happen from here on in."

4

LINKING CEREMONY

-ZANNAH-

(Earlier)

Blood hammers through my veins with a pounding sensation that echoes inside my ears as Oscar closes the trolley lid. The day of reckoning is finally upon us, and my body is surging with adrenaline.

A black unisuit has been placed inside the trolley for me to slip into before we get to the celebrations chamber, along with a full-face mask. It's a struggle to change given the confined space, darkness, and bumpiness of the ride, but somehow, I manage to get into the skin-tight suit with time to spare. The mask has fine mesh sewn in for the eyes and mouth holes. It's itchy, but it's easy to see through and will hide the colour of my irises from questioning onlookers.

There's a small hole in the front of the trolley for me to peek out of, and I use it. Frustration fills me. Oscar is wheeling this thing slower than a grandma with two bad hips. I feel like yelling at him to "HURRY UP", only I can't. Oscar needs to be standing next to Jax when the ceremony begins. *It's vital.* Jax must be protected at all costs.

We get to a set of stairs and Oscar rolls the trolley onto the pulley, which has been setup specifically for today's big event. There's a click as he locks the wheels securely into place. It's lucky that I'm a fundamental part of today's plan, or he'd probably leave the breaks off just for the fun of it. Last week, he hid my good blade and replaced it with a cardboard cut-out of a tongue that read, "Your tongue's sharper than your blade will ever be". *Jerk.* I paid him back, though, by kicking his arse during our sparring session. He's stronger than I am, but I'm much smarter, and I know the exact spot to hit, to take a grown man down.

The ride up on the pulley is jerky, but it's not the worst. My adrenaline is pumping too hard for me to feel the bumps. *It's almost time. This plan had better work.*

After arriving at the top, Oscar wheels the trolley down the long passageway and into the Celebrations Chamber, positioning it perfectly for what I need to do.

I spot Jax through my little peep hole. *Man, does he look smoking hot today!* He's dressed in a long charcoal fur coat, which bleeds with shades of white, and his dreads are tied back in a half-up, half-down style, accentuating his strong jawline. The inside of the trolley heats up as I stare shamelessly. With his height, strong jawline, and solid frame, he looks every bit the Commander he should be. If only his little girlfriend hadn't ruined his reputation.

Oscar steps up to take his position beside him. *Good boy.* If this plan goes awry, I don't want anything dire happening to Jax.

In the very corner of my vision sits Commander Azazel, looking as evil and icy as ever, in her full black fur attire which blends perfectly with her dark hair and irises. Roc and Theo stand on each side of her, guarding with watchful eyes. Theo is Azazel's personal warrior, and rumour has it he looks after her very well—even in the bedroom. It's a little disturbing given he's the same age as Jax. She used to have another personal warrior named Jasper, who she'd replaced with Theo as soon as Jasper turned forty. Jasper was heartbroken over the demotion and quit being a warrior altogether. He wasn't a bad Zeek, and he was a sharp warrior, but he was weak willed and got caught in Azazel's spell.

As for Theo, he is a cocky know-it-all creep who used to follow Nix. I'm glad it's him next to Azazel today, and not Jasper. *I can't stand Theo.*

I scan the chamber as best I can within the restrictions of my little peep hole. All is in place, and we've covered our bases well. I'm hoping none of the warriors will suspect anything is awry until it's too late.

The orchestra plays a symphony which echoes throughout the chamber. The sound is far too sweet for such a sickening union and causes bile to rise in my throat. The thought of Jax and Electra uniting sickens me to my core. He deserves much better. I give him another quick look-over, before Electra comes into eyeshot, ruining the drool-worthy view. She's wearing a long velvet purple gown, cuffed with white fur, and her long plum hair has been beautifully braided, set with florescent yellow, pink, and purple flowers which have been plucked from the depths of Spring. I hate to admit it, but she does look the part, especially with her deep plum hair and pigments. As I stare in envy, a reassuring thought replays through my mind. *You may look the part, but you'll never be the part. You're about to go down, bitch!*

Electra's arm is hooked with Feeney's, and the fool smiles smugly as he guides her down the aisle to Jax. I bet he's secretly wishing he and Jax could switch places. *Sucker.* If only he knew what was coming to him.

As always, Jax's face doesn't give much away. He's wearing his usual impassive warrior mask. I'd like to see a little bit of disgust in his eyes, but he is smart enough to keep his true feelings hidden. He needs to appear fully on board with this. Most of these guests aren't aware that he was blackmailed into this linking arrangement.

Electra arrives at Jax's side, offers a plastic smile, and the music slows to a stop.

This is my cue. I put my hand up to the lid and begin counting down.

The word "One" leaves my lips, and I burst through the top, coinciding spot-on with the first explosion. The loud blast causes some of the weaker stalactites to crack and fall. I only have a split second to make my move before Feeney reacts, and I take it, blasting a dual set of shards at Electra. She moves with alarm due to the explosion, and the shards hit her side, but they penetrate deep enough to be fatal. In the second it takes for Feeney to catch her, I send another shard spearing directly at him. The shard impales his neck, and he drops Electra, his eyes widening to the size of saucers. To his credit, he quickly retaliates, shooting a shard back in my direction. I duck instinctively, and the shard zooms past, hitting one of the warrior's shields and shattering. I'm impressed, Feeney's going down fighting. Something unintelligible gurgles from his throat. He's spilling more blood than words. He lifts his arm to shoot another shard, but the glow of his magic fades as quickly as it comes. His arm flops, his eyes roll back in his head, and he topples onto the floor next to Electra.

Oscar plays his part well, shielding Jax, and rushing him out of harm's way before any more shards can be shot.

Loud screams echo through the chamber. Some Zeeks are ducking, while others are making a beeline for the exit. Kieran is one of the few Zeeks assisting the wounded. We need him to play this role, because everyone knows if he were to come after us, he'd be able to catch us. He's much leaner than most warriors and is *by far* the fastest runner we have.

While jumping out of the trolley, my eyes flick to where Azazel sits. Her blood splattered face sags lifelessly, and the handle of a throwing knife sticks out from her chest. Luna succeeded. She killed the bitch, just as she promised she would.

A warrior rushes to the front to cradle Azazel's lifeless body.

Roc and Theo lie awkwardly on the floor beside Azazel's chair, their eyes glassy and mouths hanging wide. Destiny and Stavros have succeeded with their tasks, too.

I do a quick scan of the area. I'm unable to spot any black unisuits in the mass chaos, so I'm hoping this means they all got out okay.

There's no time to check for sure and certain because I've got two warriors coming at me. I've wasted more time than I should've admiring everyone's handwork. I need to get moving, *NOW*.

A set of hands try to snag me from behind, but I retaliate with a sharp side kick, which sends the warrior flying into the vacated seating area with a crash.

The two younger male warriors rushing towards me fire shards my way. I drop to a crouch position and the air gusts above my head with a whoosh as the shards narrowly pass, ruffling the material of my full-face mask. While I'm still down, a warrior from behind sends a dual set of shards at my back. I launch into a side flip, but the movement isn't quite quick enough to escape them completely. One of the shards nicks the side of my arm, ripping the material of my unisuit along with my skin.

I duck into a row of seats, picking up one and using it as a shield as I rise to my feet. I hold on tight, covering my mid-section, and take it with me as I race towards the exit as fast as my legs will carry me. I refuse to be killed or caught and tortured for answers. I plan on spending my afternoon celebrating victory.

A few of Jax's new recruits come close to catching me as I duck and weave through the guests and obstacles, but luckily, I'm much faster and better trained. A few more shards whoosh past, and they sound awfully close, but to my relief none make contact.

"STOP FIRING!" Kieran shouts, loud enough that it manages to echo above the chaos. "An innocent has been hit."

Handel, one of the older warriors, shouts, "Just continue to chase and use your blades."

"Everyone calm down and move to the sides of the chamber where it's safer," Kieran orders the remaining guests.

When I get into the passage, I see either Luna or Destiny—I

can't tell which because of the mask and unisuit—fighting off Tyler and Zale, two powerful warriors. There's a shard sticking out from her thigh, but it hasn't impeded her fighting spirit. Her punches are solid and ferocious.

Without hesitation, I dash over to help. Tyler's and Zale's blades are still sheathed for now, but it won't be long until they tire of fist fighting and reach for them.

I creep up on Tyler and head slam him face first into the passageway wall before he even sees me coming. The sheer force is enough to knock him out cold. Zale jerks back from my female accomplice, eyes wide as Tyler falls to the ground. I use Zale's brief moment of surprise to bring the chair down on his head. The chair snaps in two and he cries out, toppling to his knees. *Frost! There goes my shield.*

We vigilantes are in an extremely tricky position because we're not supposed to kill or severely wound any of these warriors, yet we still need to fight them off if we want to make it out alive. It's a fine line to tread, and I fear I may be overstepping it. I've never been any good at holding back, especially in a fight.

Through my peripheral, I see four more warriors running straight at us, their blades out and ready to attack.

My unknown accomplice yanks the shard from her leg and whimpers.

I take her by the hand and tug her along. "Hurry," I say, distorting my voice. "We need to move, now."

One of the warriors, Mina, catches up to us and strikes at my back with her blade. The pointed tip slices through my unisuit, nicking the surface of my skin with a bite. While the shallow cut does sting, all she's really managed to do is piss me off. I surprise Mina with a spin kick to the face. Blood sprays from her mouth and she stumbles back in a daze, dropping her blade. The warrior who'd been a few steps behind her stops to make sure she's alright, and the other two slow as they pass, giving us more ground.

"Did the others get out?" My voice is breathy as we race on.

"Yes," Destiny's voice answers, confirming who it is I'm talking to. "They were quick and got out before anyone had time to process what was happening. I wasn't as swift, and I've had a few hiccups along the way."

I can tell Destiny is struggling on her wounded leg, and I hold my arm out to help support her. "We're getting out of here too, I promise. Just keep moving."

Stavros had been given a direct order to get out A.S.A.P. He was not to stop and help anyone, no matter the cost. Had he been caught, everyone in our colony would know Jax hadn't killed him, and this would ruin everything.

When we get to the passage which has been set up for our ultimate getaway, we have to navigate our steps with care. Large chunks of fallen limestone have created an obstacle course, and rubble litters the entire walkway as a result of the explosion. I hesitate a second before tugging on the rope. "Are you absolutely positive the others are out?"

"Yes." Destiny nods adamantly, then glances at the two warriors charging towards us. Four more warriors have taken up the chase behind them. "Quick, pull it now before any of the warriors get hurt."

I pull the rope, and we both rush to cover our ears as the passageway between us and the pursuing warriors collapses with the fierce blast of the second explosion. I'm hit with flying debris, which tears at my unisuit and grazes my skin.

I swing to face Destiny. "Are you okay?"

"Define okay?"

"We don't have time." I take her by the arm. "Let's move. We need to get out of here before the warriors make it back to the other passage."

Their voices yell and curse from the other side of the caved-in rubble as we race down the passage, and I hope their cries are out of frustration, not pain. Jax won't be happy if any of the warriors are badly injured, and I'm certain I'll be the one who gets the blame.

We pass a few Purples on this side of the passage, but none of them are warriors, and they seem more eager to get away from us than chase us. One Purple sends a shard flying towards the back of my head once we pass by him, though. It scarcely misses before shattering against the passageway wall. *Coward!*

Destiny struggles as we race down two sets of stairs, even with my help. She's losing a lot of blood and leaving a crimson trail in our wake.

"You can do this," I tell her. "We're almost there."

When we get to the ground level, we are met by confused stares, but no one tries to stop us as we rush towards Saul's hunting cavern. The huskens are already hooked up to the sled, and the portcullis is open and ready to go.

I hurry to help Destiny up onto the bench seat before jumping into the sled myself. "There's a pack of clothes in the back," I tell her. "Grab something to tie around your leg and then try to stay still. You need to control the bleeding."

I'm about to prompt the huskens to start moving when a hand seizes me by the shoulder and reefs me back out of the sled. The sled has antlers fixed to both sides for decorative purposes, and as my body is dragged over the sharp jagged points, it tears my unisuit to shreds and rips my skin. Blood trickles down my torso. These cuts are deeper and more painful than the cut on my back.

"Only *I* drive this sled." Saul's magenta eyes are slitted as he brings a blade to my throat.

Saul really should've been born a Purple. He's got the build for it, and he'd make a mean warrior—perhaps a little too mean.

Thinking fast, I stamp my foot down as hard as I possibly can on his toes. During his split second of pain-filled shock, I slip away from his grasp, snatch one of the carved animal bone knifes from the workbench, and point it at him, eyes narrowed.

Saul recovers and sniggers.

This bone knife is nothing compared to his blade, but I'm low on options.

He charges towards me, blade raised, and I drop to a crouch as he swings to kill. The razor-sharp edge misses the top of my head by millimetres.

I peer up to find Destiny standing in the back of the sled with a wooden bow in her hands. She uses it to knock Saul across the back of the head. The blow stuns him into dropping his blade, but it lacked enough power to render him unconscious.

An idea springs to mind. "Catch."

I toss Destiny the bone knife, and she catches it by the handle in mid-air. *Impressive.* Before Saul can register what's happening, Destiny hurls the knife towards him, landing the pointed edge straight into the meaty flesh of his left bum-cheek. He's lucky we're on strict orders not to kill—unless absolutely necessary—otherwise that knife would have been aimed somewhere vital. He's also lucky it was Destiny throwing the knife, not me, because my version of absolutely necessary and what others deem absolutely necessary, don't necessarily align.

Saul howls and I ram at him, head butting him square on the nose. We collide and wrestle, his fingernails clawing at my open wounds. He's going for my weak spots, *scum bag.* Thankfully, it's only a matter of seconds before Destiny jumps from the sled and thumps him across the head with the bow again, this time with heavy force. The hard edge collides with his temple and his eyes flicker before his body goes lax and topples to the ground.

"Hey!" a gravelly voice shouts from outside the cavern opening, and I hear the heavy sound of footfalls charging our way.

My adrenaline kicks into overdrive. "Quick!" I shout, snatching the bow from Destiny's hands. "Get back in the sled."

We dart back to the sled at full pelt and I give Destiny a hoist. "Mush," I call before our bottoms even touch the bench seat. "Mush, mush."

The shadows of four fast moving figures splay before us on the cave walls, and the portcullis starts lowering with a clank, clank, clank. I turn to see Rae and her new hunting team at our rear. *Frost!*

The huskens eagerly propel the sled forward, barking like mad as they move under threat. As our sled flies into the open passage-way, Destiny and I need to duck to avoid being taken out by the bottommost spikes of the swiftly lowering portcullis.

I let out a strangled breath as our sled flies out of the cave mouth and onto wide open land.

It's a good thing we managed to get Saul incapacitated when we did, otherwise we'd be up for an almighty struggle.

There's a possibility Rae's team could have taken us. We are wounded, weaponless, and outnumbered. I press at the weeping gash on my torso and groan. *Bloody Saul.*

5

PROTOCOL NEEDS TO BE BROKEN

-ZANNAH-

As soon as we hit the forest border, Destiny and I rip off our face masks and throw them into the back.

My face itches like mad from the mesh, and I can tell by the vigorous way Destiny is scratching, the mesh must have been irritating her skin too. I run my fingernails down my cheeks and pull back with a wince. Sections of my skin feel raw and tender to the touch.

The sled hits a bump and Destiny cries out. Her hands fly to her wounded leg, nursing it.

"I'm sorry." I grimace sympathetically. "But it's only going to get bumpier from here on in. Maybe you should climb across the back and lay down."

She takes my advice and crawls across to the back bench seat, letting out a string of profanities with every movement.

We were supposed to leave the sled at the border, unhook the huskens, and walk the rest of the way to the Drake village by foot, but because of Destiny's injured thigh, we've had to break protocol. There's no way Destiny could do a twelve kilometre walk on her wounded leg and survive. She needs help, and she needs it fast.

Around two kilometres into the forest, we spot Stavros and Luna walking with Sphinx and Rebel. They turn when they hear us coming, and Stavros gawks in disbelief.

"What are you doing?" he shouts, and the four of them come rushing over to the sled. "You were supposed to leave the sled at the edge of the forest so that it can be easily found by the warriors."

"I couldn't," I yell back, bringing the sled to a halt. "Destiny's been hurt. She wouldn't have made it all the way to the village by foot. Quick, both of you jump in. We need to get her to help A.S.A.P."

Stavros jumps in next to me and frowns. "Your face," he says, and then his gaze drops to my bloodied torso. "Frost... What happened to you two?"

"I've only got surface wounds," I say, covering my bleeding torso with the gaping flap of material. "It's Destiny I'm worried about."

Luna hops in the back with Destiny, leaving Sphinx and Rebel to run along with the sled. As we continue towards the Drake village, we exchange tales of our exploits. Unlike Destiny and I, Stavros and Luna were lucky. They'd managed to flee quickly and escape the caves without any hassle.

We take the sled as far as we can, parking it in the usual place hidden by the large protruding roots of the forest's tallest tree. Sphinx and Rebel had raced ahead of the sled the whole way, encouraging the harnessed huskens to pull faster. Now they're all panting frantically, exhausted from the run.

Stavros gently scoops Destiny out of the sled, and I hurry over to help him.

"I'm alright," he says. "I've got her. You unhook the huskens, grab whatever you need, and venture back to the hut. I know Acacia will be fretting, so make sure you stop in to see her before doing anything else. I'm going to rush ahead and take Destiny straight to the medicine woman."

Luna comes over to help me unhook the huskens, and I give her a proud pat on the back. "Can you believe we actually managed to pull that off?" I say, grinning from ear to ear. "HALLELUJAH!" I shout to the treetops. "The two icy bitches are dead!"

Not sharing my enthusiasm, Luna goes stiff. "We might have succeeded in killing the icy bitches, but I wasn't expecting so many innocents to get hurt in the process. When that first explosion went off, those stalactites flew down like knives from the sky."

"Admittedly, there was more collateral damage than expected," I say with a shrug, "but it's for the greater good."

Luna gapes at me, like I'm callous, but I'm just being realistic. The entire colony would have suffered far greater if the ceremony had proceeded as it was supposed to. Sometimes you have to make sacrifices for the greater good.

She shakes off her shock and asks, "Do you think Jax will have any regrets now that the deed is done?"

Her question strikes me as odd. *Does she regret her decision to help us?* She shouldn't. She'd pushed for her role in the assassination.

"My life will be forever scarred because of that icy monster," she'd said. "Please. Let me take my revenge."

I'd been sceptical about her using throwing knives to kill Azazel and had argued that Stavros would be much better suited for the role. Being an ex-warrior, he's been trained to kill, but Luna was adamant that the job should be hers.

She'd dragged me outside to watch her hit targets, and to say I was impressed would be an understatement. After hearing her pleas and witnessing her mad skills, who was I to argue with her wishes?

Luna stares, waiting for my answer.

"I'm sure Jax is as upset as you are about innocents getting hurt, but I can say with certainty, he won't lose any sleep over the deaths of Electra and his mother."

"Will he still do the right thing by the Pastels now that Harlow is gone?"

I cut her a sharp glance. "This wasn't just about Harlow. Jax is an honourable Zeek with a heart of gold, just like his late father Arlo."

"Don't get me wrong. I like Jax, but I find him a little intimidating and uncomfortable to be around. He's very intense and hard to read."

This makes me laugh. "I don't think you're alone there. Quite a number of Zeeks have said the same thing to me over the years."

I go to the back of the sled, snatch up Saul's favourite crossbow, and shove it into one of the packs. I'm on strict orders to leave the hunting gear as is, but I desperately want this crossbow, and after all the trouble Saul caused me, I feel justified in taking it. I'm sure he'll be able to source another one easily enough.

"What are you doing?" Luna asks. "I didn't think we were—"

"About Jax," I say, deliberately cutting her off. "He's extremely guarded with his emotions, and always has been, but with a supreme status like his, it's paramount. Some warriors perceive emotions as a sign of weakness, and at the first sign of weakness, predators attack." A few of the hunting knives spark my fancy, so I shove them into the other pack, along with a handful of other useful tools. You can never have too many weapons. Once I'm satisfied that I've taken "everything I need", I jump back down from the sled. "Jax is actually an amazing guy when you really get to know him. Once everything has cooled down and he takes his rightful place, he'll bring about change, you wait and see."

When we held a meeting to orchestrate the prison break to coincide with the assassination, we'd also decided it would be a smart move for Sylvie to tell everyone Jax had been injured during the ceremony and has gone into hiding until he's well enough to take on his rightful role as Commander. She'll also make it known that Kieran has been appointed as Chief Warrior and is in charge of ruling the colony in Jax's place until he is fit enough to return.

Hopefully, by the time Jax claims his title, the pregnancy rumours will have fizzled out.

Luna shoots me an enquiring look. "You have a bit of a soft spot for Jax, don't you?"

"Well, he's certainly hot." I raise a brow. "And he's a badass warrior, but he only has eyes for one—and I'm not that 'one'."

Luna crinkles her nose. "I don't know what he sees in Harlow."

"Me either," I agree, and then add, "You know it's funny, because beautiful, rich, powerful women have been throwing themselves at him for years—yet never once has he shown even the slightest bit of interest. For reasons I can't fathom, Harlow is the only Zeek he's ever been interested in. Even now, after everything she's done to destroy his reputation, he's still in love with her. He's absolutely devastated that she's gone."

"I think Harlow is a seductress and troublemaker," Luna says, and I detect a hint of jealousy in her voice. "Jax might be heartbroken over losing her, but I'm glad she left with the Vallon."

I hand her the lighter of the two packs. "I'm not sorry to see the back of her," I admit. "But it hurts me to see Jax hurting."

Luna slings the pack up over her shoulder. "It could work to your advantage, you know. Now that's Harlow's gone, you might actually have a chance with him."

I shake my head. "Harlow may have left the forest, but like I said, she hasn't left his heart. Besides, I know my place with Jax. He sees Stavros as his brother and me as his little sister, and no one wants to date their little sister." Not wanting to stay on the topic of Jax's love life, I turn the tables. "Say, talking about soft spots. Isn't it about time, that you declare your love to Boshell?"

Her cheeks flush rouge. "I've been waiting for him to say something to me. I don't want to upset the balance if my feelings aren't reciprocated. I love his kids too much to jeopardise things. I think of them as my own."

"Well, speaking from an outsider's point of view, the chemistry is definitely there. You should really go for it before he curls over and dies of old age."

Luna's eyes flash wide, and she punches my arm. "Hey, he's not that old. There's only ten years difference between us."

"I know, but the sad fact is Pastels age fast, and most don't live past the age of fifty. Boshell's only got another fourteen years left in him, give or take. He's past his mid-thirties now, which means he'll start deteriorating rapidly." I notice one of my shoelaces has come undone, and I squat to re-tie it. "You should've got Jax to inject him with the ink while you had the chance. The last of it was used on Harlow's pals."

"Lovely, *Zannah*," Luna spits irritably, and I glance up to find her glaring at me. "Stavros always says you have no tact. I'm starting to see *exactly* what he means."

Annoyed by her comment, I go to shoot back, "Yeah, well, you should hear what Stavros says about you!" but I bite my tongue when I discover there's genuine hurt in her eyes. It's clear I've offended her, although I hadn't meant to. I was merely stating facts.

I rise to my feet, swallow my pride, look her level in the eyes, and say, "I'm sorry. I tend to speak without thinking sometimes." I figure it's best to keep on her good side if we're going to be living together.

She nods by way of acknowledgement, but I can tell she's still upset by what I've said.

I whistle for the huskens and then sling my arm around her shoulders, keeping it friendly. "Come on. Let's go. Acacia's probably tearing her hair out with worry by now."

6

ONE SURPRISE AFTER ANOTHER

-ZAVIER-

e've only just sat down when Zannah and a Zeek I've never met before come barging into the hut. I stare with crinkled brows. The woman with Zannah has the refined features of a Pastel, yet her body is solid and built like a Magenta. Stranger still, her hair and irises are a soft peach colour. *I wonder if she's been given special meds like Minty and me?*

Acacia sighs in relief. However, her relief quickly morphs into concern when she notices Zannah's grazed face and bloodied torso. "What happened?" She jumps to her feet. "Where are the others?"

"Destiny was hit by a shard in the thigh," Zannah says. "But she should be okay. Stavros took her straight to Roz."

Did she say Stavros? The only Stavros I've ever known—well, I didn't even know him—was the warrior who killed Nix. Clearly, she can't have meant him, because he's dead. Jax killed him.

"What happened?" I ask. "Did you succeed in stopping the ceremony?"

A satisfied smile curls Zannah's lips. "You could say that. Electra, Azazel, and a few of Nix's guys are dead, and as far as the colony will be concerned, you three helped me kill them." She draws an invisible circle around Floss, Minty, and me. "Today, everyone witnessed one male and three females, dressed in full black bodysuits, assassinate five members of the linking party, and once they discover I helped free you lot from the cell, they'll put two and two together."

I blink in astonishment. "Seriously?"

Floss simply grins and says, "Glad to be of service. Please tell me their deaths were drawn out and painful."

"I take it this means we won't be going back to the caves any time soon?" Minty cuts in, her tone more curious than upset.

Zannah drops her pack to the floor with a thud. "Not unless you want to face execution."

"Where does this leave us, then?" I ask. "Where do we go? Where do we live?"

Acacia places a jug of iced tea on the small wooden table in front of us, along with a set of cups. "You'll live here in the Drake village," she says. "Jax bought the hut next door recently, so there'll be enough room for all of us to live comfortably."

I scratch my head. "Who's 'all of us'?"

"There's eight of us living in this hut," Acacia says, pouring tea into the cups. "And now there's you four," she gestures. "Plus, Zannah, Jax and Oscar."

Minty chews her lower lip. "And the Drakes are okay with this arrangement?"

"The Drakes are a peaceful race," Acacia says. "And Jax and Dakari have a good relationship. Dakari is more than happy to take in newcomers as long as they don't pose a threat to his village or any of his tribe members. So, abide by his rules and there'll be no issues."

Floss downs her drink in one gulp. "If Azazel's dead and Jax is coming out here to live, who's commanding the caves?"

"Kieran has been appointed Chief Warrior and will be in charge temporarily until things cool down." Acacia takes a cup for herself and sits.

Floss leans forward in her seat. "What's the point in that? Shouldn't Jax stay and take control of the situation? What kind of Commander leaves his colony in the midst of chaos?"

"A Commander whose reputation has been ruined by *your* sister…" Zannah spits. "Since the pregnancy rumours took flight, he's lost everyone's respect."

"Zannah!" Acacia shoots her a horrified look.

"What? It's true. Everyone believes he's only trying to break down the colour system because he's knocked up a Pastel and doesn't want to face the consequences. He threw away everything for Harlow, and now she's gone. It was all for nothing."

"Good gracious, Zannah." Stavros enters the hut, and my jaw drops to the floor in disbelief. Either I'm seeing ghosts, or my eyes are deceiving me. "You've been here a whole five minutes and already you're mouthing off."

Zannah curls a lip in irritation. "Some of us aren't afraid to voice our opinions."

"Yeah, well not everyone wants to hear yours."

"You're dead," I blurt, putting a halt on their argument, and everyone glances my way with puckered brows. "Jax killed you."

Stavros laughs aloud. "Clearly, he didn't." A smile lights his face as he comes over to where I'm sitting to shake my hand. "You must be Zavier." His eyes flick to Floss who sits beside me. "And you're definitely Floss." He swivels to face the other two. "Which would make you Minty and Tatum."

Minty smiles in return. "Correct."

"It's nice to meet you," Tatum says politely.

When he's finished greeting us, Stavros goes over to where

Acacia sits and pulls her up by the arm to give her a loving cuddle and kiss.

Okay... They must be a couple. My mind boggles. We're not just dealing with inter-colour relationships anymore; we are dealing with inter-racial relationships. First Harlow and Alex, and now them.

"I've been worried out of my mind," I overhear Acacia whisper.

"I told you I'd come back, didn't I?" He plants another kiss on her lips.

"I'm Luna, by the way," the peach woman offers, breaking the awkwardness.

I let my curiosity get the better of me and ask, "Did you happen to be injected with special medication?"

"Do you mean vertic switz ink?"

"What? Vallon ink? No." I shake my head. "I mean Jax gave us special—"

"Jax injected you and Minty with vertic switz ink," Zannah says, cutting me off abruptly.

"He what?"

Vertic switz ink has Vallon blood in it. This means I've been injected with Vallon blood. My stomach turns. *Gross.*

I must go as green faced as I feel, because Stavros hurries to say, "Jax said there was no other choice. If he hadn't injected you with the ink, you wouldn't have made it through the night. Your Pastel body was too weak to cope with your injuries. You were dying."

"I didn't get a choice either," Luna says. "I was injected by the Vallons. But as you're probably already aware, the ink does have its benefits. You've just got to try not to think about its origin."

Minty's forehead creases. "How did Jax come across Vallon ink?"

"Harlow's Vallon left the jar with her after he'd finished doing her tattoo," Luna answers, spitting Harlow's name like it's a curse.

"Harlow has a tattoo?" Floss and I say in unison.

"Where? And what of?" I ask.

"What's it to you?" Floss grizzles, elbowing my side in a way that is definitely *not* playful.

I suppress a groan. "I'm just curious. I didn't even know she had a tattoo."

"She has a snowflake." Luna points to the inner part of her wrist and draws a small circle with her finger. "Right about here. It's small, and it has the letter J inside it."

I frown. "J… As in…Jax?"

Stavros and Acacia shrug.

"Jax was my first thought when I saw it," Luna says. "But her Vallon was the one who drew it, so it's all a bit weird if you ask me." She sniggers and then adds, "She's probably got a whole alphabet hidden in places we haven't seen. Your friend wasn't afraid to get around."

"Enough, Luna." Stavros cuts her a sharp look of warning. "You're wrong about her."

I get the feeling Harlow isn't well liked by Zannah and Luna. I'd like to back Stavros by defending her integrity, however Harlow's not here to appreciate it, and I know it'll only cause problems with Floss.

"Has Acacia shown you guys your hut?" Stavros asks.

"I was waiting for you," she says. "I thought we'd show them together."

"Let's all head over then, shall we?"

Zannah and Luna stay where they are while the rest of us stand and follow Stavros and Acacia to the door.

"Are you coming or what, Zannah?" Stavros asks.

"What do you mean?" She casts him an offended look. "I thought I was staying here with you guys. Can't I just take Atohi's old room?"

"No," he says sternly. "Jax is taking Atohi's old room. So please, whatever you do—don't go in there. I want everything left as it is."

"Why?"

"You know why. Now don't start with me."

She sets her jaw in a stubborn angle. "You guys go. I need to see Roz, anyway."

"Fine. Suit yourself."

7

LETTERS

-ZANNAH-

ax, Oscar, and RJ arrive at six-thirty the next morning, on schedule. I'm alerted to their presence by Sphinx's incessant, ear-splitting howl. Determined not to get on the bad side of our neighbouring Drakes, I hurry down to let him and the other huskens out from under the hut. Having six huskens in such a small space is bedlam.

"Shut up," I hiss through gritted teeth. Sphinx isn't used to being away from Jax for so long. He's a little too spoilt for his own good. As soon as I open the gate, all six huskens charge out excitedly. I wince as I cop several hard blows to my sides from their thrashing tails. "Calm down," I warn.

The six huskens race over to meet up with the other two, who are eagerly scurrying ahead of the guys, bringing it to an alarming eight huskens total. They sure look intimidating as a large pack. I can see why the Drakes are always so cautious of them. Their guard-hounds are puny by comparison. They look like muscly skeletons with abnormally long snouts.

I sigh inwards. I'm glad we'll be sending most of the huskens back to the caves with RJ when he leaves. As well as being noisy, they have the appetite of three men, demand constant attention, and now that we're on soil, they've discovered they like to dig. We're still keeping three of them though—which I believe is one too many. I'd suggested we should only keep Sphinx and Rebel, but Jax insisted Lucy was to stay too, and as always, Stavros sided with him.

When the guys get closer, I dash across to meet them. I'm keen to see how Jax is holding up and to find out exactly what happened after we left.

Stavros and Woody braved taking the sled back to the border yesterday afternoon before sunset. Prior to yesterday's assassination stunt, Jax said the sleds were essential for the daily work requirements of the hunters and warriors and needed to be left at the border where they could be easily found. He figured it didn't matter if the warriors knew we took off into the forest, because they'd never suspect we'd sought refuge in the Drake village. They'd presume we're as good as dead.

"You made it," I say, greeting Jax with a smile. I haven't reserved one for Oscar, so he gets a scowl.

Jax returns my smile with one that doesn't quite reach his eyes, then slings his arm over my shoulder. "Hey Zannah," he says, pulling me to him. I wince, feeling tender all over. "Thanks for everything you did yesterday."

RJ re-adjusts the straps of the large pack on his shoulders. It looks to be weighing him down. "Which of the two girls was hurt?"

"Destiny," I answer. "But Roz, the medicine woman, says that she's going to be okay."

"And what about you?" Jax side glances at my scratched face with concern. "Were you hit by any of the shards? Kieran said he saw a few get close."

"One grazed my arm, Mina nicked my back with her blade, my encounter with Saul caused some scrapes on my torso, and I got a few scratches and bruises from the flying debris of the second explosion, but you know me, I'm tough. I'll live."

"Saul?" His brows shoot up.

"I think he was a little touchy about us using his hunting sled," I say, playing it off. "Destiny sorted him out, though. She sent a bone knife ploughing into his left bum cheek." I smirk. "Mr Tough isn't going to be able to sit properly for the next few weeks."

"This is true," RJ confirms.

I'm expecting more questions, possibly even some sort of lecture from Jax, but instead I get another semi-smile.

"I'm proud of you, Zannah," he says, and my smirk grows into a full faced beam.

When we get to the base of the hut, I wait, allowing the guys to climb up the ladder first.

Stavros is all smiles and laughter as he greets Oscar with a warm hug. I can tell he's excited. He hasn't seen much of him since living here, and I know he misses being a part of the old gang.

Sphinx's loud howl must've woken Luna, because she comes out to join us, still dressed in her pyjamas with hooded eyes.

"Were there many casualties?" she asks, combing a hand through her dishevelled hair.

"Yes, mostly minor, but..." Jax lets out a pained breath and then adds, "there are three Zeeks in serious condition, and one in critical condition. Let's all pray to the stars that they pull through."

"The Zeek in a critical condition is a young teen," RJ says, expanding on Jax's answer. "One of the new warrior recruits accidentally shot her in the chest. The shard missed her heart, but it pierced her right lung which has impeded her breathing." He throws in a bit of technical jargon, before adding, "Sylvie has her on oxygen and is monitoring her closely."

Luna's peach shimmer disappears from her cheeks. "How old is the girl?"

RJ slides the large pack off his shoulders and drops it to the deck with a look of relief. The deck rattles under its weight. "Fifteen."

"Her parents are up in arms," Jax adds. "They're saying that if she dies, they want the warrior responsible for taking the shot prosecuted."

We all grimace. Fifteen is too young to die, but we don't want to see the young recruit sent to the cell. His actions might've been careless, but they weren't deliberate.

Jax and Oscar slide their packs off too, and we gather around the table on the deck while Stavros and Luna go inside to make bean-brews for everyone.

"How does Kieran feel about being the new Chief Warrior?" I ask, parking on the seat next to Oscar. He sees through the question. I'm deliberately rubbing salt in his wounds.

The title should have really gone to him—he was Jax's right-hand man—but it's because of Oscar's loyalty to Jax that he wasn't able to be appointed to the position. He'd openly defended Jax when the pregnancy rumours were circling, and he had strongly backed him when he'd put forward the very controversial idea of integrating the different colours in the workforce. Plus, Oscar is too opinionated and cocky to be a leader. He can be a meathead and often asks for trouble. Kieran will make a much better leader. He has the intelligence to rule, and he knows when to keep his mouth shut.

"Kieran is taking the position in his stride," Jax answers in Oscar's place. "But he says it's going to feel strange for a while without all of us there."

"Not having Zannah around should be an improvement." Oscar sniggers.

"You'd better watch what you say," I warn, eyes slitted. "We're going to be sharing a hut now, so continue to insult me, and I'll stab you in your sleep. As you know, I'm quite capable of murder, especially when it comes to those I don't like."

"Come on, you two." Jax leans back in his chair and presses his fingers to the side of his temples, signalling he's got a bad headache. "It's only the beginning of day one. At least give it a whole twenty-four hours before you start handing out death threats."

"I take it you didn't get much sleep," I say, noticing the dark circles under his eyes.

"No, not really. I'm worried about the young girl."

And Harlow too, I bet.

Stavros comes back out with a tray full of bean-brews while Luna brings out a plate of cream cakes and fruit spiced biscuits.

We sip and nibble away, exchanging our personal accounts of yesterday's events. None of us had expected so many stalactites to fall during the first explosion, and we all agree it's a miracle that no one was killed. I ask RJ if any of the warriors were hurt during the second explosion, and he informs me that a few of the closer ones received lacerations from the flying debris but were otherwise fine.

"The two warriors who suffered the worst injuries were the ones you and Destiny took on in the passageway." Oscar's tone holds slight accusation. "I assume it was you who smashed Tyler's face into the passageway wall and then broke a chair over Zale's head?"

I bite back a smirk and shrug. "It could have been."

He casts me a sharp levelling look, knowing full well it was me. "Sylvie told us Tyler needed fifteen stitches to close up the cut along his forehead and Zale is now bedbound and stuck wearing a neck brace for the next six weeks because you fractured his C2."

My smirk bleeds through. "I'm sure the scar will be an improvement to Tyler's ugly face."

I never did like Tyler. *He's a creep.*

Stavros reaches across the table for another biscuit. "Has anyone suspected foul play regarding Jax?"

"Kieran says a few accusations have been voiced," Oscar admits. "But no one will ever be able to prove anything unless any of us give him up, and that's not going to happen."

"Zannah's been made, as expected," Jax adds. "And the planted rumours about her and the prisoners being responsible for the assassination have started circling."

Stavros nods. "Good."

After another half hour of story swapping, RJ stands, excuses himself, and tells us he needs to get back to the caves to help Sylvie with the wounded.

"Don't forget to take all *six* huskens with you when you leave." I might be speaking to RJ, but my eyes flick to Jax when I say this.

"Watch it," Jax retorts. "Or I'll send *you* back with him."

Oscar stands too, wanders over to his heavy pack, and slings it over his shoulders with a hmpf. "Where am I staying?"

"Zannah, why don't you show Oscar to the new hut," Stavros suggests, wiping his crumby fingers on his pants.

"I know Oscar's thick, but I'm sure he can work out how to get to the hut next door without me holding his hand."

Stavros shakes his head at me. "You're awful, you know that?"

Once RJ and Oscar are gone, Stavros tells Jax that he can have Harlow's old room.

Jax's eyes flash with surprise. "Isn't it supposed to be Atohi's room again now that Harlow is gone?"

"He's alright staying in the room with Acacia and me for now." Stavros lowers his voice to a whisper, but I've got super good hearing, so I eavesdrop. "After Harlow left, Acacia came across a few things that she thought you might be interested in seeing, so we figured we'd wait and leave the sorting out for you to do."

Jax nods appreciatively. "Thank you."

We help Stavros place all the dirty mugs on a tray, and while he's busy carrying them inside, Jax stands and picks up his pack.

"Are both packs yours?" I ask, pointing to the one RJ left.

"Yes, but they're heavy. I'll have to come back for that one."

"No need." I wave him off. "I'll grab it."

"Leave it, it's too—"

Too late. I instantly regret making the offer. My arms shake with strain as I hoist the pack high enough to swing it onto my tender back. I knew it was going to be heavy, but I had no idea it would be a ton of bricks heavy! No wonder RJ was struggling. *I'm a warrior,* I tell myself, *and warriors are tough.*

I look up to find Jax eyeing me with quiet amusement. "Are you alright?"

I straighten. "Of course, why?"

The rumble of a chuckle sounds in his throat. "There's no doubt about it Zannah; you're one very determined Zeek."

He heads in and I follow. However, as I get to the doorway of Jax's new room, Stavros steps out in front of me, stopping me in my tracks. "What are you doing?"

"What does it look like I'm doing?" I glare. "I'm carrying one of Jax's packs in for him—which is pretty heavy, by the way—so move, would you?"

"Here, give it to me." He puts his hand out. "I'll take it."

Anger heats my cheeks. "What's your problem?"

"I know what you're like Zannah. You're highly opinionated and insensitive, and I don't want you commenting on all the things Harlow's left behind because—let's face it—you can be very cruel when you want to be." He gives me a pointed look. "I want Jax to be able to go through her stuff without a running commentary."

His comment cuts deep.

"Screw you, Stavros. Jax is my friend too, and how dare you call me insensitive. I have been there for Jax one hundred percent during the whole Harlow ordeal, and I've put my life on the line for that girl more than once."

Jax sticks his head out. "Look, you can both come in. It's fine. I might be upset about how things panned out with Harlow, but you don't have to treat me like I'm fragile."

Stavros steps aside and I continue in, relieved to be able to dump the heavy pack. Jax is holding a small picture frame in his hands, so, being the curious type, I glance over at it. My eyes bug out. It's a lifelike painting of him and Sphinx. "Who did that?" I ask, impressed by the likeness. "Can I have a look?"

He takes one more glance and then hands it to me. "At a guess, I would say RJ painted it."

Stavros steps in to join us, and I can only presume it's because he wants to keep an eye on me. He doesn't trust I'll be nice, which makes me all the more determined to be ultra-nice, just to prove him wrong.

I examine the detail of Jax's painted eyes in amazement. "Well, this is certainly very special. You obviously meant a lot to her."

"Acacia says you should check out the paper basket." Stavros hands it to him. "She noticed a few of the crumpled pieces of paper had your name written inside them."

Jax takes the basket and sits down on the end of the mattress.

Stavros secretly gestures for us to leave, but I pretend not to notice and park beside Jax as he picks out the crumpled pieces of paper, one by one.

I'm nosey and I want to see what's been written.

Dear Jax,
   I've given a lot of thought to what you said, and I feel

Dear Jax,
   I miss seeing your face too

Dear Jax,
   Last night was amazing

I raise a brow at this one. He never *did* mention what happened the night he stayed out here. Obviously, whatever they'd shared was "amazing". A slight feeling of jealousy washes over me as I re-read the note, but I try my best to ignore it. *Jax is my friend, and it's all he'll ever be. I'm okay with that.*

Dear Zavier,
   It's only been a week, but I already miss you, my bestie. I hope everything is working out with you and Floss, and that you are being careful to keep things under

the radar. Say "hi" to Minty and Tatum for me, and tell them that I've already finished Frenemies.
Love, Harlow
oxox

Dear Jax,
I wish I knew how you'd felt about me earlier. If I'd known, I would never have

Dear Jax,
Thank you so much for everything you have done for me. I know you've put yourself at great risk to keep me safe, and I appreciate it. I really wish there was a way I could repay you for your kindness.

"It looks like I don't get a finished one," Jax says.

I put my arm around him. "Maybe not, but the overall message is loud and clear." I keep my voice light and warm. Meanwhile, in my head, I'm secretly cursing at Harlow. If she was so grateful for all his kindness, then she should have stayed. There were four of us warriors present at the handover. We could have easily taken down Slater. I think a part of her secretly wanted to go with him, and going by those rock-hard abs of his, it's not hard to see why. She's probably been playing Jax all along. She needed him to keep her safe.

Jax's muscles bunch beneath my arm. He's obviously replaying the same scene I am.

"She was supposed to be here." His tone is a mixture of hurt and frustration. "You were right. I should have fought harder for her. I was trying to do the right thing by her, and now I've lost her forever."

8

A SPECIAL NOTE
-ZAVIER-

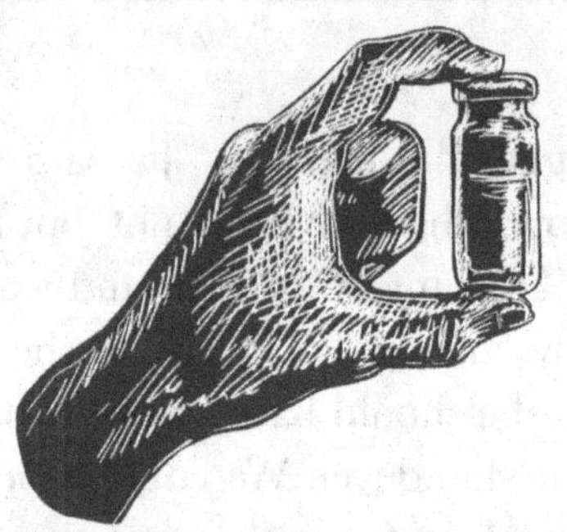

This afternoon, Acacia and Stavros brought their son across for us to meet and kindly gifted us a tray of fresh deetra meat and veggies, so Minty and I are cooking up a storm.

"His name is Atohi," Acacia had said. "Which, in my language means woods. We named him this because he was born in Spring's forest, although Woody insists Atohi was named after him." She'd laughed with a warmth that brightened the hut. "I've learnt to just smile and nod."

Tatum had rushed to Acacia's side to goo-and-ga over the baby.

She used to be a childcare worker in the caves and absolutely loves kids.

Minty was interested in meeting Atohi too, although I imagined it was more because of his blended heredities than because he was a baby. "The colour of his eyes are incredible," she'd said. "I've never seen anything like them."

Meeting Atohi made me curious about the appearance of Harlow's twins. *Will they be light or dark, pink or red?* I'm devastated that I'll never find out.

While I really miss my bestie, and I worry about her constantly, I have to admit, I'm rather pleased with my new living arrangements. Everything still feels surreal. This spacious hut is our new home. We are free to openly date outside of our colour rank, and best of all—minus my sore shin—Minty and I are fit and healthy. We've seriously been given a whole new chance at life.

After spending three weeks locked in a guarded cell, it was bliss to spend a warm relaxing night snuggled with Floss—safe—in a room of our own.

The sound of someone knocking prompts me to look up from the chopping board. Jax stands just inside the entryway, dressed in a plain black T-shirt and khaki cargos. I blink twice to make sure I'm seeing him right. The casual clothing is a stark contrast to his personality. Jax isn't a causal Zeek.

"Come in," Minty and I say in unison.

When he gets to the bench, he reaches into his pocket, pulls out a crumpled piece of paper and hands it to me. "I found this in Harlow's old room this morning. It's a note that's been written to you. I thought you might like to have it."

Here he is, sharing pieces of Harlow with me again. He's obviously a bigger Zeek than I am. He doesn't appear to hold on to any resentment.

"Thanks," I say, straightening it out to read. A lump rises in my throat at the thought of never seeing her again. *Damn it, Harlow, why'd you have to leave with Alex?*

Minty's up on her toes, trying to look over my shoulder, so once

I've scanned over the note for the second time, I hand it to her, knowing she'll be pleased to see she got a mention.

"I've just come back from speaking to Chief Dakari." Jax's gaze flicks between Minty and me. "You all need to be up and ready by six-thirty tomorrow morning. He would like to meet everyone, do a group tour of the village, and then talk about work placements. You'll need be able to work in harmony with the Drakes and contribute to their society."

Minty nods. "Perfect, we'll let the others know."

"Dakari has also spoken about doing some evening language classes with all the newcomers," Jax adds. "He believes if you are going to live in Spring on a permanent basis, you should be familiar with the Drake language."

"That sounds reasonable," I say.

Minty nods, face alight. "I think it's a fantastic idea."

Jax turns to leave, and a niggling feeling stirs inside me. The closer to the door he gets, the stronger it grows.

"Jax, wait!" I hurry over with a limp. I'm still paying for yesterday's long walk. "I want to say thank you," I say, stopping in front of him. "You've really gone out of your way to look after us, and *I personally*, don't deserve your kindness. I haven't always been very nice to you or shown you the proper respect you deserve." Jax appears to be rendered speechless, so I continue, imploring him to understand my reasoning. "My father Xander hated Purples," I say. "And after Nix blew up the factory cavern, killing all those Zeeks— along with my parents—I instantly inherited his same burning hatred.

"Harlow always said that you were different, but I refused to believe her. I thought for certain you were using her, and I resented you for it." I take a long breath and then force out the rest. "I can see now I was wrong, and I want you to know that I'm sorry."

"It's understandable. Harlow's your best friend, and you've gone to extreme lengths to protect her. I can appreciate your cautiousness. Some of the decisions I've made have backfired and put her in danger, which I assure you, was never my intention." His eyes flash with regret. "I'm sorry that you, Minty, and Floss got dragged into this mess. At the risk of sounding condescending, I'm proud of you all for not breaking during Electra's torture session. You were only hanging on by a thread when I arrived at the cell. I was honestly worried that you weren't going to survive."

"Stavros said I wouldn't have made it if it wasn't for the ink. So, thanks again. Besides my shin, I feel like a new Zeek."

"You certainly look like a new Zeek." He reaches into his pocket and pulls out two nauclea latifolia roots. "Here." he places the roots in my hand. "These should help with the pain."

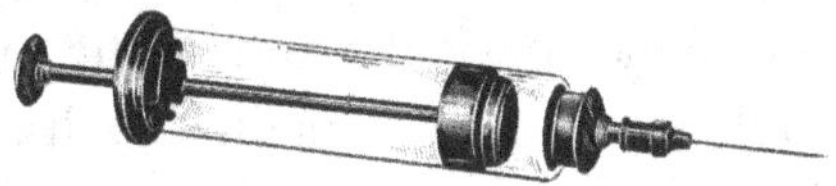

Minty, Tatum, and I are up and dressed early. I try to rouse Floss with kisses, but she merely grunts and swats me away. She's most definitely not a morning Zeek. She'd easily sleep in until midday, every day, if she could.

Minty's approach is less subtle. She rips Floss' covers off, and with a parent-like voice, she orders, "Up now, or I'll tip a cup of cold water over your head."

"I hate you," Floss grumbles, but she reluctantly drags herself up, knowing full well Minty's threats hold weight.

Dakari, Woody, and Sonja arrive at six-forty, and take us on a full tour of their village.

The ground level only gets filtered sunlight which bleeds through the gaps in the trees, but the fairy lights woven around the suspension bridges and tree houses above make the whole area glow a magical golden colour.

There are beautiful luminous gardens spread sporadically throughout the ground level of the village, and as we pass by one of the bigger ones, Woody plucks two iridescent pink flowers and hands one each to Minty and Tatum. I'd pick one for Floss too, if I thought she'd appreciate it, but she doesn't strike me as the flowers type.

At the far end of the village, the trees are widespread, leaving the area open and much brighter. There's a large open field lined with fire pits, which Dakari says is used for festivals and celebrations, and opposite it is an inviting lake with crystal clear water. I watch with fascination as a handful of Drakes, ranging in different colours, splash about at the water's edge with their children. It's so nice to see colours mixing. I'm glad there's no caste/colour system here.

Dakari is an unusual character. His accent and direct way of speaking comes across as harsh, yet every now and then he says something humorous, and then laughs at his own joke with a low, deep rumble that comes straight from his belly.

Dakari announces that this is the end of the tour, then gets our group to sit in a circle by the lake. "It's time to discuss the matter of job placements," he says.

My tummy rumbles as I sit. I wish I'd thought to bring food. It's well past lunchtime, and I'm starving. The one downfall to this new brawnier physique is it needs much more nourishment than my old wiry one.

While Dakari's accent is thick, he is much easier to understand than Sonja and Woody, who seem to have disappeared from our group somewhere along the way.

Dakari singles out Tatum first, asking her what her previous job was. She tells him she used to work in childcare, and he smiles, seeming pleased to hear this.

"We could use another childcare worker in our village, but you will have to be properly introduced to the Drake parents before we can get you started." His eyes flick to Jax's momentarily, sending a secret message. "Of course, not everyone will be happy about a Zeek stranger minding their children, but being a Pastel will work in your favour. We have many Pastel sympathisers in our village."

He zones in on Minty next, and she informs him she and I used to work together as chefs. This pleases him further. "I believe there'll be many Drakes who are interested in trying Zeek cuisine." He cups his chin in thought for a moment, and then goes on to say, "I'll organise a venue for you to set up shop and get Sonja to lend a hand for a few months. You will need her help to translate with the customers until you get a grip on the Drake language."

After further discussing a few venue and menu ideas with us, he turns his attention to Floss, who up until now has been sitting quietly next to me. I brace myself, not knowing what to expect from her. Work isn't a subject she responds well to.

"What was your previous line of work, Goeie Tweeling?"

Dakari has been calling her this all day, and I can tell by her slitted eyes, she's not a big fan. Jax told me it means good twin. I'd laughed. If Dakari thinks Harlow is the bad twin and Floss is the good twin, he is in for a very rude shock.

"I was a fruit picker, then a hunter, then a labourer," she says, plucking blades of grass and then flicking them away with a scowl. "And I hated all three jobs."

Dakari cackles to himself. "I see. Well, what is it you'd like to do?"

She shrugs. "I don't know, something interesting for once. What are you offering?"

From the corner of my eye, I notice Jax stiffen, but luckily for Floss, Dakari appears to find her abrasive attitude somewhat amusing. He laughs again and then runs her through a few job options.

It's clear from Floss' remaining scowl, she's not overly impressed by any of the jobs he has to offer. "Can you move on to the others while I consider my options?" she asks.

"Very well." He redirects his focus across all three warriors. "The Warriors," he says dramatically, and allows the words to hang in the air for a moment before continuing. "I trust our village could use some warriors to help keep guard. While we as a race believe in trying to keep the peace, conflict is not always avoidable, and I feel it would be foolish to throw away such talents by putting you all into regular jobs." He zooms his focus in on Jax. "I understand you won't be staying on a permanent basis, so I've spoken to Stavros, and as of tomorrow, he will be leaving his current position to come and train with you lot on these fields. I want him appointed as Chief Warrior in your place when you leave. I also believe it would be beneficial if you could take turns doing some extra training and self-defence lessons with our Drake guards."

"Thank you, Dakari." Jax's face is the warmest I've ever seen it, filled with pride and gratitude.

"You…know…" Zannah says, drawing her words out. "I believe Luna and Destiny would also be an asset to our team. Obviously, Destiny would have to wait until her leg is fully healed before commencing training, but those girls are agile and seriously know how to handle their weapons."

Jax nods agreeingly. "They do have extraordinary weapon skills."

"If you believe they will be an asset, then I'd be more than happy for you to discuss the idea with them. They currently work as harvesters and can be easily replaced.

"I want to be a warrior too," Floss blurts, and everyone's eyes dart in her direction, including mine.

"You're not trained to be a warrior," Zannah argues.

Floss bobbles her head with attitude. "Then train me. Duh!"

I can see where this is going, and I'm afraid it won't end well, so I give Floss' hand a light squeeze in warning.

Zannah snarls in blatant disapproval. "You're a Magenta. You're not built to be a warrior."

"Oh, I'm sorry," Floss retaliates with a snap. "I thought you were all about breaking down the colour system, or was that all just some big fat front so that Jax could make moves on my sister?" I watch as an invisible light clicks on inside her head. "Hold on…" Her shimmer darkens. "The two other girls you just recommended are former Pastels. Why them and not me, huh? Magentas are stronger than Pastels. I should have precedence."

Zannah sticks to her resolve. "They've been injected with vertic switz ink, which makes them stronger and more capable."

"Well, inject me." Floss' gaze shifts from Zannah's to Jax's, resentment radiating off her in waves. "I don't understand why I *wasn't* injected with the ink when Zavier and Minty were. Favouritism much?"

"There wasn't enough ink left for all three of you to have a sufficient dose," Jax answers. "And you didn't need it. Your body was strong enough to survive without the added help."

"Well… Would you look at that." Floss casts Zannah a challenging look. "If my body is strong enough to survive an all-night torture session without the help of ink, then I'm sure it's more than capable of taking on the intense training of a warrior."

"What is your opinion on this, Jax?" Dakari asks, his lips turned up at the corners in amusement.

"I think Floss is physically capable, and she doesn't lack courage, *but* she does lack discipline, and I don't believe it'll be easy to get her to conform."

"I'll conform if I have to," she bites back. "It beats being a lousy gardener, harvester, or labourer."

Jax cuts her a vexed glance. "Your argument is very reassuring."

"We'll give you a trial," Dakari offers, despite Jax's obvious disapproval. "You have the fighting spirit of a warrior. I'd like to see you put that spirit to good use, otherwise you might find yourself in trouble."

I don't like the idea of Floss and Zannah working together. They are both fiery and strong willed. I'll have to pull Jax aside later and ask what he plans on doing to keep them separated during training.

My tummy is still grumbling, so I'm pleased when I look up to see Sonja and Woody heading our way with two heaped baskets of food.

Minty always says food helps ease tension. I hope she's right, because the air inside our inner circle is that thick, you could cut through it with a knife.

9

A FORTNIGHT IN SUMMER

-HARLOW-

lex is back from hunting. I know, because I can hear him arguing with someone on the other side of the chamber door. Going by the high-pitched voice, I'm guessing it's a woman. Curious, I sneak over to the door and cup my ear to listen. *Dumb idea!* I quickly realise. I don't understand the Vallon language. Nevertheless, I continue to eavesdrop anyway, picking up on their tones. Alex's voice blasts with anger and frustration while the woman whines, sounding as if she's begging or pleading with him about something. *I wonder who she is, what she wants?*

He hasn't mentioned a sister, and the voice sounds too young and whiny to be his mother's, so unless she's his cousin...

Stop it Harlow! He's not your boyfriend anymore. What does it matter who she is?

The girl's whining becomes louder and more insistent before Alex explodes, growling, "Weg von mir!"

I shudder at the harshness of his tone.

Whatever he said must've been cutting and final, because there's a moment of deafening silence between them, and then I hear the tap, tap of footsteps retreating.

The click of the door unlocking makes me back up a step, and I move to the side to avoid being seen by anyone in the hall.

When Alex walks in and sees me standing close by, he jolts. "Oh…" His body is still rippling with anger. "I'm guessing you overheard that."

I'd be deaf not to. I swallow and nod. "Who was that?"

He dumps his leather holster onto the floor with a clank and sighs an exasperated breath. "Just someone who is trying to make my life extremely difficult."

"Was she a relative?" I ask, trying to sound casual.

"No, she's Jacinta's best friend. She's always pestering me lately. Don't worry, I don't think she'll be coming back."

"What does 'Weg von mir' mean?"

"It means get away from me."

I'd like to press for more information, but I don't want to appear jealous and give him the wrong idea. We're no longer together, and I'm in love with Jax, but of course I'm curious why he has women coming to his door, especially when he's the one pushing for a reconciliation.

It's exactly a fortnight today since Alex brought me here, and ever since sharing those first baby kicks together, Alex's demeanour towards me has taken a pleasant turn. He's kept his temper in check and has shown me more consideration. Every now and then when he's being playful or cheeky, I remember the reasons why I first fell for him. It's a relief—in a way—to see this side of him again, because for a long while

I'd felt completely ashamed of myself, believing I had sunk to the lowest of the low by being with him. It turns out he actually does have a likable side—I hadn't just imagined it—but regardless, my heart belongs to Jax.

I grab a cool glass of water and go back to the sofa while he heads straight to the washroom to freshen up. After he's finished, he comes over to where I'm sitting to give my tummy a rub and a kiss. He's been paying an awful lot of attention to my tummy this week. He acts as if it's all about the babies—but a piece of me wonders if it really is "all about the babies", or if he's using them as an excuse to get close to me. Either way, as long as he only sticks to my tummy, I'll allow it.

After placing his kisses, he lifts his head to peer up at me, his molten eyes glowing brightly. "If one of them is a boy, can we call him Axel? I always said if I had a son, I would name him Axel. It has all the same letters as Alex, yet it's a different name entirely. It's an anagram."

"That's cool," I say with a smile, and I mean it. "I like it." But then I think of our child being Lucas, and my smile falls flat. I know I should tell Alex the truth about Lucas, it's only fair, but I'm afraid for two reasons. First of all, admitting it makes it real, and I'm not sure if I'm ready to fully accept the idea as "real" just yet, plus I'm afraid of Alex's reaction and the consequences. He might retract his offer regarding taking me back to the forest.

"Are you sure?" He straightens and moves to sit on the sofa beside me. "Because your expression says otherwise."

"It's not that, it's just…"

His eyes stare into mine, waiting. "It's just what?"

"I already know the sexes of the babies."

"Oh…" He goes quiet a moment. "Are they both girls?"

"No, actually." I shake my head. "One's a boy and one's a girl, so you're in luck."

"Okay…?" His eyes study me. "Well, what's the problem then?" When I don't answer, his body tenses further and his gaze sharpens. "Don't you dare tell me that you've already promised Jax you'll name our son after him, or else we're going to have issues."

I roll my eyes. "Of course not, Alex. As if I would do that."

"Then why won't you tell me what the problem is?"

I pick at my nails. "Because I'm afraid."

"Afraid of what?"

Just tell him. I suck in a deep breath and force the words out of my mouth. "The boy I'm carrying is Lucas."

"What?" He jerks back, face scrunched. "How could you possibly know something like that?"

"RJ told me."

Alex knows all about RJ and his sixth sense; I've mentioned his name many times while swapping stories. Still, his molten eyes turn sceptical, so I run him through an abbreviated version of the whole "twins and their connections to other twins".

He stares ahead, chewing on his lip, and I sense a flurry of thoughts ticking over in his head. "But we slept together before you killed Lucas, so how does that work?"

"I don't know the specifics, I didn't ask. After RJ told me the news, I felt sick and started puking."

"I see." Alex's eyes darken. "This is another reason why you haven't been able to forgive me, isn't it? You blame me for this because I'm the one who has the connection to Lucas."

It's true to a degree, but I'm not about to admit it. After all, I was the one who killed Lucas, so we both had a hand in this.

"I thought you would be happy about this. In a months' time, you'll have your brother back. I took him away from you, and now I'm giving him back to you."

"Sure, I'll be glad to have him back, but not at the cost of losing you. I let my love for Lucas come between us once, and I'm still paying for it." He squeezes his eyes shut and exhales. "I don't want it to happen again. Besides, I'm fairly sure you couldn't be happy about this. I doubt you could ever really love him, could you?"

I swallow back the bile I taste seeping onto my tongue. "I am struggling with the idea, of course I am, but maybe you could help me?" This is something I need to come to terms with before our children are born. I don't want my hatred for Lucas to transfer onto my son. I can't reject him, it'd be cruel. "You still loved Lucas despite the awful things he did to us, so you obviously must have still seen some good in him, right?" My words are like a plea.

Alex looks away. "We've spoken about this before and you got angry with me, but I promise you, Lucas wasn't born a bad person, he was moulded into one due to years of abuse. Young Lucas used to be sweet and timid, but there are only so many times you can be beaten down and broken before something snaps inside you. As Lucas grew older, he conjured demons to protect himself." His eyes find mine again, and he hesitates a moment before adding, "I don't think the Lucas who killed us was the real Lucas, I think it was his demons. The real Lucas wasn't evil, he was just a broken-down soul who wanted desperately to be loved."

"Perhaps you could tell me some nice stories about young Lucas. Maybe it will help?"

"Sure…" He squirms uncomfortably beside me. "As long as you promise not to resent me for it. I've been trying really hard to make things good between us again, and I don't want to end up back at square one over this. I really love you, and I don't want to lose you."

Guilt slices through me. I love Alex too, only it's not in the same way. I feel connected to him, and I care for him, but I'm not *in* love with him. I'm in love with Jax.

"I won't resent you; I promise." In an effort to lighten the mood, I add, "As long as I get to name our baby girl Lyla."

He chuckles half-heartedly at my out-of-the-blue comment. "Okay, deal. Axel and Lyla. I like it."

10

NEWS

-ZANNAH-

*L*una carefully places the five cans back into position. She's spent a great deal of time this week helping me to master the art of knife throwing. I'm still nowhere near as good as she is, but I am improving daily.

Jax, Stavros, and Oscar sit on the deck sipping bean-brews and watch on intently as I take my next round of throws.

"I'd sleep with one eye open if I were you," Stavros tells Oscar. "She's getting better by the toss."

"Tell me something," Oscar fires back. "How is it you two are living *nice and comfortably* over here in Pleasantville while I'm stuck next door with Bitchface Zannah, Psychopath Floss, and Fussy, Bossy Rosy who's turning out to be a major pain in my arse?"

Jax raises a brow in amusement. "Her name is Minty."

"Seriously," Oscar continues, paying no attention. "I'm always getting an earful for leaving my stuff lying around or not putting items back in their 'correct place'." He air quotes. "This arrangement totally sucks. I feel like I'm back living with my mother again."

"Stop being a filth-bag, and she'll stop treating you like one. It's that simple, moron." I take my next toss, and the throwing knife hits dead-set in the middle of the can. *Heck yes!* What a perfect way to polish off that sentence.

"See what I mean…" Oscar scoffs in irritation. "How do you expect me to live with that thing?"

"Look, I'm sorry to say it, but she does have a point," Jax counters, and I smile smugly. "Is it really that hard to pick up after yourself? You do have to consider that you're living with five other Zeeks."

"Yeah, yeah," Oscar grumbles. "Leave it to you to side with Zannah."

I like having Jax around because he'll often defend me against Oscar and Stavros, even when I don't necessarily deserve it. He's always been good to me like that.

I was hoping he would loosen up a little after being out in the forest for a couple of weeks, but if anything, he seems more uptight than usual. Not only is he still struggling with losing Harlow, he's been worrying himself sick about the young teen who was impaled by the shard. Thankfully, RJ is returning for another visit today. We've all got our fingers crossed, hoping and praying he'll give us a positive update on her condition.

I pop the throwing knives down and open my pack. "Let's move on to something more exciting, shall we?" I say, gazing Luna's way with a devilish grin. I pull out the crossbow I stole, along with the case of bolts. "Are you game?"

"What do you have there?" Jax stands to get a better look at the crossbow in my hands. "Is that a hunter's crossbows?" His brows dip disapprovingly. "You weren't supposed to take that."

"Blame Stavros," I say. "He told me to grab whatever I needed —and I needed this."

Stavros throws the rest of his sandwich at my head, but I duck, so it misses. "That's not what I meant, and you know it, you little thief."

"This is my reward for the bad arse stunt I pulled off," I counter, trying—yet failing miserably—to set up the scope. "If I'm going to be stuck out here for the rest of my life, then I at least need some toys to play with, or else I'll die of boredom."

"What's so terrible about living out here?" Stavros asks defensively.

"Well, I'm sure it's not so terrible for someone like you," I spit. "But I need a little more excitement."

Stavros crosses his arms over his chest. "Someone like me?" His sharp tone signifies he's offended. "What's that supposed to mean?"

"It means you're a family man now. You've chosen your path and you're living it. You're happy to settle, whereas I'm not. I need something more 'happening' to make me feel alive."

Oscar rises from his seat. "What she needs is a man, but she'll never get one because no one's brave enough—or stupid enough— to put up with her." When he's finished taking his swipe, he picks up his mug and wanders inside the hut.

No one knows this—and if it ever came to light, I would deny it —but Oscar and I have history. We slept together once, back when I was eighteen and he was nineteen. It was on the night of Oscar's nineteenth birthday, to be precise. He and some of the other warriors decided to get loose and take some of Elgar's chemical concoctions, so feeling hyped, I joined them. Anyway, one thing led to another, and the next morning Oscar and I woke up in bed together—*completely naked*. He seemed pleased about it, but I was furious, and threatened if he ever told another living soul, I would chop off his manhood with my blade.

That was two years ago, and I haven't been with anyone else since. On the contrary, Oscar has become quite the man-whore. He seems to have a new girl lined up every month. Not that I care. I never actually wanted him; I wanted Jax.

"Frost!" I curse as I come to realise I've just finished putting the scope on backwards. That'll teach me to dredge up bad memories.

Jax jumps down from the deck and heads over to me. "Pass it here."

"It's mine," I say, digging my heals in. "I stole it fair and square."

His lips twitch into a semi-smile. "I'm not here to take it off you. I'm here to help you set it up. It's quite clear you have no idea what you're doing."

I sigh and hand the crossbow over. "Fine."

Within a matter of minutes, he's got the crossbow all set up and ready to go. *Smart arse.*

"Do you even know how to use it?" he asks.

I shrug. "I'm sure I can work it out."

"Here." He passes it over and then steps around behind me, helping to position my arms correctly for the shot. "Now see this here," he says, pointing. "Pull it back this way, but make sure to keep your arms steady and your eyes on the target."

He guides me with the first shot, and together we hit the can.

"Nice work," he says with approval. "Now give it another go without my help."

I consider asking him to help me once more, just to feel his strong arms around me again, but then I decide not to torture myself. Besides, I don't want to look incompetent.

Jax and I will only ever be friends. I've come to terms with that. I just wish I could find someone who compares to him, because I'll die an old maid before settling for less.

My first shot isn't the best, but by my third go, I at least hit the side of the target.

"Cool! Can I have a turn?"

I look over my shoulder to see Floss and Zavier standing behind us. "No," I answer, deadpan.

She pouts. "Why not?"

"You need to work on making your body a lethal weapon before you start using lethal weapons."

"Come on," she snaps. "I've been training hard for two weeks straight. That should count for something."

Jax frowns, grunts by way of response, and then leaves. It's funny, because Jax is usually very controlled with his emotions. I've seen cocky new recruits push him to the brink, and he's remained his expressionless stoic self—no worries at all—yet for some reason, he has no tolerance for Floss, *whatsoever*.

Floss' bratty attitude gets on my nerves too, and there's been several occasions this week where I've been tempted to punch her face in, but at the same time I can't help but feel a little respect for her. She's tough, brave, and doesn't take crap. Plus, she managed to stay strong and keep her mouth shut during Electra's all-night torture session—which is a pretty big feat, I reckon.

As I take my next shot, a loud scream rings in my ears, distracting me, and I miss the target completely. I spin to find Floss sniggering—hands on hips.

"Oh, I'm sorry," she says. "I thought I saw a bug."

Stavros laughs. For some reason he and Dakari seem to find Floss' bratty behaviour somewhat amusing.

"Bitch!" If she keeps this behaviour up, my respect for her will dwindle in no time. "Try that again, and you'll become the target."

"There's still some sandwiches and cakes on the table," Stavros says. "Why don't you two come up, and I'll fix you each a warm mug of bean-brew."

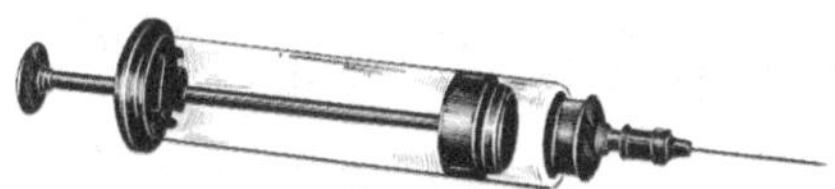

RJ arrives at midday, and we're all over the moon to hear that the young teen has gone from a critical to stable condition. He also mentions that the rest of those injured, including the warriors I took down, are all on the mend.

RJ fills us in on everything that has happened since the ceremony, and I find it interesting at first, but once he and Jax start diving heavily into politics, I zone out. I'm all about breaking down the colour system, and I'll support whatever decisions Jax makes regarding the matter, but I'm not interested in the nitty gritty of it all, and RJ is prone to rambling.

Feeling restless, I go to check in on Destiny only to find Oscar lying alongside her in her bed, chatting, flirting, chuckling—the usual. *Typical.* She's the only available Zeek here—besides me—so like a fuegor, he's pounced.

"I wouldn't go getting *too* close if I were you," I say, casting Destiny a look of warning. "This one here is a lady-killer."

Oscar glares up at me, his face tight. "Shut up, Zannah."

Ignoring Oscar, I ask, "How's your leg? Is it feeling any better?"

"It's slowly getting there." Destiny's face is flushed, and there's stardust in her eyes.

Poor girl, she's already under his spell.

"That's good." I glance between the pair, making them squirm. "Okay, well, I'll leave you both to it then, but don't say I didn't warn you, Destiny."

SECRETS UNCOVERED

-HARLOW-

I lie in bed, watching as shadows flicker across the carved ceiling, set in motion by the dancing flames of the candle chandelier. I've spent so many hours daydreaming about Jax and the magical evening we spent together wrapped in each other's arms. I remember the way he'd set my nerves on fire with a single touch, and how he'd traced his strong fingers along my body, like he was worshiping my every curve. I know deep down inside that Jax is the one I love and want to be with, but after opening up to Alex last Thursday, the dynamics between us have changed. He's been really sweet and attentive, and I worry about it complicating things.

I was worried he was going to be a complete jerk about the whole Lucas thing, but surprisingly, he considered the situation from my angle and has been compassionate and supportive. For the first time *ever*, he put me and my feelings first.

He shared a couple of nice stories about young Lucas before saying, "I'm not going to keep harping on about him. I don't think it's beneficial. I'm sure you get the picture. Lucas started out sweet and innocent and changed for the worse. The way I see it, if we love, nurture, and treat our son right, he won't turn out the same." Alex had taken my hand in his, sparking my insides to churn with mixed emotions. "I believe we can restore Lucas back to the sweet boy he once was. We just need to let go of the past and give him the loving childhood he never had."

I broke into sobs, and he'd quickly backpedalled. "Perhaps what would really be best is if we stop thinking of the baby as Lucas and start thinking of him as Axel," he'd suggested. "Let's sever the connection in our minds and start fresh." He'd tipped my chin up so he could look into my eyes, and with complete sincerity, he'd added, "I love my brother, but I love you more, and I want to do what's right for you—for us."

What Alex hadn't realised was I was no longer crying because of Lucas, I was crying because we were never going to be the family he wants us to be.

Now, alone in his bed, I rehash our conversation over and over.

The prospect of leaving Alex in less than a month scares me as much as the thought of being locked in this chamber with him forever.

I don't want to lose him entirely. I wish he could come with us and live in the forest. I'm not suggesting we reconcile and share a hut, but I'd like him to be close enough that he could remain a part of our twins' lives. My heart twists, knowing this is an impossible dream. There are so many reasons why this plan could never work.

I care deeply for Alex, and I want him to be happy, just not with me. An image of human Alex flitters through my mind, and I wince. He's already been through so much, it would be cruel for me to turn my back on him now, especially when he's been trying hard to mend things between us.

My gaze wanders across the wide-open chamber, taking in the lush furniture and added luxuries most others here on Zadok can't afford. I suppose this wouldn't be the worst place to be trapped for the rest of my life, and Alex would make a decent partner and doting father. He can be completely irrational at times, but of late, his good points have outweighed the bad. And let's face it, creepy irises aside, he's definitely appealing.

My chest tightens painfully as I truly consider the idea. To fulfil Alex's hopes and dreams, I will be giving up my freedom, my friends in Spring, and a promising future with Jax.

However, if I leave as planned, not only will I be robbing Alex of his happiness, I'll be robbing our kids of their chance to get to know their birth father, and I know firsthand how detrimental that can be.

What's the right choice? Is there one? The worst thing is, no matter what choice I make, someone is going to get hurt. *Why does everything have to be so damn complicated?*

Frustrated, I roll over and squash my face hard into the pillow.

As much as I don't want to hurt Alex, the thought of never seeing Jax again is almost too excruciating to bear. I've never felt this way about anyone.

The door clicks and clanks, and I jolt. I hadn't expected Alex home so early. Not wanting him to see me depressed and miserable, I quickly pull the covers up high, pretending to be asleep. I don't want to have to explain myself. I've still got another few weeks to figure everything out, *so why upset the applecart by bringing up issues now?*

The door opens with a drawn-out creak, and my breath catches. I listen intently. It sounds as though it's being pushed in a slow, cautious manner. The tap-tap of footsteps entering the chamber has me tensing in fear. These taps are light and feminine like. My heart pounds. *This isn't Alex. I'M IN DANGER!*

The taps grow louder as this "someone" heads straight over to the bed where I'm lying. My body trembles involuntarily, and my fists clench tightly to the blanket coving me. I need to keep my identity hidden. *Vallons are my enemy. They abuse and kill Zeeks like me.*

As tight as my grip is, it proves useless against the Vallon's sheer strength. In less than a second, the bed covers are reefed back, exposing my shimmering Zeek skin. A young woman with wavy blood-red hair stands above me, and she gasps in horror at the sight of me.

"Ein sklave!"

I hurriedly scoot up to the head of the bed and cower like a wounded animal. I have no idea what her foreign words mean, nor do I have any idea of how to respond. There's no chance I could beat this woman in a fight. She's built like a boxer, and there's nowhere safe for me to run. I'm trapped like a mouse.

Her molten eyes shoot lasers at my tummy. "How far along is you are, slave?"

I blink, shocked. She speaks Zeek. Clearly not very well—and her accent is super thick—but I recognise those words, just as I recognise her voice.

It's the same woman I'd heard arguing with Alex a few days ago. *Who is she really? And why is she sneaking into Alex's chamber when he's at work?*

She leans closer, her body language fierce in warning. "Tell, slave."

Her scornful use of the word slave cuts deep and makes my heart bleed for the poor Pastels being kept here against their will.

I consider my predicament. Given she hasn't laid a hand on me yet, I figure it's probably in my best interest to cooperate.

I hold up three fingers. "Three months."

She shakes her head. "You too big." She spreads her fingers out over her tummy to indicate what she means. "I say you mean longer."

"I'm just over..." My words wobble past my lips, "but only by a—"

"Longer," she shouts over top of me. She doesn't believe me, *and why would she?* My tummy is huge. I look full term.

I shake my head. "No."

Her reaction to the timeframe of my pregnancy has me questioning if she and Alex are… *No!* I freeze at the thought. I've known Alex to do lousy things, but I can't bring myself to believe that he would stoop this low, especially after the big song and dance he'd made about Jax and the letters.

Her face hardens. "Is no matter how much, if when is longer than three months or no. Is still time with me," she puts her hand to her chest, "and must be overlap."

Her speech might be broken and hard to decipher, but the message is loud and clear.

My heart slows to a near stop. I don't believe it—or at least I don't want to believe it. I wouldn't have picked Alex as a cheat. Only last night, before we went to sleep, he'd said, "You, and the twins mean everything to me. I hope you know that."

Taking in a deep breath, I build up the courage to ask, "Are you and Slater…" I stumble. Each word stabbing at my throat. "Are you together?"

She snarls in disdain. "I no believe he cheat on me with slave whore. He more disgusting than I thought."

Her words are like a double slap to my face. My heart twists and then sinks. I need to swallow, or I'm going to puke. I can't believe it. I've spent all day worrying about Alex, and his feelings, only to learn that he's been playing me this whole time. And to think, I was seriously considering the idea of sacrificing my own happiness, to keep him happy.

"Screw you, Alex!" I curse under my breath. Every time I let him in, he hurts me. I should never have let my guilt influence my decision to stay here. I should have insisted that he take me straight back to the forest.

I slink back uneasily as the woman goes around to the other side of the bed and sits. To my bewilderment, she doesn't say anything else, she merely stares ahead, her brows dipped in a V, indicating she's brewing inside, just as I am.

12

UNEXPECTED

-ALEX AS SLATER-

 arrive at my chamber door to discover it partially open, and alarm bells ring in my head.

Ruby…

A wave of sickening images come crashing to mind, nearly knocking me off my feet. She'd better not be hurt—or worse. *I can't lose her.*

Panicked, I quickly draw out my blade and charge inside, expecting to find either a blood bath or an empty chamber.

My feet come to a screeching halt when I spot her in our bed, alive and unharmed. "Rubes?" *Oh shit… No!* My heart leaps into my throat when I register Raven sitting near her. This woman doesn't let up. I curse Jacinta and the day she introduced us.

I can tell by the puffiness of Ruby's eyes she's been crying.

"Rubes." I rush over to her side of the bed, afraid of the irreparable damage Raven might have caused our fragile relationship. "Are you okay?" I go to put my hand on her arm, but she recoils.

"Don't." Her stony-faced expression confirms my fears. It's official. In one afternoon, Raven has managed to destroy two-and-a-half weeks' worth of progress.

"She didn't hurt you, did she?"

Ruby doesn't get a chance to answer because Raven leaps at me like a maniac from the other side of the bed.

"You're a disgusting predator!" She hits my chest with the heal of her hands. "How could you degrade me by cheating on me with one of the slaves? You've always said you were against using the slaves as whores, but you're a liar. You're just as sick and evil as your mother's guards."

I'm glad Raven is using our Vallon language to scream all of this at me, although chances are she's already said far worse to Ruby before I arrived. Another quick glance at Ruby's stony, tear-streaked face tells me my assumptions are accurate. Raven is semi-conversant in Zeek. The irony is, I taught her the language, believing one day we would be linked. All royals need to be familiar with the Zeek and Drake languages, it's a requirement. Little did I know what seemed like innocent lessons might, one day, come back to bite me.

Raven continues to pound into me, screaming and crying hysterically. I find her tantrum infuriating.

Air comes out through my nostrils in loud angry bursts. "Raven stop!" When I repeat this twice, and she still doesn't let up, I grab hold of her wrists to restrain her. "What are you doing here?"

"I thought you were keeping a teenage girl locked in your chamber. Jacinta said she saw you at the markets with teenage girls' dresses, but it turns out you've been hiding away a pregnant slave whore." Her eyes gleam darkly "I don't know what's worse."

The fact that she can say something as appalling as this—and honestly believe it—sickens me to my core.

"Did you speak to her?" I ask, trying my best to ignore that she just called Ruby a whore.

"Yes, I spoke to her," she says, and something shrivels inside of me. "She told me she's three months pregnant, which means you must have slept with her around the same time we got back together. How could you do this to me, to us? How could you be so disgusting and stupid? I thought you were better than that." She glares at me hatefully. "You can't hide her in your chamber forever. You know what has to happen. She needs to be destroyed, just like the others."

"No!"

"There's no other choice. She can't have that baby. If you allow that half-breed child to be born and it gets discovered, your mother will kill all three of you, no questions asked. Are you really prepared to lay your life on the line for a slave whore?"

My anger spikes. "Stop calling her that."

"It's what she is."

"No, it's not what she is." The volume of my voice rises, and my grip on her wrists tightens. "She is going to be the mother of my children, and I'm in love with her, so show some respect."

"Respect?" Raven gawks at me in disbelief. "Slate, listen to what you're saying. This girl is not a Vallon from a rich and powerful bloodline, she is a Zeek and a slave. She is not worthy of a prince. If you have any ounce of self-respect left, you will hand her over to the guards to be executed before anyone in the kingdom comes to know about your indiscretions." Her eyes plead with me. "If you do this right now, with me, I might even consider taking you back."

"Are you kidding?" I let go of her wrists and take a step back. "I don't want to get back with you. I want you out of my life. We are over. I keep telling you, but you don't seem to be able to get it through your thick head. I don't even know how you keep getting in here. Did you have a key made?"

She thrusts a pointed finger towards Ruby, her eyes bulging with fury. "Are you honestly choosing this wretched slave over me?"

It suddenly occurs to me that insulting Raven might not be in my best interests right now. As much as I want her out of here, chances are as soon as she leaves this room she'll go running straight to Kenneth and Jacinta and betray me. I need her to keep my secret under wraps, at least until I can work out a solution. This means, I need to keep her onside.

There is only really one true solution, I realise with a pang, and I don't like it one bit. *Ruby won't be able to stay here anymore. It's not safe. I'm going to have to take her back to the forest.* My heart breaks just thinking about it. I can't believe it's come to this. Things were finally improving between us; I could feel it. The way she'd gazed into my eyes last night, warm and wistful, suggested she was starting to feel something for me again. I'd been so close to winning her back.

I stare into Raven's bulging eyes, my insides boiling with pure and utter rage. I used to feel sympathy for her, but now all I feel is burning hatred. She has no idea what she's cost me.

Using every bit of inner strength I can muster, I fight back the string of outraged curses I'd been about to let rip. "I don't know actually," I backtrack. "Maybe not. I'm confused. I need more time to decide. Can you please give me twenty-four hours to think about this?"

Her face twists. "Excuse me?"

"You're asking me to sacrifice my kids. I don't really think twenty-four hours is too much to ask."

"Kids?" Her eyes glance to Ruby's tummy and then back at me. "Are you suggesting she's pregnant with twins? Is that why she's so big?"

"Raven, please." I soften my tone to hide my resentment. "Just give me twenty-four hours without mentioning this to anyone. If I'm going to do as you ask and hand them over, then I at least need a chance to say goodbye."

She frowns, taking a second to think it through. "Okay, fine. Twenty-four hours, but that's all the time I'm giving you." Then without warning, she leans in and presses her lips firm against mine. I imagine this kiss is more to prove something to Ruby than because she actually wants to kiss me, and it takes all the strength I have not to pull away. "Just remember, those babies inside her aren't Vallons.

They are half-breeds, and if you don't get rid of them now, they will be the death of you."

Raven gives Ruby one last look of disgust before turning on her heels and strutting out the door. I rush over to lock the door behind her. The last thing we need is another surprise visitor.

As I head back to Ruby, she pulls the blanket up to her chest, using it like a barricade. She's sending me serious "back off" vibes, but we don't have the luxury of time for me to give her the space she wants.

I sit down in front of her and reach for her hand. "Rubes, I—"

"Don't," she says, raising her palm in warning. "Don't you dare touch me." She turns her face away. "I'm so upset with you right now; I can't even stand to look at you."

"I can explain."

"Explain what?" Her small hands ball into fists as she grips the edge of the blanket, scrunching the fabric tight beneath her fingers. "That you're a liar and a hypocrite? You absolutely grilled me about Jax and the letters, yet never once during our fight did you mention that you have a girlfriend."

"I had a girlfriend," I correct. "Past tense." I lean forward trying to gain eye contact, but she jerks back. "Raven and I are over. We've been over for a long time."

"Not according to Raven or that parting kiss I just witnessed." Ruby's red swollen eyes finally snap to mine. "Raven's Zeek language skills aren't exactly up to scratch, but the sentences we 'must be overlap' and 'I no believe he cheat on me with slave whore' got the message across loud and clear."

"She actually called you that to your face?" My teeth clench in anger. "I'm so sorry, Rubes, she had no right to say that to you."

A bitter laugh escapes Ruby's throat. "But you have the right to lie and cheat on me?"

"No. Please, let me explain." My voice catches against the lump in my throat. "I *was* with Raven the day we first met. We'd been dating for a year. But like I've told you before, ever since the first moment I laid eyes on you, I've been crazy about you. When I finally saw you on Earth again after all those years—I knew in an instant that my feelings for you were real—and that Raven could never compare, so to be fair, I came back and ended things with her."

Ruby's frosty gaze penetrates mine. "And then what…? I know that's not where the story ends. Raven was upset about me being three months pregnant. She said we overlap."

I wince. "I did sleep with her once since then," I admit thickly, and the wounded look in Ruby's eyes hits me like a freight train. Regardless, I force myself to hurry on before I lose my nerve. "That day I took off on you was a big mistake, and I only got so far before racing back to apologise. But when I returned, I saw Jax kneeling in front of you, and…" I flinch at the memory. "He was so close, and his hands were all over you, yet, never once did you tell him to back up. I got jealous."

"Oh, come on, Alex," Ruby scoffs. "Are you seriously trying to justify your actions under the banner of jealousy? I'd hardly say that Jax's hands were 'all over' me. He was just being kind. He was showing me concern."

I'm sure, I think bitterly, but I leave it alone. I don't want to make things any worse between us. "It's not just that. Please, let me finish," I say. "When I saw Jax carrying you away, I figured I was never going to see you again. You'd severed my link to Earth, which meant there was no longer a safe way for us to stay in contact. I was a mess, Rubes." I swallow hard before continuing. "And at a loss for what to do, so in that moment, I forced myself to believe that things were truly over between us."

Ruby's gaze remains hard and cold. "So, it's my fault then?"

"No, of course not. That's not what I'm saying." I lower my eyes, feeling ashamed. "When I got back to my chamber, Raven was inside waiting for me. She'd said that she was upset with the way we'd ended things, and that she thought we owed it to ourselves to give our relationship a second chance, so I…we…" I stop short, unable to finish the sentence.

"Let me get this straight," Ruby says, looking green. "Are you telling me that you slept with Raven less than twenty-fours after you slept with me? I can't believe you, Alex. That's disgusting."

This is the second time in one day that I've been referred to as disgusting, and it stings.

"I know it was wrong, but I was hurt and confused, and she was there throwing herself at me. It was a terrible mistake." My eyes plead with Ruby's for forgiveness. "I promise you, it only happened the once, never again. And it meant *nothing*."

"I was really upset when I got back, too." Her tone is cold—not forgiving. "But do you know what I did? I slept alone, crying into my pillow every night for the following week. I didn't jump in bed with the first Zeek I came across, even though you have blatantly accused me of doing so. I love how you magically seem to remember that you broke up with me when it works for you." The next part she mutters under her breath. "Hypocrite."

"You fell for Jax. That's worse. Jax actually means something to you. Raven means nothing to me. You're all I want, I promise you." I reach for her arm, and she pulls back.

"Don't touch me."

My heart twists as her face fills with disgust.

"I can't do this anymore, Alex," she says. "I'm done with being your prisoner. I want to be taken back to the forest."

"Prisoner?" *Does she really consider herself to be my prisoner?* My heart rips in two. I hadn't known she felt this way. If she'd said something earlier, I would have taken her straight back to the forest. I would much rather lose her to Jax than have her think of me as some kind of monster. A sick sinking feeling invades my stomach. Maybe Raven's right. Maybe I am as evil as my mother's guards. *I should never have brought her here.* I should have respected her wishes and walked away, but I was too selfish to give her up. *Who am I kidding*, I still am. Even now, I don't want to give her up. She's supposed to be with me. After all the years I've longed for her, I only got to be with her for a moment and now I have to let her go again. *It's not fair.*

Noticing my internal struggle, a look of regret flashes in Ruby's eyes. "You belong with someone like Raven. Clearly, she still loves you, so maybe you should take me back to the forest and then try to work things out with her when you get back."

"If you understood anything Raven just said to me, you

wouldn't be suggesting this." I narrow my eyes. "She was begging for me to take you to the guards to be destroyed. That's what happens to Zeek slaves who get pregnant here. They are taken away and executed by order of the Queen. She doesn't want Summer to be tainted with half-breeds.

"And to be clear, that kiss you just witnessed was me bartering for an extra twenty-four hours. I asked Raven to keep our secret to herself for a day. I said I needed a chance to say goodbye."

Ruby's eyes spark with fear.

"Oh, come on, Rubes," I say, resenting her lack of faith in me. No matter what I say or do, she's always going to think of me as a monster. "It's not what's really happening here. I'm going to take you back to the forest. I just can't do it right now, there's too much activity going on at this time of day. Most Vallons finish work around now. The streets will be too crowded. Our best chance to get out unseen will be at midnight, when it's the changing of the guards."

She nods, acknowledging what I've said, and then lowers herself down under the blankets, turning her back to me. Devastated, and unable to console her, I get up and head for the washroom with a heavy aching heart.

13

FIRE AND ICE MAGIC INTERMINGLE

-HARLOW-

$\mathcal{A}$fter half an hour of being left alone with my turbulent thoughts, Alex comes over with a plate of sandwiches and places them on the bed beside me. I think it's his way of a peace offering.

"I know you're still upset, but you should really eat something. We have a long walk ahead of us tonight, and if you don't, you're going to end up getting lightheaded and passing out."

My throat constricts at the thought of eating anything, but it's not just me I have to worry about anymore, so I force myself to pick up a triangle and take a bite.

Alex walks around to the other side of the bed and sits heavily. "On a scale of one to ten, how much do you hate me?" His eyes weigh mine. "Is there any chance of us parting on friendly terms?"

While a part of me is still seething below the surface, I care about him enough not to spend our last several hours together fighting. "I don't hate you, Alex," I say. "I'm just upset with you." I allow my eyes to meet his. "I keep letting you in, and you keep hurting me. You're like Dr Jekyll and Mr Hyde. There's a kind, funny, caring Alex who makes me laugh and sweeps me off my feet, but there's also a selfish, spiteful, jealous Alex who says and does horrible things."

"I'm sorry. I don't want to be Mr Hyde."

"I know," I say, believing him. "And I know you've been trying really hard to keep your Hyde side in check." I force a semi-smile. "Besides our rough beginning and ending, I have actually enjoyed spending time with you."

"Even as my prisoner?" he says defensively.

I cringe. "I didn't mean that literally. I was hurting, and I..." I pause, seeking the right words for a soft delivery. "Take a minute to think about this from my perspective. I've been confined to your chamber indefinitely because I'm not safe beyond these four walls. How is that a life?" Softening my voice, I hurry to say, "I do honestly care about you, Alex, and if there's a way that we can still meet up now and then without putting you in danger, I think we should do it. I'd really like you to remain a part of our twins' lives."

"A part of our twins' lives but not yours?" The look in his eyes says it isn't easy for him to accept this.

Even after everything he's done to hurt me, a twinge of guilt grips at my heart. "We don't belong together, Alex. We were brought together by our twin connection, but the reality is we're not suited. Besides, we have too much painful history to make this work."

He stays silent for a long moment before asking, "Do you think there'll be another life after this one?"

I shrug. "RJ once told me that he remembers his life before

being a human, so if there was life before Earth, I'm sure there will be life after Zadok."

"Do you think if we were to meet up in the next life, we could start afresh?"

I conjure a weak laugh. "Sure. Although, who knows where we'll end up, or who or what we'll come back as? It's kind of scary to think about, isn't it?"

"Not as scary as the thought of losing you forever." His voice is low, thick and sounds far away.

The depth of his words unsettles me, but I don't have time to dwell on them, for a loud blasting sound vibrates through the chamber, and I watch as the large chamber door rips off its hinges and goes flying across the room with a crash. A sense of horror sweeps over me. *Raven must have given us up.*

Alex surges upright, his muscles coiled and ready to fight. "Ruby, get under the bed now!"

"What about you?"

"DO IT NOW!" His voice is loud, jarring and filled with panic. I obey.

I spot four guards charging through the opening as I slip to the floor.

"TÖTE SIE!" one of them shouts.

I quickly slither under the bed—fully aware that I'm only buying myself seconds—*if that.*

The beats of my thudding heart fill my ears, muffling out the sound of pounding fists and pain induced grunts. Please let Alex survive this, I pray. I know he's strong, but I don't know that he's strong enough to take on four guards at once, especially as he doesn't have his blade. It's not long before a glowing red arm tries grabbing at me from the side of the bed. A rough finger grazes me, and I hurriedly slide further to the middle, where I'm out of reach.

"Hündin," the guard's gruff voice spits like a curse. His arm retracts, and then the next thing I know the whole bed is lifted and tossed on its side. The two lower posts crack loudly against the stone wall, snapping like toothpicks due to the sheer force.

My body trembles like a leaf. I'm exposed, and there's nowhere left for me to hide.

The guard's guttural laugh vibrates above me, and I look up to find his molten red eyes blazing down on me like globes of fire. His lips quirk up wickedly, revealing a crooked set of teeth. This Vallon looks nothing like Alex. His face is beyond demonic. I would try pleading with him if I thought it would help, but I can see it in his eyes—he's here for the kill.

"Du kannst dich jetzt nicht verstecken," he says, and then he reefs me up with a jarring force.

The grip of his hand is secure like a clamp, crushing the flesh of my upper arm to the bone. I'm trying to keep a brave face, but it's impossible. I whimper in pain, tears spilling from my eyes.

Dread grips me tighter than his hands ever could, making my thoughts go straight to Luna and Destiny. If this was the kind of manhandling they endured while being held here in Summer, then I can certainly see why they despise me so much for the choices I've made. No one in their right mind would choose this. But what they hadn't understood was Alex is not your typical Vallon—and I hadn't fallen for him as a Vallon, I'd fallen for him as a human.

My hands claw at the thick fingers gripping me, when suddenly, I feel a spark of heat, and I'm blinded by a burst of bright light.

To my astonishment, the guard lets go of me with a yelp and shakes his hand. "Sie hat mich verbrannt."

Shock jolts through me. *Did I cause that spark?*

Now aggravated, he gives me a kick to the side of my stomach, which sends me flying headfirst into the stone wall. I grit my teeth, holding in a cry. That hurt—*a lot*—and I'm worried about what damage his kick might have done to the babies. Chances are I won't live long enough to find out. I try to scramble back to my feet, but the chamber swims around me. The skin just below my hairline burns, and I can feel warm blood trickling down my forehead.

"Ruby!" Alex kicks and fights his way over to me.

The other three guards come at him from all angles, jabbing, punching, and kicking, yet somehow Alex manages to push through them, only stopping when he comes face to face with the guard who'd just kicked me. A dangerous glint flashes in his eyes, and with one solid king hit, he thumps the guard across the temple so hard I swear I hear his skull crack. As the guard stumbles back, Alex snatches his blade handle, unsheathing it. The guard tries to snatch the blade back, but his reflexes are slow after the powerful hit. Alex takes advantage of his disoriented state and swings the blade to his throat, slicing it wide open. Blood splatters everywhere—including on me—and I scream.

The remaining guards unsheathe their blades in a flash, pointing the sharp tips towards us, threatening.

Alex's eyes snap to mine fierce with warning. "Get behind me and stay behind me."

I press my trembling lips shut and hurriedly step behind him.

One of the guards speaks to Alex. Going by his hand actions and toned-down approach, I believe he's trying to reason with him.

There are a few moments of semi-civil discussion between them before Alex's rage reignites. Clearly outraged by what the guard has said, Alex lunges forward and stabs him through the stomach, causing him to drop and squeal like a stuffed pig.

The two remaining guards slip back into attack mode, and one of the two manages to strike Alex across his ribs, leaving a deep and painful looking gouge. I shudder.

Blood spills from Alex's side, but he simply groans and continues to fight.

As soon as Alex starts gaining on them, the guards throw fireballs, bringing this fight to a whole new level. I crouch behind Alex and watch as he struggles to duck and weave two sets of fireballs along with two sets of blades. He's on the defence now instead of the attack. *I have to do something.*

While Alex ducks the fireball from one guard, I dive at the other hoping to distract him long enough for Alex to win back his edge.

"Ruby, don…"

As soon as my hands hit the guard's body they spark, filling the chamber with blinding white light. *What in the world?* He makes a choked, throaty sound and convulses, dropping his blade scarily close to my bare foot with a clank. Next his knees buckle, giving way, and I leap sideways to avoid being fallen on and crushed.

Shocked, my gaze flicks to Alex's. He and the other guard are both staring gape-mouthed.

"Keep fighting, Alex!"

He reacts instantaneously, lunging and slicing the distracted guard clean across the throat.

The electrified guard recovers and takes a dive at me, but thankfully Alex is quicker. He spins, and then faster than my eyes can register, he ploughs his blade through the guard's back and tugs it like a lever, ripping him wide open.

I cast my eyes away from the gore, sickened with relief.

Alex stands unmoving for a moment, trying to catch his breath. His skin is a sheen of sweat and blood. Lots of blood.

"Alex, your side." My voice wobbles at the horrendous sight of his gaping gash. "It looks bad, really bad."

I step closer to get a better look, but he turns away, hiding it from my view. "Don't. It's fine. We don't have time for this. We have to move."

"We need to make time, or you're not going to get very far. You're losing too much blood." When he doesn't listen, I say, "Hey! You need to listen to me. I ate the sandwich, didn't I?" *Okay, so not my best argument.*

He grunts in frustration. "Fine, pick that up." He points to the fallen guard's blade, and I frown, confused. Nevertheless, I do as he says.

The guard's blade is heavy, and my hands are shaky. "Now what?"

He grabs the blades edge and holds it between his hands. As the edge heats up and goes from silver to a glowing orangey-red colour, my confusion morphs to panic, followed by nausea. *Oh no!*

Alex's expression is dead serious. In this very moment he reminds me a little bit of Jax. *A warrior.* This isn't a side of Alex I'm used to seeing. "When I let go, you need to place this edge across the cut."

I shake my head. "I don't think I can."

"Do you want the bleeding to stop or not?"

I grimace. "Yes."

"When I let go, you need to press the side to my wound and leave it there for two seconds, regardless of my reaction, okay?"

"I'm nervous."

"I'm the one who should be nervous," he says, keeping a brave face. He releases the blade and repeats. "Two seconds, now."

I wish I could close my eyes, but I need to line up the heated edge with the wound. Even as it is, I'm struggling. My hands are shaking, and the blade is heavy; I can hardly hold it still. There's a sizzle as the heated metal hits his skin, and he roars in agony. Tears prickle my eyes, and I have to fight the urge to pull away.

I count aloud, "One, two," and then draw back, relieved when the moment is over.

He looks down at me, jaw clenched, and eyes filled with agony. "You did good," he says through clenched teeth.

"Are you okay?"

"I'm fine," he says, sweating profusely, "but I'm afraid you're not." He glances across the chamber, examining the bodies of the fallen guards and his expression darkens. "When these guards don't return, they'll send more. If we stay, they're sure to kill you, but if we leave..." he pauses. "Chances are we won't make it to the border, let alone past it." His hard exterior crumbles a moment, revealing his softer, more compassionate side. "I don't know what to do, Rubes. I'm so sorry. I've sentenced you to death."

"I'm not dead yet, and I don't want to stay here and give up," I say, trying to sound braver than I feel. "Even if our chance of escaping is minimal, I want to take it. If I'm going to die anyway, I'd rather die trying."

"Me too." He offers his hand and I take it, and then together we run.

BATTLE ON
-HARLOW-

$\mathcal{S}$weat drips from my hairline down into my eyes, stinging them, and I need to keep blinking to see straight. The hallways are beyond boiling. The stone walls are lined with large blazing torches, each with flames burning high towards the ceiling. It seems ridiculous to use fire as a light source in a stone castle situated in the blistering heat of the desert. This castle would already be naturally overheated without adding fire.

We Zeeks use the zofts to light up the inside of the caves and power up everything. I don't understand why Vallons don't use voltz.

Admittedly, red light isn't as effective as purple light, but Vallons have supreme vision, so it shouldn't be a problem.

I stagger, slightly woozy from sweating so much. I understand why so many Zeeks die of heat exhaustion here. Our bodies aren't made to endure such high temperatures.

Alex and I make it down two hallways, and a set of stairs, before running into another group of guards. There's six of them, and they look even more terrifying than the first four. There's no way we can take them. We are severely outnumbered.

Alex jerks to a halt and curses, while I do my best not to cower in fear.

The guards are fast to react. They spring on us like a pack of savage wolves.

"Quick Rubes, aim to kill," Alex yells, and within a split second he's already sliced through one of the guard's throats.

I've never been taught how to use a blade, and I swing it around with absolutely no precision. Besides, it's much larger than any Zeek blade I've seen, and is way too heavy for me to use properly.

I strike one of the guards in the stomach, but the force isn't hard enough to do any real damage.

It gets his attention though, and he lunges at me, knocking me to the floor. He tries to restrain me, but I zap him, only to have another guard reef me up by my dress strap. The material tears as I'm lifted, but he seizes me by the waist before I drop.

The guard I'd just zapped finds his feet again and comes rushing over to seize my wrists. He says something to the guard holding me, and then with his free hand he produces a leather pouch and slides it over both of my hands. Once they are fully covered, he uses a leather strap to fasten the pouch in place. I've finally been gifted with powers, and now I won't be able to use them.

I glance over at Alex. He is trying to fight his way over to me, but the two guards still on him are big and powerful. Alex might be just as big, if not bigger, but he's slowing and weakening due to his injuries.

As the shorter of the two guards lugs me away, Alex screams my name. The hysteria in his voice makes my heart bleed.

"Keep fighting," I scream back. Even if I die, I want him to survive.

As I'm dragged through the castle, the guards' stinking sweat dripping all over me, my mind becomes my worst enemy. *How will they kill me?* A multitude of sickening possibilities tick over inside my head. A few months ago, I wasn't afraid to die, but now I am. I've finally found reasons to want to live.

We enter what looks to be the Great Hall of the castle, only it has a prison cell built into the back wall. *Vallons must like to keep their prisoners in full view.*

The ceiling above is vaulted with hundreds of wooden beams carved into intricate patterns, and on the side walls there are stained glass windows depicting their Vallon Gods.

I recognise these Vallon Gods, because the Vallon bible was the only book Alex had in his chamber for me to flick through. I couldn't read it, but I liked looking at the pictures, and when Alex got home from work, I would ask him questions about them. Vallons have different beliefs to the Zeeks. They don't believe in reincarnation, they believe in 'Stadt der Götter' and 'Dämonen landen' which are their versions of heaven and hell, only these magical places are not governed by a single God or Devil, they are governed by many, all with different purposes and powers.

The brute carrying me lugs me over to the cell while the other stands guard at the entrance. "Geh in die hure," he spits, and then tosses me carelessly onto to the hard cell floor.

I'm unable to use my bound hands to protect my tummy, so I swivel mid-air, forcing my hip and shoulder to take the brunt of the fall. I hear a loud crack, and I cry out, afraid I might have broken a bone.

The brute laughs. *Evil bastard.* I might not know the Vallon language, but I strongly suspect he just called me a whore.

I remain limp on the hard floor where I've landed. The pain in my shoulder is agonising. It's the same shoulder the shard had sliced through less than two months ago. I'd only just started to get full range back, and now I've injured it again. My whole side feels brutalised. If I live to see tomorrow, I'm sure to be black and blue. I don't understand why the guards haven't killed me yet. They must have a plan for me. I hope the plan isn't to torture me slowly and painfully until eventually, I die. A chill runs down my spine as I envision it.

My disturbing thoughts are acutely interrupted by a pain-filled bellow, and as excruciating as it is, I force myself to look up.

The brute races over to the guard who's shrieking at the entry, unsheathing his blade, but before he's able to get to him, the guard gives a final screech and falls to the floor. I hold my breath, waiting, praying… And then to my delight, Alex rounds the corner.

Seeing him alive gives me a new sense of hope, and I scramble to my feet. "Alex. You're alive."

I press my cheeks to the evenly spaced bars of the cell and watch in fear as he and the brute battle it out. The brute nicks Alex's arm and thigh, seeming to aim for the limbs, but Alex doesn't muck around. As soon as the brute drops his defensive arm and leaves an opening, Alex goes straight for his heart. A strangled squeal escapes him, and then his eyes roll back into his head as he falls.

I hear a squelch as Alex yanks his blade out of the brute's fallen body, and my stomach turns. I've never seen so much gore in one day. *It's sickening.*

"Alex," I call, and he comes rushing over.

He slides his blood smeared arms through the bars, wrapping them around my waist and crushing me to him—and against the bars. "I'm so sorry, Rubes. I wasn't able to fight the others off in time to stop them."

My body shakes against his, a mix of fear and relief flooding me all at once. "I'm just glad you're okay. I was so worried."

We stay this way a moment longer than we should, neither of us wanting to let go.

"The keys," Alex mutters, releasing me from his grasp. He takes off back to the fallen guard, searching each of his pockets.

"Where did he put the keys?" Alex yells.

I try to recall but I can't even remember seeing the brute with any keys. "I don't know."

Alex leaves his body to search the guard at the front. He hadn't come over at all, so I don't see how he would have them, but I leave Alex to search him anyway. Maybe in my moment of despair, I missed something.

Nope. Alex comes up empty handed.

"Did you see either of them go anywhere?" he asks, frustration leaking into his voice. "Is there somewhere they could have hidden them?"

"I didn't see anything."

He curses, kicks the dead guard, and then boom, something clicks inside him, and he comes rushing back over. "I've got an idea. Stand back." His hands grab hold of two of the bars, and within an instant, they start glowing orange. The bars are thick and set approximately fifteen centimetres apart. His face hardens with strain as he forcefully tugs at them, trying his best to pull them apart. Eventually the metal begins bowing and bending, but I'm afraid Alex will tire before the gap is wide enough for me to fit through. My large swollen tummy is going to need a decent sized opening.

Suddenly, a flash of movement catches my eyes. I gaze beyond Alex and gasp. Another guard has entered and is charging straight at him with a fireball in hand—ready to throw.

"Alex, behind you!"

Alex lets go of the bars, spins, and sees the fireball coming towards him. "Duck!"

We both duck in time and the fireball zooms past. It hits the cell wall behind me and blackens the stone.

Alex bounces back to his feet, ready to attack, but to both of our disbelief, something hits the guard from behind. He shrieks, jerks, and then falls, revealing another Vallon standing behind him. This Vallon is the same size as Alex, only his face is much broader.

Alex stares, frozen in shock. "Kenneth?"

15

BIG BROTHER

-ALEX AS SLATER-

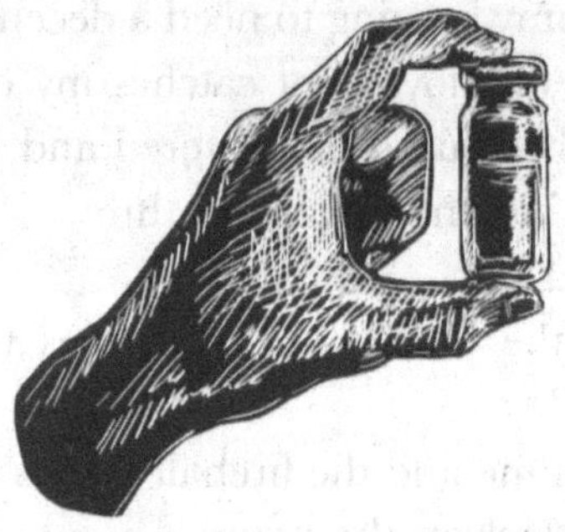

*E*ither this is a trick, or my eyes are deceiving me, because there is no way in hell Kenneth would side with me over a guard, especially given the circumstances. He is a mama's boy and a stickler for the rules. He has killed Pastel slaves for far less.

"Run, little brother."

"What do you mean run?" I gaze past him, expecting a group of guards, or our mother to enter. "Is this like a game? The thrill of the chase?"

"I mean get out of here before our mother sees you. Raven told her about the slave, and it's sent her into a fit of rage. She's done with your reckless behaviour. And after what you've done to the guards, she wants you eliminated."

I suspected Raven might tell Jacinta, who would then tell Kenneth, but never, ever would I have thought she'd go running straight to my mother. It seems I severely underestimated her. She's more vindictive than I thought.

"There is a secret passage behind the wooden shelf in the cellar beneath us," Kenneth tells me. "Use it, go to the forest, and don't ever come back."

I nod. "Okay." I can't say that I completely trust him, but right now he's all I have. I turn back to the cell and re-grab the bent bars, summoning the power of fire to my hands. "Quick, help me get her out."

"No."

Shocked, I spin back to face him. "No? What do you mean no?"

"I'm here for you, and *you* only. She stays in the cell."

"I'm not leaving without her."

Kenneth doesn't bat an eyelash. "Then stay and face the consequences. It's your choice."

"Please," I urge. "Help me get her out, and you'll never see or hear from us again."

"You know I can't do that, Slate, even if I wanted to. Besides, now that our mother knows about her and those babies, she'll have her hunted down within the hour. To take her with you now while the guards are in pursuit would be suicide. The slave poses a risk to you and everyone else on Zadok. Those half-breeds she's carrying will tarnish and endanger the future of our race. They can't be born."

"Our children won't be a threat."

"You can't promise that."

"Kenneth, please," I say, laying down my pride. "I'm begging you. I need her alive. I can't live without her."

I detect conflicting emotions warring within him, but he holds his stance. "You're running out of time, Slate. Forget about her. She's the property of the Queen now and won't be around for much longer. You should go."

"What's our mother planning on doing with her? Is she going to make a spectacle of her? Is that why she's still being kept alive?" When Kenneth doesn't answer, I roll out my next question—the most important question. This one I need answered. "How long does she have?"

"A day or two at most."

"Drag it to two. Please. If you keep her safe for me while I get external help, I will repay you. Ruby has a useful connection. We could strike a bargain with the Zeeks. Think about it. This is something you've always wanted. Think of her as an opportunity."

Kenneth walks over to the cell and taps his blade on the bars. "Tell Slate to go," he says in Zeek. "Tell him to save himself."

A look of fear mixed with dread flashes across Ruby's face as she realises what is happening. However, she's quick to hide it.

"You should go," she says, her words wobbling past her lips. "I want you to go. I want you to survive."

16

GOODBYE

-HARLOW-

*A*lex steps over, slips his arms through the bars, and tugs me to him—eyes wild and intense. "I love you so much," he says, and then kisses me so deeply it almost hurts.

The anger and resentment I'd felt earlier melts away in an instant.

A small part of me still loves Alex, even after everything he's done, and if this is the last time we're going to see each other before I die, I'll give him this moment without pulling away. I have no future, let alone a future with Jax.

After what feels like only a matter of seconds, he reluctantly draws back and moves his head to the side. His lips brush my ear. "Try to hang on for me, okay?" he whispers. "I'll be back soon, and I'll be bringing help with me."

"No." There's a squeak to my voice I can't control. I don't want anyone else involved. "Don't worry about me. I'm as good as dead. Just worry about yourself."

"I promise I'll be back," he whispers once more, and then Kenneth takes him by the shoulder and pulls him back.

"Geh jetzt."

Alex spares me one last pain filled glance and then takes off, leaving me alone with his brother.

As soon as he's gone from sight, I drop to my knees, and Kenneth turns to face me. He doesn't look anything at all like I imagined he would. While Alex's features are handsomely defined, Kenneth's are flat and broad. It's hard to believe they were born of the same parents.

"You're not one of our slaves, are you?"

Now conscious of my torn dress strap, I angle my body away from him and shake my head. "No."

"I didn't think so." He regards me curiously. "So, does this mean that you are here of your own free will?"

Again, I nod, although I wouldn't exactly call it free will that's brought me here.

"Slater is begging for me to help keep you alive as long as possible, so tell me, is there a particular reason I should oblige?"

I shrug. "I don't know."

"Slate says you have a useful connection, but I can tell by your delicate facial features you were originally a Pastel." He cocks his head to the side, brows puckered in curiosity. "How does a Pastel come to have a useful connection?"

"I am the only Pastel to be born from two Magentas. It's made me stand out among my race."

"And this is useful to us, how?"

I think long and hard before answering. If Alex wants me to use my connection to Jax to buy me time, it's not happening. I refuse to do it. I've already caused Jax enough trouble. "It's not really useful."

He stares intently, seeming unconvinced. "Your hesitation tells me otherwise. I think you are more important than you're letting on, but I don't understand how or why."

"I don't understand why you feel you can use Pastels as you please, only to kill us when we become pregnant. It's cruel and barbaric." My eyes lift to his, and I try my best to keep a strong, brave face. "Even if I did have a connection, why would I help you? Your race treats my kind like dirt."

"Your own race treats your kind like dirt." His voice takes on a scathing edge, and I shudder under his frightening gaze. "If you want to live, you will co-operate and help us get what we want."

I don't know exactly what it is he wants from me, and I don't care. I refuse to be used as his barging chip. "No," I say adamantly. "I'd rather die."

17

I NEED TO FIND HELP

-ALEX AS SLATER-

I glance over my shoulder for the hundredth time, still half expecting Kenneth's getaway tip-off to be a setup, but there's no one following me, and as far as I can tell, nothing's suspicious or out of place. I enter the cellar slowly and cautiously, my blade raised, ready to swing at the first sight of a guard. To my relief, the cellar is empty, and I find the passageway hidden behind the wooden cupboard, just as Kenneth said it would be. *I wonder how long he's known about this secret escape. I wonder if he's ever used it.*

I enter the passageway and close the wooden cupboard behind me. It's dark inside, but luckily, I have night vision. Plus, the glow of my vertic switz is bright and lights up the whole passageway in a soft shade of red. I follow the dusty old passage for quite some time. The floor is ancient, uneven, and a major trip hazard. I watch my step, not wanting to add a snapped ankle to my list of injuries. My side burns like fury, and my limbs throb from gashes. The gash on my left leg is deep. It dripped a crimson trail all the way to the cellar. I hope Kenneth plans to get it cleaned up, or the secret passage won't be so secret anymore.

The further I head in, the more sweltering the passage becomes. The air is sultry, and the walls are covered with clumps of green and black mould. The ghastly smell of mould brings back awful memories of my human childhood. A time where the pain I feel now was all I ever knew. It was the only thing I could rely on.

The passage is long and gets rougher and narrower with every passing step. Eventually, I see a glimmer of light and, after crawling through the last several metres, I find myself at a drain grate near the forest's edge. I wish I'd been told about this passage earlier. It would have made sneaking out to the forest a hell of a lot easier.

My thoughts drift to Ruby. Had I known about this passage, I could have snuck her out as soon as Raven left our chamber. I would have carried her down to the cellar, hidden in the rug. No one would have been any the wiser.

Could haves, would haves, aren't going to save her. *Hurry up,* I think instead. I need to get out and get help before the unthinkable happens.

I push on the grate, and it budges first go. There is a thick broken chain and lock hanging from it. *I wonder if it's always been broken, or if Kenneth had it broken for me to make for an easy escape.*

Once I'm out and have scouted to see if the coast is clear, I set the grate back in place and charge towards the border. I need to get to the Drake village and find this Stavros guy Jax mentioned in his letters. Ruby's life depends on it.

There's a lot of ground to cover, and pain grinds at me with every stride.

I'm only a few kilometres from the Drake village when the forest around me starts swaying, and I stagger.

Please. I beg my limbs to co-operate.

It's not far now. You can do this. Ruby's life depends on you.

The further I push myself onwards the more distorted my vision becomes, and soon I stumble…

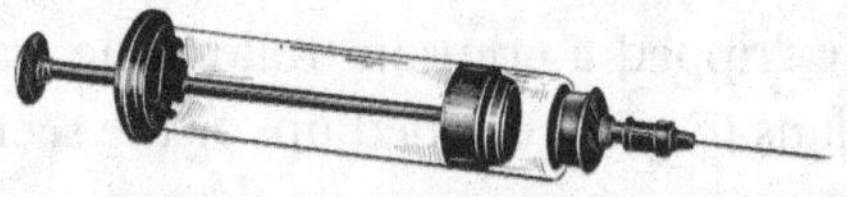

I don't remember passing out, but my eyes snap open to the feeling of someone's hand on my neck, and my body instantly jerks upright, ready to attack.

A frightened yelp rings in my ears, and as my vision clears, I see a scrawny young Pastel darting away from me. *What?*

"Wait!" I yell. "Come back."

The Pastel stops and slowly turns to face me, his eyes wide. "You speak Zeek."

Going by his face, he's not very old—he'd be twelve at most, but his body is buckled, bony, and bears many scars. He must've been a slave. *I wonder what he's doing in the forest. Did he escape during the chaos?*

"I'm not going to hurt you," I assure him. "In fact, I need your help."

I stand and take a few steps towards him, holding my hands up in a surrender pose.

His broken-down body starts to tremble. "I'm sorry, I thought you were dead. I was just checking to see whether you had a pulse."

"What is your name?" I ask, trying to ease his fear.

"Koby."

I notice Koby is wearing a watch. "Koby, my name is Slater, and I can assure you I'm not going to hurt you. I just need your help. Now, please, can you start by telling me what time it is?"

"Slater?" His eyes bulge further, recognising my name. "The prince?"

I nod. "Yes. Now what's the time?" I prompt.

"My watch is broken. The only reason I still wear it is because it was my father's. He gave it to me before he died."

Frustration fills me, but I muster enough decency to say, "I'm sorry."

He shrugs it off.

I glance around the forest floor searching for the guard's blade I'd taken. I can't see it anywhere. I must have dropped it somewhere along the way. *Damn it!* Now I'm weapon-less.

"It was around seven P.M. when the guards snatched me up out of bed and dragged me to the forest's edge," Koby offers. "So, at a guess, I would say it's currently around nine A.M. here—give or take."

I curse and he flinches. I left at around five P.M., and I'm much faster than a Zeek, especially a Pastel. This means I must've been passed out for several hours. I've wasted precious time.

Suddenly curious I ask, "Why did the guards send you to the forest?"

Despite all my efforts to try and calm him, Koby's body still trembles. "I've been chosen to send a message to the Drake Chief. The guard who dragged me to the forest, handed me a note written in Zeek which said, "If you succeed in getting this message to Chief Dakari, you'll be set free, but if you fail, the guards will hunt you down and drag you back to Summer". I tried asking the guard how to get to the Drake village, but my Vallon isn't fluent. In the end he just handed me a map, compass, and a scrolled message for the Drake Chief, and then told me to go."

"What's in the message?"

"I don't know." His eyes lower, and his cheeks flush pink. "I had a peek but can't read it. It's written in another language."

I put my hand out. "Show it to me."

He pats his pocket cautiously. "You will give it back, won't you? As I said, if I don't deliver this message to the Drake Chief, the guards will hunt me down and take me back to Summer. I've never been outside of Summer before. I was born there. I want to see what the caves look like."

The guard wouldn't bother to hunt him down, I think to myself. *He is using scare tactics on the poor kid to get him to co-operate.*

But to ease his anxiety, I say, "Don't worry, I'll give it back."

He plucks the scroll from his pocket and hands it to me with shaky fingers. The message has been written in Drake.

Chief Dakari,

I am writing to inform you that my youngest son Slater has gone AWOL and is officially considered a traitor to the kingdom of Summer. Slater is no longer classed as an affiliate in our current working agreement as I fear he may pose a threat to your village and tribe. I'm requesting for him to be killed on sight, and as a token of my gratitude, the Drake who's successful in eliminating him will be generously rewarded with royal jewels.

Queen Sjaan.

Another curse escapes me. I hope Dakari and his tribe aren't driven by greed, or I'll be dead before the day is out.

In a meek inquiring voice, Koby asks, "What did it say?"

"It says that I am to be killed on sight."

A look of fear takes over Koby's features once more. "Why? What did you do?"

"I fell in love with a Zeek." Admitting this finally seems to calm him down a fraction. "Come on," I prompt. "The village isn't very far from here, let's get moving."

"You're coming with me?" His brows bunch. "Why? Won't they try to kill you?"

"Maybe, and that's why I need your help. Will you help me?"

His hands fidget at his sides. I can tell a part of him wants to help, but given what my race has put him through, it would be hard for him to trust a 'big bad Vallon'. "What do you want me to do? I can't fight, I've never been taught."

"I don't need you to fight. I need you to speak for me. There will be patrols at the entrance of the village, and chances are they won't speak Zeek." I turn to face Koby as we continue to walk. "Repeat this after me 'Persoonlike boodskap vir Dakari'."

Koby gives it a try, and we repeat it back and forth a few times until he's got the hang of it.

"What does it mean?"

"It means 'Personal message for Dakari'. After you say this, they're probably going to want to see the message. Show them the scroll, but don't hand it to them. Hold onto it tight and tap a finger to your chest while repeating the saying. This will tell them that you want to deliver the message to Dakari personally."

"And then what? I don't know how much of this language I will remember."

"Hopefully one of the patrols will take you to Dakari, and he speaks Zeek, so the rest of what I need you to say will be in Zeek. I need you to tell Dakari that I'm outside, that I'm not a threat, and that I want to see Stavros." We run through these messages repeatedly until I'm confident he's got it all down pat.

The closer to the village we get, the darker and denser the forest becomes, and Koby's nerves get the better of him.

"Are you sure this is the right way to the village?" His voices quavers.

"Yes."

Unwilling to take my word for it, he reaches into his pocket to pluck out the map.

"Oh, come on, Koby," I say with offence. "I'm not luring you into the dark to kill you. Trust me, this is the way to the village." His cheeks flush, and he reluctantly slides the map back into his pocket. "If anything," I add, "you should be glad to have me near, no creature will dare to touch you with me around."

A few glowing creatures make flash appearances, and Koby shuffles closer, to the point where our arms graze as we walk. He might not trust me, but he's quite happy to use me as his shield.

When we get within thirty metres, I catch sight of one of the patrols and hurriedly duck behind one of the many giant trees. It's lucky the patrol wasn't looking our way. "I'm going to wait here," I tell Koby. "Now quickly, before you go, let's run through everything one last time."

His body trembles, and his words are shaky, but his Drake pronunciation is good enough to pass.

"Okay, that's good. The patrols you'll be talking to are extremely tall, but don't let that intimidate you. Drakes are peaceful unless provoked."

He looks at me and gulps. Poor boy, he's clearly scared out of his mind.

"Don't be afraid. You can do this, Koby."

SLATER IS HERE
-ZANNAH-

"Nice right hook, moron," I mutter under my breath.

Floss looks my way and grins.

Jax and Oscar are sparring, and Oscar, Mr Act Before Thinking, has just dropped his guard to make a failed right hook. Jax takes advantage of his lapse of defence and lands a solid kick to his stomach, causing him to buckle. I enjoy watching these two spar. When it comes to size and body shape, they're well matched.

Jax always ends up winning though. Not because he is stronger, but because he's smarter.

Stavros and Jax were good to watch together too. That is before

Stavros let his strength and fitness slip. Stavros isn't as broad as these two, but he's super agile and focused, plus he's always had the ability to calculate his opponents next move before they've made it, which gives him the leading edge in a fight. *I'm completely envious of this skill.*

We all have our own unique abilities. Jax is strong, intelligent, and switched on to everything going on around him. Oscar is strong, confident, and daring. Stavros is focused, agile, and calculating. I am quick, determined, and cutthroat. And let's not forget our cave member, Kieran. He's a super intellect with long legs made for fast running and a killer kicking circle.

Luna and Destiny are no match to us warriors when it comes to sparring, but they are more weapon savvy than all of us combined.

I glance back at Floss and groan. While I do have mild respect for her, I also find her bratty, lazy, and unpredictable, and an unpredictable warrior can be a liability.

Power cracks through Jax's body as he moves swiftly and fiercely within the fighting circle, landing blow after blow on Oscar. Oscar gets in a few good hits too, but eventually Jax knocks him down with an unexpected left.

Jax holds him in place, pinned to the ground, while Stavros calls, "One, two, three, out!"

I laugh, and Oscar shoots me a filthy look. His pride would be extra bruised today because Destiny's here watching. Despite my little warning, they seem to have gotten hot-and-cosy at an accelerated rate, but this is typical of Oscar, The Charmer. I just hope he doesn't break Destiny's heart.

"Zannah, Stavros, you're up," Jax says between pants, and then takes a swig from his water canteen.

"What about me?" Floss pouts. "Why won't you put me with Zannah?"

"Because you're not ready," Jax argues. "Zannah will eat you alive."

I stand and give my arms a good stretch, not bothering to hide my smug expression.

Floss' fists ball, and her jaw clenches. "But you've been happily pairing me up with Stavros and Oscar, what's the difference?"

"The difference is I know that Stavros and Oscar will take it easy on you while you're still building up your body strength and endurance."

"I don't want Zeeks taking it easy on me. I'm not a charity case. I'm training to be a warrior. I want to be treated like a warrior."

"Okay, fine," Jax snaps. "If you want to take on Zannah, be my guest. But when she beats you to a pulp, you'd better tell Zavier that this was your idea, not mine."

Floss rolls her eyes and stands. "Whatever you say, boss."

Stavros glances between us with knitted brows, his eyes eventually settling on mine. "Don't kill her," he warns.

We step up to the circle. I take the left of Jax, and she takes the right.

Despite what the guys think of me, I'm not going to beat her senseless. I do plan on giving her a wake-up call though.

"Ready, set…" the word "fight" doesn't come. Jax must be having second thoughts.

I whip around, ready to let him know I don't actually plan on killing her, when I see Woody hurrying our way.

"At ease," I tell Floss. "It looks like you'll get to live a little longer."

"Bite me," she retorts.

I leave the circle and make my way over to Jax. Stavros and the huskens are quick to join us, but Oscar's too busy rolling around on the grass with Destiny to realise we've got company.

Woody rushes to say something, but it's all in Drake, so unlike Jax and Stavros, I'm out of the loop. I've barely managed to master "hello" and "goodbye", despite a fortnight's worth of language classes.

The alarmed look on their faces tells me this is serious. Eventually Jax curses and storms off towards the village with Sphinx. *Frost,* if Jax is swearing, this must be bad. Woody and Stavros follow, and Rebel and I join them.

"Not to be rude, but can we switch to Zeek for a minute? I have no idea what's going on."

"Slater is here," Stavros says. "And he's asking for me. He says that Harlow is in trouble."

"Why is he asking for you?" I ask, confused.

"I don't know, but it looks like we are about to find out."

Oscar rushes up behind us, voice breathy. "What's going on?"

I glance over my shoulder to cast him a glare. "How nice of you to give up playing sucky face with Destiny and come and join us."

"Slater's here," Stavros repeats.

"Frost…" Oscar mutters under his breath. "This can't be good."

Dakari stands in the centre of the village waiting for us, and alongside him, stands a young Zeek boy around the same age as Will and Daisy. He's in poor condition, pale, scarred, hunched, and all skin and bone.

It's clear he can still see though, because when he catches sight of the huskens, he gasps, and takes a step closer to Dakari.

Slater must have brought a slave with him to deliver the news. *Coward.*

Dakari hands Jax a fancy scroll and he unrolls it to read, allowing Stavros to read it over his shoulder. I rise to the balls of my feet and take a quick peek, but just as I presumed, the letter is written in Drake.

"They must have been caught together," Stavros says. "Why else would the Queen want him dead?"

Oscar steps forward, brows creased. "Who does the Queen want dead?"

"Slater," Stavros and I say in unison.

When Stavros shoots me a questioning look, I say, "Unlike sludge for brains, I don't need to read the scroll to pick up on the obvious."

"Where is he?" Jax asks the boy. His tone is deep, frightening, and scares the life out of the kid. "Is he alone?"

The boy's head shrinks into his shoulders. "If I tell you, are you going to kill him?"

"That all depends on what he has to say," Jax answers, and the boy gulps. "I need you to take me to him, now."

The boy glances at Dakari for guidance. He's so afraid he's shaking. "It's okay, Koby," Dakari assures him. "All you have to do is point Jax in the right direction, and then you can come straight back to the village where it's safe."

Koby nods, but he's still shaking. "He's alone."

I wonder if he's worried about his master.

Stavros notices his unease and gives him a pat on the shoulder. "It'll be okay, kid."

"This matter is to be settled outside the fence. I don't want any of my tribe involved, is that understood?" Dakari warns.

Jax is on the verge of losing it, we can all see it. His fists are balled, and his jaw is set. "Understood," he manages, steam rising from his body.

"If that Vallon steps one foot into this village and starts causing problems, you and I are going to have problems," Dakari adds, firmly, but not unkindly. "And I don't want that."

"It won't come to that point," Stavros assures him. "I'll make certain of it."

19

KEEP IT TOGETHER, JAX

-JAX-

My temples pulse, and my mind fills with dread as Koby leads us to an enormous tree trunk just outside the village. If Harlow isn't with Slater, it means she's in trouble. I should never have trusted that he would protect her. I curse myself for letting him take her without a fight, but I was worried if we fought, it'd be to the death, and Harlow would never have forgiven me if I'd killed him. It was the wrong decision, and I've regretted it every day since. I'll never forgive myself if anything has happened to her.

I spot Slater as he peers around the trunk, eyes cautious.

When those glowing red globes catch sight of me, he jolts and leaps out from his hiding spot, biceps coiled. "You! Why the hell are you here?"

Sensing a threat, Sphinx hunkers beside me, baring his razor-sharp teeth with a growl.

Blanking his question, I ask, "Where's Harlow?"

He roars like a wounded fuegor and charges at me, fist raised, causing poor Koby to yelp and scurry back towards the village.

I duck Slater's potentially powerful blow and kick him full force to the stomach, sending him flying. He hits the ground gasping, and I grit my teeth, resisting the urge to continue kicking him while he's down. I doubt he'd show the same restraint in my place, but I'm not about to lower my standards to meet his.

It would usually take more than one kick to knock down a Vallon—especially a Red—but by the look of Slater's battered body, I'm guessing this isn't his first fight today.

The huskens rush at him, barking and snapping.

"WHOA," I shout, and they retreat on command. As much as I wouldn't mind seeing them rip him to shreds, I still need answers, and you can't get answers from a dead man.

"Where's Harlow?" I ask again.

Slater scrambles to his feet, fists clenched, ready to take his next hit.

"ENOUGH!" Stavros jumps between us. "ENOUGH!"

He turns to Slater. "I'm Stavros. I'm the one you asked for. Now tell me, where's Harlow?"

Slater's eyes flicker, and his expression grows dark and anguished. "She's been captured," he says, and my heart twists painfully inside my chest. "The Queen has her locked in a cell."

I stare, jaw clenching. *If she's been arrested by the Queen's guards, she's as good as dead.* Fuelled by hatred, I lash out, the harsh tone of my voice reverberating through the forest. "This is all your fault; you should have let her stay!"

"I didn't know—" he begins, but he doesn't get to finish because I lunge at him, pummelling his face with my fists. He manages to land a right to my jaw before Stavros, Oscar, and Zannah jump between us, shoving us apart.

"Stop," Stavros warns. "If you want to find out more about Harlow, we need him to be able to speak. Now take a deep breath and calm yourself, or I'm going to have to ask you to leave."

The rational part of me knows that what he's saying is right, so I suck in a deep breath and raise my hands in surrender.

Slater spits out a mouthful of blood and cuts me a hateful glare before speaking directly to Stavros. "I need your help," he says. "I need you to come back with me and freeze the bars so I can smash them. I tried heating and manipulating the metal, but it took much longer than I'd anticipated for the bars to give, and to be honest, I don't know if I'll be able to pull them wide enough apart for her baby bump to fit through. The bars are closely spaced."

I step forward, pushing my anger aside as my sense of reason returns. My only concern is rescuing Harlow. "Let's go now. You lead the way!"

Slater snarls, lip curled. "I wasn't asking you."

"Stavros has a wife and child to worry about. I don't want him anywhere near Summer."

"I think we should all go," Zannah says. "Strength in numbers."

"Nobody is going anywhere until we have a plan," Stavros barks. "We can't save Harlow if we're all killed. And barging into Summer without a plan would most certainly be a suicide mission."

"What's going to happen to her?" I ask. "Are they planning on killing her?" It hurts just asking this.

"Kenneth says we have two days at most."

"Why two days?"

Slater averts his eyes. "The Queen plans to make a spectacle out of her first."

His words are like a dagger to my chest. "Forget the plan," I tell Stavros. "We need to go now!"

"Yes, let's go now while it's still night in Summer." Slater's head nods eagerly in agreement. "If we don't go now, we'll need to wait until tomorrow night, and who knows what the guards will do to her in that time."

Stavros gazes at me sympathetically. "We all love Harlow, but we are no good to her if we're dead. You need to stop thinking with your heart and start thinking with your head. We have two days. So, let's put our heads together, draw up a plan, and we'll leave tomorrow morning, which will be their evening." He motions his head towards Slater, who's wavering where he stands. "Look at him," he says under his breath. "He's in no condition to go anywhere right now. He'll pass out before we get to Summer, and then we'll be totally screwed. We need his intel and directions, and for him to be of any use to us, he needs first aid, some food and drink, and a good night's rest."

"Stavros is right," Oscar says. "We all want to save her, but we need to do this right."

I can't stand the sight of Slater, but after scanning him over, I reluctantly agree. He's a wreck.

If I could rescue Harlow on my own, I would, but as Stavros said, I'm no good to her if I'm dead. Unfortunately, I need this moron, and I'm prepared to do whatever it takes to get Harlow back. I'm in love her and have been for a very long time.

I would've shared my feelings with Harlow much earlier, but I wasn't prepared to put her life in danger for a relationship that needed to be kept top secret. I wanted our relationship to be accepted and legit, which meant I needed to wait until the colour system was broken down, or at least, that was the plan before *he*—my eyes shoot daggers in Slater's direction—came along and destroyed everything.

I sigh an exasperated breath. "How exactly do you propose we deal with him? He's not welcome in the village, and I doubt the medicine woman will be willing leave the village to tend to him."

"I'll tend to him," Zannah says, surprising me. "I just need someone to fetch me a bucket of soapy water, towels, and a first aid kit."

"Fine." I wave a pointed finger between her and Oscar. "Both of you stay and keep an eye on him. Stavros, you come with me."

20

PLAN OF ATTACK

-ZANNAH-

By the time the guys get back with the goods, Slater is slumped against a tree trunk looking dazed and dejected.

"Are you certain you're okay about doing this?" Jax asks, handing me a basket of food and medical supplies.

"Sure, he didn't steal *my* girlfriend." It's a bad joke, and I can tell by the hardness of Jax's brow he doesn't appreciate it.

"Acacia packed a heap of iron-rich food and a few bottles of water. Can you make sure he ingests some of it? We need him strong enough to travel into Summer with us by the morning."

"Certainly. If he doesn't eat willingly, I'll shove the food down his throat," I say, grinning.

Stavros pops a bucket of soapy water and a fresh towel over where Slater sits. "Cooperate and keep your hands off my sister."

Slater meets his eyes but doesn't respond.

"Okay, Tough Guy," I say, stepping over to him. "Let's get you cleaned up, shall we?" I pluck the sponge from the bucket, and he tries snatching it from my hand.

"Leave it, I can do it."

He's only a head space away, and his glowing eyes are looking right at me. I find it so intriguing the way the colours of his irises swirl.

"No." I stare him down. "You eat and drink while I wash. We need you strong for the morning. There's plenty of iron-rich food in the basket, so sit back, shut up, and take your pick."

Surprisingly, he doesn't argue. He grabs out a bottle of water and chugs down half its contents in three big gulps.

"Impressive," I say.

Ignoring me, he digs into the basket again, plucking out a container of dried fruit and nuts along with a deetra sandwich. He squishes the bread between his fingers a few times before taking a bite. *Weird,* but at least he's eating willingly. It looks like I won't need to shove the food down his throat, after all.

He winces while I wash over his wounds. This might be torture for him, but I'm secretly enjoying it—*and no, it's not because I'm a psycho.* I haven't been this close to a set of rock hard abs since… well…Oscar. *Yeah, let's not got there shall we.*

I gaze between Jax and Slater, soaking in their individual features and rock-hard physiques. I still don't understand why these two smokin' hot men are both so taken by Harlow. Her pretty face doesn't make up for her insipid personality.

I dab at the nasty wound at Slater's side, and he curses.

"Watch it!" he yells, shoving my hand away.

"I'm sorry," I say, "but I need to get rid of all the dirt or else your wound will get infected." I lean forward to get a better look. Now that some of the dried blood is gone, I'm able to see how nasty the wound truly is. "What happened anyway?" I ask. "It looks like you got branded with the side of a stake."

"Close." His voice croaks. "It was the side of a blade. Ruby did it to stop the bleeding."

"Huh, I didn't think she had it in her."

I try dabbing his side again and he flounders. "Fuck this!" He jerks upright. "I don't care if it's clean or not, just leave it."

"I can't leave it." I don't know what route Slater took to get here, but his whole body is covered in dirt and grime. If I don't finish cleaning the wounds, it'll only be a matter of time before he gets an infection.

"Jax," I call, breaking up the D&M he, Stavros, and Oscar are having.

Slater's whole face crumples. "What are you calling him over for?"

Disregarding Slater's question, I yell, "Chuck me some nauclea latifolia roots."

Jax snuffs and cuts Slater a slitted glance. "I don't see why I should. He deserves to suffer." But regardless of his hateful comment, he slips his hand in his pocket, grabs a couple of roots, and hands them to me.

He's always got a stash of roots in his pocket. He's like a nauclea latifolia root dealer. I'm forever teasing him about it—calling him a closet chewer. He claims as Chief Warrior—now Commander— they are a necessity. Warriors are always getting hurt.

"Here." I hand the roots to Slater. "Once you've finished your sandwich, chew on these."

He twirls the roots around in his palm, eyeing them with suspicion. "Why? What will they do?"

"They'll ease the pain."

Hearing this, he places the rest of his sandwich down and pops the two roots in his mouth at once.

I wait a minute or two for the roots to take full effect before dabbing his side again. He still winces, but he's no longer thrashing or swearing.

"Zannah, that's your name, right?"

"Since birth," I confirm.

His eyes lift to meet mine, raw and open. "Thank you, Zannah."

The gratitude in his voice is way too warm and familiar for someone who is supposed to be my enemy. It causes my defences to rise. I can't have Slater mistaking my kindness for weakness. I'm a Zeek, and he's a Vallon. We are enemies. His race keeps Pastels for slaves. He even had the audacity to bring a slave with him as a messenger boy. An image of the poor beaten and broken boy flashes to mind.

Jax is right. I shouldn't've shown Slater any kindness. I should've made him suffer. It was those damn abs and mesmerising irises that got to me. Not again. *I am a warrior, and warriors aren't weak.*

"Don't thank me. We're not friends. I'm only helping you because you're still useful to us. If Jax decides he wants to kill you after we're done rescuing Harlow, I won't stand in his way."

Oscar fetches a mattress and pillow while I'm stitching up some of the deeper gashes on Slater's limbs and then leaves to help Woody with a task in the village. Once I'm finished, I tell Slater to go rest for a while. He nods, bleary eyed, and stumbles over to the mattress without having to be told twice.

Jax and Stavros are sitting on a mossy log nearby and after rinsing my hands off in the bucket, I wander over to join them. "Is Slater going to be sleeping out here all night?" I ask, taking a seat next to Jax.

"He's a Vallon," Jax says. "And a hunter. Sleeping out here won't be an issue for him."

"What's the plan so far?"

Stavros leans forward. "We have no idea what we're up for. We'll need Slater to help us with the plans."

"I'll give him two hours rest and then I'm waking him up to talk," Jax says. "He should be feeling a bit better by then. He has a faster recovery rate than us because of the vertic switz ink."

Rebel comes over and rubs her muzzle against my leg, begging for a pat. "How does that work?" I ask.

"I'm not sure exactly, but take Minty and Zavier for example, they were battered and broken a month ago, and now look at them —they're fully healed like nothing ever happened."

I notice he doesn't mention Harlow and her quick-to-mend-shoulder, and I find myself wondering why. I know he still really loves her, *but does he still want to be with her?* She's spent two-and-a-half weeks living with her ex—or perhaps he's her current again—*who knows.* That's got to be pretty tough for him. A lot can change in two-and-a-half weeks.

I wonder if Harlow has any idea how lucky she is. She's had a piece of Jax, a piece of Slater, and to top it off, she's been injected with vertic switz ink—talk about winning the trifecta.

Had someone suggested the idea of "being injected with Vallon ink" to me, a few months back, I would have been disgusted, yet these days, I find myself wishing that someone would hurry up and inject me already. Imagine the things I'd be capable of with a bit of added power.

"We need to get our hands on some more of that ink," I say.

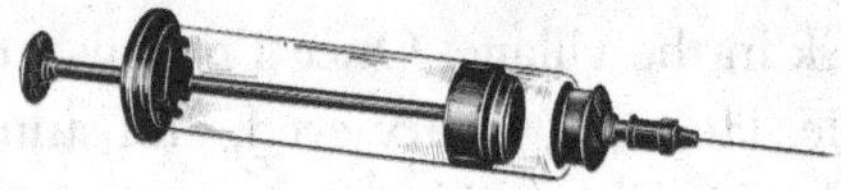

I'm the lucky one who gets to wake Slater when the two hours are up. He jerks up with a fright and karate chops my neck, just about knocking my head clean off my shoulders.

I gasp and my hand goes flying to my throat, expecting to find an indent. *That was one heck of a powerful chop.*

"Shit! I'm sorry," he says, and he looks it, but still I glare. "I thought you were…"

"I don't care what you thought." I croak. "Try that again, and I'll pop all your stitches back open."

"What's going on?" Jax calls.

"Nothing," I manage, and then my eyes snap to Slater's. "Come on. It's time to get our plans in order."

Stavros has brought out a flat piece of board, along with a pencil and a couple of sheets of paper. The first thing the guys do is get Slater to draw a map. He draws a rough sketch on the paper showing us where the border is, where the castle is, where the guards will be situated, and what route we're supposed take if we want to get into the castle undetected.

"Getting into the castle will be the easy part," Slater says, adding a few more squiggles. "Kenneth let me in on an old hidden passageway, which I used to escape. It has a grate opening not too far from the border's edge. It leads to the cellar."

Right away Stavros is suspicious. "If Kenneth is the one who told you about it, how do we know it's not a trap? He might have guards set in place in case you return."

"I got out without a fuss, didn't I?" Slater barks in defence. "He saved me from one of the guards and told me to run. If he wanted me caught or dead, the opportunity was there. He could have taken it, but he chose to let me go."

"What about Harlow?" Jax asks. "Why didn't he let her go?"

"She'd already been locked in the cell by the time Kenneth got to us. I wanted him to help me get her out, but he said there was no time, and that if I was to leave with her, our mother would have us hunted down within the hour."

Jax's face reddens with rage. "So, you left her, like a coward."

Slater opens his mouth to retaliate, but Stavros raises a hand in warning. "Enough." He doesn't appear sold on Slater's story. "If you want our help, I think it's about time you told us exactly what happened, starting from the beginning."

Slater drops the pencil and lets out a frustrated huff. "Fine."

He tells us that a girl named Raven snuck into his chamber while he was out hunting with Kenneth, and that she found Ruby— as he calls her—curled up in his bed.

Jax stiffens beside me, and I swear I hear his heart shattering inside his chest. I think a part of him wanted to believe that despite the distance and hopelessness of the situation, Harlow was still holding on to him. He wanted to believe she was only in Summer with Slater because her hand was forced. He falls quiet after this.

Luckily, Stavros is here, he's a master at rolling out the questions.

He likes to leave no stone unturned. "Who's Raven, and why was she in your chamber?"

"Raven is my ex," Slater admits. "She got jealous when she discovered Ruby was pregnant and ratted us out to my mother…the Queen," he adds, like we don't already know this. "She assumed Ruby was one of the slaves, and pregnant slaves are to be destroyed. The Queen doesn't want any half-blooded children tainting Summer."

Jax's fists clench and unclench repeatedly as Slater continues to tell his story. Eventually, we get to the end, and Stavros frowns.

"I still don't understand," he says. "If Kenneth wouldn't help you save Harlow when you asked, then what makes you think he is going to let us sneak through the castle and break Harlow out now? It doesn't make any sense."

"I honestly don't know what Kenneth's motives are, and I can't say if he'll let us take her without a fight, but I know he was right when he said the Queen would've had an army of guards hot on our tails had I taken her with me when I left. Ruby wasn't in any condition to keep fighting. We would've been killed before we made it out of Summer."

"What's the difference now?" Stavros presses. "We still run the risk of being followed by the guards."

"The difference is even if the guards are alerted to our presence, you can protect Ruby while I slice them open. I can't navigate offence and defence at the same time. I need someone to help keep Ruby safe while I fight."

"This doesn't sound like a very well thought out plan. Do you have any idea how many guards the Queen will have stationed outside her cell? She could have a dozen assigned."

Slater glares at Stavros, eyes narrowed. "Look, I've told you everything I know, so either help me, or go back to your wife and kid, while I take Jax." If Slater's willing to team up with Jax, he must be feeling desperate. "We don't have time to go around and around in circles. If we don't get to Summer by tomorrow evening, Ruby is dead… Dead." He repeats the word with more emphasis the second time around, forcing it to sink in.

When no one says anything, Slater picks up the pencil and starts drawing again. "Even if Kenneth does plan on betraying me, or the Queen does have a dozen guards stationed, we can take them. I took out ten guards today while trying to protect Ruby at the same time. The guards are strong, but they lack true fighting skills. They don't train daily like you warriors."

"Let's pretend for a moment that the passage is clear, and we make it to the cellar undetected. How do we make it from the cellar to her cell without being noticed?"

"Luck," Slater answers honestly. "And if luck isn't on our side, we fight our way there. Like I said, we can take them."

"If we have to fight, there will be a lot of noise, and noise attracts attention. We don't want to be discovered before we get to her, or we may never get to her. Plus, it's going to take a lot of time and effort to freeze and smash the bars. Going by what I've read in past documents, Winter magic doesn't work well in Summer. The climate is hot and dry, which means there's limited moisture in the air to summon."

"Well, there's a balcony off to the right side of the Great Hall with a set of arched double doors, but I don't see how you could possibly get to it. First, you'd have to run across the heavily guarded ground level to the castle, swim across the filthy moat, and then scale a twenty-metre stone wall without a rope."

"What if we skip the ground level and zoom straight to the balcony?" I ask, and I'm met by four sets confused of eyes.

"What do you mean?" Slater asks.

My gaze falls on Stavros. "Acacia could fly in."

His expression goes hard. "That's not an option."

"And anyway," Oscar pipes in. "She wouldn't be able to freeze the bars."

"She could strap one of us to her," I suggest. "And then she could fly Harlow out of there so that she doesn't get hurt."

"But she wouldn't be able to fly both Zeeks out," Oscar replies.

"The warrior would have to stay and escape through the castle."

"Like I said," Stavros' voice is much harsher than I've ever heard it sound. "It's not an option."

Slater cocks his head. "Who's Acacia?" he asks.

"None of your business," Jax warns.

"Are you Zeeks friendly with the Rukes too?"

"Just shut up and keep drawing," Jax spits. "And you," he says, turning his wrath on me. "Next time you want to throw out dangerous suggestions like that, pull one of us aside. You're always opening that big mouth of yours and causing trouble. You never consider the consequences."

His words are like a rock-solid punch to my chest. Jax has never snapped at me like this before. Usually it's Stavros snapping at me, and Jax defending me.

"You should give her a little more credit," Slater says, stepping to my defence. "Her plan makes a lot of sense."

"Oscar, watch him," Jax commands. "Zannah, Stavros, and I need to talk."

21

JUST AS I THOUGHT
-ALEX AS SLATER-

The three warriors step away, close enough that I can still see them, but far enough away that their words become indistinct. I can still make out their harsh tones though. Stavros, the Zeek of calm and reason, is not so calm anymore. He and Zannah are shouting at one another, pushing and shoving, and then next thing I know, their argument turns into a full-blown sparring match.

"Hey," I yell, but nobody listens. I'm surprised Jax is allowing this. You'd think he'd jump in to protect the girl. I turn my sights to Oscar. "Aren't you going to step in?"

He huffs out a laugh. "They're siblings. This is how they settle things. If you're worried about Zannah, don't be. You should be worried about Stavros. Zannah can hold her own. That bitch is cutthroat."

As if on cue, Zannah slams Stavros into a tree trunk and lands a solid headbutt to his face. Jax finally steps in to pull her back, and I notice lines of blood trickling down from Stavros' nose.

"We should discuss this with Acacia." Jax's voice is deeper than the other two and travels far enough for me to hear. "It should be her choice."

Just like that, the fight is over, and the three head in the direction of the village. Their obedient huskens rise from where they were laying—on my mattress!—and race over to join them.

"Who's Acacia?" I ask.

Oscar scratches the midline between his cornrows and sighs. "It's not my place to say."

I watch as Zannah struts alongside the guys, shoulders squared like she's one of them. She's certainly strong enough to be one of them. I'm struggling to figure her out. I've seen glimmers of kindness inside her, but I've also seen the glimmers of a born killer. She seems like the kind of girl who would stroke you with one hand, while stabbing you with the other.

The three amigos are gone for a long time, and I find myself lost in worry. *Ruby.* Guilt courses through me at the thought of her lying scared and alone in that awful stone cell. It's my fault she's there. I should have protected her better.

I wish these Zeeks weren't so damn cautious. I would have preferred to rescue her tonight. The longer we wait, the worse it will be for her. A lot can happen to someone in twenty-four hours, and you can't always undo what's been done. I should know.

Vile thoughts seep into my mind, and I try my best to shake them off. I hope Kenneth will keep the guards in line. If I find out anyone has so much as touched her while I've been gone, they're dead.

The trio finally return, and I'm flabbergasted to see they've brought an unexpected fourth. I stare in awe as I take in the woman's folded wings and marble veined skin. Just as I suspected, Acacia is a Ruke.

"You must be Slater," she says as she nears, and I'm thrown to discover her eyes are the colour violet.

I nod. "And you must be Acacia." My eyes lift to Stavros', finally putting all the pieces together. "Stavros' wife."

22

UNEXPECTED VISITOR DURING THE NIGHT

-HARLOW-

Panic rips through me as the pressure of someone's hand pressing against my shoulder stirs me awake. My eyes flick open to find Kenneth standing above me, and I scream—well at least I try to. He drops to his haunches, and cups my mouth, smothering the sound.

His hand smells sweet like sugar, which dramatically contradicts his terrifying presence. I want to fight him off, but fear turns my limbs into jelly. Not that it matters, he's much stronger than I am. I'd never stand a chance.

"Shhhh…" he warns. His other hand holds me firmly to the

lumpy cell mattress, sending a stabbing sensation through my wounded shoulder. My hip and knees hurt too, but it's the pain in my tummy that's been worrying me the most.

Kenneth's head lowers towards mine, and my heart quickens to an unnatural rhythm. He'd better be here to kill me. I know my time is limited, and I'd much rather be killed than face the alternative.

"I'm not here to hurt you." His accent is thick, harsh, and not at all reassuring. "I'm also not here to help you escape, either. I'm here because I need to show you something." His eyes blaze down into mine, holding me captive. "I'm going to move my hand, and you're not going to scream, or else I'll have to forcefully silence you. Got it?"

I nod against his hand.

"Okay, good." He releases me, stands, and picks up the hessian sack he dropped. When he shakes it out, small granules go flying. Sugar, I realise. This must be why his hand smelt so sweet.

He holds the lip of the sack open and nods to it. "I need you to get in."

I eye the sack, my insides squirming. I've heard of people putting small animals in sacks, tying the top, and then throwing them in a river to drown. I don't trust Kenneth. He says he's not here to hurt me, but I know what he's capable of—what he's already done. Alex never shied away from the truth when it came to talking about his mother and brother. I've heard horrendous stories.

"Now!" he says impatiently.

There's no point in arguing with him. He could easily force me in. I'm too sore to be manhandled, so I slip off the bed and do as he says.

The sack scratches at my sweaty skin as Kenneth lugs me away. I know we've left the cell. I heard the tap of the metal door shutting, and the click of a key, re-locking it. Kenneth's footsteps echo as he walks, the crude stone walls and floors reverberating the thudding sounds. Soon the echoes are replaced by the squeaks of sandals on sand. We must be outside the castle. I wonder where he's taking me. Eventually the sack is placed down—with far more care than I would have expected—and Kenneth opens the top tie.

The sack drops around me and I gaze about, curious with unease. The night sky is dark, but the moon is full and reflects brightly off the yellow waves of sand. Rows of stone houses surround us, old, warn, and covered in cracking red clay—transporting my mind to pictures of Uluru.

"Where are we?" I ask, but Kenneth doesn't answer the question.

"Can I trust you to follow me and keep things civil?"

I nod, and he unties the leather pouch that holds my hands captive.

Pain shoots through me as I force myself to stand. He walks over to the house closest to us and I follow, wincing with each step. My ripped dress strap hangs down, revealing more skin than I would like. I fold my arms over my chest self-consciously.

Kenneth knocks on the wooden door with a light rasp of his knuckles, and an Amber Vallon in his thirties comes to greet us. His hair isn't as closely shaved to his skull as Kenneth's, and the amber peppercorn hair that shows, is a stark contrast to the dark colour of his skin. He says something to Kenneth in Vallon and then smiles down at me. I'm too stunned to smile back. I've never seen an Amber Vallon before. He is less intimidating than the Reds I've come across, both in looks and persona.

"This is Jye," Kenneth says.

"I'm Ruby," I offer. It feels weird to introduce myself as Ruby in my Zeek form, but it's the name Kenneth knows me as, and if I introduced myself as Harlow, it would only confuse things.

Jye nods. "Hello, Ruby."

He says something else to Kenneth after this and then leads us inside to a small kitchen-dining room. "You sit." He says, pulling out a chair for me. "You eat?"

I'm not hungry, but I haven't eaten since Alex gave me the sandwiches. I give my tender tummy a light rub. I really should eat something for the sake of the babies. "Please."

He nods and wanders over to the kitchen bench, where a loaf of bread lies uncovered on a chopping board.

Kenneth pulls out the chair across from me and sits. "Jye speaks a little bit of Zeek. But he's not fluent."

"Why am I'm here?" I ask. "I know you didn't carry me all this way just for Jye to feed me." An awful idea springs to mind. "Are you selling me to him?"

"No." A non-humorous laugh escapes him. "I need to show you something, but we have to wait for Sylus to bring the horsens around. He was supposed to meet us here at midnight. It seems he's running behind schedule."

A small wave of excitement hits me when I hear the word horsens, and I mentally slap myself for being so foolish. I haven't seen one since that horrid day I witnessed the Red stealing the young Pastel. As terrifying as the situation was, I was mesmerised by the sight of the horsen. It was so big and colourful.

Jye comes back over and hands me a dried meat sandwich. I smile politely, forcing myself to take a bite. It's tough and doesn't taste very good, but I'm not exactly in a position to be picky. I'm glad when he hands me a cup of water soon afterwards. It helps to wash it down.

Kenneth stares at me with dipped brows while I eat. It makes me feel uncomfortable, but I lower my gaze pretending not to notice.

"I don't believe you're ready to die," he says eventually. "So, I'm going to ask you again, who is your useful connection?"

I'm not ready to die, but also not willing to involve Jax. I curse Alex for putting me in this tight, awkward position. "What do you need my connection for?"

"We Vallons have been trying to negotiate a trade deal with the Zeeks for years, but your Commander won't budge on the terms she's set, and her price is unreasonable."

I shrug with my good shoulder. "I don't believe I can help you. I have no pull with the Commander." If only he knew the awful truth, I'm sure I'd be dead already.

"But you have pull with somebody high up, don't you?"

"Maybe."

He flashes me an enquiring look. "Maybe?"

"You Vallons have done vile things to Pastels like me. I've heard the stories; I've met the victims. Give me one good reason why I should help your race."

"Your race is just as cruel. I've heard vile stories about what the warriors have done to Pastels. Furthermore, your Commander sent many of the Pastels here, gifting them as a peace offering. Did you know that?"

"So what? You think because they were gifted to you as an offering, that gives your race the right to beat and rape them?" I'm surprised to see that my words make him flinch.

"Not all Vallons are as evil as you think. Take Jye for example." He gestures in Jye's direction. "The Queen's foot guards are the worst offenders. However, thanks to Slate's little killing rampage, the cruellest of the bunch have been taken out." He leans forward in his chair, his voice dropping an octave. "And as for the other vile offenders who have been caught taking advantage over the years—they have been dealt with by me personally. Nobody likes the Queen's foot guards. Even the Queen's elite horsen guards despise them."

"You can pretend like you're on our side, but I know you're not. You've killed Pastels like me. Slater told me about the ink trials. He's told me about everything."

"Slater only saw what I wanted him to see. What I wanted everyone to see. I love my younger brother, and I'm all for what he believes in, but he's an unstable rebel who runs around causing more harm than good." Kenneth's tone lightens slightly. "I liked it when he was with Raven. She kept him calm and in control. They seemed to be a good fit. They were set to be linked, but then all of a sudden Slate came home from work one day and ended things. He wouldn't give her a proper reason why either, he just told her it was over and then turned cold." He looks me over, eyes narrowed with judgement. "The reason is clear now."

"I didn't know about Raven until yesterday. Ale…" I shake my head. "Slater never told me he had a girlfriend. Had I known, I wouldn't be here. I wouldn't be waiting to be destroyed because I fell pregnant to him." Tears sting my eyes.

"Raven isn't a bad Vallon," Kenneth says in her defence, and I find my body stiffening with resentment. "She got jealous and made a bad decision in a fit of rage. She feels awful about what she's done and has been crying on Jacinta's shoulder ever since."

I hmpf. "Yeah…well her tears aren't going to save me now, are they?"

"Perhaps not. But your connection might," he says pointedly, and then stands and leaves.

23

DON'T JUDGE A BOOK BY ITS COVER
-HARLOW-

Kenneth steps back into the dining room just as I've finished the first half of my sandwich. "Sylus is here. It's time to go."

I leave the other half of my sandwich on the table. I should really stash it in my dress for later, but it was such a struggle to eat the first half, I don't know that I could face the second.

Outside stand three magnificent looking horsens, all brightly coloured with eyes like fire. The one closest to me swishes its tail revealing a bright mix of reds, oranges, and yellows.

"You're with me," Kenneth says, and he picks me up by the

waist to place me on the horsen's saddle. I wince but manage to hold in a yelp. I don't think he realises how incredibly sore I am all over.

Sylus is sitting on the horsen up front, reins in hand, waiting to go. We haven't been introduced yet, but I can see by the bright colour of his vertic switz tattoos he's an Orange.

Kenneth climbs up onto the saddle behind me, while Jye hoists himself onto the horsen next to ours. "Let's move," Kenneth commands.

We ride through the sandy streets for quite some time, passing various clay coated houses in various shapes and forms. The further out we get, the smaller the houses become, until suddenly, a large out-of-place building appears. It looks to be an ancient church, which has been forgotten about over time. Its windows are boarded shut, and the roof is sagging lifelessly in the middle. I'd say it's in desperate need of a little love and care.

Kenneth pulls the reins, bringing the horsen to a halt by the bottom of the front steps.

"We're here." He slips his hands around my waist and slides off the saddle, bringing me with him. As soon as his feet hit the ground, he places me down. "Follow me."

The stairs of the hall are partially eroded, and he warns me to mind my step when climbing them. "There have been a few accidents on these stairs over the years," he says. "One girl tripped and hit her head on that jagged edge, right there." He points to a particularly rough section. "She almost died."

I eye him curiously. "I thought you wanted me dead, so why bother with the warnings?"

"It's our mother who wants you dead. I want your help."

The large, arched double doors open as I reach the top step, revealing another Orange—only this time it's a woman. She looks to be a year or so older than I am and rocks a wild afro like the singer Diana Ross. The tight curls spread out from the top of her head, full and fluffy, like a bright orange-seeded dandelion framing her pretty face.

To add to the brightness, she wears a vibrant peach dress which contrasts nicely with her dark skin. I glance down with burning cheeks. My torn dress strap hangs awkwardly off my battered shoulder, and most of the fabric has been stained by blood and dirt. *I'm a mess.*

"This is Sienna, Sylus' sister," Kenneth tells me. "Sienna, this is Ruby," he adds, gesturing towards me.

She smiles politely, then waits for the other two while I follow Kenneth's lead and enter.

Inside, the church is lit with soft glowing candles which flicker yellow, allowing me to see two long rows of triple-bunk beds, lining each of the side walls. A few heads pop up from the pillows as we enter, revealing pale white skin and pastel pink hair.

I gasp loudly, and more heads rise. "What is this? Where are we?"

A few of the newly risen Zeeks have peach-coloured hair, the same as Luna and Destiny. I'm shocked. Slater told me that all the Peach Zeeks were destroyed after a guard was found killed. He said that Kenneth helped to destroy them. I never told Alex that I had the displeasure of meeting those two escaped Peaches. I knew if I told him, questions would follow, and I didn't want to reveal I'd met them in the Drake village.

A Zeek with reddish hair slips out from the lower bunk furthest from us, and races over, prompting a few other Pastels to follow. My breath catches in my throat. Her hair isn't as red as mine, it's more of a pastel red, but it's still a shade of red, nonetheless. This can't be real. My body sways, threatening to fall sideways. I truly think I've gone into shock.

"These here," Kenneth says, putting his hand on my arm to stabilise me. "Are the Pastels we have saved."

"Saved?" I repeat the word, forcing it to process. "But I thought you…"

My aired thoughts are interrupted by the Pastel-Red Zeek who practically dives at me. She throws her arms around me tightly. It hurts *a lot*, but I try not to let the pain show on my face. After a moment, she pulls back, her eyes regarding me with sympathy. "You poor thing. Rest assured; you can get past this. I've been in your position. I can help you."

My insides clench. I'm sensing another Luna moment about to arise. This poor Zeek thinks I'm a rape victim, like her. I clamp up, tears forming in my eyes. I don't know how to respond. These Zeeks would have been through hell, yet they surround me with sympathy written all over their faces. If they find out the truth, I'm sure they'll turn on me. *I'm afraid.*

"Give her some room, all of you," Sienna orders, stepping up beside me. Clearly, she speaks Zeek. "We don't want to overwhelm her. Kiyra," she eyes the Pastel-Red Zeek. "You come with us."

Great. Kiyra was the one I was hoping to get away from. I don't want her to find out the truth about Slater and me. I don't want her to hate me.

There's a lounging area along the back wall made up of mismatched lounges and cushions. Sienna leads us there and gets us to sit so we can talk.

When Kiyra asks, "What happened?" I tell her I'm not ready to talk about it, which isn't exactly a lie, so she opens up to me instead.

I cringe as she relays her horrific encounter with a guard which resulted in an unwanted pregnancy. She's been through so much and yet here I was a few days ago, crying at the prospect of being locked in a five-star chamber with Alex, who loves me. Guilt fills me. My problems, which seemed so big at the time, seem inconsequential compared to what Kiyra has been through.

"What did Kenneth say will happen with the baby?" she asks, her gaze dropping to my stomach. "Will he let you keep it? You look like you are ready to pop."

"He hasn't said," I answer carefully. "Why, what happened to yours?"

"Kenneth made me abort it for my own safety. I wasn't very far along though, not like you are. And I didn't know how I was going to raise a child here, so I did as he said and saw the doctor."

I swallow. "I'm sorry."

"Don't be. There are a couple of other girls here who are in the same boat. We lean on each other for support. We Reds band together."

Kiyra tells me a bit about the other girls, in our situation and I cringe. "Kenneth says of the thirty slaves still working in the castle, the majority are males. We tried persuading him to rescue them as well, but he felt it would be best to leave them where they are. He said this old church is unstable and doesn't have the capacity for thirty more bodies. However, he assured us that on most counts, the guards tend to leave the guys alone. Is that right?"

I glance between the two rows of eight triple bunk beds lining the walls. Forty-eight Zeeks in total, living in a broken-down old building. As much as I hate to admit it, I understand where Kenneth is coming from. This place is already dangerously overcrowded as it is.

Kiyra mistakes my internalisation for fear. "Don't worry," she says, her hand squeezing mine. "The Vallons who care for us here are very kind. Sienna is my favourite." She smiles. "She likes to teach us acrobatics and dance moves. She knows a lot about performing. Her mother runs the open-air circus in town. I've heard it's so popular, even the Queen herself attends once every few months."

"That sounds cool." I force a smile.

Kiyra's mouth opens to say something else, but then a shadow appears over us, and the words die in her throat.

"We need to go," Kenneth says, putting an end to our conversation. "I need to get you back to your cell before anyone notices you're missing."

"Cell?" Kiyra's eyes widen. "You're taking her back?"

"Ruby's pregnancy has been discovered by the Queen. She can't stay."

"What does that mean?" Her eyes flick between us, and my insides shrivel.

Please don't tell her my story, I think.

Kiyra swallows. "Is she going to be killed?"

"Not if she can prove she's useful," he answers, his gaze locking firmly on mine.

There's a swap over. Jye stays to watch over the Pastels while Sienna rides back with us. She and Sylus banter in Vallon on the way back, each doing a neat rotation of acrobatic tricks as they ride. You can tell their mother runs a circus and that they're siblings, going by how fiercely competitive they are. I presume trick riding takes a big part in the open-air circus. A slight pinch of envy swirls within me. I wish I could attend one of the shows.

As we get closer to the denser part of town, Kenneth tells the siblings to rein it in and quieten down. "We don't want to attract any unwanted attention."

Eventually we pull up in front of Jye's place again, and Kenneth leaves me with the siblings while he goes inside to grab the hessian sack.

"Thank you for what you are doing to help the Pastels," I say to them. "I am grateful to you both."

Sienna's playful expression grows serious. "Now that you can see we are not all evil, will you help us in return?"

"I'll try, but I can't promise anything. Our Commander isn't easily swayed."

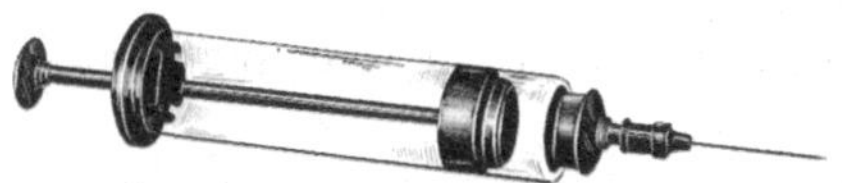

Kenneth gets me back to my cell without any hiccups.

"So?" he says expectantly as he helps me out of the sack.

"So..." I repeat, letting the word drag out. I know what he wants from me—and after what I've seen, I'm considering cooperating—but I still have a few questions I want answered first.

"Now that you can see I've been helping to save Pastels, not kill them, are you willing to help me in return?"

"Why have you never confided in Slater?" I ask. "Why did you want him to believe that you were evil? He would have helped you if he'd known. Together you could have achieved a lot more."

"Slater has good intentions, but like I said before, he is an unstable rebel who causes more harm than good. When someone upsets him, he goes off like a firecracker. I couldn't trust him to keep my secret rescue operation under wraps. He's a liability."

"How do you know you can trust me?"

"I don't, but I'm hopeful." He sighs. "I'm not a fan of war. It costs too many lives, and thus far, it has achieved very little. I want the trade deal, but I don't want to fight for it. I'd rather it be a peaceful agreement than a forced agreement. Our races have fought for too long. It's time that we unite as allies, just as your race has done with the Drakes."

"I agree with what you're saying, and I'm sure my connection will agree too, but like I said to Sienna, our Commander is not easily swayed. Even with my connection we might not be able to get you what you want."

"Who is your connection?"

I freeze up. Kenneth might not be the evil Vallon I thought he was, but it still feels wrong to willingly hand him Jax's name.

"As a part of the agreement are you willing to release the Pastels from Summer?"

"I could easily sway the Queen to release the slaves for the trade deal, but are you sure this is what you want? The Pastels were sent to us by your Commander for a reason. They weren't wanted in Winter."

"Things are about to change. Jax is fighting to break down the colour system."

"Jax," he repeats with a curious glance. "He's your connection, isn't he?" He pauses a beat and then adds. "Going by your expression, I'd say Jax is more than a connection." His eyes bore into mine. "Is Slate aware?"

"Yes, Jax is my connection," I answer, frustrated by my transparency and his probing question.

Kenneth's eyes light up. "A useful connection indeed." He cups his chin in thought. "Tell me, if I do you a solid and turn a blind eye when Slater comes back to rescue you, will you do me a solid and help set up a meeting with Jax in the forest? Slater knows all the best places to hunt. He could easily bring Jax to me during the evening while I'm working. That way the Queen's suspicion won't be aroused. I want the deal signed off on by Azazel before I put it to my mother. It needs to be a sure thing."

I nod. "I can do that."

"Good."

Kenneth stares for a moment, his look of satisfaction slowly fading to something much darker. "There's something else I need to discuss with you, and you're not going to take it well, but know it needs to be done."

I tense, suddenly afraid that I may have fallen into a trap. He'd better not be planning on hurting Jax in order to blackmail the Commander, or the deal's off. There is no way I'm putting Jax in danger.

"We're going to have to get rid of those babies."

My heart stops. "What? NO! No, no, no."

"I'll be back in the morning to escort you to the doctor. The procedure needs to be done before Slater and his rescue party come back for you, and I can only presume they'll be back tomorrow night.

"You can't..." I shake my head. "No."

"I'm sorry, but this is for your own good," he says, and then turns and leaves, locking the cell shut behind him.

HARLOW IS IN TROUBLE

-ZAVIER-

*M*inty and I arrive back from work to find Floss sprawled on some cushions, half snoozing. I'm surprised and a little worried. She's usually home later than me these days.

"Hey," I say, kneeling in front of her. My eyes scan over her body for any signs of an injury. "Are you okay?"

She raises her head, eyes blinking. "Yeah, I'm okay."

"Why aren't you at training then?"

She sits up. "Our training session was interrupted. Woody came rushing to the fields to tell Jax something, and then he and all the

Purple warriors took off and never returned. Luna, Destiny, and I waited for around for a couple of hours, sparring and practising moves, but when it didn't look like they were coming back, we packed it in."

My brows pucker. "What was the message?"

She shrugs, not seeming all that concerned. "How should I know? They were speaking in Drake."

A few light taps sound at the hut entrance, and Minty yells, "Come in."

Jax's tall figure rounds the corner, and my heart pounds. I have a gut feeling that whatever is up has something to do with Harlow.

"I hope I'm not intruding," he says. "I saw you and Minty arriving home as we were heading back to the fields."

"Oh, so now you're heading back to the fields," Floss grumbles. She glances at her watch and scowls. "It's almost four. I'm not going back for the sake of an hour."

Jax's grits his teeth and glares at her. "I'm not here for you," he says coldly. It's clear he's not too fond of Floss. This bothers me, but I can't really blame him. Her bratty side seems to shine brighter whenever he's around.

"I have bad news about Harlow," he says confirming my fears. "She's in trouble."

My body tenses and I gulp. "What kind of trouble?"

"She's been discovered by the Queen and locked in a cell. Slater says the Queen wants to make a spectacle out of her before killing her, which buys us two days. Well, one and a half now."

My heart twists. "Where is Slater? Can't he help her?"

"Slater is here. He showed up near the entrance of the village this morning, asking for our help. He wants us to break into the castle with him and help break her out."

Minty stops what she's doing and looks over, her face crinkled with concern. "That sounds highly dangerous. Are you going to do it?"

"We have to. There's no other option. We'll be leaving at seven A.M. I just thought you all should know."

"Will you be bringing Harlow back here?" Floss' voice wobbles with the question.

Jax nods. "That's the plan."

Without warning, Floss bursts into full-fledged sobs and storms into our room. I'm shocked. I hadn't expected such an emotional reaction from her. Going by Jax's expression, he hadn't expected it either.

"Just one more thing before I go," he hurries to say. "If all goes to plan and we manage to bring Harlow back, it's inevitable she's going to have a lot of questions about why you guys are here and why your colours have changed. I was wondering if you'd do me a favour and allow me to explain everything to her. I know you two are best friends and you tell each other everything." His gaze lowers to my shared friendship necklace. "But I want the chance to explain myself regarding Electra and the whole linking ceremony."

I nod. "That's fine. I get it. Just, *please* bring her back."

"I'm prepared to die trying." As he turns to leave, he adds, "Let Floss know, there will be no training tomorrow." Discontentment stains his voice. "She can sleep in as long as she wants."

As soon as Jax exits, I head to the bedroom to console Floss. She is sitting on the edge of the bed, her face buried in her hands. I plop down next to her and run my hand over her hair. "It'll be okay, Jax won't fail. He'll bring her back." I don't know who I'm trying to convince more, her or myself.

"That's the problem," she sobs. "I know he will."

It takes me a second to register the meaning of her words.

My hand drops from her hair, and I stand. "Let me get this straight," I say, anger spiking inside me. "You're not upset because Harlow's in trouble, you're upset because Jax is planning on bringing her back, am I right? Tell me I'm not." She doesn't answer, which is an answer in itself. I shake my head in disbelief. "What is wrong with you, Floss? Harlow's your twin sister. I thought you were upset for her safety."

"I don't want Harlow to die," she sobs, "but I also don't want her brought back here. I'm happy for her to be alive and happy, just so long as it's somewhere else, far, far, away."

Frustrated, I turn for the door. I've known Floss to be mean and selfish, but this is next level.

"Your whole body reacts to the sound of her name," she says with a sniff, and I pause mid step to look back at her. "You're still in love with her. I can tell, and I know as soon as she's back, I'll go back to being invisible again."

I sigh, some of my frustration ebbing away. That's what this is all about. She's jealous. "That's not true. Harlow is my best friend, and I care about her deeply. But I'm in love with you." Relenting, I head back over to where she sits. "Please don't do this, Floss. Jealousy isn't a good look on you. I thought we were past this. I thought we were happy. These few weeks have been amazing, haven't they? I thought you and I were solid."

"You don't look the same as you used to. You're buff now, the way Harlow seems to like her men." She sobs. "Harlow might see the new you and decide she's made a horrible mistake."

A dry laugh escapes me. "I very much doubt that, but if on the off chance it turns out to be correct, it would be her loss." I take hold of Floss' hands and pull her up off the edge of the bed, drawing her to me. "I have you now, and you're all I want."

"Promise?"

I plant a soft kiss on her lips. "I promise."

25

NOT HAPPENING!

-HARLOW-

When Kenneth arrives to collect me at dawn, I swoop on him from my cell cot like a mummy plover bird protecting her young. I'm aware that with each hit I take, I'm causing more pain to myself than to him, but this doesn't stop me. The idea isn't to injure him; or I'd zap him. I'm trying to appeal to his compassion.

"I won't honour the deal," I scream. "If you take my babies, I won't honour the deal."

"Ruby stop," he says, taking a firm hold of one of my wrists. "It has to be done."

"No, it doesn't." I try to tug away from his grip, but it sends a stabbing pain through my shoulder, and I whimper. "I know you believe my babies will tarnish our races, but what if you're wrong? What if they are the key to bringing our races together? Think about it, they are the half Zeeks, half Vallons of a prince. That's important. They're important."

"This isn't just about the babies being half breeds, it's about your safety. If those babies aren't removed soon, you will die."

"Then let me die. It's either all of us or none of us. Those are my terms."

He clamps his arm around me to pick me up. *Not happening.* I refuse to go easy. I start kicking and throwing myself about. The pain jolting through me is immense, but I'll take all the pain in the world if it means there's a chance I'll get to save my babies. "I won't help you if you do this to me. Do you hear me? I won't help you."

"Enough," he shouts. He lets go and points to the cot. "Sit down."

Refusing to obey, I keep whacking into him until he seizes me firmly and forces me down in a tackle.

His torso is like a slab of concrete crushing down on top of me. Pain shoots through my entire body, and I let out a cry that rings off the walls.

"This doesn't have to be a painful process." His eyes blaze into mine. "If you listen and co-operate, this will all be over very shortly."

"How can you say that?" I ask in disbelief. "You are asking me to give up my babies. What could be more painful than giving up my unborn children?"

The hard set of his face softens slightly. "If you leave this castle with those babies inside you, our mother will have you hunted down and killed within a day."

"Slater's strong. You saw what he did to those guards. We can fight off whoever the Queen sends."

"This might be true, but even if you do manage to fight them off, it'll only be a matter of a week before those babies start crushing you from the inside. Zeek bodies aren't made to carry Vallons, they're too small. Trust me, I know." He levers off me and takes a seat on the cot beside me. "The first two Pastels I ever saved were pregnant. Jacinta noticed their pigments were off, and that they appeared to be struggling, so she pointed them out to me. I didn't have anything setup back then, so I hid them away with Jye in his home. They said they wanted to keep their babies and Jacinta agreed that they should be allowed to. She thought it would be barbaric to force them to get rid of them after everything they'd already been through." He lets out a pained breath. "Three months into their pregnancies the Pastels started struggling. They began vomiting constantly and complaining of tremendous pain. The first Pastel died at three months and a week, and the other died at three months and two weeks. I got the doctor to run an autopsy, and he said both of the girls' insides had been crushed."

A strangle noise gurgles in my throat, and he turns to face me.

"Raven says you are just past three months."

"My body is bigger than most Pastels." I say, trying to reassure myself as much as him. "I should be able to make it through the next few weeks."

"You are bigger, but you are also carrying two babies. That's double the load." His gaze lowers to my tummy. "Are you in pain?"

"Yes, I'm in pain, but I've been manhandled and kicked in the stomach by one of the guards."

"If you die, my hopes of a peaceful trade agreement are gone."

"If you take my babies away your hopes of a peaceful trade agreement are gone. Please, if you let me keep my babies, I promise to track down Jax and arrange the meeting as soon as I'm out. If I die after that, it shouldn't matter to you. You will have gotten what you wanted from me."

He seems to consider this for a moment. "I think you're making a mistake, but I'll give you one more day. If Slater comes tonight, you get to keep the babies, but if he doesn't, you'll be taken to the doctors in the morning. I'm telling you right now, your time is running short. If those babies aren't taken out soon, they will kill you." He stands and slips his hand into his pocket, pulling out two biscuits. "Here," he says handing them to me. I look up in surprise. "I thought you might find these a little more appealing than a tough meat sandwich."

26

RESCUE MISSION

-ZANNAH-

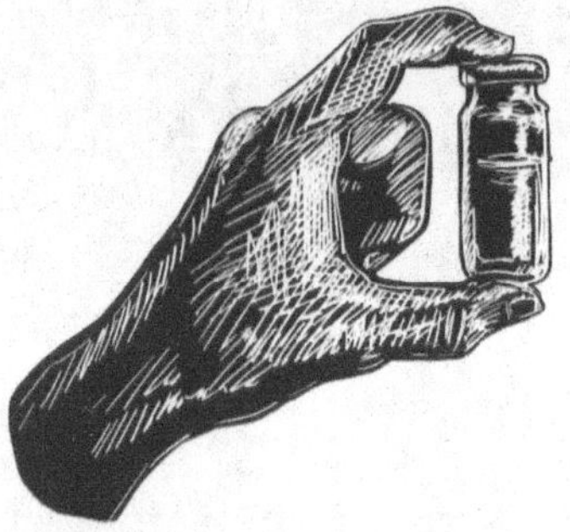

*J*ax trips backwards as soon as his heels hit the ground, dragging Acacia down on top of him. The harness holding them together has them landing in a very intimate position. *Awkward.*

"What's this?" Stavros shouts with a mocking grin. "You're lucky I'm not a jealous man, my friend."

Jax blushes, and I chuckle. I find it endearing how easily he flushes at suggestive comments. For someone so badass, he can be such a prude.

We'd gotten up early so Acacia could have a few more practice runs, flying with Jax strapped to her, before the rescue mission. She has the flying part and turning part down pat, it's the constant crash landing that seems to be an issue, and that's on Jax.

Woody sprayed Acacia's wings with liquified coal dust, to make them blend with the night sky, and she and Jax are wearing long sleeve black clothing to cover their pale, shimmering skin.

Stavros helps them up, all smiles. Meanwhile, he's been shooting daggers at me all morning. He's still super pissed at me for getting Acacia involved, but as long as no Vallons see her flying overhead and start hurling fireballs, I honestly believe she's our best shot at getting Harlow out unharmed.

I glance at my watch. It's six-thirty, almost time to leave.

Oscar's beside me, anxiously plucking out blades of grass while he watches Destiny goo and ga over Atohi on the other side of the field. I laugh inside. It seems someone's freaking out.

"Has anyone checked on Slater since we left him yesterday afternoon?" I ask. "Do we even know if he's still out there? If he's still alive?"

"No, I thought you'd be all over it." Oscar's words are biting. "You're the one who seems to have taken a fancy to him."

Wow. Snappy, snappy.

"Leave me alone, man-whore."

"You know..." He looks at me pointedly. "When you were giving Jax a mouthful about Harlow 'heading off to Summer with her super-ripped ex-lover,' I thought you were playing it up to be a bitch, but you actually do find Slater hot, don't you? I saw the way you were drooling over him yesterday. I think you were enjoying playing 'Medic Zannah'."

"Well, he's certainly hotter than you, Meat Head," I bite back.

He laughs like I'm joking, but I'm being serious. Oscar isn't bad looking, but Slater's sex on legs.

Unable to resist, I nod in Destiny's direction. "*Awww, look.* How sweet. Hold up..." I cup my ear. "Do you hear that?"

Oscar frowns and cocks his head to listen.

"CLUCK." I shout in his face, making him jolt. "Cluck, cluck, cluck, cluck."

Air explodes from his nostrils in a puff of anger. "There's something seriously wrong with you!"

Now it's my turn to laugh. "There, there, Oscar," I say, in sickly sweetness. "Don't go getting testy, I think you'll make a great dad."

I'm one up on him for the day, so I hurriedly snatch up my pack and leave before he can take his next swipe.

Besides, I'm pumped and ready to go. Life here is a little too monotonous for my liking. I'm craving some action, even if it is highly dangerous.

Slater is awake when I get to him, but he isn't up. He's lying on his back gazing up at the trees. This isn't how I expected to find him. I thought he'd be fired-up and pacing. Instead, he seems deflated—broken.

"You made it through the night, I see."

"Yeah." He sits up, wincing as he does. "Where's everyone else?"

"They're coming. Acacia and Jax wanted to do a few more practice flights before we left."

He grunts. He'd fought against this arrangement yesterday afternoon—and lost. He wanted Stavros to be the one strapped to Acacia, not Jax. If Jax is the one being flown in, it'll be his face Harlow sees first. I'm guessing this leaves a sour taste in Slater's mouth. I wonder which face she'd prefer to see first. I'm hoping for Jax's sake, it's his. He hasn't been the same since she's been gone; he's been a shell of himself. Even Oscar has noticed—and he's barely around; he's always too busy knocking about with Destiny.

"I come bearing gifts," I say, handing Slater a pack with two sandwiches, two bottles of water, and my spare blade.

He grabs out the blade and unsheathes it, running his fingers along the newly sharpened edge. The faint curl of his lips tells me he's impressed. He's probably imagining lopping Jax's head off with it.

"You dare turn that blade on one of us and I will make you extremely sorry, you got that?"

"Got it."

I plonk down on the end of the mattress while he tucks into the sandwiches I'd made. He should be impressed. Little does he realise I'm not in the habit of making breakfast for others.

After the conversation I had with Koby, I'm feeling a little more generous towards him. It turns out I was wrong with my presumption. Koby isn't his personal slave. Koby said he'd never met Slater before yesterday. Apparently, he'd found him passed out by a tree on his way to the village. He said he'd accidentally woken Slater while checking to see if he had a pulse.

Slater devours both sandwiches and a whole bottle of water before Sphinx and Rebel come bounding over. They stay down by my end, eyeing Slater with suspicion.

Slater rises to stretch and Sphinx growls. "Tell me we aren't bringing those things," he grumbles. "They'll be slaughtered in Summer."

I shrug. "It's Jax's call, not mine. But I think you're underestimating them. They're fast, and their teeth are razor sharp."

He rolls his eyes. "Whatever. Where are Jax and the rest of his team? I wish they'd hurry up. I want to get to Summer before the night's out."

"It's just on seven now." Jax's voice rumbles through the trees. "We'll make it to Summer with plenty of time." His figure emerges, followed by Stavros, Oscar, Acacia, and Woody. *I wasn't expecting Woody.* "Besides," Jax continues, "aren't you the one who said the later in the evening we enter Summer, the better?"

Slater does a double take at Woody and tenses. "What are you doing here? This mission doesn't involve your race."

Good question, I'd been wondering the same thing. Dakari made it crystal clear he didn't want any of his tribe members involved.

"You came to our village asking for help," Woody says in his super thick accent. "So, I'm here to help."

"While I appreciate the gesture," Slater says, sounding more frustrated than pleased, "I think it's a bad idea. If you're seen helping us, it could cause tension between our races. We have a good trade setup in place. I'm not looking to ruin that; I just want Ruby back."

"Why do you care about what happens to your race when clearly they don't care about you?" Woody cocks his head, his face curious. "Your own Queen has put a generous bounty on your head. You're lucky I'm not here to kill you."

Slater glares a moment and then sheaths the blade I've lent him. "To hell with it," he mutters. "Let's go."

We've only trekked a matter of metres when we're disturbed by the pat, pat, of rushing footsteps charging up behind us. We stop and pivot. Slater has his blade out and raised, ready to attack. I think the mention of the bounty on his head has put him on edge.

I gawk in disbelief. Floss and Zavier are rushing towards us.

Slater gawks too, but not for the same reason. "What's going on with that Zeek's colouring?"

I shrug. It wasn't my decision to use vertic switz ink on Harlow's friends, so I'll be damned if I'm left having to explain it.

"What are you two doing?" Jax commands.

Their pace slows to a walk. "We're coming," Floss says between pants.

I sigh internally. This had better be a joke.

"No, you're not." Jax, points a finger in the direction of the village. "Go back. NOW!"

"I'm a warrior." Floss straightens. "And Harlow's my sister. I'm coming."

Jax turns his focus on Zavier, who in turn is staring at Slater with gauging interest. "This is madness, Zavier, and you know it. Floss hasn't had enough training, and you haven't had any. You will only be a nuisance and slow us down."

"I don't plan on entering Summer with you. I just want to wait by the border. I'm too anxious to stay here and work."

"Then don't work," Jax replies flatly.

"We're coming with you whether you like it or not," Floss insists. "You can't stop us."

Actually…we could, I think, pumping a fist. I'd only need to give them one good knock to the head each, and they'd be out cold for the next few hours.

"Why do you even want to come?" Jax argues. "I happen to know you care very little for your sister."

"I might not be close to her, but he is." Her eyes slit for a moment as they flick to Zavier. "Besides, I'm interested in seeing Summer."

"Hold up." Jax thrusts a palm. "I thought you said, you were going to wait at the border."

"No…" She tilts her head in Zavier's direction. "He said he'd wait at the border. I'm coming along for the mission."

"We don't have time to debate this," Slater grumbles. "Just let them come."

"Easy for you to say," Jax snaps. "You don't care if they're killed."

"Sure, I do. Floss and I are old friends, aren't we, Floss?" He winks at her.

"Friends?" A bitter laugh escapes Jax's throat. "You used her as your hostage to get your hands on Harlow."

Slater nods, face smug. "Yes, and what a brave and *willing* hostage she was."

Jax's head snaps in Floss' direction, his eyes wild with fury. Floss is lucky she's a female and Harlow's sister, otherwise she'd be out cold on the ground right now. Noticing the crazed look in Jax's eyes, Zavier slings a protective arm around Floss, although it's clear from the distinct crease in his brow this comes as news to him too.

"Jax." Acacia lightly touches his arm, snapping him back to himself.

"I say let them come," Slater insists.

Jax turns his heated gaze on Slater instead. "Fine, let them come. But from here on in, they are your responsibility. If anything happens to them, it's on you."

27

PREDATOR ALERT

-HARLOW-

The click of a metal door rouses me, and my eyes fling open to find a guard entering my cell. My blood runs cold as his eyes roll over me hungrily, like I'm a tasty treat he's about to devour. He runs his tongue along his teeth, then sucks it back into his mouth with a slurp.

Terrified, I scream, and he dives on me, crushing me to the cot with his body weight. His slimy hand clamps over my mouth, reeking of sweat and sour fruit. I'm guessing he's been into the hooch tonight. Alex told me that the foot guards like to drown in it.

He rips at my tattered dress, and I scream again, but it only comes out as a hoot through my nose.

After a moment of agonising struggle, I manage to get a hand free from under him, and without hesitation I reach for his face. The entire Great Hall lights up white and he convulses, letting go of my mouth only to headbutt my cheek. To my distress, his heavy body remains on top of me as he jerks and thrashes, bashing into my body with a force that's bound to leave nasty bruises. His studded belt grazes up and down my legs with the movement, setting my skin on fire as the sharp points tear into my flesh.

I scream repeatedly, although I don't know what good it'll do me. Chances are, any guards I alert will either let him continue and watch—or even worse—join in.

The predator's convulsions eventually cease. I try zapping him again, but my energy levels have depleted. I panic as I'm unable to make a spark. He snatches my wrists and holds them down above my head, hissing something in Vallon. I know what's in store for me, and I'm terrified. My entire frame shudders.

I manage another scream before he stuffs a rotten tasting cloth into my mouth, making me gag.

As his hand slides down my body in the direction it shouldn't, I feel a zap rip through my tummy, sending us both into convolutions. *It was the twins*, I realise. Every jerk my body gives sends a stabbing sensation through me, but I'm grateful, nonetheless. *My children are looking out for me, they know I'm in trouble.*

"Ryze!" Kenneth bursts through the cell door and rips the guard off me, throwing him to the floor, before pounding him with his fists.

Ryze attempts to fight back, but Kenneth draws his blade and ploughs it up through his abdomen to his chest. "Du bist eine Schande für unsere Rasse," Kenneth says with hostility.

The guard spits blood in Kenneth's face and gurgles something back before choking on his last breath.

I sit up, hands shaking, and remove the filthy cloth from my mouth. "W…what did you say to him?"

"I told him he was a disgrace to our race." The glow of rage leaves Kenneth's eyes, and he assesses my current state in concern. "Are you okay?"

"I think so." My words are as shaky as my hands.

"How much faith do you have in my brother?" he asks.

I blink. "What do you mean?"

"I mean he'd better return with his rescue party tonight, or we're in serious trouble. My mother wants you executed before the entire kingdom at dawn. She's got her horsen guards sending out the word to the citizens of our kingdom as we speak."

SUMMER

-ZANNAH-

The walk to the Summer border takes forever given the overly intense dynamics of our group. Slater soars ahead the whole time—leading the way—while Jax treks silently next to me, his warrior mask firm in place. Even Stavros, Oscar, and Zavier remain quiet. Floss, Acacia, and Woody are the only ones undeterred by the tension in the air. They take up the rear of the group, chatting amongst themselves.

Last night, just as I was about to jump into bed, Jax swung over to apologise. He said he was sorry for lashing out at me and gave me a hug. Jax isn't much of a hugger, so I'd made a point to enjoy the embrace while it lasted. We sat together on the end of my bed for quite some time, talking about the mission. He didn't mention anything about the comment Slater made, regarding Harlow sharing his bed, all Jax said was how worried he was about Harlow —and how irate he was at Slater for getting her into this mess.

"I swear, if anything's happened to her by the time we get there, I'll kill him," he said. "She told him she wanted to stay, but he wouldn't listen, and now she's paying the price for his selfishness."

Now at the border, Slater tells us all to wait while he sneaks ahead and scopes out the area out. Jax eases the pack off his shoulders and takes out the harness.

"Are you positive you're up for this?" he asks Acacia. "Because if you're having second thoughts, you can stay here with Zavier, and we can go back to the original plan."

"I didn't get my wings sprayed with coal dust for nothing," she says with a smile, although her hands are shaking nervously at her sides, and rightly so.

Stavros gives Acacia a long hard kiss before helping to strap the two together. "You'd better take good care of her, my friend," Stavros says, eyeing Jax with warning. "This woman is my world."

"I'll protect her with my life," Jax promises.

Slater comes over to fill Jax and Acacia in on the position of the guards. "Do you remember the directions I gave you?" he asks Acacia directly.

"I spent all night studying the course on the map you drew."

"Good. Because if you stick to the course, you shouldn't have any problems." He turns and points a finger at Zavier. "You," he says. "We need you to wait a few metres back, behind a tree. If the guards' suspicions are aroused, they will investigate around the edge of the border." He points to the huskens next. Sphinx notices and growls. "What's happening with these things?"

"They're coming," Stavros replies.

"I think you should leave them with the boy for protection. They'll only get in our way."

"Boy," Zavier repeats in offence. "You do realise I'm the same age as Harlow."

"Fine, we'll leave them," Jax says through the balaclava.

I laugh. Jax and Acacia look like true criminals.

"You look badass, Casey," I tell her with a wink.

I detect a smile beneath the mask. "Be safe, Zany. And make sure to watch your brother's back."

"Always."

Jax orders the huskens to stay and protect Zavier, and then he and Acacia take off, leaving a puff of dust in their wake. I stare in fascination as they launch up past the trees and disappear.

"Come on." Slater tugs Floss' hand and signals for the rest of us to follow. "Everyone, keep low to the ground. We don't want any guards spotting us before we get to the grate, or it's game over."

Slater keeps Floss beside him, watching over her in a protective manner. I hadn't expected that. Stavros crawls close behind followed by Woody and Oscar, and then I follow at the rear.

Summer's hot wind slaps my face with a wallop as I commando crawl behind the others, blowing sand granules in my mouth and eyes.

The sky is dark, but the full moon glimmers faintly off the ripples of sand, giving us enough light to see by.

The grate isn't far, as Slater promised, and all six of us manage to slip inside the narrow passageway without alerting any guards. Slater gets me to pull the grate back over the opening once I'm inside. I slide it carefully in place and then pause to listen. *Not a sound.*

Crouched, due to the tight confinements of the passageway, I glance ahead, squinting. The area is dully lit in red, courtesy of Slater's glowing ink.

Oscar shuffles forward on his hands and knees, and groans. "Well, this is going to be fun."

"Man up, Tiny," I taunt. "I don't hear Woody or Slater whinging."

"Woody might be taller, but he's wirier," he bites back in defence. He doesn't mention Slater.

To my relief, Stavros unzips his pack and plucks out a glowing rag, which he unravels to reveal two iridescent zofts. They light up the passageway in purple, showing a worn jagged pathway and tight stone walls.

"The passageway widens as it goes," Slater's voice echoes from up front. "Now hurry up."

We crawl on all fours over dirt, grit, and patches of mould. It's understandable why Slater was in such a horrid mess when he arrived at the village yesterday. He's lucky I took the time to wash out his wounds thoroughly. I imagine mould residue would cause a nasty infection. No doubt, I'll have to wash them out again when we get back—*if he makes it back*. Once this is all over, Jax might actually kill him, and if he doesn't, I'm sure there'll be plenty of others who are eager to do the job. Like Woody said, Slater has a hefty bounty on his head.

This thought bothers me more than it should. *What do I care whether he lives or dies? He's nothing to me.* Only a few short weeks ago, *I* was gearing up to kill him myself.

Dammit! Living out in the forest is turning me soft.

The further into the passageway we get, the worse the air quality is. I scrunch my nose and keep my breaths shallow. The only bonus at this point is the passageway has widened to something more manageable. Oscar sighs a breath of relief once he's finally able to stand without bashing his head on the jagged stone ceiling above.

"Watch your step," Slater warns, and I can see why. The pathway below our feet is old and rugged.

Eventually we get to a wooden door, which Slater pushes on firmly. It creaks as it swings opens, revealing three Vallons, one Red, and two Oranges. They jump to attention, like we've startled them, but they're not the only ones who are startled.

My hand dives straight for my blade. *There's six of us. We can take them.*

One of the Oranges is a female with big hair and a skimpy dress. I hope she's not planning on fighting us in that little number, or we're all going to cop an eye full.

"Frost," Oscar curses, clutching for his blade too. "It *was* a setup."

"Easy…" Slater says, rising a hand. "If this was a setup,

Kenneth would've brought guards." His head lifts to the Red in question—presumably Kenneth. "Am I right?"

"We're not here to stop you," Kenneth assures him, his voice rich with authority. "We're merely interested in seeing who you've brought." He glances curiously at Floss—who doesn't budge—and then turns his attention to Woody. "I wasn't expecting to see a Drake in your rescue party, much less the Chief's son."

"I'm only here for Harlow," Woody says. "Allow us to take her without a fight, and there'll be no ramifications."

"Harlow?" Kenneth's brows crinkle.

"He means Ruby," Slater corrects.

The girl with the orange afro smiles like she's in on something I'm not. *I don't like it. I don't like any of this.*

"I was hoping to find Jax among you?"

Kenneth's words spark my attention, and I push forward to the front. "What do you want with Jax?"

"I wanted to strike a deal."

I raise my blade. "What kind of deal?"

"I'm willing to go against Queen Sjaan's orders and hand Ruby over without a fight if he's prepared to approach Commander Azazel about a peaceful trade deal."

"Jax's mother is…" Oscar is directly behind me, so to shut him up, I stomp on his toes with my heel. He yelps like a child, and all four Vallons—including Slater—eye us with suspicion.

The news of Azazel's death obviously hasn't reached Summer yet, and it's not up to us to share it.

"If you want your conversation with Jax, get us to the Great Hall untouched," Slater bargains. "He's up there now, freezing the bars."

My eyes narrow and zone in on Slater, my mild fondness for him instantly disintegrating. This had better not be an elaborate setup to capture Jax, or else I'll slice him into a thousand pieces myself.

HELP HAS ARRIVED

-HARLOW-

I jerk upright and gasp, awoken by a loud thud. Trembling, I shrink my back against the head of my cot—praying it's not another one of the Queen's guards.

Every inch of my body throbs, but at least I was spared from the same fate as Luna. The idea of what might have happened to me if Kenneth hadn't come is too nauseating to consider.

There's a bang followed by a clank, and then the double doors at the side of the Great Hall fly open, revealing two dark figures.

Alex? I think. I hope. I keep my mouth shut in case I'm wrong.

Kenneth is under the impression Alex will be back to rescue me tonight. I hope he's right, because as of this afternoon, the Queen's ordered that I be executed in front of all the kingdom at first light.

Moonlight streams in from the open doors, painting everything a pale shade of blue. The smaller of the dark figures stays put, while the larger figure slowly enters, unsheathing a blade from their belt. The curve of their blade shimmers as they near, and I hold my breath, praying they're here to rescue me, not kill me.

When the figure gets closer, I detect long dark dreadlocks hanging out the bottom of a balaclava and my heart leaps inside my chest.

"Jax?" I leap from my cot and stumble over to the bars, emotions warring in the base of my belly. He shouldn't be here; not for me. It's not safe. Nevertheless, am I over the moon to see him.

He tears off his balaclava and rushes over, his feet coming to an abrupt stop just before the bars.

"Harlow." He plucks a zoft from his pocket, and I catch the briefest of smiles, before he takes in my current state, and gapes. "What have they done to you?" Horror floods his expression as his eyes roam over my body taking in the severity of my injuries.

I'm ashamed to be seen like this. My barely there, stained dress is badly ripped, and my pale skin is a mural of cuts and bruises.

I fold my arms over myself and lower my face. "It's okay, I'm okay."

Jax lays down his blade and zoft, and steps up to the bars, bringing us closer. "You should never have come here," his tone is gentle, but holds slight accusation.

"I had to."

"No, you didn't." He shakes his head. "You could have stayed. I wanted you to stay. I was willing to fight for you. You should've let me." A pained breath escapes his lips. "I should've fought for you regardless. It was stupid of me not to."

"You did the right thing. I asked you not to fight."

"Look at you." His eyes trace over the cuts and bruises marring my face. "How could you possibly say it was the right thing?" He slips a hand through the bars and gently caresses the side of my battered face. "I knew Summer was a dangerous place for Zeeks,

but for some insane reason, I thought Slater would keep you safe."
His violet eyes gaze into mine, with such burning intensity, it
scorches me from within. "I'm sorry, I should've known better."

Why is he saying sorry? I close my eyes, unable to meet his gaze any
longer. The memory of leaving with Alex, instead of staying with
Jax fills me with such guilt, it breaks my heart all over again. It
wasn't a choice I wanted to make; it was a choice I needed to make.
If I hadn't left with Alex when I did, one of them would've been
killed—maybe even both. If Alex killed Jax, the warriors would
have killed him, and I would have died right there with them.

His eyes lower to the broken strap of my dress, causing my
cheeks to flush again.

Embarrassed, I lift my arms higher trying to cover more skin.
"My dress was ripped," I say, stating the obvious.

Anger flashes across his face. "Yes, I can see that."

He slides off his pack and tugs off his shirt. "Here," he says,
handing it to me through the bars. "I'm sorry, it's a bit sweaty, but it
will save you from having to hold your dress up."

Grateful, I take it from him. "Thank you."

I struggle to lift my bad shoulder through the sleeve, so Jax helps
me through the bars.

I feel much more comfortable standing in front of him fully
covered. My little revealing number had me feeling like the "whore"
I've been accused of.

Jax's shirt is baggy on me and a little sweaty to touch, but I don't
mind. It smells like him.

The smaller figure who'd arrived with Jax, leaves the balcony,
and comes into view. She peels off her balaclava as she strides over
to us, revealing two thick black braids.

"Acacia?" Her wings aren't their usual pearly white colour,
they're a greyish black. "What are you doing here?"

She shouldn't be here risking herself for me. She has Atohi to worry about.

As she gets closer, her eyes trace me, mirroring the same horror
I'd seen written across Jax's face. Her hand reaches for mine and I
take it, the corners of her eyes twinkling with tears. "I'm so glad
you're still alive."

"You shouldn't be here." I gaze between the pair, my voice strained. "Neither of you should be."

"You shouldn't be here either," she replies. She waits a beat and then places her other hand on Jax's shoulder. "You need to get started before the others arrive."

Jax kneels and rummages through his pack, pulling out two water canteens, a large hammer, and two pairs of protective goggles. He hands a pair of goggles to Acacia, followed by both canteens of water.

He rises, and his goggled eyes lift to mine as he takes hold of the bars. "Stand back and look away. I don't want you getting hurt."

It's near impossible to look away. My eyes wander from Jax's face to his chest, to his arms—and then back up to his face again. He looks so beautiful, yet so powerful all at once.

Acacia flicks both canteens open and slowly pours the water down the bars.

When the liquid meets Jax's hands, frost and condensation emit from them like an open freezer. The stressed metal crackles and pops, echoing loudly off the stone walls.

Jax lets go of the bars and grabs the hammer. "Look away."

I turn away, covering my ears. There's a loud smash followed by another, and then the clank of the hammer being tossed back to the stone floor.

As they move on to the next two bars, I glance over my shoulder to take another sneak peek at Jax, and it's a good thing I do, because a guard has entered the hall, and is headed straight for them.

"Behind you," I yell.

Jax immediately lets go of the bars and spins, snatching up his blade off the ground in one swift movement. A fireball is thrown and all three of us duck. Acacia grabs hold of the hammer while she's down, her hands quivering.

"Wait here!" Jax launches up full force, and flies at the guard, running up his body ninja-style, like Neo from the Matrix. When he gets to the guard's chest, he squats, slices through his throat, and then backflips off him—sending the guard's bleeding body stumbling backwards.

I gape, wide eyed. *I can't believe it.* Jax just took out that guard in the blink of an eye.

I've heard Zannah referring to Jax as a badass, but I've never seen this side of him.

Guilt tugs at me. I'd secretly thought if Jax and Alex came to blows, Alex would have overpowered him. Now I'm not so sure.

He strides back over, blood dripping from his blade. "Are you okay?" he asks us both.

Acacia and I nod, too stunned to speak. I take it Acacia's never seen this side of him, either.

He lets out a long loud breath and sheathes his bloody blade. "We'd better hurry up and get the next set of bars done before anymore guards come."

Two tries later, and the bars are completely destroyed. Jax throws down the hammer and carefully assists to manoeuvre me through the opening. I've barely made it out the other side when his strong arms wrap around me, pulling me to him with a sense of urgency. "I'm so glad you're alive." His grip tightens "You have no idea how worried I've been. I didn't know what I was going to do with myself if something had happened to you."

I press my cheek to his chest, breathing him in. "I'm sorry for leaving. I didn't want to. It's just that—"

"Shhh…" He runs a hand over my hair. "None of that matters anymore. I'm going to get you out of here."

SUCKS TO BE SLATER

-ZANNAH-

Slater comes to an abrupt halt by the entrance of the Great Hall, and I slam headfirst into his sweaty back. *Eeewww…* It's like hitting a stone wall, only slimy.

"What the…?" I scrunch my nose and wipe my face with my sleeve.

When Slater doesn't budge or say anything, I duck around him, blade raised, expecting to find a pack of guards inside, waiting to trap us. What I find is a shirtless Jax. I blink, momentarily stunned. His strong muscular arms are wrapped around Harlow and their bodies are pressed together in an intimate hug. *Wow,* the chemistry between the pair is undeniable. This scene must be torture for Slater because it's enough to make my chest tighten and I've got no claim on Jax.

Dropping my gaze, I spot a guard on the floor behind them. His eyes are glazed over, and blood pools from a gash across his neck.

Slater moves behind me and I whirl on him pointing the blade at his chest in warning. We didn't risk our arses to save Harlow, only for him to kill Jax in a fit of rage.

"Don't even think about it," I warn.

His swirling irises glow redder than ever. "Already stripping off for her, I see." He says to Jax, and there's a raw anger to his voice. "You don't waste any time, do you?"

I'd been expecting more of a volatile reaction from him. Instead, his comment is almost laughable, and certainly rich coming from him. I've seen him shirtless more times than I've seen him clothed. Jax on the other hand... I glance over my shoulder, trailing the ripped muscles of his back with delight. My cheeks flush with heat. This is a very pleasant surprise.

Harlow jolts. "Alex?" Going by her wide-eyed expression, I'm guessing Jax hadn't mentioned Slater's involvement.

Slater stares back, his body ridged, his lips drawn tight. I wonder what's bothering him most, the fact that his girlfriend just had her face pressed intimately against Jax's bare muscular chest, that she's wearing Jax's shirt, or that she looks like she's been put through a blender. Jax's long sleeve shirt is giving her a lot of coverage, but her face and lower legs are a mess of cuts, grazes, and bruises. Lots and lots of bruises.

"Look at her." Jax points to Harlow while fixing his accusing gaze on Slater. "Take a good look at her. You did this. You should never have dragged her here against her will."

Slater stalks forward, intense anger pouring off him in waves. I stay on him, hoping to keep him in check. "I didn't do this. The guards did this. I tried my best to protect her."

"Don't." Harlow hobbles between them, raising her arms. "Please." Her voice is raspy. "No fighting."

Kenneth seizes this moment to step around us and enter the Great Hall. His fellow Oranges flanking his sides while the Amber walks behind him protecting his back.

175

NEGOTIATIONS

-JAX-

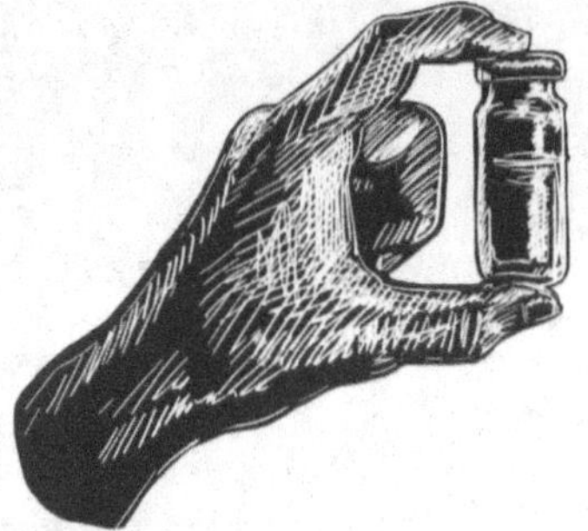

"Now, now, Jax. This Zeek is here of her own free will, she told me so herself."

I jerk up straight, squaring my shoulders. "Kenneth."

I haven't seen Kenneth since my mid-teens, but I recognise him instantly. He looks exactly like his late father, Alfonzo. I step in front of Harlow, blocking her like a shield, and assess the situation before us. Kenneth has three Vallons with him, two Oranges and an Amber. I'm surprised; I would've expected him to be surrounded by guards.

"Harlow doesn't belong in Summer, and we're here to retrieve her." My eyes flick to the fallen guard. "Whether there will be any more bloodshed or not is up to you."

Kenneth cocks his head to look around me. "Harlow, is it?"

Much to my consternation, she moves to my side. "Harlow is my Zeek name."

Harlow doesn't appear scared of Kenneth, leaving me uncertain what to make of his presence.

He and his crew stride closer, prompting Oscar, Stavros, and Floss to jump into action. They surround the Vallons with their weapons raised. The Oranges and Amber counter defend, spinning outwards to face them.

"I'm not here to fight," Kenneth says, lifting his hands in surrender. "I'm here to negotiate."

My eyes swivel between Slater's and Kenneth's, now narrowed with suspicion. It appears Kenneth knew he would find me here and has come prepared. "I'm listening."

"I want you to persuade your mother to sign the trade agreement. I want it to be a peaceful agreement, no war. Our races have been warring for too long. I think it's time we set our differences aside and unite as allies."

I gesture to Harlow, my pulse quickening with anger. "Is this how you treat your allies?"

"I'm not responsible for her current state, and the Vallon who was responsible is no longer breathing."

"Let me put this plainly," I say, voice harsh. "I don't trust you. Nor do I trust Vallons in general. There is nothing peaceful about your race. You have used and abused Zeeks for centuries. Why would we ever want to align with you?"

"Only a small percentage of Vallons are responsible for the ongoing abuse in Summer, and of those abusers, most of them are, or shall I say, *were*, royal guards." Kenneth clears his throat. "As of the past couple of days, the worst of the remaining offenders have been killed. We've lost twelve royal guards in total." His eyes lower to the fallen guard. "Make that thirteen, including your little contribution."

Slater opens his mouth, looking as if he wants to say something, but he seems to think better of it, and closes it again.

When I don't respond, Kenneth continues. "Besides, if you are intent on playing the blame game, maybe you should start with your own mother, she's the one—"

"I know what my mother has done," I snap. "But I am not my mother. My mother is dead, and from here on in there will be no more Pastels offered as peace trades."

Kenneth's face grows wide with surprise, while Harlow makes a choking sound beside me.

After a taking a moment to collect herself, Harlow places her hand on my arm, seeking my attention. "Kenneth isn't like his mother, either," she says. "He wants to make positive changes, but he needs your help to do it."

Her eyes beseech mine, genuine and full of hope. I'm shocked beyond words. *Why is she standing up for Kenneth—a Vallon, and our enemy?* Look at her. Look at the shape she's in. She's been severely brutalised.

"If you're the Commander now," she continues, "you can set the terms. You can make this trade deal work to the Zeeks' advantage. You can request the return of all Pastels."

I shoot her a look that says, "This is not the time or place for this discussion". I don't know what story Kenneth has concocted, but I'm certain he hasn't told her the whole truth. I suspect he is using her to get to me.

"Precisely," Kenneth jumps in, which only furthers my suspicions. "Set your terms, get the paperwork done, and meet me in two days' time on the outskirts of the Drake village. Dakari should be a witness to our new agreement. Let's make it nine P.M. to keep within the Drake border agreement." Kenneth glances at Woody, seeking his approval with this arrangement like this is a done deal. "Does this work?"

"The time and location work, and my father would happily be a witness, but what Jax decides regarding the peace agreement has nothing to do with the Drakes."

"I haven't agreed to this arrangement," I challenge, not appreciating his presumption.

"Then I think it's about time you did. The quicker you agree, the quicker you get out of here without any trouble. This is not a trick. I want the trade deal, but it's about much more than that. I want harmony between our races."

"I don't care what is or isn't being decided or agreed upon, we're taking Ruby with us, even if I have to fight you myself," Slater says through gritted teeth. "She didn't look half this bad when I left her with you yesterday. I thought you'd protect her."

"Ryze was sly and took advantage of his position, but I guarantee you, he has been taken care of *permanently*. And as for the trade deal, if you help bring Jax and Dakari to me in the evening hours for our meeting, I will see what I can do about retracting the bounty our mother has placed on your head."

I swallow hard at the phrase "took advantage". Does this mean... I wince, not wanting to imagine it. I need to get Harlow out of here, *now*. "Fine, I'll agree to the meeting but that's it. Whether the trade deal goes through or not will depend on if you're willing to meet my terms."

Kenneth's glowing eyes meet mine. "Speak to Harlow. Ask her what she's witnessed, what she's been shown. We are not all the animals you paint us to be. Just like you Zeeks have corrupt warriors, we Vallons have corrupt guards."

Frustrated by his arrogance, I merely respond with a nod and then sling a protective arm around Harlow and lead her to the balcony.

"Where are you going?" Kenneth asks.

"I'm getting Harlow out of here."

"It will be much safer to carry Harlow through the castle then to have her abseil off the balcony. The grounds below are heavily guarded."

"She won't be abseiling," I say, exiting the double doors.

Kenneth follows us out and stops with a jolt at the sight of Acacia. "A Ruke," he says, eyes bulging.

Acacia nods in acknowledgement but keeps her head down and purple eyes lowered.

"I didn't know the Zeeks had ties with the Rukes too."

"Our ties are none of your business."

I place Harlow in front of Acacia and begin strapping them together. "If you get scared, close your eyes," I say, "but whatever you do, don't scream. We'll meet you in Spring."

"Wait," Kenneth says, stopping me with his hand. "If the guards below detect these two soaring above, they will shoot them down with fireballs."

"We flew in without raising any attention," I argue. "I don't see why flying out will be any different."

"You got lucky. I sent most of the foot guards out to protect the grounds only a matter of moments before you arrived. I figured if Slater returned, he would take the secret passageway and I wanted the passages to be kept clear for an easy getaway. I assure you, it'll be much safer for you all to leave together through the castle."

I shrug his hand off. "Is this some kind of trick?"

"No. I want this trade agreement, and if Harlow dies, I'm certain you'll retract. I'm covering my own back."

Slater bursts out onto the balcony with Zannah hot on his tail. "We're wasting time," he growls. "Let's move now before we attract attention."

LET'S GET OUT OF HERE
-ALEX AS SLATER-

Jax concedes and scoops Ruby up in his arms. Of course. He's going to carry her out of the castle like a fuckin' hero. *Son of a bitch.* I should never have agreed to letting him come with us, but I was desperate.

Sadly though, the look on Ruby's face tells me she's exactly where she wants to be.

As we pile out of the Grand Hall with Kenneth and his crew leading the way, Jax's accusation burns inside me. "Take a good look at her. You did this". *I wonder if Ruby feels the same way? If she hates me for bringing her here?* I have no idea what Ryze did to her, and I'm afraid to find out. I told her I would protect her, and no one would ever hurt her. *I promised I would keep her safe.*

I was hoping Kenneth would keep the guards away while I was gone, but I realise now, the only one Kenneth's been looking out for is himself. He could have easily let me take Ruby in the first place. He wasn't really worried about our mother hunting us down within the hour or our children posing a risk to everyone on Zadok. He must have sensed Ruby was important even before I told him and wanted to keep her as a bargaining chip. Our mother would give anything for that trade agreement and Golden Boy knows it. If he can strike this deal with the Zeeks, she'll be forever in his debt.

I don't know what story he's spun to get Ruby to back him up. He might be playing Mr Nice Guy, but she should know he can't be trusted. I've told her. Kenneth has as much Zeek blood on his hands as the guards. He told Jax "only a small percentage of Vallons are responsible for the ongoing abuse", but what he's failed to point out was he's a big part of that small percentage. I'd considered pointing this out, but I figured it would only hinder the situation. The best solution was to let Jax agree, get Ruby out safe and sound, and then spill the facts once we're out.

My eyes trace the side of Ruby's face as Jax moves beside me and guilt shreds me to my core. He's right. It's my fault she's in this mess. I've been selfish. I am selfish, but I don't know how to give her up. She's the only connection I still have to the person I once was —*to Alex*. And what's more, she's carrying my children—*she's carrying Lucas*. If I have to let her go, I'll be letting go of a chunk of myself. Without her, I'll be empty. I might as well be dead.

Zannah steps up to my other side and taps me with the flat of her blade. She's been on me like a screw the entire time. She doesn't trust me. She's waiting for me to lash out and betray them.

"Stop looking," she says. "And keep your head clear until we're out."

We get back to the passageway which leads to the cellar without running into any trouble, but as we get to the entryway three dark figures exit. Kenneth and his crew stop in their tracks and Kenneth curses in Vallon.

"Where is he? Where's Slater?"

Shit! It's Raven.

Zannah's grip on her blade tightens. She doesn't need to understand our language to know there's a problem.

"You're not supposed to be here," Kenneth says with more compassion than Raven deserves. "And you most definitely shouldn't have brought guards."

"They won't tell. They've promised. I was too afraid to come alone."

I force my way to the front and Zannah follows.

"What do you want Raven? Haven't you done enough already?"

She rushes over to throw her arms around me, but I ward her off. "Stop."

Her guards move closer and unsheathe their blades.

Tears fill Raven's eyes. "I'm sorry, I'm so, so, sorry. I shouldn't have told Sjaan, it was a mistake. I didn't know she'd put a bounty on your head."

"But you knew what she'd do to Ruby."

"I'm sorry, I was angry and…"

"Stop. I don't care. Leave."

"Please, I…"

"No." My tone is firm and full of hate. "I don't care what you have to say. Your words mean nothing to me. You've cost me everything."

"Raven, you need to leave," Kenneth warns from behind me. "You've said your apologies, now leave."

"You scumbag." Kingsley, Raven's guard, and my former friend lunges towards me, his blade aimed at my heart.

"No…" Raven dives between us, right as he takes the deadly plunge.

Her scream fills my ears and my anger drains from me, along with the blood of my face.

"Raven!" She falls forwards, and I catch her in my arms. "NO! NO!"

Chaos explodes around me. Voices shout and bodies blur in my peripheral. From the corner of my eye, I see Zannah fly at Kingsley, ninja style like Jackie Chan. I should be helping her, but I can't function. *I can't think.*

A second ago, I'd felt like strangling Raven myself, but now that she's bleeding out in my arms, I'm conflicted. I'm the one who should be bleeding right now, not Raven. That blade was meant for me. *She sacrificed herself to save me.*

"I'm sorry." She lifts a shaky hand to touch my cheek. "I never meant to hurt you. I love you." Her hand drops and her eyes roll back.

Tears fill my eyes. "Shit... No..." I shake her, and when she doesn't respond, I shake her some more. "Raven... Raven." This is my fault. Everything is my fault. Ruby's hurt and Raven's dead, all because I didn't listen.

"Slater stop, she's gone." Kenneth's hand cups my shoulder. "Pass her to me, you need to leave."

I stare blankly, unable to focus.

"Slater, now!" His stern tone draws me back.

"How did she know I was here? Did you tell her I was coming back?"

"No."

"Did you tell Jacinta?"

His eyes answer for him.

"Telling Jacinta is the same as telling Raven, you know that!"

"Jacinta is my wife; I tell her everything. Now hand me Raven and get in the passage before you share the same fate. Your friend is waiting for you."

I glance towards the cellar. Zannah is standing by the opening, her left leg bouncing impatiently. Raven's two guards lie in puddles of blood on the stone floor between us, and I don't know whether to be impressed or intimidated. Rowen and Kingsley are both double Zannah's size in body mass.

Catching my glance, she says, "I have no idea what you pair are arguing about, but you've got exactly two seconds before I'm leaving without you."

I swallow hard and pass Raven to Kenneth, spying another two dead guards behind where he stands. "I'm sorry it's come to this."

"I'm sorry too."

As I hurry over to Zannah, Kenneth calls. "Brother wait…" and I turn. "Harlow, Ruby—whatever her real name is—needs those babies removed, or she's going to die."

"How do you know that?"

"Ask her."

Zannah tugs my arm impatiently. "Enough. Come on."

We enter the passageway, and the Amber closes the shelf behind us, leaving only the glow of my tattoos to lead the way. The dim red passage blurs in and out as my head pulses, and I'm tripping, hyperventilating. I feel like I'm running under water.

Zannah pulls my arm around her shoulder to support me while we run. "Pull yourself together or I'm leaving you behind."

I'm surprised she's helping me. I'm of no use to the Zeeks anymore. I got them into the castle, and they have Ruby. My usefulness has reached its limit.

Images of Raven's last moments flash through my mind, along with images of Ruby's battered face. I hurt Raven so she hurt Ruby, and now Raven is dead, and I've lost Ruby to Jax.

Zannah should leave me behind I have nothing left to live for anymore, and nowhere to live.

33

ZAPPED

-HARLOW-

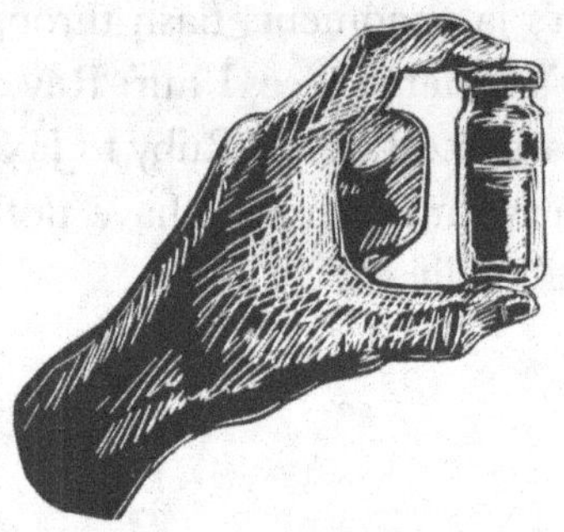

(Ten minutes earlier)

The taller of the two guards facing our group roars something at Slater and then lunges. Simultaneously, Raven dives into Slater's arms and releases a blood-curdling scream.

Heavy footfalls reverberate behind us and Jax whirls on the spot, revealing another two guards charging our way. They each have a fireball in hand and as they hurl them towards us, I scream in panic.

Jax ducks the fireballs with proficient speed, and then tosses me to Stavros. "Get everyone out of here. Now!"

Kenneth's crew rush to cover him, as he calls, "Waffenstillstand."

Stavros lugs me away, and I watch as Jax runs at the guards head on, shooting dual shards from both hands. Once he's closer, he drops and slides in front of them, trip kicking one, while ploughing his blade into the stomach of the other. Fear claws at me as we round the corner and they're out of sight. From this angle, all I can see is Zannah. She's standing just outside the opening, tugging her bade from a fallen guard's chest.

"Put me down," I shout.

Stavros holds me firm. "No."

I wrestle against his hold. "I need to go back." Not only am I worried about Jax, I'm worried about Alex too.

Stavros refuses point blank as he charges past the cupboard and into the dark passage.

I wrestle harder tugging at his hands. "Please," I beg. "I can help them, I have pow…"

A zap leaves my hands before I can finish, and the passage flashes bright white. Stavros' body shudders and falls backwards, bringing me down with him.

"What the…" Floss spins, shinning a zoft on us. "Did you just…" She frowns. "What did you do?" She, Woody, and Oscar are all staring at me with furrowed brows.

"It was an accident." I roll over and shake Stavros' shoulder. "Stavros, Stavros."

Acacia falls to her knees beside us.

"I'm okay," he croaks, levering himself up with a groan. His eyes narrow in on mine. "New powers, I take it?"

I nod sheepishly. "I'm sorry. I didn't mean to do that."

"Do what?" Jax enters the passageway and relief fills me, although his bare chest and arms are slicked in blood. I look him over, trying to determine whether he's been injured.

"It's the guards' blood," he says, when he notices me looking.

Woody takes Stavros' hand and pulls him to stand. "It seems Harlow has a new power."

Jax lifts a brow in question.

"Where's Alex?" I ask, and his face falls flat.

"He's not our concern."

Despite everything that's happened with Alex, I can't leave him to die. "We need to go back."

"No." Jax's eyes trail over me. "Look at you. Look at what's been done to you because of his selfishness. You shouldn't be worried about him." He sighs, and then adds, "He'll be okay. All four guards are dead and Zannah is with him. She'll have his back, *not that I believe he deserves it*." He mutters the last part under his breath.

I nod, understanding his antipathy. "I'm glad you're okay. I was worried."

"Come on." He steps forward and scoops me up in his blood smeared arms. "I'm getting you out of here."

I keep my hands together behind Jax's neck as he carries me along the narrowing passage, afraid if I touch him, I'll zap him. It gets super tight towards the end, and I have to crawl the rest of the way by myself. My open cuts sting from dirt and grime, and as we exit the tunnel and commando crawl our way across the sandy terrain to the forest, the grittiness of the sand stings them further.

I swallow hard and gaze ahead. Floss and Oscar disappear into the trees, closely followed by Stavros and Acacia.

Woody's directly in front of us and glances over his shoulder to say, "Keep moving."

Having Woody and Acacia as a part of my rescue team was an unexpected delight, but I almost fell over when I saw Floss standing by the entryway of the Great Hall.

When we get to the trees, Jax helps me to my feet. "I've got a surprise waiting for you."

"A surprise?"

He scoops me up again and carries me to where the rest of the group is waiting.

"Harlow." I recognise the voice right away, but the guy running at me doesn't match the familiar sound.

"Zavier?" Zavier is built like a Magenta and his hair and irises are a pastel red.

He throws his arms around me tightly. They're bulkier and

firmer than they used to be. It hurts, but I don't care. I throw my arms around him too, breathing him in. He might look different, but his scent is exactly the same as I remember. He smells like friendship and stability.

"I've been so worried about you," he whispers in my ear. "I was afraid we'd be too late." He pulls back to look me over, leaving his hands clasped around my arms, holding me in place. "Are you okay?" He grimaces and adds, "I'm sorry to say this, but you look terrible."

"I'm sore, but I'm alive."

Floss comes over to break us apart. "Okay, that's enough hugging for one day."

"Don't start," Zavier says, but he lets go and steps back, regardless.

I scan him from head to toe. "My goodness Zavier, you look so…" Floss' eyes snap to mine, slitted like daggers. "Different," I say, keeping it safe.

"Yeah, well don't go getting any ideas," Floss warns. "You missed your turn."

"Floss!" we say in unison.

Her eyes examine me. "You look downright awful. What did they do to you? Did that guard…you know…" She screws her nose up.

I shake my head. "No. He tried but my babies zapped him, and Kenneth killed him."

Jax is standing nearby, and it's clear he's listening in, because he sighs a breath of relief.

Floss' forehead crinkles. "Your babies did what?"

"There they are!" Stavros shouts, and races over to Zannah. Alex has his arm slung across Zannah's shoulders. However, when she shrugs him off to hug her brother, he stumbles over to where I'm standing and falls to his knees.

His chest and arms are coated in blood, but he's covered in so many wounds it's hard to tell which are fresh and which are old.

"Are you okay?" I ask.

Something in his expression doesn't read right. He's not himself.

He looks fragmented. He tugs my hand pulling me forward, and I assume he wants to whisper something, but instead, he presses the handle of a blade into my palms. It's a Zeek blade. I can tell by its shape and weight. I'm confused. He puts his hands around mine and points the razor-sharp end to his chest.

"Kill me."

His words rattle through my brain, sparking fear and guilt. I shake my head. "No."

His grip on mine tightens. "Look at what's happened to you because of me. I should have let you stay in Spring. I deserve to be killed."

"I don't blame you."

"You don't get it!" His tone is forceful. "I don't have anywhere to go, and I don't have you. I have nothing to live for, so do it." He forces my hand forward enough for the tip of the blade to bite into his chest, and I cry out in fear.

My eyes fill with tears. "Alex, stop! Please. Don't do this. Think about the twins. I'll speak with Dakari about granting you sanctuary and letting you stay in the Drake village."

"Kenneth says the twins need to be removed now or you'll die." He swallows hard, like there's a lump caught in his throat. "Chances are, they won't survive the early delivery, so kill me know and you'll be completely rid of me.

A tear dribbles down my cheek. "Don't say that."

Jax steps up behind me and snatches the blade from our hands.

Alex's eyes lift to meet Jax's. "Go on then. I'm sure you'll enjoy it."

Jax shoots him a look that could kill but lowers the blade. "No one else dies today, now get up."

Zannah snatches the blade from Jax's hand. "It's my blade, allow me."

"ZANNAH, NO!" I reach to take it from her, but Jax snakes an arm around me and draws me back.

"She won't kill him." His words muffle in my hair. "Trust me."

Zannah charges straight up to Alex and jabs the biting end of the blade into the spot where he'd already forced me to cut him. He winces but doesn't cry out. I cry out instead.

"What are you waiting for," Slater growls. "Do it."

Zannah lowers the blade and spin kicks him across the head, knocking him sideways.

He jerks back upright, eyes flared. "What the fuck?" Blood dribbles from his lip to his chin.

"Did you feel that?"

"*Yeah*, I felt it."

"Good. That means you're still alive, and as long as you're alive you are going to pull yourself together and make the best of it. Not everyone gets what they want. You're the most intimidating looking guy in this group, and you're acting like a baby."

Alex blinks, appearing too stunned for words.

"I didn't waste my energy dragging your sorry arse through that tight passageway only for you to give up now. You need to get up and stop bitching. We'll work out a place for you to stay."

Zannah offers Alex her hand and surprisingly he takes it.

"You see," Jax says. "I told you Zannah wouldn't kill him."

34

SANCTUARY

-HARLOW-

*B*esides Floss giving Zavier a detailed run down on what Summer was like, not much is said on the trip back to the village. Zannah keeps to the rear with Slater while Jax treks on ahead of the group, holding me securely in his arms.

We stop several metres out from the village fence, where a blood-stained mattress lies.

Woody looks at Zannah while pointing to Alex. "You stay here with him. I'll have a talk with my father and see what I can arrange."

Once we're inside the fence, Jax kisses my forehead and whispers, "I'm so glad to have you back," before holding me out for Stavros to take. "Can you please carry Harlow to Roz, I need to go with Woody. There are things I need to discuss with Dakari."

"No." I cling to him like a limpet. "There are things I need to discuss with you all too."

"What you need first and foremost, is medical attention. If Dakari sees you in this state, it will only hinder your cause. He doesn't trust Vallons, and with good reason. Even as it is, I'm not so sure that Slater should be given sanctuary. He is selfish and unstable, and I'm afraid if I support this decision and it turns ugly, it'll cause a rift between the Zeeks and Drakes."

"This isn't just about Alex, I assure you. I understand your angst and predicament, but I have other information about the Vallons that I need to share with you all. Please. I need to be a part of this discussion."

"You should take her with you," Stavros says, and slips his hand around Acacia's. "I think we should all be a part of this discussion."

Woody is already inside speaking to Dakari when we arrive at his hut. Dakari gawks as Jax places me down, and his wife Tahlia gasps in horror.

He shakes his head, and says, "Vreeslike," before continuing with whatever he and Woody had been discussing before we entered. I don't understand what's being said but going by their tense body language and brittle tones they are not in agreement. Stavros and Acacia stand beside us and speak up a few times during their conversation, but Jax doesn't say a word until Daraki addresses him directly.

When Jax finishes speaking, Dakari's eyes zoom in on mine. "You can't be serious," he says, as if I'm the one who'd just spoken, not Jax. "There is no way I am allowing a Vallon into my village. You were lucky I allowed you to stay given your circumstances."

"Queen Sjaan has placed a bounty on Alex's head, and he's been banished from Summer. I understand the significance of what I'm asking, and I know this isn't an ideal solution, but he has nowhere else to go."

"This isn't my problem, and what's stopping my tribe members from killing him? It is a very generous bounty, after all."

"Alex isn't a threat to you or anyone else in the village, I assure you. He is a Pastel sympathiser and the father of my children. I'd like my children to have a relationship with him while growing up. I think it's important."

Stavros and Acacia swap compassionate glances.

"If I were to offer this Vallon sanctuary, it will put me in an awkward position with the Vallon Queen." Dakari doesn't look moved. "Our relationship is already shaky at best."

"The Queen doesn't need to know. You've given Zeeks sanctuary for years and Commander Azazel was none the wiser. I doubt Chief Waya knows about Acacia being here, either. Your tribe members are good at keeping secrets," I say.

"My answer is no." His eyes roll over my battered body. "Your current state speaks for you. Vallons are predators, and predators are unwelcome in my village."

"Not all Vallons are evil," I say, which earns me a frown from everyone. "Many of them share the same views as we do when it comes to keeping Pastels as slaves."

I can see an argument forming on Dakari's lips, so I rush on to tell them about the church Kenneth had taken me to and the forty-eight Zeeks he and his crew have rescued over the years. Everyone's frowns disappear, and they stare wide-eyed in disbelief. "Kenneth says it's the Queen's foot guards who have done the most damage to the Vallon name, and once he's finally in power, changes will be made." I turn to Jax. "You and he aren't so different."

Jax bristles at my comment, clearly not appreciating the comparison. "Even if this were all true, it doesn't change where we stand at present. Kenneth isn't in power yet, Sjaan is." Jax's tone is crisp. "He might be the one instigating the peaceful trade agreement, but it's Sjaan who will be signing it, and she doesn't share his sentiments."

"I'm not telling you to go forward with the agreement. It's not my place. I'm only telling you what I know and what I've been told, because I think it is worth considering. You have the power and the upper hand. You have the opportunity to set the terms in a way that will benefit Zeeks."

Jax's eyes leave mine and swivel to meet Dakari's, concern and questions written on his face. They go back to speaking in Drake again, and I'm sure it's to deliberately keep me out of the loop.

My battered legs tire and the hut starts to sway around me, so I crouch before I fall.

Jax bends forward to pick me up, but Stavros stops him.

"You stay. I'll carry her to the medicine woman." He heaves me up carefully and warns me to keep my hands to myself.

"Wait." My gaze snaps to Dakari's. "Will you at least consider giving Alex sanctuary?"

"This isn't a decision I'm taking lightly. I need more time to discuss the matter with Jax and my tribe. Your Vallon can remain where he is for another night, and I will give my verdict tomorrow morning."

I wish Dakari hadn't referred to Alex as my Vallon, especially in front of Jax. I'm not satisfied with his answer, but I thank him anyway, out of respect.

Once we're away from the hut, Stavros jumps straight into interrogation mode. The playful, jovial Stavros is gone. He's all warrior.

"Do you truly understand the gravity of what you're asking?" When I stumble on an answer, he continues. "Inviting a Vallon to live in the Drake village could cause an uproar with the tribe, not to mention the angst it will cause Luna and Destiny. And what about Jax? Have you given any consideration to how he might feel about this?"

"I'm stuck between a rock and a hard place," I say. "My feelings towards Jax haven't changed. I love him, and I want to make things work with him—if he'll still have me—but I can't stand the thought of Alex being killed. I know that what I'm asking is pushing the boundaries, but what choice do I have?"

"Slater tried slicing Jax's throat when you told him you wanted to stay here, so how do you think he's going to react to actually seeing you two together for the next several days?"

I draw in a pained breath. "He's going to hate it, but at least he'll be alive. Don't worry, If Dakari awards him sanctuary, I'll warn him not to touch Jax. He's changed a lot, and I believe I can reason with him."

My brain swirls with a thousand thoughts, when suddenly, an insane thought springs to mind. It's a desperate thought, and a long-shot, but I'm desperate enough to consider it.

"Wait." My hand touches Stavros arm, and he tenses, waiting for a zap. "Before you take me to the medicine woman, we should stop at the hut. There's something I need to do."

"Like what, exactly?"

"I'll explain when we get there."

He shakes his head. "No. Jax will kill me. You need medical attention A.S.A.P."

"You can take me straight afterwards. Please, Stavros. It's important."

He huffs and then changes direction. "Fine, but you'd better make it quick."

When we get to the entry of the hut, I ask Stavros to put me down. I don't want to be seen as completely weak. Inside, Luna, Boshell, and the kids are lounging in the common area playing a game of cards with another young Zeek I don't recognise. The kids squeal when they see me, and come rushing over, but stop short when they notice what a frightful mess I'm in.

Daisy covers her mouth, stifling a gasp, while Will studies me with blatant curiosity. "Did you get attacked by a fuegor, Harlow?" he asks.

Boshell hurries over to lend me a hand, but Luna doesn't move. She merely gapes at me in horror.

Together, Stavros and Boshell help me to a seat.

"Can I get you a drink?" Boshell asks.

"A water would be nice," I say.

Luna's expression is conflicted. It's as if she's torn between consoling me and telling me, "I told you so".

I look her straight in the eyes, which appears to unnerve her. "I need to talk to you," I say. "I'd like to ask something personal."

Her eyes flick to Stavros' and back to mine. "What do you want to know?" Her voice is uneven.

"When you took care of that Vallon guard for what he did—" I chose my words carefully, as to not alarm Will and Daisy or their new friend "—did a Red walk in on the incident, and then allow you and Destiny to escape?"

Her breath catches. "How do you know about that?"

"Alex told me." I don't mention that Stavros shared a part of her story too, and this is how I was able to match them up. "Alex is the one who turned a blind eye while you both escaped. He's against Pastels being used for slaves."

Luna tenses and her face turns red. "What's this about? Why are you telling me this?"

"Alex is in trouble, and he needs your help."

"No." She shakes her head. "I'm not helping a Vallon."

"He helped you. Please, just hear me out."

"NO!"

"Harlow, that's enough," Stavros warns.

Boshell hands me a cup of water, and Luna shoots off to her room. "What exactly is going on?" There's a cautious edge to Boshell's voice.

"Alex has been banished from Summer, and the Queen has put a bounty on his head." I take a sip of the water before continuing. "I've asked Dakari to offer him sanctuary, but he's hesitant to do so, and I'm afraid if he declines, Alex will die."

Boshell's eyes scan over my broken body and he shivers. "Did Alex do this to you?"

"No. I was attacked by a few of the guards. Alex tried to save me. He isn't a monster. I thought if I could get Luna and Destiny to come forward and tell Dakari that he allowed them to escape from Summer, it would help his cause."

"I don't know Alex," Boshell says. "And I don't mean him any harm, but I don't know that allowing him sanctuary is such a great idea. At the end of the day, he is still a Vallon, and Vallons can't be trusted."

His comment stings, considering there's a good chance I could be carrying Vallons. I don't want my children to be ostracised because of their heritage.

"If Alex couldn't be trusted, Luna and Destiny would have been killed." It's a harsh thing to say but I'm desperate to prove a point. "He showed them mercy. All I'm asking is for them to show him mercy in return. Besides, think about it. Alex is the reason your children are fit and well. His ink has given them a second chance at life. You should be grateful to him, not condemning him."

Guilt clouds his face. "This isn't—"

I refuse to hear his argument. "Please, Boshell, you need to talk to Luna and Destiny. Convince them to speak to Dakari. Alex doesn't deserve to die, and you can do something about it."

"Okay, you're done." Stavros comes around and hauls me into his arms.

"But I—"

"You've said more than enough. It's time to get you to the medicine woman before you find yourself banished from the village."

GOOD KARMA
-ALEX AS SLATER-

$\mathcal{I}$ didn't want to follow Ruby and her friends here, but I couldn't stop myself. I've been completely spellbound by her since the first night I saw her dancing by the firepit. She was like a bright beam of light that shone away all my darkness. She made me believe there was beauty in the world. *I don't know how to let her go. There's a thread between us that I can't seem to sever.*

Zannah sits on the end of the mattress near my feet. She hasn't said anything since she booted me across the head and told me to get a grip. I'm still unable to figure her out. *Does she see me as an ally or an enemy?* I never know if she's planning on saving me or killing me. I know she doesn't trust me. None of them do. *So why bring me back here to the outskirts of the Drake village? Why not leave me by the Summer border to die?*

After a long while of wallowing in self-pity, I hear the crunching of footsteps descending upon us.

Zannah gives my calf a squeeze. "We've got company. Sit up and play nice."

I reluctantly do as she says. There's a small group heading towards us, and Chief Dakari is amongst them. I haven't seen the Chief since I was eighteen, back when I was brought to the forest for an introduction. Kenneth handles all the trades and politics under our mother's command, so he's the one who sees Dakari and Woody bi-annually to discuss any problems, changes, or new ideas. I was never trusted.

Dakari and Woody flank three Pastels, one male and two Magenta sized females. The females have a peach hue, which tells me they must have been a part of the vertic switz ink trial done in Summer. On closer inspection I realise I recognise them. They're the Pastels who killed Ash with his own blade.

"Luna?" Zannah's brows shoot up to her hairline.

The male holds the hand of the prettier of the two females, and as they get closer, he leans in to whisper something in her ear.

Her eyes cut to mine, and she trembles, before looking at Dakari to nod. "It's him."

The other female Pastel nods in agreement. "It's him."

Dakari thanks them and tells Woody to walk them back to the village.

I glance at Zannah in silent question, and she shrugs.

The Pastel male steps forward. He's slim but not nearly as scrawny as the male Pastels I've seen in Summer. He eyes me warily yet offers a smile. "Hi, I'm Boshell." He raises a hand for me to shake. "Shall I call you Alex or Slater?"

"Slater," Zannah answers before I get the chance. I don't know what it matters to her, but Slater works fine.

I take Boshell's slender hand and shake it. If he's disgusted by the dry blood coating mine, he doesn't let it show.

"I hear you're in trouble and in need of a place to stay."

"You could say that." My words come out slowly and cautiously.

"Did Harlow ever mention my twins Will and Daisy?"

I frown, puzzled by his question. "No."

"They were frail, blind, and arthritic, so Harlow suggested we use your magical ink on them. Since being tattooed their lives have changed for the better. They can see, run, swim..." Joy lights his eyes. "Your ink gave my children a second chance at life."

While I *am* glad to have inadvertently helped Boshell's kids, it cuts deep that Ruby never mentioned it. Still, I say, "That's good to hear."

"Will and Daisy wanted to come out and meet you, but I wasn't sure if it was a good idea. Are you a threat to us?"

His question irks me, but I suppose I can't blame him for asking. The two escapees would have had horrifying tales to share about Summer and the Vallon guards. "I'm no threat to anyone but myself."

"In that case, I'm happy for Dakari to award you sanctuary. I only ask that you keep your distance from Luna and Destiny. I understand you allowed them to escape, but they're scarred from their experiences and feel little trust for your kind."

"They have no reason to fear me," I say. "But I'll stay away."

"Thank you."

Boshell drops back to Dakari's side, prompting the Chief to speak. "I am here to award you temporary sanctuary while we devise a more permanent solution."

I stare, not speaking.

"You will behave and conform to the rules of our village. Pull any stunts or start any fights, and you will be executed on the spot as your Queen has decreed."

"I'll keep him in line," Zannah assures him.

Dakari eyes me with revulsion. "Get yourself cleaned up before entering. You look like something a fuegor's dragged back."

"Boshell, can you have Oscar bring us two buckets of soapy water?" Zannah asks.

He nods. "Sure thing."

"Be at the fence entry by a quarter to six," Daraki continues. "My guards and the warriors will escort you through the village to the fields. You will camp there tonight, away from the huts and my tribe."

I force myself to nod and thank him.

Quarter of an hour later, Oscar comes trotting over with two buckets of soapy water. He dumps the buckets in front of Zannah with little care and water splashes on her boots. "Ask and you shall receive." His tone is dry, mocking.

"Oh, and this is for you." He slides a clump of material off his shoulder and tosses it to me. "It's one of Woody's. He said you might have to readjust the waist."

I shake out the material. It looks like a nappy crossed with a skirt. I screw my nose up and toss it back to him. "I'm not wearing that."

"Whatever, it's your funeral."

Zannah jumps to her feet and snatches the nappy-skirt back off Oscar. "Thanks for the buckets, it's all we needed from you, now run along."

"Perhaps you should reconsider." Oscar glances my way with a sneer. "I think Zannah's excited to see you in Woody's little number."

Zannah gives him a hearty shove, sending him back a few steps. "Tell Stavros to come relieve me in an hour. I need to have a wash and change as well."

"What am I? Your slave."

"Just do it!" she growls.

After Oscar leaves, Zannah plucks a wet cloth out of one of the buckets and presses it to my chest. She squeezes it so the water trickles down, washing away Raven's blood.

I consider telling her that I can wash myself, but I'm hurting, and I like the attention. Her touch feels nice, comforting. *Who would believe she's the same Zeek who'd booted me across the head only hours ago?*

"I take it Oscar is your ex?"

She rolls her eyes. "Please..."

I sense there's more to the story than she's letting on, but I don't push the matter. While I'm curious, it's really none of my business.

Zannah's eyes spark with an emotion I can't quite grasp and then evade mine.

"Promise me that you won't provoke or harm Jax. I didn't save you only for you to kill him." When I don't answer, she insists. "Promise me."

I chose my words carefully. "I promise on my life I won't touch Jax." It's not a lie. It's the price I will pay if I lose control.

CLEARING THE AIR

HARLOW

*W*hile Roz, the medicine woman, checks me over, she and Stavros converse in Drake. *I really need to learn this language.* After cleaning and dressing my wounds with natural herbs, Roz hands Stavros a jar of ointment and some extra dressings, which he repeats is for me to put on after I've had a good wash.

Roz palpates my black and blue tummy and frowns.

"Wat is dit?" Stavros asks, which sounds similar enough to Zeek, that I understand.

Roz's answer, however, is completely undecipherable. Acacia swings by the hut mid conversation and joins in on the discussion, adding something further that seems to shock both Stavros and Roz. Once they've finished speaking, all three glance my way, their faces tight with worry.

I have so many questions.

Acacia doesn't stay long, and as soon as Roz is finished with me, I roll my questions out one by one. "What did Roz say about the babies?" I ask. "She looked concerned."

Stavros' lips tug in deliberation before answering. "She said these babies aren't compatible with your body, and she's worried that if they aren't taken out soon, they could cause you internal damage. She's also concerned about the bruises and wanted to know what happened to you. She's afraid whatever hurt you may have hurt them. I told her I would get Jax to fetch Sylvie tomorrow. We'll see what she suggests."

Kenneth's warning rings in my ears, and I think of the two original Pastels he'd saved only to die a couple of months later because of their incompatible foetuses.

Stavros scoops me up and says "Dankie" to Roz before exiting the medicine hut with me in his arms.

"What did Acacia say?"

"That the little stunt you pulled earlier paid off. Luna, Destiny, and Boshell spoke to Dakari about Slater, and then went out and sighted him to confirm he is indeed the Vallon who allowed them to escape. Dakari has awarded him temporary sanctuary."

I breathe a sigh of relief. I can't believe Luna went out and saw Alex. I never thought she'd listen to me. I thought my pleas were in vain.

"Dakari has warned that if anything happens to Jax, or anyone else in the village, Slater will be killed on the spot."

A shiver runs through my aching body.

When we arrive at the hut, Stavros warns me not to speak to Luna and Destiny unless spoken to first. "You've already said more than enough, and in case you've forgotten, we all have to live together."

He leaves me with Acacia, who offers to help me get cleaned up, while he heads off to relive Zannah. I'm pleased to have some alone time with Acacia, even if I am sitting nude in a bath. Unlike Stavros, she's doesn't grind me for my decisions. She says she's worried about further conflict arising between Alex and Jax, but as a mother, she can also understand why I pushed for Alex's safety.

Jax has taken yet another risk for me by not fighting the idea of Alex being given sanctuary. I owe him the world.

I close my eyes while Acacia gently dabs my face with a moist flannel. "Have you seen Jax since the meeting with Dakari?"

I shake my head. "No, and I'm worried I've ruined things. I know my actions look bad, but I'm not trying to make things difficult for Jax. I just don't want Alex to die."

"Hopefully when this is all over, you and Jax will have a chance to talk. I know he's missed you. He hasn't been the same since you've been gone." She grimaces as she washes over my lower bruises and wounds. "Do you want to talk about what happened?"

I tell her a bit, but not everything. I'm not ready. I'm too stressed out about Jax.

After the bath, Acacia helps me into an ankle length royal blue dress. It's flowy around the waist and doesn't constrict my tummy.

Once it's on and I've taken a look, I sit at the end of Acacia's bed and let her tie my dreads into a fish braid.

"Where's Atohi?" I ask.

"Minty and Tatum are minding him."

I blink, confused. "What do you mean?"

"Didn't Floss and Zavier tell you that Minty and Tatum have moved to Spring too? The four share the hut next door with Zannah and Oscar."

"No, they didn't even tell me that they live in Spring." It seems a lot has changed in a matter of a few weeks. "Since when? What happened in the caves?"

Stavros is back and was obviously listening in, because he sticks his head through the doorway to say, "Hold it there. That's a story for Jax to tell."

"Have you seen Jax?" I ask him.

"He and Dakari were still heavy in discussion when I stopped in on my way back."

"Is he angry with me?"

"No." Stavros leans on the door trim with his arms folded. "He's just got a lot to consider. Between Kenneth pushing for an alliance, Slater being awarded sanctuary, and running a colony from a distance, he has his plate full."

An excited squawk breaks the tension, and Minty and Tatum emerge from behind Stavros, carrying Atohi. Minty steps inside the room and my eyes bulge. She's the same colour as Zavier. *How? Why?*

Stunned, I blurt. "You're red."

"Not as red as some." She grins and crosses the space between us, leaning down to give me a hug me. It takes me a second to process what's happening. *Minty is giving me a hug. And not just any hug, a warm hug.*

"Frost, Harlow," she says into the crook of my neck. "You look dreadful."

Tatum hands Atohi to Acacia and joins our hug. "You have no idea how worried we've been."

Jax arrives a quarter of an hour later and leans on the doorjamb, taking Stavros' place. His face is unreadable like granite. *I wonder what he's thinking—what he's feeling?* When he rescued me from the cell, I could feel his love wrapping around me like a warm blanket, but ever since I pushed for Alex's sanctuary, I've felt his walls go back up.

"As you may have guessed, a lot has happened since the mask festival," he says, his eyes flicking to Minty's.

Tatum takes this as a cue and grabs Minty by the hand, tugging her to her side. "We should really go," she says, and then glances between me and Jax with an anxious smile. "I'm sure you two have a lot to catch up on."

Once they've left, Jax comes and sits on the bed beside me, leaving a small gap between us. He's quiet for a moment, before saying, "I'm sorry I didn't let you in on everything that was going on before you left. I held onto certain secrets, believing I was protecting you from the truth."

"I still don't know anything," I say, "except that Minty and

Zavier are Reds, and now live in the neighbouring hut with Floss, Tatum, Oscar and Zannah. Stavros wouldn't let anyone tell me anything. He said it was up to you to tell me."

Jax lets out a long breath and then dives straight in, not bothering to sugar-coat anything. "The morning after the masks festival, I arrived back at the caves to find Zannah fired up and waiting for me. Electra had wreaked havoc during my absence, and Zavier, Floss, and Minty had been taken to one of the cells and tortured throughout the course of the night. Electra and my mother set your friends up as bait to blackmail me into linking with Electra. Zavier was near death and Minty wasn't far behind, so to relieve them from their suffering, I accepted my mother's request and asked Sylvie to inject them with the last of the vertic switz ink, hoping it would be enough to get them through the night."

Bile rises in my throat. "This is my fault. I upset the balance."

"No." His voice is firm, but there's a hint of compassion behind it. "This is exactly why I didn't want to tell you. I knew you'd draw to this conclusion. My mother and Electra were the ones responsible, and they've been taken care of, along with the warriors who took part in the brutal torture session."

He gives me a detailed spiel on everything that happened, including how they brought Tatum into their escape plans, and Stavros, Luna, and Destiny into their assassination plans. My jaw nearly hits the floor when he tells me Luna was the one who assassinated Azazel. She's a real surprise package, that one.

When Jax finishes speaking, I ask, "Do you have any regrets?"

"I have a lot of regrets, but I feel no love lost for my mother or Electra."

"If you're now the Commander, why aren't you living in the caves? Why are you here? Acacia told me you've taken Atohi's old room." *My old room.* When he doesn't answer, I say, "It's because of me, isn't it? You lost everyone's respect because of the pregnancy rumours."

"It doesn't matter why." He pauses a moment and then adds, "I was hoping you'd be staying here, and that we'd get to spend some proper time together before I needed to return. As it is, I'm only here for another few days."

My breath hitches in my chest. "I wanted to stay, I really did, but Alex—"

"Alex is selfish, although it's plain to see you still care about him."

"Only as the father of my children. Alex and I aren't together," I rush to add. "We haven't been together since..." I stop, not wanting to extend any further. "We've been sleeping in the same bed—because it was the only bed—but nothing's happened. All I could think about was you. Alex and I bickered continually because of you. He knew you were the reason I wanted to stay."

"And now we're all in Spring, living together."

"I'm sorry, but I couldn't let him die."

"I understand that, but I don't know where this leaves us. I want to be a part of your life, but I'm not willing to share your attention with someone like him."

"Alex knows how I feel, I promise. He and I are completely over. You're the one I want to be with."

Jax stares without responding. *Ouch.*

"The only reason I left with Alex was to protect you." My eyes flick to the thin pink scar on his neck. "I didn't want you getting hurt. I didn't want either of you getting hurt."

"You should have stayed. Look at you." His eyes roam over me and he winces. "Your body has been severely brutalised. You're the one who ended up getting hurt."

"If I hadn't gone, we wouldn't be aware of all the Pastels Kenneth helped to save. Now that your mother and Electra are out of the picture, we can get them back. You can write it in as a condition of the trade deal. This could all be for the greater good."

Jax's jaw ticks. "I don't know about that. As much as I want to save the Pastels, I'm not sure what to make of Kenneth's proposal. Unlike you, I don't entirely trust him."

"I know it's not my place, but I really do believe we can trust Kenneth. I think he has a decent set of morals and truly cares about the future of his race. Not all Vallons are evil, and the whole race shouldn't be punished for the crimes of the foot guards."

Jax continues to examine the marks on my face, frowning like he disagrees. "Dakari thinks it's best to see what Slater can tell us about his mother, brother, and the way Summer is currently being run before I make any rash decisions regarding the trade deal. He has a variety of animals on spits roasting over the firepits and has suggested we chat with Slater as a group over dinner—try to keep it civil. I don't imagine it will be a pleasant conversation, but I'm willing to give it a shot."

My heart races with nerves. I don't think Jax should be approaching Slater just yet, especially while he's still raw and hurting inside.

"I doubt Slater will be able to tell you anything useful," I say, and it's the truth. "He isn't like you. He didn't have a lot to do with the politics, and Kenneth kept him out of the loop when it came to his rescue operation. I'm afraid I know more about Summer's politics than he does."

I take this opportunity to tell Jax more about what I've learnt since my stay in Summer, and he nods, his face still stony.

"Are we going to be okay?" I ask when I'm done. "I mean… Do you still want to be with me? You're a Commander now, so that means—"

His face softens, and he brushes a wisp of hair from my face. "Me being Commander makes no difference to us. My only issue is your tie to Slater, but if you can promise me that there's nothing to worry about, I can accept him as the father of your children, and we can move forward."

"I promise with all my heart, you have absolutely nothing to worry about."

"You have no idea of the heartache and regret I've felt since you left," he admits. "I was livid at myself for letting Slater drag you off the way he did, but it was clear there was still chemistry between you two, and you didn't say one word to me during the handover, in fact, you didn't even so much as look at me. It gave me the impression that your heart still belonged to him."

My insides bunch. "It was quite the opposite, I assure you. I was afraid if I looked at you, my true feelings would show on my face, and I didn't want Alex to know that you were the reason I wanted to stay. I didn't want you guys to fight. I'm so sorry that I hurt you."

"Come here." Jax wraps his arms around me, and I nestle my cheek into the crease of his bare chest. "Ek het jou lief," he whispers in my hair, and I wish I knew what the words meant.

We stay this way for a long magic moment before he draws back. "I shouldn't be hugging you in this state. I need to have a proper wash and get ready for tonight's group dinner."

I fidget, feeling awkward about asking, "Am… Am I invited to the dinner?"

"Of course. Chances are you'll need to mediate for me. I don't imagine Slater will be very pleasant or forthcoming when it comes to speaking with me personally."

I don't know that he'll want to speak with me either, I think, but I nod regardless.

Before six o'clock rolls around, Stavros gathers everyone up. "Dakari said dinner will be served at six, so we need to make our way to the field.

He takes one look at my arms as I exit and asks Acacia to fetch me a shawl. "A number of Drakes will be attending tonight's dinner, so I think it's best if Harlow covers up as much as possible," he says.

Acacia passes me a shawl, and I tie it like a cloak around me before hobbling to the deck ladder.

Jax steps out behind me and curls an arm around my waist, pulling me back to him. "Don't even think about it. I'll carry you down."

I hold on tight as Jax carries me down the ladder and to the field. I imagine his arms would be burning with strain after already carrying me all the way from Summer to the Drake village, but if he's hurting, he doesn't let it show. Stavros leads everyone to the end firepit where we'd sat for the mask festival, and my heart squeezes as magical memories float to mind. So much has happened since that night. *Everything has changed.*

There are more Drakes present than I'd expected, and all the field's firepits are alight. Four of the firepits have animal spits turning above them, while the others have grates set across the top with veggies simmering. Whatever the veggies have been marinated in has my tastebuds dancing with delight.

Boshell spreads blankets out for everyone to sit on and then takes the end one with Luna and Destiny. Jax places me protectively between himself and Acacia on the middle one, and Will and Daisy play at the end of our blanket with Atohi.

I'm pleasantly surprised that Luna and Destiny have made an effort to be here. Given their experience in Summer, I imagined they'd want to sit it out. Boshell puts his arm around Luna, and she leans against him, resting her head on his shoulder. *I wonder if they're officially a couple yet. It looks as if they are.*

"When are we going to see the Vallon?" Will asks impatiently, and Boshell tells him to hush.

Zavier, Floss, Minty, and Tatum take the blanket on the other side of us. I haven't seen Zavier since I've returned. Minty says he and Floss have been fighting about me ever since they arrived back at their hut from the rescue mission.

I avoid looking at him as they sit to save causing any further problems between them, but I resent it. *Zavier was my friend first,* I think, my fingers twiddling with the halved magic rock of my friendship necklace.

The sun slowly sets as we wait, bringing the flickering flames to light. Eventually the Drakes break into a chant, and Alex is led into view by Dakari, Woody, Oscar, Zannah, and two Greens.

His harem shorts are gone, and he is dressed in a tribal garment which doesn't leave much to the imagination. My cheeks burn. I feel awkward even looking his way.

Dakari steps forward and makes an announcement, first in Drake, and then in Zeek. "I hereby grant Slater sanctuary on a trial basis. However, let it be known, if he shows any form of aggression towards anyone in this village, he will be executed on the spot, no questions asked."

I sigh a breath of relief. Alex is safe—*for now.*

Murmurs fill the field as the Drakes take in Dakari's news. Some leave right away, while others stay and sit by the firepits with family members and friends. Jax leaves my side and heads across to speak with Dakari, while Zannah and Oscar make their way over to our firepit, Alex in tow. When Luna and Destiny see Alex approaching, they tense, and then quickly scamper off to fetch some dinner.

Alex pinches Jax's spot next to me, and I tense as he sits close enough that our sides touch. It makes sense that he would choose to sit by me. I'm the main reason he's here, but I'm not at all comfortable about it. I glance Jax's way to see if he's noticed that his spot has been taken. I don't want to be rude to Alex by telling him to move right away, but I also don't want Jax to get the wrong impression.

Acacia must feel me tense because she gives my hand a friendly, reassuring squeeze which says, "I'm here if you need me."

"I take it I have you to thank for this," Alex says.

"I wasn't all me. A few others stuck their necks out for you too, so please promise me that you'll keep your Hyde side in check. This is a peaceful village, and Dakari doesn't want any trouble."

He nods, head lowered, and I bite my lower lip, considering carefully, before adding, "Stavros told me what happened to Raven; I'm sorry."

"Don't be." His Adam's apple bobs. "I'm sorry about everything. Are you okay?"

I nod. "I don't blame you, Alex."

"You should."

"I don't."

Will rushes to our blanket excitedly, and Daisy follows, but hangs back, fidgeting with her dress.

"Hi, I'm Will." Will puts his hand out. He seems to have grown tremendously in every aspect since I left.

Alex shakes his hand. "Hi, Will."

"Your tattoos are super cool. I wish I had as many as you do. I only have one." He twists his wrist to show Alex his star. "I wanted a blade, but my dad said I had to get a star." He rolls his eyes. "Boring."

"I like the star," Alex says.

Will's gaze darts between us, and he examines our wounds with knitted brows. "Did you two get into a fight?"

Thankfully Boshell joins just in time to tell Will to hush and mind his own business. Daisy waves to Alex and mouths a meek "hi" but stays close to her dad's side.

Boshell gives an embarrassed smile. "The kids were eager to meet you."

Boshell rounds up Will and ushers him back to their blanket as Luna and Destiny arrive back with plates of food.

Soon after, Jax strolls back with Woody and Dakari, but instead of demanding his original spot back, he parks himself beside the Drake Chief, facing us—watching us. *Awkward.*

"Will and Daisy are fraternal twins." Alex says, glancing at my tummy. "Like ours."

There's that dreaded word "ours" again. My eyes flick to Jax's to gauge his reaction to Alex's comment. *Nothing.* He's got his unreadable mask on again.

"Have you picked out any names for the babies yet?" Acacia asks, making small talk.

"Alex has chosen to call the boy Axel because it's an anagram of Alex," I say, "and I've chosen to call the girl Lyla."

"Lyla?" Jax repeats, his eyes sparking with recognition. *Hold on, does this mean he remembers her? Is this why he believes in humans?*

Alex is quick to react. He cuts me a questioning glance, teeth grinding. "What haven't you told me?"

I swallow hard, feeling uncomfortable. Everyone is watching us.

I hadn't expected this to happen. RJ said that Jax wouldn't remember Lyla. If I'd known that Jax would recognise the name, I wouldn't have blurted it out like that. I thought this was my own little secret tribute to him.

When I don't answer right away, Alex's eyes blaze, and his voice takes on a scathing edge. "What does Lyla mean to Jax? Tell me!"

I lower my voice to a whisper. "Alex, not now. We have an audience."

Without saying anything, Alex jumps to his feet, snakes his arms around me and carries me away from the group.

"Oi," Jax tries to leap up, but Dakari holds him back.

"Leave it," he warns. "This is between them." And then after a beat he adds, "I take it the name Lyla means something to you?"

I would like to know what Jax's answer is, but I don't get to hear it.

After clearing several metres, Alex puts me down. "We have no audience now. Tell me, what does Lyla mean to Jax?"

"Lyla was Jax's human twin."

He stares for a long moment, his eyes still blazing. "As in you are naming our baby after Jax's human twin that you've heard about or as in you're actually having Jax's fraternal twin?"

"Lyla was Jax's actual fraternal twin."

"How convenient?" He huffs with scorn. "I take it this means you and Jax already had a strong connection before we slept together, given this whole twins thing works on connections. Am I right?"

"Alex, please don't do this."

"Do what? Ask for the truth?" The betrayed look in his eyes tears me to shreds. "Tell me something. It's clear I've lost you to him but was any of this—" He gestures between us. "—ever real to you?"

"Of course, it was real, and you know it was. That night we spent in the forest together was incredible, but what happened afterwards broke me." I place my hand over my heart. "We've both made hurtful mistakes." I step forward, taking his hand in mine, and squeeze my eyes shut for a moment. "I still love you as the father of our children, and I want you to be happy, but you and I are over. You need to accept that and move on."

He snatches his hand back. "Jax is looking pretty worried over there." His voice is cold. "You might wanna head back to him and let him know that the big bad Vallon hasn't hurt you."

"Let's go back together. He and Dakari want to speak with you about the way Summer is being run. They want you to fill them in on all the ins and outs before they meet with Kenneth to discuss the trade deal."

He shakes his head. "I don't care about Kenneth or the trade deal, if there's no chance of us ever sorting things out, I'm leaving. I don't belong here."

Fear claws its way up my throat. "What do you mean? I fought for your sanctuary."

"I didn't ask you to."

"What about our twins?"

"They won't need me if they have you and Jax. I'll only be a complication." His voice is low and thick and sounds far away. "They'll probably be better off without me. What do I know about being a good parent? I've never been blessed with any." Tears glisten from the corners of his eyes. "I'll probably only mess them up."

"That's not true. I'm sure you'll be a good father. Please don't go, Alex. They'll need you." He doesn't say anything, so I press on, hoping to convince him. "What about Lucas? Don't you want to see him again?" Alex and I might be standing close, but the distance between us feels immeasurable. "Stay, please, I'm begging you. We might not be together, but I still want you to be a part our kids' lives."

His hand cups my cheek, and for a split-second I'm filled with hope. "My life is not worth living if I can't have you too, Rubes." The desperation in his voice is gut-wrenching and my hope deflates. A tear finally escapes him. "You're all I've ever wanted."

His hand drops back to his side, and he takes off towards the thick of the forest.

"Alex, wait!"

"Just let me go."

I'd go after him, but I'm too sore, and what's more, I'm worried about how it would look to Jax. *Damn you, Alex. Why do you have to be so difficult?*

When Jax sees me hobbling back to the group, he hurries over to help me.

"I'm sorry," I say as he scoops me up. "So much for mediating, I've ruined your chances of even getting that talk."

"It was Dakari's idea, not mine. As soon as he suggested it, I figured it'd be a long shot."

After Jax places me down on the picnic blanket, I call to Floss.

"Is there any chance you could go and talk some sense into him?" I ask.

A stubborn expression comes over her face. "Why should I? He's your problem, not mine."

You were more than willing to pose as his hostage when it suited you, I think bitterly.

Instead, I say, "Jax and Dakari need to speak with him. It's important."

Zavier wraps his arm around Floss in a loving, protective manner. "I'm sorry, Harlow, but I'm with Floss on this one. I don't think she should go. Alex doesn't seem very stable."

Ouch. There was a time when Zavier hated Floss, and now he's siding with her over me.

Zannah jumps to her feet. "I'll go," she says with a huff, and then sprints off after him.

A small wave of panic washes over me. I don't know that Zannah is the right Zeek to be going. She's very tough love, but she's the only one offering, so I'll have to take what I can get.

Come to think of it, if Alex tries to do anything rash, Zannah won't have any qualms about knocking him out. This could work.

KICKED INTO LINE

-ZANNAH-

My legs aren't as long or as fast as Kieran's, but I'm still significantly faster than most, which means I'm able to catch up to Slater in no time.

When he hears me gaining on him, he whips around. "What do you want?" His eyes spark with pure hurt and rage. "Are you here to give me another boot across the head?"

"No." I suppress a grin. "I'm here to stop you from doing something stupid. *However,* if booting you across the head again is the only way to achieve this, then so be it."

"Let me go." His breath comes out in angry gasps. "I'm not going to cause any problems; I just want to be left the hell alone."

He goes to take off again, but I do a low sweep kick that clips his ankle and trips him mid stride. He lands in a plank position, but springs back to his feet with a quick flip manoeuvre which brings us face to face.

His eyes glare into mine wild with fury. "I don't know what you're playing at, but I'm not in the mood, so you need to back off!"

"Or what?" I challenge.

"Don't push me!"

I *literally* push him, trying my best to provoke him. "Or what?"

No one can see us—we're hidden by trees—and I figure if I can get him to fight me, it might help to release some of the hurt and anger built up inside him.

He grabs for my arms, but I duck, delivering a solid punch to his abdomen.

Winded, he curls over and thrusts out a palm. "Stop!"

I hit him again—harder. He grunts and kicks my stomach, knocking me backwards. I quickly rebound though, delivering a circular kick to his jaw.

A curse word erupts from his lips, and he retaliates with a kick that sends me flying back first into a nearby tree trunk. The force of the blow knocks the wind out of me for a split second, but it doesn't keep me down.

There's a fallen branch resting on the roots where I've landed. I pick it up and run at him, jabbing his side. He grunts and reaches for it, but I'm too quick. I spin away only to run at him from another angle and whack him firmly across the back of the head.

This time as I'm pulling back, he catches it and reefs it from my hands to snap it in half.

"Stop!"

I don't stop. I give him a right hook followed by an uppercut, which finally provokes him into fighting back. Kicks and punches are thrown left, right, and centre. He gets in a few good ones, but so do I, and it's only a matter of time before I've tripped him with a low spin kick and pin him to the ground.

"You're pretty good." A sly smile plays on his lips. "But you seem to have forgotten something." Before I even have the chance to register what's happening, he's got me flipped onto my back, straddling me, and his strong hands have my arms pinned above my head. "I'm a Vallon, and Vallons are much stronger than Zeeks."

"Everyone has a weak spot," I counter. "Even Vallons." I send my knee upwards with force, hitting him right where it hurts.

His body contorts, and his grip on my hands loosens allowing me to pull free. I push my fingers firmly to his wounded side, making sure to apply enough pressure to make it hurt without digging my nails in—*because I'm not an outright bitch.* When he groans and buckles, I shove him off and flip him over.

The tables turn once more, only this time, I've managed to slip my pocketknife out of my boot, and I press it firmly against his throat.

"Do it," he says, giving up any fight that's left in him. "I want you to."

I press down, only enough to nick the skin. He winces ever so slightly and closes his eyes, waiting for me to press down harder. Keeping the knife where it is, I lean forward, align my lips with his ear, and whisper. "That's for Jax."

I roll off him, and when he doesn't budge, I lie next to him, gazing up at the stars through the gaps of the tree branches while the insects around us buzz.

After a long while of only heavy pants escaping us, he says. "I've lost her. Jax has stolen her from me."

I turn to face him, using my elbow to prop my head up so I can look him straight in the eyes. "The way I see it, you are the one who tried to steal Harlow from Jax."

He bolts upright, infuriated by my comment. "Ruby was mine first. Jax swooped in and took her from me."

I jerk up alongside him. "Ruby might have been yours first, *but* Harlow belongs with Jax. He treats her right, and they are better suited, so stop being a selfish prick and let her go." His face falls. *Oops.* This is precisely the reason why I got him to fight me. I'm no good with words. I'd rather fight things out than talk things out.

"Listen," I say, lightening my tone. "I don't fully understand the backstory between you two, but you are no longer the humans you once were. She's not Ruby, and you're not Alex. She is Harlow, and you are Slater, and Harlow belongs with Jax.

"But she's pregnant to me."

"Okay, yeah, that sucks, but this kind of thing happens all the time. Your kids shouldn't be the glue keeping you together. It should be your love for each other." I nudge him with my shoulder. "I'm sure you two could work out some sort of system. I'm not a massive Harlow fan, but given what I know of her, I believe she'll be fair when it comes to sharing the kids. Just because you two can't make it work, doesn't mean the kids need to miss out. Think about it. Is it really worth doing something stupid in a fit of rage and losing your kids too?"

He casts me an inquiring glance. "If you aren't a big fan of hers, then why did you kill one of your own warriors to save her?"

"I didn't do it for her, I did it for Jax. I wanted to spare him the heartache of losing her."

"Why?"

"Because I'm in love with him," I admit, and it's the first time I've ever said these words aloud.

He blinks. "I don't get it. If you're in love with him, then why didn't you just stand back and let her die? With Ruby gone, you'd stand a good chance. You're hot, feisty, and you seriously know how to kick arse. He'd be crazy to pass you up."

"You should really try calling her Harlow," I say. "And I don't want to win Jax's heart by default. I love him enough that I'd rather see him happy with someone he loves than miserable with me."

"I'm familiar with the whole 'if you love somebody let them go' saying, but it doesn't make sense to me. If you love someone, you fight for them."

"That's only half the saying. The full saying goes, 'if you love somebody let them go, if they return, they were always yours. If they don't, they never were', and Harlow didn't want to go to Summer with you, you forced her to go. She wanted to stay with Jax."

"How are you even familiar with this human saying?"

"I saw it written on one of RJ's drawings, so I asked him about it. RJ is——"

"I know who RJ is," he says curtly, giving me the impression that I've touched on another sore subject.

Not willing to let him lie here wallowing all night, I jump to my feet and hold out my hand for him to take. "Come on. The night's still young. Let's forget about Jax and Harlow and have some fun. I've got a crossbow; some throwing knives, and a set of targets for us to play with."

He looks up at me in confusion. "But it's dark. I didn't think you Zeeks could see in the dark."

"My sight might not be as keen as yours." I help tug him to his feet. "But I'm a Purple, not a Pastel, so my vision is reasonable. And besides, I enjoy a good challenge."

"I hadn't noticed." His voice drips with sarcasm. Slater cradles his side and winces as he straightens. "You fight dirty."

"I fight to win. Oh… And by the way…" My eyes drill into his, and I stab a finger at his chest in warning. "If you repeat anything that I've just told you, about my feelings towards Jax, I will slice you open."

A short bitter laugh escapes him. "I don't doubt it."

SETTLING BACK IN
-HARLOW-

*J*ax and Stavros grab two big plates of food each and set them down on the middle of the picnic blanket for the four of us to pick at as we please. We chat while eating, exchanging stories about the wild fortnight that's passed.

So much has happened in such a short period of time, and so many lives have been affected, it's hard to believe.

As dinner winds up the guys venture over to the other side of the fire to speak with Dakari and Woody. I'd asked Jax to apologise to Dakari for me, but he'd waved me off, saying, "It's fine. Zannah's on the case. She might be able to draw some useful information out of Slater."

Atohi lies snugged at the end of the blanket, so with only the two of us girls remaining, Acacia moves closer and opens her wings out, wrapping them around us like a cocoon. "How are you feeling? Are you okay? Your shimmer appears to be paling."

I lean my head on her shoulder and allow my eyes to flutter shut. "I'm tired, sore and ready for bed."

"How about we leave the guys to their discussions, and go back to the hut for a girls' lay in? I'll put Atohi straight to bed, so it'll be just us."

"I think that sounds perfect."

I'm glad to have Acacia's kindness and support. I could really use a good friend, especially now that my former best friend has been stolen.

Acacia asks Herc, one of the Drake guards, if he'd be kind enough to carry me back to the hut. Jax springs to his feet, saying he'll do it, but Acacia shakes her head.

"You should stay here and carry on with the discussion," she insists.

The Drake guard carries me all the way to into the common area of the hut before putting me down.

I smile and say, "Dankie," showing off the one Drake word I know.

My eyes are hanging out of my head, but I'm too unsettled to sleep. I glance restlessly around the room before finally resting on some cushions to wait for Acacia. When she comes back from putting Atohi to bed, she plonks herself beside me, covering us with a blanket, and we have a heart to heart. We speak about everything, including my human life and my sister Jade.

I tell her how Jade was struggling with the fact that she was the only one who could see me and had pleaded desperately for me to prove my existence to her husband. She was sick of Byron and her best friend Carrie believing she was hallucinating, so last week, while sleeping in summer, I finally managed to move a glass across the coffee table in front of Byron, convincing him of my presence.

He'd leapt from the lounge and cursed, eyes bulging. I hadn't wanted to go down this road and scare him, but I'm glad I did. When I saw Jade a few nights later, she told me that it's brought them closer, and she's feeling much happier in herself.

She's taking control of her life again and living it to its fullest, which means I no longer need to worry about her between visits to Earth.

Jax and Stavros arrive back an hour later, and Jax offers to carry me to bed. He takes me to Atohi's old room, which is now his room, and places me down on the mattress with care.

"Zannah coaxed Slater back to the field," he says and then clears his throat. "He's okay. I thought you'd like to know that."

Relief fills me. "Thank you."

"Zannah thought it would be a smart idea to bring him back with a set of throwing knives for target practice, so I kept my distance not wanting to become the target. Dakari was able to speak with him though. You were right, the information he had to share was useless."

He kisses my forehead and levers up to leave. "Good night, Harlow."

I take hold of his forearm. "Where are you going?"

"I wasn't sure if—"

"Stay," I say before he can finish. "I want you to stay."

Just like last time, he strips his shirt off before sliding into the spot next to me. There's only one single mattress this time though, not two, so he has to shuffle in nice and close. My bulging belly rests between us, and he runs a hand over it gently, his brows creased in thought.

"Sorry. I take up a lot more room now days," I say, trying to make light of the situation.

His eyes meet mine in all seriousness, and I gulp, afraid of what he's going to say. "I have Oscar leaving early tomorrow morning to fetch Sylvie. I heard what Slater said to you outside of Summer, and Stavros filled me in on Roz's prognosis, which aligns with the story you told me about the original Pastels Kenneth rescued. I'm sorry to say it, but these babies need to be delivered tomorrow."

"I'm nervous," I admit. "I don't want to lose them."

He takes my hand in his. "I'll be there for you… And I'll see what I can do about getting Slater to be there for you too."

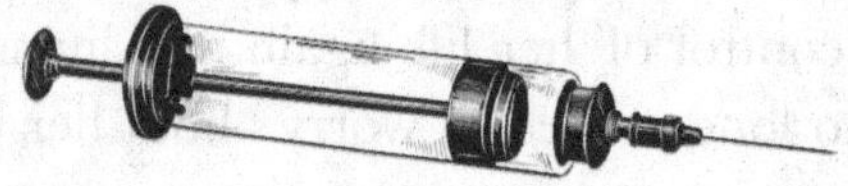

My eyes flutter open to find Jax's face in front of mine. His eyes are already open, and he's gazing at me adoringly.

"Good morning," he says, his lips curling up in a smile. "How do you feel?"

Soft golden light filters in through the window behind him, and the scent of damp wood and earth, along with his arms around me, brings me undeniable comfort.

"Much better, thank you." I rub my eyes and stifle a yawn, thankful for a decent night's sleep on a soft and comfy mattress.

"I've been awake for a while," he admits. "But I didn't want to move because I didn't want to wake you." He strokes the outline of my cheek with his thumb. "And in all honesty, there's no other place I'd rather be."

My insides flutter. His walls are back down. It seems a decent night's sleep did us both some good.

"I'm so glad to be back. I thought about you constantly while I was gone." I nestle in closer. "Alex said if I still wasn't happy with him after the babies were born, he'd bring me back, but I didn't entirely trust that he would. I was worried I'd never see you again."

His hand moves to my hair, stroking his fingers through my dreads. "I'd like to be the one to perform the c-section with Sylvie's assistance, but only if you're comfortable with it. I want to do everything in my power to make sure you and the twins get through the delivery procedure as safely as possible."

"I'd like that."

After another five minutes of snuggling, Jax says, "Oscar will be arriving back with Sylvie soon. We should really get up so I can prepare the area."

I reluctantly draw back and lever myself up to a sitting position at the edge of the mattress. Noticing me struggling, Jax springs to his feet to help ease me up. As I stand a stab of pain shoots through my tummy, and I give it a light rub.

Atohi is giggling and gurgling in the background.

My mind races with nervous energy. By the end of today, I will have two Atohis. I will have an Axel and a Lyla. I'm terrified about becoming a mother, but I'm even more terrified at the thought of losing them. I'm praying they'll be strong enough to survive the delivery.

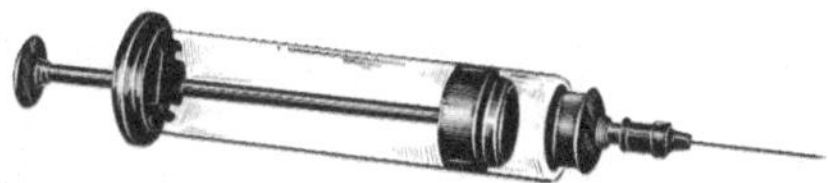

Oscar and Sylvie arrive at nine, and I'm pleased to discover RJ is with them. He's stating random facts about Spring's luminescent wildlife and why they glow so brightly as he enters the room. Apparently, it has something to do with a certain bacteria that grows on their skin.

He stops to take a breath when he sees me, his eyes looking everywhere but mine. "The babies are okay," he says, matter-of-factly. "But you'll die if we don't take them out soon."

Sylvie mouths, "Sorry," and she and Jax share an *oh, RJ* look, before Sylvie gives her own less confrontational greeting.

Oscar dumps a heavy looking pack onto the wooden floor with a thump. RJ has a pack on his shoulders too, which he slides off to place beside it.

"I've set up that room for the delivery," Jax nods towards Atohi's room.

He and Stavros dragged in the deck table earlier, which earnt them a look of disgust from Luna.

RJ and Sylvie make their way to the room, and I stand to follow.

"I've got you." Jax takes me in his arms, and carries me into the room, gently placing me on the deck table.

His eyes, full of compassion, meet mine, and I'm glad when he holds onto me a moment longer than is necessary, before letting go. "You're going to be okay; I'll make sure of it."

I swallow bile. My heart is racing. "And the babies?"

"I've done plenty of these procedures during my medical training, and as I said before, I'm going to do everything in my power to make sure you and the twins get through the delivery as safely as possible."

He straightens and glances at RJ. "Fetch us the pack with the supplies and the extra sheets."

THE BABIES ARE COMING
-ZANNAH-

I'm on my way back from the markets, carrying a drink and some sandwiches for Slater, when Oscar spots me and calls me over.

"What do you want?" I ask, making my way over to him. He must've gotten less sleep than I did. His hooded eyes are hanging out of his head.

I've had about three hours, tops. I stayed up until the early hours talking trash and playing target practice with Slater. He's competitive, I like that. It makes it all the more rewarding when I win.

"Sylvie and RJ are here to deliver Harlow's babies. Jax asked me to inform Slater that Luna and Destiny have cleared out so he can be there for the delivery. But if he comes, he's not to cause any trouble."

"So, what? You want me to tell him." It's really more of a statement, than a question.

"It saves me having to. I don't like the guy."

"You don't know the guy."

"And you do?" He eyeballs me. "I know he tried killing Jax in front of us, and that Harlow's come back from being with him looking like mincemeat."

"You're being dramatic."

"You're being reckless. Where'd Slater sleep?" He raises his brows in question. "On the grass, or on your mattress?"

"That's none of your business."

I'd dragged my mattress to the field early this morning, and Slater and I topped and tailed on it. The mattress he'd been given to use the night before was too bloody and gross to re-use, and what's more, I'd felt odd about leaving him alone on his first night with no hut to call home. I'd slid my blade under my pillow and told him if he dared touch me, I'd slice his throat.

He'd laughed and said, "I wouldn't dream of it."

I wasn't sure whether to be offended or not, and found myself questioning, *am I that intimidating or that unappealing?*

Either way, he kept his hands to himself as promised.

"Whatever… Just hurry up and tell him so I can settle a bet with Woody. I've got a gemstone encrusted knife riding on this. Woody says Harlow's having a set of Zeeks, but she's too big, I recon she's having Vallons for sure."

I roll my eyes. "Okay, okay…enough. I don't care about your petty bet. I'll tell him."

40

I'M HERE FOR HARLOW

-ZAVIER-

Oscar stopped by specifically to let me know that Harlow's twins were being delivered soon, so I immediately woke up Floss and dragged her out of bed so we could be there for the birth of her niblings. I feel a little guilty. I haven't had much to do with Harlow since she's been back, but it's tricky now that I'm with Floss. No matter how many times I assure Floss that she has nothing to worry about, she's still ridiculously jealous of my friendship with Harlow.

Floss and I arrive at our neighbouring hut to find Zannah and Alex in the middle of a deep discussion by the ladder. Alex's eyes are flaming with emotions, but unlike yesterday, he seems to be keeping himself under control.

"Are you two here for Harlow?" Zannah asks, and we nod. "Perfect, you can take Slater in with you and make sure he behaves himself. I don't need to be here for this."

I never know if I'm supposed to call this guy Alex or Slater. Zannah's calling him Slater, so I guess I'll stick with that.

Slater casts her a "don't you dare do this to me" look, to which Zannah shrugs and says, "You've got this. Just remember why you're here and keep yourself in check."

41

DELIVERY

JAX

Zavier and Floss slip into the room and say a quick "hi", before heading to the top end of the deck table, where Harlow's head rests partially hidden behind a low hung draw sheet. Slater follows wordlessly on their heels, cutting me a hateful glance as he passes. I bite my tongue as he parks himself at the opposite side of the room, leaning against the back wall with his arms folded across his chest, and his eyes blazing. Floss and Slater are my least favourite Zadonians. I resent them both with a passion because of the awful way they've treated Harlow. Regardless, I'm glad they both made the effort to be here, because I know it'll mean a lot to Harlow.

Her face brightens when she sees Zavier, which has me smiling on the inside. Zavier seems to have a positive, calming effect on her which is precisely what she needs right now. Plus, I know I can count on him to help her through this, especially if Slater lets her down—which I'm afraid he might.

I pull back the sheet covering Harlow's abdomen and gulp. The sight of her multicoloured tummy is far more confronting than I'd expected. I pray to the stars RJ is right, and that these babies are okay.

I glare at Slater accusingly while wiping her skin with disinfectant, only to find he looks just as appalled as I feel.

I reassure Harlow continually as I prep her, telling her to relax, leave the worrying to us, and everything is going to be okay.

RJ busies himself organising instruments for the procedure while Sylvie gets Harlow to roll over so she can inject her lower spine with anaesthesia as a spinal block.

"This might pinch a little, but it'll be over before you know it," she says, her tone gentle. "Now take a deep breath and hold as still as you can for me, okay?"

After she's done, Sylvie rolls Harlow onto her back again and after several moments, I check to see that her lower region is numb, before proceeding.

I take a calming breath before placing the scalpel on Harlow's lower abdomen, and then run the blade in a straight line across the skin above her pubic bone.

Despite the fact that she's numb from the waist down, Harlow feels the pressure of the incision, and her breathing becomes laboured. Her complexion takes on a green hue, and her features grow sweaty with stress. *Frost!*

"Harlow," I call but she merely groans. "You're okay," I reassure her. "If you can survive Summer, you can survive this."

Zavier takes her hand, as I hoped he would, which earns him a sharp look from Floss.

I'm usually good under pressure, but it's hard to remain calm and collected when I can see that the woman I love is physically struggling. I can't be the one delivering her babies as well as the one holding her other hand.

My eyes snap to Slater's. "Be there for her," I growl. "She's distressed. Come and take her other hand."

Slater jerks up straight. "She doesn't want my hand, she wants yours."

How old is this guy, five? "Stop being childish and get here now. She needs you. If you were man enough to get her in this situation, you can be man enough to see her through it."

He takes one look at Harlow's stressed face and concedes.

With both guys comforting her, Harlow's breathing regulates again, allowing me to concentrate on cutting through the uterus wall and getting these babies out.

There's a squelch as I pull out the first baby, and Slater straightens to peek over the curtain. The infant is covered in blood and placenta, but he's alive and moving with dark skin and a male anatomy. *Axel is a Vallon.* On closer inspection I detect a slight shimmer through the muck. It seems there's some Zeek to him, too.

"It's your son," I say to Slater as I hand the baby to Sylvie to cut the cord. "And he appears physically fine."

Slater repeats this to Harlow, and once the cord is cut and clamped, Sylvie brings their son over to them, placing him on Harlow's chest. My heart swells as I catch a quick glimpse of her smiling before I dig back in for baby number two.

There is another squelch as I pull the second one out, and I'm frozen to the spot for a moment as an explosion of memories of my human life as Levi rush to the forefront of my mind. I see Lyla—not this baby Lyla—my human twin Lyla.

"Jax." Sylvie places her hand on my arm, bringing me back to myself. "Is everything alright?"

My eyes trace over the small baby in my hands. She's slighter and pale skinned like a Zeek. *Harlow's had one of each.*

"Lyla's fine too," I say loudly enough for everyone to hear, and then hand her to Sylvie with a tug of my heart strings. I don't know what's come over me.

I pull myself together and remove the placenta so I can get on with the sutures.

A tear dribbles down Harlow's cheeks as RJ whisks Axel away for a wash and Sylvie replaces him with Lyla.

Slater gives Harlow's arm a semi affectionate squeeze. "She's beautiful, like you."

LYLA
-HARLOW-

The twins' delivery swirls through my head like a blur. I can hardly remember it; my mind was a mess of out-of-control emotions. The last thing I remember clearly was Sylvie placing Lyla on my chest and Jax stitching me up. I must've passed out afterwards, because I've woken up to Jax sitting in a chair next to me with Axel in his arms, and Lyla cocooned beside me.

"Hey." Jax runs a hand over my hair. "How are you feeling?"

"Next question." I force a soft chuckle, which hurts. *I feel like I've been hit by a truck.*

"You did really well," he says.

"Thanks for saving me—again. I promise to try and stay out of trouble for a while and give you a break."

Now it's his turn to laugh. "We'll see."

Our voices must've woken Lyla, because she whimpers. Jax's hand leaves my hair, and he stands to swap the twins over.

"Lyla," he says once he's seated again, rocking her gently in his arms. "Is there a meaning behind the name?"

I get the feeling he knows there is.

"RJ told me that human you, Levi, had a twin named Lyla, but he said that you probably wouldn't remember her because you were fraternal twins."

Jax glances between me and Lyla, eyes questioning. "Is there a particular reason why RJ told you about Lyla?"

I give a slow anxious nod. "You know, don't you? You feel the connection."

"It hit me as soon as I delivered her." He takes a minute to process this before asking, "How long have you known about this, about Lyla?"

"A while."

"You should've told me." There's slight accusation in his voice. "I would've never—"

"RJ said you wouldn't remember her."

He goes quiet for a long moment, and I'm afraid I've hurt him again, but then he says, "I know Slater is the father of Lyla and Axel, and he's always going to be a part of your life, but I want to be here for you and the twins too." He slips his hand around mine. "Link with me."

"What?" I'm glad I'm lying down or else I would have fallen over. My heart thumps. "But you're the Commander and I'm just—"

"You're the only one I want to be with. Honestly, Harlow, these past few weeks without you have been gut wrenching."

"But what about the colony? What will everyone say?"

"With my mother and Electra gone, it shouldn't be as hard to make changes. I've got plans in place for integrating the colour system, and depending on what Kenneth and the Queen make of my proposal, we may be entering into a peaceful trade deal with the Vallons. A lot needs to change, and I'm willing to stand up for what I believe is right, but I need you by my side."

"You can count on me to stand beside you." I squeeze his hand and add, "Whatever it takes."

43

EVENING MEETING WITH KENNETH AND HIS CREW

-JAX-

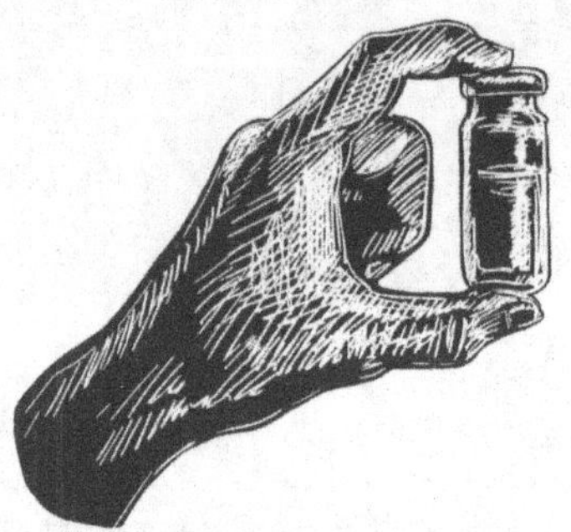

stick to the rear of the group with Oscar and Dakari as Slater leads us through the pitch-black forest, with only his ink and Stavros' two glowing zofts to light the way. We raise our blades as we pass several large luminous creatures. Their skin textures vary from smooth and slick to rough and scaly, all with reflective eyes and long razor-sharp teeth. Some snap at the air as we pass, while others hunker and hiss.

"These creatures are far more vicious than the ones lurking around the village." Oscar observes. "I feel like it's danger training all over again."

"Only this time we've got a Vallon with us," Zannah says, keeping to Slater's side. "So, we've got the advantage."

I do find it interesting how whenever a creature gets too close, Slater only has to yell, "Bleib zurück," and they cower or scurry off. It's puzzling that they're so afraid of Vallons, yet they see us Zeeks and Drakes as a meal. Vallons might be bigger, with glowing tattoos and the power of fire, but we are all humanoid in appearance, so you'd think it'd be all of us or none of us.

Eventually, I sight Kenneth and his crew in the distance. They're not hard to miss. They've brought horsens with them and together they burn brightly, like a raging fire in the forest.

Slater scoots ahead to converse with his brother in Vallon, and I'm pleased to overhear Kenneth asking after Harlow and the twins.

Slater gives a brief, "They're fine, they survived," and then goes on to ask about the removal of the bounty on his head. When Kenneth doesn't give him the answer he wants, he growls and turns away from his brother, kicking at a protruding tree root with aggression.

"You came," Kenneth says to me in Zeek as I near. "I wasn't sure you would."

Dakari and Woody step up beside me, proving where their loyalties lie.

"You wanted a proposal for a peaceful trade, here you have it." I pluck the prepared scroll from my pocket, and hand it to Kenneth. "These are my terms."

The line between Kenneth's brow deepens as he reads through the proposal. Eventually his eyes lift to meet mine, filled with frustration and defeat. "My mother will never agree to this."

"She will if she wants the trade deal," I press. "It's time to see what means more to her—her kingdom or her title."

Kenneth curses in Vallon, and then sucks in his lower lip, seeming to contemplate something. "I have limited control over what happens to the Pastels in the castle. The only way they will be released is if my mother agrees to these terms, which I'm not entirely sure she will. You've put me in a very difficult position." A moment passes before he adds, "Would you be willing to bring this proposal to my mother personally if I set up the meeting? I can't hand this proposal to her myself, or she'll believe I concocted the idea."

"I'll agree to the meeting if you allow us to retrieve the Pastels you have hidden in your safe house, first. They don't belong in Summer, and I want them back."

He nods in agreement. "I'll get things set up for you and Slater to retrieve them tonight. Bring as many helping hands as you like, but only the two of you are to cross the border; the others must remain at Spring's edge."

44

PLAYING WITH FIRE
-ZANNAH-

Slater's eyes are blazing, and his fists are clenched. He looks like he wants to slice someone's throat open.

He pipes up with something in Vallon, and all those who understand the language glance in my direction.

"What?" I ask.

"He's not prepared to work with me," Jax says. "The only way he's willing to help rescue the Pastels is if he can take you through to Summer instead."

I shrug like, *whatever,* but on the inside I'm gloating. "That's fine by me."

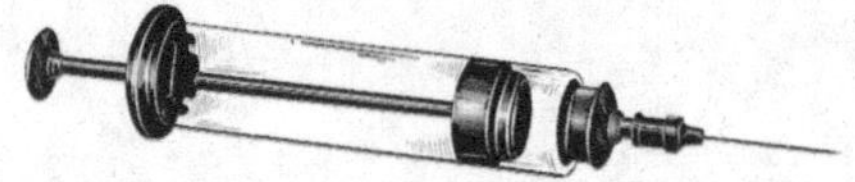

When we get back to the village, Slater stalks towards the field while everyone else veers towards our huts.

"I'll keep an eye on him again," I say to Stavros, and then part with them.

Oscar sniggers, and mutters, "Yeah, I bet you will."

I'd turn back and tell him to shove it, but it'd be a waste of my breath.

I double my pace to catch up with Slater's long powerful strides. I can tell by his bunched muscles and thundering breaths he's in a foul mood, and I want to know why. "What happened back there?"

When he ignores me, I grab his arm and jerk him around to face me. "Hey…" My voice comes out much louder than I'd anticipated, and a few Drakes turn to suss out the situation, a shimmer of yellow and green bodies glittering in the dark. "Talk to me."

"After what happened with Raven, Kenneth says there's no chance *whatsoever,* that he'll be able to convince our mother to lift the bounty on my head. He says Raven's death has sealed my fate, because everyone in the kingdom believes I killed her… Me." He stabs a finger at his chest. "She dove in front of that blade to save me, and yet I don't even get to go to her funeral."

"What happened with Raven was awful, tragic and unforeseen, but she's the one who got you in this mess, don't forget that. She set that blade in motion." *For crying out loud, I sound like my brother. Mr Rational-and-Reason.*

Alex raises his hands to the back of his head, looks up at the stars, and sighs. "I don't know what to do, Zannah. I want to be a part of my kids' lives, but I can't stay here. I don't belong here. Drakes see me coming and they tuck their kids away like I'm a predator. I might have been given sanctuary, but I'll never be welcome. I feel like a monster."

"I'm not entirely happy here either, but I'm trying to make the most of it. It's all I can do. The Drakes will warm to you eventually.

Just keep your cool, concentrate on what's important and try not to worry about what others think."

"If you're so unhappy here, then why don't you go back to the caves?"

"I have a bounty on my head too. I've killed important Zeeks."

"Well, if that's the case, then why haven't Jax and his warriors locked you up or wiped you out?"

"Because we're all in this together. We did what needed to be done for the sake of the colony. Azazel, Electra, and their Purple followers were set to tear the caves apart, so we eliminated them, and I took the fall."

A sarcastic laugh escapes his lips. "And you Zeeks like to call us Vallons untrustworthy and underhanded. Talk about hypocrisy."

"I don't profess to be perfect. I'm partially rotten and I know it. Everyone tells me as much, but I can't help it. I wasn't born to be nice."

"Yeah, you and me both."

His burning irises meet mine and something sizzles inside me. *I don't like the way he makes me feel.* That's not entirely true. *I don't like that I like the way he makes me feel.* I'm playing with fire—*literally*—and I know it, but Slater is the most exciting thing to enter Spring in weeks. Now that I'm not so intent on trying to kill him to protect Jax, I'm quickly discovering he's actually far more my type than Jax. After spending the past couple of days hanging out with him, I've found he's grown on me—*a lot.* I appreciate his raw openness, competitiveness, and the thrill of danger in his wild eyes. *Oh,* and don't even get me started on how my body responds to that smokin' ripped torso of his.

Slater shifts uncomfortably, and I realise I've been staring. I break eye contact, nod in agreement, then continue to the open field where my mattress lies skewwhiff by one of the firepits.

"I take it we're topping and tailing again?" he asks, forehead scrunched.

Burn. I thought he'd appreciate the company. Right now, I'm all he's got. "I don't have to stay."

"I'm happy for you to stay. It's your mattress, but do we have to top and tail? I had to forgo my pillow during the night and use it as a blockade. You kick in your sleep, and I've got a lot of wounds up this end." He gestures from his waist up.

I narrow my eyes, pretending to be suspicious, but deep down I'm totally fine with the idea.

"I'll keep my hands to myself, I promise," he adds. "I've spent the last few weeks sleeping alongside Rub… Harlow," he rushes to correct himself. "And I've behaved myself just fine."

Interesting. "Are you telling me nothing happened between you and Harlow while she was in Summer?"

"Nothing worth mentioning." He chews his lip. "I messed up pretty badly, and I tried hard to fix things between us." A sad laugh escapes him. "You know, for a moment there, I actually believed she was warming to me again. I thought we would mend things and become a proper family, but I realise now, it was all in my head. I never stood a chance. I'm an idiot. I should have let her stay with Jax like she asked. All I've done is cause turmoil."

"True… You should have let her stay, but some good came out of it. Yesterday you got to watch your children being born."

I lower myself to the mattress, and he follows suit, groaning and shifting to get comfortable. His burnt side is swollen and looks angry. I bet it hurts to touch.

"How was that by the way?" I ask, rolling to my side and propping my head on my hand to face him. "Watching your kids being born?"

"Surreal. It feels like it was a dream." He gazes up at the stars with a faraway look in his eyes. "I'd like to spend more time with them, hold them, but I'm not ready to be near Harlow and Jax when they're together. Seeing them together still makes me want to kill him."

"I get it, but don't kill him. I don't want to have to kill you."

My comment makes him laugh again. "Why not? At least you'd get your mattress back."

"I don't mind sharing, and I've kind of enjoyed sleeping out here, under the stars. It's been nice." Suddenly embarrassed, I add,

"But we'll need to find you a proper place to stay soon. It's only a matter of time before it rains."

He shifts to his side looking at me earnestly. "You don't mind coming into Summer with me tomorrow, do you?" The question is genuine. "It'll be dangerous, and there's a chance we could be killed, but I get the feeling you're not afraid of danger, and I couldn't bring myself to work with Jax."

"I'd prefer it. I hate being sidelined." My eyes trail over his glowing chest and biceps, and my pulse quickens. I wish he wasn't still so caught up on Harlow. He and Jax both. There must be something more to her than I'm seeing, because I don't find her all that special.

I close my eyes and lower my head to my pillow, not wanting to give him the wrong idea. While I might be growing fond of him, I'm no one's rebound or one-night stand. My one-off evening spent with Oscar was a drug-induced mistake I've sworn never to repeat. I hate myself for it, and in a way, I resent him. It was my first and only time, and I don't even remember it. I promised myself from that moment onwards, the next time a guy wants to touch me, he needs to earn it.

"Good night, Slater."

"Sweet dreams, Zannah."

I wake up in the morning with my back pressed up against Slater's bare chest. The heat of his glowing vertic switz feels nice against my sore muscles, and his heavy breaths near my ear make me think of him in ways that heat up the rest of my body. I wiggle away before these thoughts manifest into an inferno of steamy images.

He grizzles when I move, but he doesn't wake—which is good—because I decided during the night that I'd like to do something nice for him this morning as a surprise. The idea is a little out of my comfort zone, but I know he'll appreciate it.

"Nice bed hair," Oscar says, when I get to Stavros' hut. He's sitting at the deck table with Destiny, sipping a bean-brew.

I don't appreciate the implication, and this time around, I *do* tell him to shove it.

Stavros and Acacia are in the kitchen, and I say a brief "hey" as I pass them on my way to Jax's room.

Jax is sitting on a seat next to the where Harlow lies, cradling Lyla. I stare a moment. It's a strange sight for me to absorb. I hadn't expected him to look so comfortable in his new stepfather role.

Harlow has put him through absolute hell these past few months, and yet he's still so deeply in love with her. Going by the affectionate way he's gazing down at Lyla—it seems this love has extended to her children.

Harlow notices me first and greets me with an awkward, "Hello."

"Hey," I say in the friendliest way I know how. "I was wondering if you'd like a small break. I could take the babies out to Slater for an hour or so? It'll give him a chance to spend some time with them before we have to head to Summer."

Jax cuts me a sharp look, but Harlow says "sure" like it's no big deal.

Thankfully, the babies aren't crying. I don't think I could have gone through with this if they were. I don't have a problem with babies, I like them fine, but I can't say I'm particularly maternal.

Harlow points to two carry sashes, hanging at the end of the cot Axel is lying in. "Acacia gave me those. You might want to use them if you're walking all the way back to the fields. The twins might be small, but I'm sure they'll get heavy."

Jax, goes ahead and grabs the sashes inspecting them carefully to see how they work. When he figures it out, he tucks the twins into them carefully, before strapping them tightly to me.

"Please be careful," he warns. "If anything happens to either of them—"

"Nothing is going to happen. Trust me."

"It's not you I don't trust."

"It'll be okay." I take hold of his forearm and give it a reassuring squeeze. "Enjoy the peace while you can. I'll be back in an hour with them, safe and sound."

"Not to be rude," he says, surveying me quizzically. "But this seems out of character."

I laugh. "Look who's talking, Insta-dad. We're all maturing and changing." I turn my gaze to Harlow before leaving. "There's one other thing I'd like to ask," I say, forcing my tone to stay light. "Would you mind calling Slater by his Vallon name from now on? He's not your Alex anymore, and I'm sure it tears at him every time you call him by his human name. I've told him the same in reverse, so expect him to call you Harlow for now on."

When Stavros sees me exiting Jax's room with Harlow's babies strapped to me, he rushes to block me in the hall. "What are you doing, Zannah?"

"I'm minding my business, big brother. What are you doing?"

"What is this?" He uses his finger to draw an invisible circle around me and the babies. "At first I thought you were sticking close to Slater to keep him in line, but now I'm worried there's more to it." His eyes cut to mine with a scrutinising gaze. "Oscar and Destiny saw you two this morning when they went out to the lake with Boshell and his kids. They said you looked cosy together."

Annoyed, I clench my jaw. "Have I ever interfered with you and Acacia?"

"No, but it's not the same thing, and you know it. Slater is selfish and dangerously unstable. I don't trust him, and I don't want you getting hurt."

Axel wiggles frantically against the material of the sash and makes a distressed squeally noise. *Oh no, no, no, no… Don't you dare cry on me.*

"There's nothing going on," I snap. "We're just sharing a mattress. Now back up out of my way before these kids start crying."

"You need to be careful," he warns, stepping aside. "Think before acting."

"You need to back off," I shoot back at him. "You're always acting the authority on everything, and you're not always right."

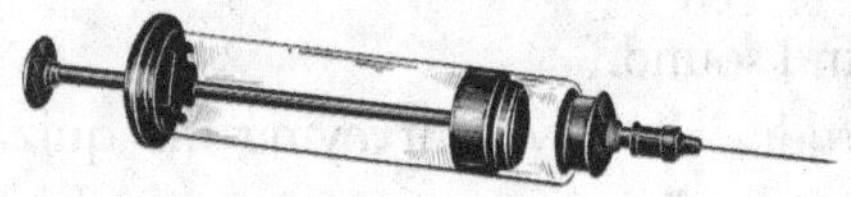

By the time I get back to the mattress, Slater is gone, and my breath catches in panic. Axel's squeals are intensifying by the minute, causing me to seriously regret my decision. I bounce my legs, telling him to shoosh, but this only seems to egg him on further.

My heart pounds and my breathing quickens. This is far more stressful than I imagined. *I'm completely out of my depth here. I don't know what to do with babies.* I consider returning them and forgoing the surprise, but then I spot Slater stepping out from the lake's edge and I hurry over to him, desperate for his help.

His whole face lights up when he sees the small bundles strapped to me. "What's this?"

Water drips from his dark skin, making him sparkle in the early sunlight. I drink in his broad shoulders and ripped muscles. He really is visually spectacular.

"I thought you might want to spend a bit of time with them before we head to Summer. Just in case… You know."

He reaches to unstrap Lyla, and I stop him. "Unstrap Axel first, he's the one causing all the fuss."

Slater's lips split from ear to ear as he unravels his son from the sash and holds him close to his chest. I've never seen him smile like this before. It looks good on him.

"Thank you, Zannah," he says, directing his smile at me. "I needed this."

45

PASTEL RESCUE MISSION
-SLATER-

Zannah treks close beside me the whole way to Summer, her muscles tensed and eyes alert. She hasn't said anything, but I can tell by her body language she's worried we're walking into a trap. I can't blame her for being suspicious; I don't trust Kenneth either. I can't understand why he's kept his Pastel rescue operation a secret from me all these years, especially when he knew my stance on the matter. I've always been against keeping the Pastels as slaves. I could have helped him.

Oscar and Woody follow quietly behind us, and I can feel Oscar's eyes burning holes into my back. I take it he's jealous of the attention Zannah is giving me, but if they're not ex's and he's dating that Destiny chick, then I don't see what his problem is. It's not like there's anything going on between Zannah and me. She's hot and feisty, and I appreciate her ongoing help, but I haven't forgotten where I stand. She might have been all smiles when she brought my kids out to me this morning, but she's threatened to slice me open more times than I can count, and I know if it ever comes to the crunch with Jax, she won't hesitate to gut me like a fish.

Jax is her number one, just like he's Harlow's number one. *I'm the nuisance.*

Jax called a meeting before we left to ensure that we're all on the same page with who's who. Several of the Zeeks staying in Spring are fugitives, so he's given them aliases to use when the Pastel rescues stay the night. He wanted to come with us today, but I forcefully told him to stay with Harlow and the twins. As much as I'm dirty with Harlow for choosing him over me, I need to know she and the kids will be looked after if I don't make it back. I was surprised when he backed down and listened to my argument, and I was even more surprised when Zannah agreed with me. She even made a point of telling Stavros he should stay too.

"We've got Oscar and Woody, and only the two of us can cross the border, so there's no need for all of us to go. It's unnecessary."

When we get to the border, Kenneth and the Amber are waiting for us with horsens hitched to a cart. The Amber finally introduces himself as Jye.

"What's with the cart?" I speak in Zeek to include Zannah and Oscar in the conversation.

"It's how I'm getting you in and the Pastels out. I've told the guards on duty that we are trading supplies with the Drakes, and we will be passing across the border several times over the course of the evening."

He reaches into the cart and tosses me my hunting suit. "You need to cover up your ink. It's too recognisable. Also, I've loaded a pile of sacks in the cart, so once you've changed, you and Zannah need to lie down in the back so we can cover you."

Zannah has come prepared. Dressed in an all-black suit that

reminds me of Catwoman minus the cat mask. Her hair, which is usually a mix of twirls and braids, has been pulled back into one thick, tidy braid which she twists into a bun. She pulls out a black bandana I'd seen Jax handing to her before we left and ties it over her hair, covering the purple. She looks sexy in a unisuit but knowing the bandana she's wearing is Jax's ruins the image for me.

I slip behind a tree and swap the ridiculous nappy skirt for the hunting suit. I'll have to see if Kenneth can scrounge up a few pairs of shorts for me while I'm here.

"If we're not back by three, it means something terrible has happened, and you should head back without us," I tell Oscar and Woody when I re-emerge.

"They'll be back," Kenneth assures them and gives me a slitted glance. "Where's the trust little brother?"

"What trust?"

"If it wasn't for me, Harlow and your children would be dead."

"Harlow came back from your care looking like she'd been put in the ring with a fuegor," I growl at him in Vallon. "So don't throw that bullshit in my face. You could have helped me break her out of the cell, but you didn't. You tricked me into believing we'd be hunted down so that you could use her to your advantage."

A sick feeling forms in my gut as I remember the shocking sight of Harlow's black and blue exposed body the day she'd delivered the twins.

"That's not entirely true. Yes, I knew she wasn't a slave given your opinion on keeping slaves, and yes, I saw her as an advantage, but I was being honest when I said that our mother's guards would've hunted you both down before you got to safety."

"We're both out now, and our children still pose the same threat to the Vallon race." I glance about dramatically. "Where are all these guards trying to hunt us down?"

"That's the thing, our mother now believes that the ba—"

"You know what, I don't care what you have to say, it's all lies as far as I'm concerned. Let's just hurry up and get this over and done with."

I jump into the back of the cart, roll up two sacks, and hand one to Zannah. "It's for you to use as a pillow," I say, reverting back to Zeek. "Kenneth wasn't kind enough to consider our comfort or safety. The cart would only have to hit a few bumps and we'd be knocked out cold."

Kenneth leans towards Zannah, and whispers loud enough so I can hear, "Slater has a way of dramatising situations."

After setting down our make-shift pillows, we lie flat on our backs. Zannah has her blade out and is holding it firmly against her chest.

Kenneth smiles and says, "It seems Slater isn't the only one who doesn't trust me."

Dust and fibres tickle my nose as he lays the hessian sacks over the top of us.

"No talking or moving," he warns.

The cart jerks on the spot as Kenneth and Jye climb aboard the bench seat up the front, and after calling out, "Weitergehen," the horsens pull forward.

The ride is bouncy for a few metres through the forest but smooths out when we cross the border and hit sand. I sense the soft quiver of the horsens straining as they struggle to pull the heavy cart across the soft terrain, but their speed soon picks up again, telling me we've hit the red earth road.

As always, the Summer evening air is sweltering, and my body beads with sweat beneath the itchy sacks. After a while of traveling, Kenneth calls the for the horsens to halt, and I feel the cart lift as his weight leaves it. He pulls the sacks back and we sit up. Zannah keeps a tight grip on her blade while she gazes about, taking in her surroundings. Her eyes are narrowed and alert, yet they sparkle with curious wonder.

Small, red clay-clad houses, cracked and weathered, line the road. In front of us is another cart along with four individual horsens hitched and ready to go.

"This is the poorer section of Summer's kingdom," I tell her, recognising where we are. "This is where most of the Ambers live."

The wonder fades from her eyes and she scowls. "Their houses don't look much better than the Pastel caverns."

"I've never seen the Pastel caverns."

I've never even entered the mouth of the caves.

I think back to the first time I'd visited Winter with my father Alfonzo and Kenneth. It was five years after the war had ended between our races, which had claimed thousands of lives on both sides. Vallons are much stronger than Zeeks and had the war have been fought on our land—or even Spring—the Zeeks would have been annihilated. But our bodies aren't made for the cold, and the thick, frosty moisture in the Winter air made it near impossible for our army to summon a spark.

Our father Alfonzo said the only reason the Zeeks were able to overpower the Vallons was because they had the advantage of using Winter's elements as their weapon. That, and their bodies held up in the in the frigid temperature without buckling.

We'd gone to negotiate for the trade deal, but unlike Kenneth, our father came in hard and threatening, which got the Zeeks offside right away. Not that I believe gallantry would have done him any good with Azazel. She was firm with what she wanted, and it was a price we couldn't pay.

Azazel refused to even come out and meet us. She sent her sons out on her behalf.

"Our mother is not interested in negotiating," Nix had said. "Either pay the price she's asked or be on your way."

Jax and I were only in our mid-teens back then, and we didn't have much say in the matter. I hadn't taken much notice of Jax besides thinking how exceptionally long and dark his dreadlocks were. I was busy watching his brother Nix. He had dark sly eyes and a menacing angular face. I didn't trust him, and for good reason. Little had I known back then that Jax would be the one to cause me the most grief in years to come.

My father had stepped forward to argue the point, causing the warriors to circle in on us, blades raised and hands glowing purple with winter magic.

Nix's lips had twisted in into a smug smirk. "Go home Alfonzo, and don't return unless you have voltz to trade."

I snap out of my memory and jump down from the wagon.

Kenneth offers his hand to Zannah, but she sidesteps it and leaps off the cart, landing with the grace of a ninja.

"Is this where the Pastels are?" I ask.

"No, they're in the old church, but we need both carts and the extra horsens to get them all out. Even then, it'll take a couple of trips."

"The old church?" I scoff. "That building is ancient. It's a safety hazard."

"True. But right now, that ancient building is the only place keeping them alive."

Jye brings over two saddled horsens. He hands me the reins of one, and Zannah takes the reins of the other without question, acting confident, but I sense a slither of unease.

"Do you know how to ride?"

She casts me a slanted look. "I'm sure I can figure it out."

"O—kay." The horsen is much too tall for her to mount without assistance, so I interlace my fingers to make a stirrup, and kneel. "Here," I say, and surprisingly enough, she accepts my help without argument.

The two Oranges we've met twice before now, exit the small clay-clad house beside us and mount a pair of horsens up front.

"That's Sienna and Sylus," Kenneth says. "Just like Jye, they've dedicated a lot of time to keeping this operation afloat."

"Why was I never told about this? As you mentioned before, you knew my stance when it came to keeping slaves, I was against it. I wasn't quiet about the matter. I could've helped you."

"That's the problem. You're reckless and unstable with a big mouth. I was worried you'd expose the operation."

His accusation stings. Ruby had deemed me as untrustworthy on several occasions too. She was wary of sharing her secrets with me.

My heart squeezes painfully at the thought of her. Even after all that's happened, I'm struggling to let go.

I force myself to repeat Zannah's words in my head. "She is Harlow here, not Ruby. Think of her as Harlow."

Thank goodness for Zannah. She's been a Godsend during this

heartbreaking ordeal. She might be all tough love and endless threats, but she seems to get me in a way that others don't.

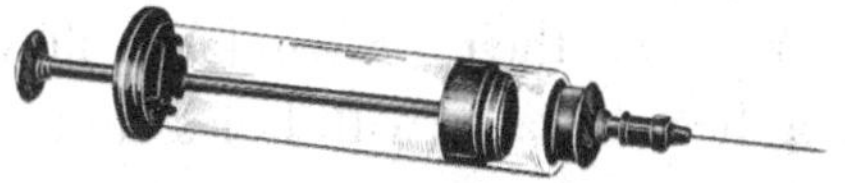

During our ride to the church, I notice Zannah struggling on her horsen, so I trot up beside her and offer some tips.

She listens and does as I suggest, and soon she and the horsen move as one. Regardless, I keep alongside her, afraid she'll inadvertently lean forward and prompt the horsen to break into a gallop.

"If it makes you feel any better, I've had the same thing said to me more times than I can recall," Zannah says.

Her comment comes unexpectedly, and it takes me a second to register what she's referring to.

"Yeah?"

"They say we're reckless with big mouths, I say we're passionate." Her eyes flick to mine momentarily. "I wouldn't let Kenneth's evaluation of you get you down. I love the way you wear your heart on your sleeve."

"Really?" Scepticism drips from my voice. I'm not sure if she's being sincere or mocking me. I hadn't expected such a kind and supportive comment from a girl who has threatened to slice me open countless times over.

"I've spent a lot of time with stone-faced warriors who keep their true emotions hidden behind expressionless masks. It's refreshing to not have to guess what someone's thinking or feeling."

When we get to the church, we dismount and tether our horsens to a weathered post.

Zannah examines the ancient building, her forehead crinkled. "Exactly how old is this building?"

"It was built close to three thousand years ago in honour of the union of Judith and Noah," Kenneth says.

"They are two of our high Gods," I add, in case she's unaware.

Kenneth leads us up the stairs to a set of double doors, warning us to be mindful of loose, eroded steps.

As soon as he pushes the double doors open, Zeeks come rushing over to greet us, their drawn faces lit with excitement. They're all wearing hessian sacks with holes cut for their heads and arms, camouflaged and ready to go.

Zannah curses at the sight of them all; there are so many.

Beyond the Pastels, handmade triple bunks line both walls of the room. The windows are sealed shut with large wooden boards, leaving the place dim and reeking of body odour. This church brings back memories of my human childhood. I've stayed in foster homes similar to this when I was Alex.

I spot a couple of Pastel Reds and several Peaches. I'd seen Kenneth lug these Peaches away and believed he'd destroyed them as our mother had ordered. I'd hated him for it. Everything I thought I knew about my brother was a lie. He'd saved these Pastels, and he helped save me. Yet regardless of his kind acts, a gut feeling still tells me to remain cautious. I still don't fully trust him.

"Enough," Kenneth commands. "I know you're all eager to get out of here, but I need you to return to your bunks, keep quiet, listen, and do exactly as I say."

Sienna and Sylus enter and help to usher everyone back to their beds.

"I'm going to call out the bunks one by one, starting from the left." He points. "When I say your bunk is ready to move, you will make your way out the doors and down the stairs in a calm sensible manner. No rushing, no speaking, no arguing. We don't want any unnecessary injuries, and we don't want to attract any attention."

"How many are we taking this round?" Sienna asks.

"As many as we can safely fit."

When everyone is back in their beds and settled, Kenneth tells the first bunk of three to grab their things and follow Sienna. He waits a moment to be sure that they are safely down the stairs before repeating the same thing to the next lot, only this time he tells them to follow Sylus.

Kenneth beckons Zannah over to lead the next group, who are

tweens, and flutter about excitedly gawking and pointing at Zannah's eyes and shimmer. The word "purple" is whispered among them, and they stare, their young faces piqued with curiosity. They would've been born in Summer, which means they wouldn't have seen a Purple in the flesh before now.

Kenneth tells them to hush as Zannah leads them outside and then gets me to follow suit with the next group.

Outside, Jye is busy playing Tetris with the Zeeks, trying to fit as many as he can in one cart.

Sienna takes two tweens from Zannah's group of three and leads them to the bench seat up front. "Kenneth says we are to place a pair of the younger ones on each of the bench seats."

The leftover girl twiddles her thumbs nervously until another tween is brought out, and they're led to the front of Kenneth's cart.

Sienna, and Sylus do another round each, and Kenneth exits with one extra, bringing it to a total of nineteen Zeeks for the first round of our rescue mission.

We fit seven in one cart and eight in the other, including the tweens up front. I roll up sacks for pillows and Sienna hands them out.

There are only four Zeeks left standing, three males and a female. The female has faded red hair and irises like Harlow's friends and stands tall and broad. The men are wafer thin, scarred and badly buckled, but two of the three have kept their angelic faces.

"You can each double a Zeek on horsenback," Kenneth tells those of us riding.

The Red female automatically follows Sienna to her horsen, and Sylus beckons the broken guy closest, leaving us with the two angelic faced ones.

An irrational part of me doesn't want Zannah riding with either of these pretty boys.

"Zannah rides with me," I say. "She's not a strong enough rider to double someone else. Chuck me one of the leading ropes, the two guys can double on the other horsen while I lead it."

I'd half expected Zannah to take offence and argue, but her lips remain sealed. I get the feeling the ride out here proved to be much harder than she'd expected. Not that she'd ever admit it. She's too proud.

After boosting the two guys up on one horsen, I help Zannah onto the other, then grab the reins and swing around behind her.

A tingling sensation spreads through me as she leans back resting her spine against my chest. I'd felt this same strange sensation last night when I'd awoken to a noise and found her body pressed against mine.

For a second, I forgot about Harlow and thought about wrapping my arm around her. I might have actually gone through with it too, had I not seen the glint of her blade lying beside her, warning me to keep my hands to myself.

The way she'd looked at me earlier that evening had me wondering if she was only sticking around to keep me in line, or if there was something more to it. Her eyes had traced over me with admiration, not disgust.

She's a complicated Zeek to get a true read on. Part kind-hearted and part killer. I think back to when Harlow had called me Dr Jekyll and Mr Hyde. The same reference could apply to Zannah. Perhaps I should pursue her. We'd make a good match.

Her Dr Jekyll side had shone through brightly this morning when she'd brought my kids out to me. It was an act of kindness I hadn't expected from her.

She's gone out of her way to stick by me since everything turned to shit, and she's helped ease the pain of my broken heart by giving me loads of attention. *I wonder if she's been hurting over Jax too?*

Just thinking Jax's name burns holes inside me. Despite knowing he'll be good to Harlow and my kids, I still hate him with a passion for what he's taken from me.

Let it go, my inner voice tells me. *Let her go.* Brushing all thoughts of Jax and Harlow aside, I focus on the task ahead. This mission is dangerous, and I need to stay focused and alert.

When we get to civilisation again, Kenneth stops at the front of the small clay-clad home we'd stopped at earlier and tells those of us on horsenback to go inside and wait for them to return with the carts.

I eye him with distrust. I don't like the idea of being left here waiting.

"We can't keep you hidden from the guards' inquisitive eyes on open horseback. We're going to have to make three trips to the border with the carts. Don't worry, it's Jye's place. You're safe."

46

NO TRUST

-ZANNAH-

Slater clearly doesn't trust his brother, which means I don't trust him either.

Inside the stone, clay-clad home, Sylus offers to make those of us remaining something to eat and drink.

The three male Pastels are keen and hoe in, but I screw my nose up, and Slater follows suit. We're hot and thirsty but we use our canteens to drink from. At least we know they're not poisoned.

The size of the kitchen and living area are bigger than I'd imagined they'd be going from the external appearance of the small, dilapidated building. It's closer to the size of a Magenta cavern rather than a Pastel cavern. But even with the thick red clay cladding on the exterior of the eroded building as insulation, it's still ridiculously hot inside. I run my finger along the benchtop, and it comes away a reddish-black colour. There's sand and red dust coating everything, even the plates the Zeeks are eating off, although they don't seem to mind.

After a few moments of standing around aimlessly, Slater frowns and goes back to the front door to open it ajar and peeks out. "Where are Sienna and the Red Pastel?"

Sylus replies in Vallon and Slater glowers at his response.

"Taking care of what?"

I don't understand the answer, but Sylus' clipped tone has me cautious.

Eventually Kenneth and Jye return with their emptied carts, and Slater and I exit, ready to retrieve the next lot.

"The first lot of rescues have been safely transported across the border," Kenneth informs us.

Jye leaves his cart to poke his head through the doorway, "Stay, and no answer door. We get more and be back for you."

He's not as fluent with the Zeek language as Slater and Kenneth.

Slater glances at Kenneth, eyes narrowed with suspicion. "Why not take them across now?"

"There'll be extras this round too, so we'll take them all together as a third group. It'll save us a fourth trip across the border," Kenneth says. "Now let's get the next lot before you're noticed."

Accepting this, Slater swivels his gaze to mine. "Do you want to take your own horsen or double again?"

The first ride out had been a thrill, but it wasn't nearly as easy as I'd expected it would be. "I'll ride with you."

Sienna returns just as we're about to take off, but the Red Zeek is no longer with her, she's alone.

"Where's the Red Zeek?" Slater asks.

"She's safe."

He grunts and then whispers in my ear. "Keep alert."

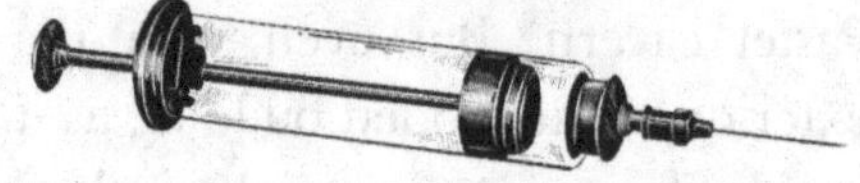

Slater and I stick close, watching each other's backs, but to our combined relief, round two of the church rescue mission runs smoothly, and we get the Zeeks back to Jye's place safe and sound.

However, our suspicions arouse once more when Kenneth tells Slater to remain on horsenback and wait while he ushers the three Zeeks who were brought here on horsenback inside.

Kenneth beckons me over, but I don't budge. "You should wait inside too. Jye will come back for you and the remaining six when he's done taking this lot across."

Slater slings a protective arm around me. "She stays with me."

I don't need protecting. I can fight my own battles, but I like the feeling of being worth protecting.

After closing the Pastels safely inside, Kenneth heads over to us, taking the leading rope from Slater's hand and drawing the lone horsen to himself.

"What's going on?" Slater's grip on me tightens, and my fingers wrap around my blade handle, ready to draw it out if necessary.

"Relax little brother. Raven's funeral is tomorrow, and since you can't attend, I thought I'd take you to the morgue to see her and say your final goodbyes."

A strangled noise sounds in Slater's throat. "Shouldn't you be concentrating on getting the rest of the Zeeks across the border?"

"My crew has it covered. This is your one and only chance to see Raven before she's cremated. Take it or leave it."

Sienna dismounts, ties up her horsen and slides into the driver's side of Kenneth's cart. "I need you all to keep quiet until we're safely past the border," she tells the Zeeks lying in the back, and she and Jye take off.

Sylus steers his horsen our way. He must be coming with us.

"Fine." Slater's teeth mesh. "You lead the way."

Kenneth's eyes zoom in on mine before mounting his horsen. "There's no need for you to come. Are you sure you don't want to be taken back across the border with the remaining Pastels when Jye and Sienna return?"

I'm hot and bothered, and ready to get out of this disgusting oven known as Summer, but there's no way I'm leaving Slater alone with Kenneth. Especially when he's got a generous bounty on his head.

"I'm coming."

"Very well."

I want to point out that this isn't smart, that we're putting ourselves in unnecessary danger for a corpse, but I know how upset Slater was about missing Raven's funeral, so I clamp my mouth shut and go along for the ride.

The ride is long, and the closer we get to the castle, the more the buildings grow in size. We eventually stop at a large block-style sandstone building signposted "Leichenschauhaus", which sits next to a much newer, architecturally magnificent church.

Large statues of their many gods line the stairs of the church, weathered but not too eroded, with tall actual flames shooting up from their hands. The flames light up the entire area around us in bright flickers of orange and yellow.

We dismount and Slater ties our horsen to the pole by the church next to Kenneth's. Sylus doesn't stop with us; his horsen trots on into the distance.

Kenneth leads us up the stairs to the morgue—which are plain and simple by comparison to the church's—and through a set of metal double doors into a metal-sheeted hall that glows purple.

The air inside is much cooler and a relief to my Zeek skin, but my insides quickly heat up when I spot zofts lining the ceiling— stolen zofts.

There is a large circular room at the end of the hall with a slate bench, where Raven's lifeless body rests. She's been encased by zoft infused glass, which is foggy and frosty around the edges.

Slater touches the glass, and a shiver runs through him.

"Take your time." Kenneth cups his shoulder with his hand and gives it a squeeze. "I'll wait outside."

I keep back, allowing him a moment of semi privacy with her. I'm not exactly sure how much she meant to him. I've never asked.

"This is my fault," Slater says, and I don't know if he's talking to me or her. "I did this."

I take a single step closer and console him. "I saw what happened, and like I've told you before, this wasn't your fault."

"I never loved her the way I should have," he admits. "I was always in love with Ruby, human Ruby. I never gave Raven the chance she deserved." He thumps his fist on the glass in frustration, but without any true force. "Now she's dead, human Ruby is lost to me forever, and Harlow's with Jax. It was all for nothing. Raven died for nothing."

I could easily argue this statement and point an accusatory finger directly at Raven, but it seems inappropriate while standing in front of her corpse, so instead I say, "You both made regrettable decisions that lead to her death, but it was her guard who killed her, not you, and I killed him. She's been avenged. Now say goodbye and stop shouldering all the blame or it'll eat you alive."

Slater shares a few words with her in Vallon and runs a hand over the glass as a final goodbye.

"Thank you for this." He turns to face me, eyes glassy. "Thank you for everything."

"We should go," I say.

When we open the double doors to exit, we're blinded by a fiery ball of light. "Get down," I shout, snatching Slater's hand and tugging him down with me. I spot at least eight guards, but there could easily be more hiding.

One comes flying at us, and I shoot a shard, but it liquifies before it gets to him, so I leap to my feet and run at him head on, embracing the challenge.

Slater tries calling me back, but he's too late. I refuse to hide in the morgue like a coward only to be captured, tortured, and killed. If I die, then I'm going to die fighting.

More fire balls are thrown, but I duck and weave through them before side stepping the guard and jabbing my blade deep into his side. He yelps, but I don't stick around to finish him off because I have another guard coming at me, blade raised, ready to strike. I flip out of the way as he brings it down and kick his knee from side on. There's a crack followed by a howl, and his legs buckle, so I continue with a low spin kick to take him all the way down, and then drive my blade through his back. Through my peripheral I see Slater taking on one of the other guards. I'm glad he's out here fighting with me. I would've lost all respect for him if he'd hidden.

Another fireball comes at me from close range, and I duck and roll. It must singe Jax's bandana, because within seconds, the smell of burnt fabric invades my nostrils.

I bounce back up and run at the guard who threw the fireball at me, but he falls before I can get to him, *what?*

Thumps fill my ears as the other two remaining guards, standing furthest from the chaos, fall. Puzzled, I scan the area, and come across the red Zeek we'd met earlier, crouching by the steps of the church.

"What's going on?" My eyes snap to Slater.

He plucks something from one of the fallen guard's backs, and then frowns. "It's a dart," he says, oblivious to the red Zeek standing behind him.

"Six o'clock," I warn, and he spins, raising an arm which glows completely red with Summer magic.

"At ease," Kenneth calls from behind us. "She's on our side."

Slater turns his glowing arm on his brother. "There is no 'our side'. You set us up."

Sylus appears on horsen with the limp body of a female Zeek draped across his lap. He dismounts and places her body on the ground by one of the dead guards. Going by her ashen skin colour and lack of shimmer, I'm fairly certain she's dead.

"What is this?" Slater curls a lip. "What are you playing at?"

"I needed the last of the corrupted guards taken out without arousing suspicion," Kenneth says. "And you need to be set free of your bounty. If our mother thinks you and your Zeek girlfriend are dead, we can all move forward without having to look over our shoulders." Noticing Slater's disgust, he adds, "Don't worry, Slate. I didn't kill this Zeek; she was found a couple of days ago by one of the guards."

"If you wanted the guards killed, you could have asked us. You didn't have to set us up. We could've been killed." Slater glances between the tranquillised guards. "And what's with these ones? If you wanted the guards 'taken out', then why'd you shoot them with darts?"

"These three guards were told to stand back in case of a trap, but the truth of the matter is I wanted them spared. They are decent guards, and I needed witnesses to report what they saw here tonight. Our mother must be made to believe, beyond a doubt, that these bodies." He points to where the dead guard and Pastel lie. "Belong to you and your 'slave'."

Sylus plucks the darts from the tranquillised guards' bodies, disappears, and then returns with a sash and blade, which I'm guessing was Slater's. He lifts the dead guard's head and slings the sash around him.

"If you're using Grant as my body-substitute, you'll have a guard and a Zeek—" Slater nods to me "—unaccounted for."

"These guards were tranquillised before you took your fatal blow on Grant, and Sylus and Sienna saw Grant chasing a Purple towards the border on horsenback."

"Clever, but you forgot about something. The dead Zeek isn't pregnant."

"As I'd tried telling you earlier, as far as our mother is concerned, Harlow's babies were removed and terminated the morning before you came back for her. She believes the twins' corpses were given to our family doctor to be tested and experimented on. Why do you think she hasn't sent guards out for her?"

Slater's face falls flat. "You still took a gamble with our lives."

"It was a calculated gamble. You took out ten guards on your own the afternoon Harlow was caught, and your new girlfriend—" he nods to me. "—wasn't supposed to come, but I figured she could handle herself. She killed Raven's guards simultaneously in two slices. These guards didn't stand a chance."

"It was still a gamble."

Sylus tosses Kenneth a pack, which he then hands over to Slater. "A gamble that paid off."

"What's this?"

"It's enough to get you settled elsewhere, wherever that may be."

"What about ink?" I ask.

Slater's back straightens and his eyes flick to mine in question. "What about ink?"

I turn my gaze on Kenneth. "We want two jars of ink."

His answer is a flat, firm, "No."

I wordlessly step away and kneel by one of the tranquillised guards, pressing the tip of my blade to his chest between his ribs. "We want two jars of ink, or this guard doesn't wake up."

"Saxon is an honourable guard with a wife and child on the way. If you kill him, you'll be killing an innocent."

"Innocent?" I laugh. "Only moments ago, Saxon tried roasting me with a fireball, so I'm afraid your argument carries very little weight. Get us the ink and nobody else has to die. I only want two small jars, it's not a big ask."

47

FEELING USED

-SLATER-

"What do you want the ink for?" I ask, even though I know the answer.

"What does it matter?"

"Your new girlfriend is a force to be reckoned with." Kenneth says to me in Vallon. "You'd better watch yourself because if that girl goes red, you'll only have to step out of line once and it'll be the end of you. She's the most lethal Zeek I've ever come across."

I cut him an irritated glance. "Yes, I know."

"I'll get her the two jars, but that's it. Neither of you are to come back for more in the future, am I understood?"

"Loud and clear," I reply through gritted teeth.

Zannah's little surprise stunt has me burning up on the inside as well as out. "Any chance you can add a pair of shorts to that list? I'm dying in this suit."

He nods before returning his focus to Zannah and switching back to Zeek. "Put your blade down, there's no need for any more violence. Stay put. I'll get you the ink."

Kenneth and Sylus take off on their horsens, leaving us alone with Kiyra and the scattered bodies of the fallen guards. Zannah and I stand guard, waiting on edge for another surprise attack which never comes.

When Kenneth returns, he tosses me another bag. It's soft, light, and hopefully filled with shorts. "All rescues are safely across the border now." He dismounts and hands the jars to Zannah personally. "This ink isn't a toy. Use it wisely and once you're a Red, try not to kill anyone, especially my brother. These are the only two jars you'll *ever* receive from me. Don't waste them and don't make me regret my decision."

She takes the jars and slips them into her pants pocket, nodding in response.

"Oh, and tell Jax and his crew to be at the border by nine for the meeting tomorrow evening. My mother doesn't like to be kept waiting, so I insist they arrive on time. I don't want any trouble."

Sylus moves the tranquillised guards' bodies back, while Kenneth tips an accelerant over the dead guard and Zeek. We all step back as he hurls a fireball at their bodies, setting them ablaze. *Alex and Ruby are dead—finished.* It's time for me to let go once and for all.

"You three had best get going before you're spotted," Kenneth says, and helps Kiyra up onto his horsen. "Leave the horsens free by the border. It'll corroborate our story."

"What about the border guards? How do you propose we get past them?" I ask.

"The border guards are napping, so you'll have a free run and nothing to fear. Now go live your best life and never return."

"If this is legit, then I want to thank you. However, if this is a trap, let the words 'Brenn in der Hölle' be the last you ever hear from me."

An amused smile curls Kenneth's lips. "I wish you well, little brother."

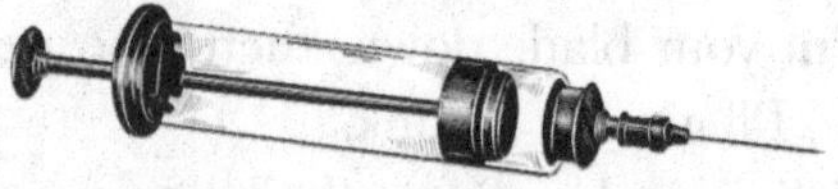

We return to the Spring border without any trouble and leave the horsens loose as Kenneth ordered. Hot and grouchy, I quickly duck behind a tree and shuck off my hunting suit in exchange for a pair of shorts. It's lightly drizzling, which is an instant relief to my sore sweltering skin. I draw in a deep breath taking in the smell of wet earth and mulch. *This is my new home now.*

Zannah tries speaking to me when I re-emerge, but I'm too pissed off to respond so she resorts to speaking to Kiyra instead.

I'm afraid the only reason Zannah has been playing nice with me these past few days is so she could get her hands on some vertic switz ink.

I'm such an idiot. Here I was thinking that she was looking out for me because she actually cared about me. *She was using me.*

Oscar is waiting beside a large tree root, blade out and ready. He stands when he sees us, dripping from the rain.

"What happened to you two?" He asks, his gaze cutting between Zannah and me. "And who's this?"

"*This* is Kiyra," Kiyra answers.

"We got held up," Zannah says, playing it down. "Where are the others?"

"Woody has taken the Pastels back to the village where it's safe."

Despite the wide space, Zannah deliberately shoulders past him. "Well in that case, let's get moving."

It's Zadok's longest, *most awkward* walk back. Not to mention the closer we get to the village, the heavier the rain gets and the further the sun falls. Zannah and Oscar converse with Kiyra along the way, and my insides knot as she shares the horrendous experiences she'd been made to face in Summer. Oscar's eyes flick in my direction every now and then, and he curls a lip at me, like it's my fault. I resent it, especially when Kiyra is referring to Kenneth like he's some kind of hero. Admittedly, Kenneth isn't the ruthless Vallon I'd thought he was. I'm confused about how I feel about him now. I've spent so long hating on him, believing the worst of him, that it's hard to let those feelings go. I loved Lucas despite the vile things he did because I'd seen the hell he'd been though, and I knew he had a mental condition, but I'd never felt any brotherly love for Kenneth, because he'd hurt and killed vulnerable Zeeks in cold-blooded calculation. I was wrong. He saved them, and he saved me. *I'm the lesser brother.*

When we get to the fence, the Hazel on guard tells me the Pastels have all been divided and taken in by willing Drake families who have offered to give them food, shelter, and a bed for the night. He eyes Kiyra carefully and says, "They had trouble placing the last Red, so you may want to ask Woody what to do with this one."

Switching to Zeek so he'll understand, I tell Oscar to take Kiyra to his hut and get someone to round up Woody for her, before stalking towards the fields without saying anything to Zannah.

Zannah stays to discuss something with Oscar, and it isn't until I hit the fields—metres from the mattress—that I hear the sloshing of her footsteps chasing after me on the wet grass. "Where are you going?"

"Where do you think?" My tone is clipped, sharp.

"The mattress will be soaking."

"Then don't join me."

"Hey!" She tries to jerk me around, but I shrug her off. "Hey!" She tries again and this time I spin to face her, my whole-body pulsating with anger.

"WHAT?"

She backs up a step. "What's your problem?"

"You're my problem. This whole place is my problem."

"Screw you!" She shoves me hard, hurting my wounds. "I don't deserve that. I've been far kinder to you than I should've been given the circumstances." Her teeth mesh. "The day you showed up here

—cut to smithereens and begging for our help—I could've killed you, but I didn't. I fed you and tended to your wounds. The next day when we rescued Harlow, you were a pathetic blubbering mess. I could've left you in Summer to rot, but I didn't. I dragged your arse the whole way back to the Zeek village, where I cleaned you back up *again* and showed you support. I gave you my mattress, and I've kept you company for the past few nights so you wouldn't feel ostracised and alone. Frost, I even brought your children out to see you this morning, which was completely out of character for me, and most definitely out of my comfort zone."

I couldn't tell, I think sarcastically. Holding my children is the only time I've ever seen her look afraid.

"You didn't do those things because you care about me. You kept me close for selfish reasons. You used me to get your hands on the vertic switz ink. You want to be a Red and have the ultimate power."

"I didn't need you to get me the ink, I got it without your help! And so what if I want the ultimate power? It's not a crime. I'm a warrior and warriors are meant to be powerful. Anyway, how come you were willing to share your power with Harlow, but not with me? That's double standards."

"Harlow was weak and had Zeeks trying to kill her. She needed it, you don't. You're already lethal enough without adding two jars worth of ink to your body."

She plucks one of the jars out of her pocket and forces it into my hand, rough with anger. "I got the second jar for your kids. And I plan on sharing the first one with Boshell and Tatum, so don't presume to know who I am and what I'm about, because you don't know me at all. I might be lethal and have selfish wants and needs, but I'm kind and generous to those I care about." Her eyes lift to meet mine, burning with anger and—surprisingly—a hint of desire. "I've been kind to you because I feel something for you, you idiot. I know I shouldn't, but I do."

My anger shatters and falls away, leaving me with a new feeling of appreciation and warmth. *She does care.*

Desperate to feel wanted, I wrap my arms around her waist,

and pull her to me, planting a hungry kiss on her lips. She flinches a moment and then responds with unleashed passion and force. Her kisses are hot, wild, and nothing at all like Ruby's or Harlow's. She's in charge. My hand glides up her waist and tangles in the loose wisps of hair falling from her tousled braid, drawing her body hard against mine. Despite the cool rain beating down on our bodies, the heat between us pops and sizzles. I lift her up and she clamps her legs around me, allowing me to carry her to the mattress, and lower her down with a splash. I hover above her face, admiring her for a moment. She is beautiful, fiery, fierce, and someone I could easily fall for if I allow myself to let go of Ruby/Harlow. As I lower myself to keep kissing her, I feel a sharp jab against my abdomen and automatically pull back. I retreat further when I notice the silver pocketknife glinting in her hand—blinking at the sight of it.

"What the fuck, Zannah? You give me the green light, then you pull a knife on me. What the hell is wrong with you?"

"I don't know what you mean by 'the green light', but I'm not your rebound."

"I'm sorry, I thought you were enjoying the moment. You were responding as if you were. If you wanted me to stop, you could have told me. You didn't need to pull a knife on me. And for the record, I wasn't using you as my rebound. I feel something for you too."

"But you're still not over Harlow. I can see it in your eyes, and you're emotional about Raven's death."

"So..." I retort. "You're still not over Jax. I can tell by the way you act around him, and I'm pretty sure there's more intimate history between you and that Oscar guy than you're letting on. He looks at you like you're the one who got away, not to mention, he's been eyeballing me the whole time I've been here."

"Oscar is a womaniser, and Jax was never mine to get over."

"Well, Raven is gone forever—and as it turns out—Harlow was never truly mine either, so our situations aren't that dissimilar."

"You and Harlow have kids together; it's totally different."

My spine straightens. I hadn't expected Zannah to consider this as an issue. Jax doesn't seem to have a problem taking on Harlow with the twins. He's there for my children more than I am. He'll probably hear the word "Dad" before I do.

"So, Harlow and I have kids, that's no reason to pull a knife on me. A simple 'back off' or 'no' would have sufficed."

She sits up and lowers the knife. "I'm not saying *no* indefinitely. I'm saying if you want to be with me, prove it; and if you want to sleep with me, you need to earn it. I want you to treat me with respect."

The tension eases from my shoulders. "I can appreciate that, but what about the twins?"

She frowns. "What about them?"

"Are you willing to take me on in the future, knowing I have a set of twins to Harlow? You don't seem very kid friendly, no offence."

"As long as you take care of the nappies and nurse them when they're squawking, there's no issue. It'll save you pestering me to have any."

Her answer isn't exactly reassuring. "But you will have something to do with them, won't you? You will grow to love them?"

"Of course I will, but they don't need a second mother. Harlow is their mother. I'll be their friend, and when they get older, I'll teach them how to fight."

I huff out a laugh. "I'm sure you will."

She reaches for me, and I flinch, worried she might stick me with some other weapon she has hidden on her.

"Relax." Her hands slide around me, sending goosebumps across my skin. "I'm prepared to start something between us, but I need you to move much slower. I want you to be thinking about me, and only me, before we take things any further."

I consider pointing out that she was the one moving hard and fast just now but think better of it. After all, everything she's pointed out is true. I'm not entirely over Ruby/Harlow, and I am upset about Raven's fate.

Zannah's lips brush my cheek and then she stands, extending her hand to me. "Come on, let's go."

I take her hand but don't budge. "Go where?"

"To the hut, it's too wet out here."

I shake my head. "I'd rather be cold and drenched than be anywhere near Harlow and Jax."

"I don't live in the same hut as Harlow and Jax." Her words are biting. "And if you want to start something with me, you'll need to get over seeing them together or else we're not going to work. We all live on top of each other here, so we need to keep things friendly."

48

UNEXPECTED

-HARLOW-

$\mathcal{I}$'m sitting on a cushioned chair chatting to Tatum, when Zannah enters the hut, hand in hand with Slater. I do a double take, unable to hide my shock. A nauseating feeling stirs inside my stomach. I hadn't known they'd become *so* friendly. They're both completely drenched and dripping a pool of water all over the hardwood floor.

Minty and Zavier give an awkward "Hey" in unison as they continue preparing dinner.

Slater's whole frame stiffens when he sees me sitting here. He was supportive during the delivery of our twins because Jax forced him to be, but now that it's over, things are super prickily between us.

"Slater will be staying here with me tonight. Does anyone here have a problem with this?" Zannah asks. Her eyes encompass everyone in the room, eventually landing on me with a penetrating gaze. The look she's giving is practically daring me to protest, and it makes me squirm.

"This has nothing to do with me," I say. "I don't live here."

49

NEW HUT-MATES

-ZAVIER-

$\mathcal{H}$arlow's face turns whiter than snow as Zannah stares her down, deliberately trying to intimidate her.

"It's fine by me," I state, in an effort to alleviate the tension. Admittedly, I feel a little weird about Slater staying here too, but not for the same reasons as Harlow. I've spent my whole life being told "Beware of Vallons, especially Reds", and now here we are, inviting one into our home.

"Floss," I yell out, hoping she'll hear me. "Can you bring out some towels?"

Floss exits a moment later carrying two towels in her hand. She jolts, nearly dropping them, when she sees Zannah and Alex standing hand in hand in the doorway.

"Well, this is new." She rights herself and tosses them a towel each. "And may I say, much more believable."

"Slater's staying here with Zannah tonight," I say. "Are you okay with this?"

She shrugs with a smirk, then cuts a glance at Harlow. "Sure. He's not my ex."

Harlow's face tightens, but she doesn't retaliate.

"Knock it off, Floss," I warn.

Zannah wraps the towel around herself. "Do any of you have any spare blankets you could lend us to sleep on? My mattress is waterlogged in the field."

"You can always take Oscar's bed," Minty suggests. "He moved in with Destiny last night, and the rescues who were going to stay with us ended up being taken in by a Drake family. Jax thought it was better to keep them away from us as much as possible in case we accidentally slipped up and used our real names in front of them."

Zannah humfs and screws her nose up.

"Don't worry; the sheets are fresh," Minty adds.

"How many Zeeks are living in the hut next door now?" Zannah asks with a frown. "It must be packed beyond measure."

"Jax bought the other neighbouring hut." Harlow's voice comes out scratchy. "We moved in last night, and Acacia and Stavros moved in with us, although Acacia and Atohi are hiding out at Sonja's temporarily because Jax doesn't want it common knowledge that there's a Ruke living in the Drake village. He's worried if word gets back to Chief Waya, it could put their lives in danger and cause conflict between the races. We've also got a couple of rescue Zeeks staying with us temporarily." She clears her throat. "Talking about that, I should probably get going." Her eyes flick to Slater's, displaying a vast array of emotions. "Minty and Tatum have agreed to mind Axel and Lyla while the rescues are here so they're not seen, but being as you're staying, you might want to help them out."

"We will," he says, including Zannah in his answer, and Harlow's face blanches at his reply.

"I'll be back later on with a couple more bottles of expressed milk," Harlow says.

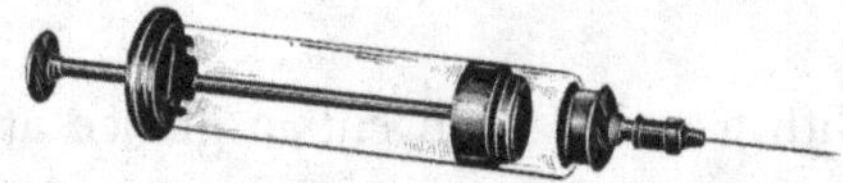

During dinner, Zannah recounts some of the day's events in Summer and Slater chips in occasionally adding to the story. I'm surprised at how comfortable he is in our company; I hadn't expected him to fit in so well. He responds well to Floss. They banter like old friends, which alters my opinion of him. While I prefer Jax for Harlow as a partner, he always brings out the worst in Floss.

Towards the end of the conversation, Zannah turns her attention to Tatum. "Before we left, I asked Kenneth for two jars of vertic switz ink. The one jar is for these two." She gestures towards the twins snuggled on a fluffy throw rug close by. "But I wanted to share the other jar with you and Boshell. Luna and Minty are already enhanced and are going to age slower and live longer, so I thought you'd both like to be enhanced too, otherwise you'll fall apart and die by fifty." Tatum's eyes widen at Zannah's comment, prompting her to add, "Well, you might get to sixty if you're lucky, although you'll be blind, decrepit and praying for death."

Talk about being brutally honest.

Minty's face is bright with excitement, but then Tatum says, "I really appreciate the offer, but I'd like to reward my dose to two others, if I may?"

"What?" Minty's expression falls flat. "No Tatum, she's offering it to you. Take it, please; if not for yourself, for me."

"Quinn is in terrible condition," Tatum argues. "And so is Beau. Half a dose each could mean a better life for them. Take Zavier for example. He would have been permanently crippled if it wasn't for the ink, and look at him now. You'd never believe he'd been savagely beaten and tortured."

"Hey," I cut in. "You're killing my pride here."

Zannah leads forward in her chair. "Who are Quinn and Beau?"

"Two of the rescues you guys brought back. They're staying with Jax and Harlow."

"Keep your dose," Zannah says. "The jar Slater gave Harlow was split five ways, so this jar can be split the same, small tattoos for all five Zeeks."

"This means there should be one dose left," Tatum says. "What about Koby, he's way too broken for a boy so young?"

"The fifth dose is mine."

Tatum's face turns crimson. "Oh, sorry, I didn't realise you were keeping a dose for yourself."

Minty, being less diplomatic, asks, "What do you need a dose of the ink for? You're a Purple; you're already strong."

"Call me selfish, I don't care. I sourced the jar, and I want at least one dose for myself. Quite frankly, I didn't have to share it at all. Think yourself lucky that I'm offering it to your girlfriend."

The conversation falls flat after this and we finish our meals off silently.

50

VERTIC SWITZ INK PROPOSITION

-ZANNAH-

Just as Slater and I settle on one of the cushioned chairs together to relax for the evening, Harlow arrives with the extra bottles of milk—and my brother in tow.

Cutting straight to his reason for accompanying her, he says, "I hear we have a new neighbour to welcome." He shoots me a look of warning, which I return with a look that says, "Mind your business and don't you dare say a word".

"How long will these rescues be staying in Spring?" I ask, deflecting his comment.

"Most of them will be leaving tomorrow. We want to make

room as we're hoping that the next lot will be coming back with us from the castle tomorrow. However, Dakari is allowing a certain number of them to stay by request. Some are afraid to go back, and others are too ashamed to return as they are, battered and broken."

"What about the two staying with you?" I ask, standing to meet his gaze. "What have they decided?"

"They've put in a request to stay, but they are still currently undecided. Beau is ashamed of what he's become, but Quinn misses her family and would love the chance to see them again, even in her current state. They are going to let us know for sure in the morning." His eyes narrow in suspicion. "Why are you interested?"

"I have an offer I'd like to make them."

Stavros eyes spark with curiosity. "What's the offer?"

"I've sourced some ink I'd like to share with them," I say. "And by the sounds of it I'm running low on time. Go and get Jax to dig out some needles from his medical stash. Slater, Tatum, and I will stop by next door and grab Boshell. I've got a dose with his name on it too."

"Do me a favour—when you go next door, don't take *him* inside." My brother tilts his head towards Slater and Slater curls a lip. "You know how Luna can be, and according to Boshell, she's struggling harder than ever at the moment after seeing the shocking state some of the rescues are in."

"I'm about to offer her 'should be boyfriend' ink, so I'm sure that'll help bring a smile to her dial. She'll get to keep him around for much longer if he's a Red."

"Regardless don't—"

"I won't, okay! I have no desire to cause trouble. I'm attempting to do something nice. Now hurry up and do as I've said, because you're starting to annoy me."

Furthering my annoyance, Stavros turns to Slater and says, "I don't mind you coming to our place, but I don't want any trouble. If you're not happy with something you see, then leave. Don't start anything or it won't end well."

Slaters eyes flash with burning resentment. "I'm not coming."

"Yes, you are," I urge. "Harlow's chosen to be with Jax. Accept it and cut your losses. You have children to share, and we all live in the same village, so it will be much easier if we can all get along."

Stavros steps between us, blocking Slater from my view. "If he doesn't want to come don't push him."

"Stay out of it, Stavros!" I warn.

Slater jumps to his feet. "Enough!" He moves around Stavros to stand at my side. "If Zannah wants me to come, I'll come."

"I think Minty and I should come too," Zavier chimes in. "We can assure Beau and Quinn that the red ink is safe to use."

Floss folds her arms over her chest and scowls at him. "Oh, yes, that's a wonderful idea. Everyone should go to Jax and Harlow's hut, and leave the pathetic Magenta behind. She's of no value to anyone. She's only a middle-class nobody."

"Don't be silly, of course you're coming with us." Zavier slings his arm around her stiff set shoulders. "I think we should all go."

"Brilliant!" I slant my eyes at Stavros. "See, we're all coming. Now run along and tell Jax to get those medical supplies ready. Chop, chop."

51

SIMPLE INGREDIENTS
-HARLOW-

Slater stays with our twins while Zannah heads to the neighbouring hut to speak to Boshell. She said she'd bring Will and Daisy back to watch over our sleeping babies. Now that they're capable, Will and Daisy love to help out, especially when it comes to the twins. They must feel the twin connection.

Zavier and Floss follow Stavros and me to our new hut. The rain has stopped for now, but the ground is still squelchy under my boots. Sphinx, Rebel, and Lucy are a mess. Their coats are covered in a layer of brown mud from racing through the puddles. For once, I'm thankful that they sleep under our hut, not in it.

Zavier hastens his steps to meet my pace and Floss hurries alongside him, curling her arm around him possessively, proving to me that Zavier's hers. *She really needs to get over it and stop seeing me as a threat.*

"You kept quiet throughout Zannah's big announcement about the ink," Zavier says. "Are you okay?"

"I'm glad Zannah has ink to share. I just wish she had enough ink to share with all the rescues."

"I'm sure seeing her hand-in-hand with Slater earlier this evening, must've burnt," he adds with a sympathetic glance. "Do you want to talk about it?"

Seeing Zannah with Slater did pinch, but more because I know how much Zannah detests me. Regardless, I say, "There's nothing to talk about. I'm happy with Jax, so it's only fair that Slater finds happiness too." *I secretly wish he'd find happiness with someone other than Zannah, but I'm not about to say so, especially in front of Stavros.*

Floss glances across Zavier to look at me. "You have to admit, Slater is better suited to Zannah."

"Floss!"

"It's okay, Zavier," I assure him. "Like I said, I'm fine with it."

"He'd better not hurt her," Stavros bites.

Floss laughs. "I think your sister is every bit as dangerous as he is. I'm sure if he hurts her, he'll pay for it two-fold, especially if she's going red."

"What?" Stavros stops in his tracks. "Zannah's going red?"

"*Yeah…*" Floss confirms. "So good luck sparring with her during our training sessions from here on in. She's likely to snap you in half."

"Yikes." Stavros exhales a breath, gazes skyward and exclaims, "Stars, help us all."

Once inside our hut, Stavros enlightens Jax about Zannah, the ink, and what her plans are. I also hear him whisper about Slater and Zannah appearing to be an item now.

I keep my face angled away as they speak. I don't want Jax thinking I'm listening in because I'm jealous—*I'm not.* I just feel weird about it.

Stavros goes in to see Beau and Quinn and guides them out to the common area, telling them his sister Zoe—her alias name—has an interesting offer she'd like to put forward. Jax digs into his bag of medical supplies, placing syringes and needles out on the bench.

The others arrive soon after Beau and Quinn are comfortably seated. Slater enters, shoots Jax a dirty look, and then positions himself as far away from him as possible. Boshell enters close behind and glances about curiously while greeting us all in a cautious friendly manner. He mustn't've been told about what's happening yet.

Once everyone, bar Slater, are closely congregated, Zannah lets it rip about injecting Beau, Quinn, and Boshell with the vertic switz ink. She arrogantly skips the reassuring build up about how the ink will have positive effects on the user's bodies, and I can tell by Beau and Quinn's wide, terrified gazes they're ready to run screaming. They may have been living with Peaches who'd been injected by the amber ink, but this doesn't mean that they fully understand the benefits associated with the ink, and the only red Zeeks they've met, besides me, are those who'd fallen pregnant to a Vallon.

"May I cut in?" I step forward to address Beau and Quinn directly. "Before you freak out, let me show you something, and then I'll explain how the ink works." I turn to Slater. "Unless you want to?"

He shakes his head.

I give them the same spiel Slater gave me about the tattoo versus injection, show them my tattoo, and tell them how much stronger I feel since getting it. Minty and Zavier share their story too—only slightly altered—telling them how Zavier would have died without the help of the ink. Boshell joins in, sharing his story about his kids and how the ink has dramatically changed their lives for the better.

"So, are you interested in receiving a dose or what?" Zannah asks, still as blunt as ever. "You can choose to be tattooed or injected, whatever method you'd prefer."

They discuss the offer between themselves for a few minutes, and I'm astonished when they choose being injected with the ink, over getting the tattoos.

"Are you sure?" I ask.

They share a look, squeeze each other's hands and nod in unison. "We're sure," Quinn says. "No offence, but we wouldn't like to turn out as red as you, nor do we want the constant glowing reminder of the Reds marked on our skin. The Oranges and Amber were kind to us, but besides Kenneth and him—" she does a quick eye flick towards Slater "—all the other Reds we came across were pure evil."

"Also, this way we can return to our families tomorrow already looking strong and healthy," Beau adds.

I glance over at Zavier and Minty. "How much does it hurt?"

Zavier shrugs. "I don't really remember. I was pretty out of it by the time I received my dose."

"To be honest, it was actually quite painful, but fortunately the feeling didn't last very long," Minty shares.

"We injected them with morphine at the same time," Jax says. "Perhaps we should do the same with these two. Sylvie left me a couple of vials in case of an emergency."

"What option are you two going with?" Zannah asks Tatum and Boshell.

Tatum grimaces, spares an apologetic look at Minty and then says, "I might hold off one more day. I want to see what state the next lot of rescues come back in. My pigments are reasonably good for a Pastel; I'm not far off from being a Magenta. I'd hate a dose being wasted on me if there's another poor soul who needs it more."

"I'll wait too, just in case," Boshell says, although it looks as if it hurts him to say it.

"They raise a good point, wouldn't you say Zoe?" Stavros glares in Zannah's direction. "We should wait and use the ink on those who need it most."

"I sourced the ink, so I'm getting a dose no matter what. If you want the ink spread further, you source a jar."

"You're going red?" Jax doesn't hide his shock.

While he, Zannah and Stavros continue to debate the matter further, I wander over to Slater. His fists bunch when he sees me coming, and he looks like he wants to back away, but he stays put.

"How exactly is the vertic switz ink made?" I ask.

Zannah pauses mid argument with Stavros, and jerks around to listen in.

Slater glances about cautiously before answering my question. "They mix the dust of our ancestors with the blood of our family members, add a crushed voltz, and then blast the ingredients with the power of fire."

"That's it?"

"Pretty much."

"What would happen if we used only your blood, a crushed voltz and the power of fire. Do you think it would do anything?"

His top teeth graze his lower lip as he considers the idea. "I wouldn't know."

"Would you be willing to test the idea?"

"I didn't bring any voltz with me."

"Jax and I still have the two you gave my father," I say, avoiding Saul's name, "to help bring me back."

Zannah's brows shoot up. "You did what?" Before Slater can respond, she whirls on Jax. "Another little secret you forgot to include me in on, huh? So, Saul knew about Sla..." Stavros gives her a sharp look, and she stops short of using our actual names. "These two?" Her lips purse like she's tasted something sour. "That would've been good to know at the time being as I'm supposed to be a part of your trusted warrior circle."

Jax sighs in exasperation. "The man doesn't know what he knows, and don't take it personally, Zoe. I didn't share this information with anyone."

"What's your verdict?" I ask, stealing Slater's attention back to me. "Will you allow us to use your blood to test the idea?"

He shrugs, nonchalant, his eyes evading mine. "Fine. But I can't promise anything, and you won't know for sure if it's effective unless you have guinea pigs who will allow you to trial it on them."

Tatum raises a hand. "If 'guinea pig' means a test subject, then I volunteer. You can trial the ink on me."

"What?" Minty whacks her hand down. "No. Are you crazy? You should take the legit ink Zoe's offering. She wants you to have it. I want you to have it. Who knows what side effects the new ink will have on your body? It might make you sick—*or worse.*"

"I doubt it'll do any damage," I say. "It'll have all the same ingredients as the ink we used, only it'll be minus a few. If anything, I imagine it'll just be less effective."

Minty crosses her arms over her chest. "You imagine, but you don't know for sure!"

Jax walks over to join us, and I feel Slater's inner tension rise in waves. "What do you think would happen if we mixed my blood with a crushed zoft and then freeze it with winter magic?"

Slater cuts him a glare. "How the hell should I know?"

"Hey, that's not a bad idea." Stavros' eyes spark, keen with excitement. "Imagine if we could give all Zeeks the health and power of Purples. Pastels would finally be strong enough to stand up for themselves."

"And it would make breaking down the colour system a whole lot easier," Oscar adds.

Slater sneers. "I think you're going to need a few more guinea pigs to put their hands up if you're planning on testing this theory."

"I would do it," Boshell says. "But I'm worried if something happens to me, my kids will be left without a father."

I sympathise with his position.

Beau puts his hand up. "If you are able to create the purple ink, and you think it will work, I'll be your test subject." He curls an arm around Quinn and squishes her to him. "I have nothing to lose besides Quinn, and I'd rather be a Purple than a Red, even if it was a Purple who sent me to Summer in the first place. At least if I'm Purple in the caves, I won't stand out like a sore thumb."

"Make that both of us," Quinn agrees. "My family aren't expecting me. If I come back with the other rescues, it will be a bonus to them, and if not, they'll assume I died in Summer like many of the other Pastels."

Jax leaves the common area and returns a few moments later carrying two zofts in one hand and two voltz in the other. He places them on the bench and beckons Slater over. "Come and sit down so I can take your blood."

Slater doesn't budge. "I want Zoe to do it."

"You'd best let him do it," Zannah says. "I'm not medically trained."

"Zoe," Jax calls, eyeing the crystals. "Why don't you and your brother see what you can do about getting these things crushed."

Zannah picks up a zoft and a voltz in each hand, twirling them at eye level. "I wonder what would happen if we mixed them together?"

I humf. *Trust Zannah to want to turn this experiment on its head.*

"We don't even know if they'll work singularly—never mind mixing them," Jax replies, echoing my thoughts. "Let's save your insane idea for another day, shall we?"

Stavros picks up the remaining two. "How are we supposed to crush them without bits of crystal flying everywhere?"

I step forward. "I have an idea. Sis, can you please pass me that," I say, pointing to the bucket on the floor next to Floss.

I take it from her, place it on the bench, and then pluck the zoft from Stavros' hand, holding it above the brim.

I close my eyes and take a deep breath, forcing myself to concentrate. I haven't got full control of my power yet, but Jax has explained that I need to focus and summon the elements around me.

I draw in the heat and moisture from the air and send that energy back out through my hands. My arms glow white, and a loud zap fills the room as the crystal explodes and crumbles into fine pieces, settling at the bottom of the bucket. I cough as a glow of purple dust flies in my face and Jax comes rushing over to make sure I'm okay.

I clutch my lower abdomen. The stitches tug painfully with the movement.

"That's super cool—yet totally unfair," Floss says with a prickly edge. "I want that power."

"So do I," Zannah seconds. She fans the haze of purple dust glittering in the air and then glances at the glowing mess settling on the floor. "I'm sure I'd be able to handle it better."

I roll my eyes.

"Is there going to be any zoft dust left to use for the ink?" she taunts.

"There's still heaps inside the bucket." I tip it diagonally to show her in defence. "Next time I'll cover the top."

"And perhaps you should do it outside," Stavros advises.

Minty, Mrs Squeaky Clean, goes straight for the broom to sweep up the mess.

Tatum moves a chair out of Minty's way, and says, "It's a shame the floor can't stay this way. It looks quite pretty."

Jax empties the crushed zoft into a metal mixing bowl and then hands the bucket back to me, along with the other zoft, covering the top with a tea towel. "You two," Jax says, nodding to Zavier and Floss, "can you go outside with her," he doesn't use my name, "while she zaps the next one. Make sure she's careful. I don't want her overexerting herself."

My next attempt goes much smoother, and when I'm done, Zavier takes the bucket inside to be emptied, leaving me alone with Floss.

Floss' hands fidget at her side and then she flexes them a few times before saying, "I know I've never said it, but I'm glad you're okay, and I'm enjoying being an aunt more than I'd thought."

I stare at her pinched face. "Then why does it hurt you so much to say it?"

"Because although I love you, I hate being your shadow. I feel like I hardly exist when you're around. Admittedly, Zavier has been trying really hard to make me feel special, but I still get the feeling he loves you more."

"Zavier loves me as his best friend, that's it. And as you can see, I'm happy with Jax, so you shouldn't keep treating me as though I'm a threat. I'd really love us to become close. Twins have a special bond; they're meant to be close."

Her open expression tells me she's considering the idea, but her internal defence mechanism must kick in, because to my disappointment she changes the subject. "If they're successful in making the purple ink, I'm thinking of putting my hand up for it," she says. "Although, I'm worried how Zavier will react. I know how much he hates Purples, but I'd prefer to go purple than red because I don't want us looking identical."

"I don't think Zavier holds the same hostility against Purples as he once did. You should speak to him about it."

"I could go for the mix if Zannah's able to talk Jax into it." She waggles her brows.

"*You could…*" The words drag off my tongue. I don't know that I want Floss or Zannah getting their hands on that mixture. I'm scared enough of Zannah going red, let alone mixed.

"I'd let Zannah trial it first, though," she continues, "and if she turns out deranged, then I'll just stick with the purple ink."

I laugh. "Nice."

Zavier returns with a fresh bucket and the two voltz. "Let's see if you can work your magic on these crystals too."

52

ADD A TOUCH OF MAGIC

-SLATER-

I sit across from Jax and force my mind elsewhere while he takes my blood. I'm not squeamish about the needle or blood itself, I'm squeamish about him. I've only agreed to do this out of curiosity. If we're able to make an ink that will benefit Pastels in need, then I'm all for it. I know what it's like to feel beaten, broken, and helpless. It was only as I got bigger and stronger as Alex that I could fight the adults off.

Zannah stands beside me, resting her hand on my shoulder. I can't tell if it's to support me or piss off Jax, but either way I like it there, and I hope Harlow sees it as well.

After taking my blood, Jax gets Stavros to assist him with taking his own, and Harlow, Floss and Zavier return with the bucket of crushed voltz.

Zannah glances inside the bucket. "Did they explode the same way?"

"Mostly." Harlow's hands glitter red, while the rest of her glitters purple due to her first crushing fiasco.

She notices me looking, and I quickly turn my face away.

After Jax's blood is taken, he carefully empties the tube of crimson over the bowl of crushed zofts. "Here." He hands me the bowl with my blood and the crushed voltz in it. "Now for the next step."

"I believe the 'next step' is another outside job," Minty says, broom still in hand. I don't know her very well, but given what I've seen of her this evening, I get the feeling she's a control freak.

Zannah exits the hut with us, and a few of the others pile out behind, their faces wide and alight with anticipation.

"How long do I freeze it for?" Jax asks.

"Count to ten," I answer. "It's what we Vallons do."

I watch him blast his contents first. His extended hands flash bright purple and prickle with frost. The purple glow extends up his forearms as he continues blasting, while frost crackles down from his hands coating the entire bowl.

At the count of ten he pulls back, and as the frost dissolves we are left staring at iridescent purple ink.

"It worked," Zannah says, eyes enlarged.

"Don't get too excited yet," Jax warns. "We still don't know how effective it will be."

I blast my contents next, and everyone watches with the same intensity.

Once I'm done, Zannah bounces on her legs, face eager. "How long until we can trial them?"

"As soon as they've returned to room temperature."

53

AN HOUR TO KILL

-ZAVIER-

*A*fter both sets of ink have been made, Jax tells us all to meet back at his hut in an hour.

As soon as we get home, Floss lures me into our room, and I grin, believing it's going to be an hour well spent. But instead, she drops a bomb on me, telling me she wants to put her hand up for the purple ink trial.

I no longer resent all Purples. I've learnt to accept Zeeks for how they treat me, but it's the fear of adverse side effects that's got me worried. We have no idea exactly what this ink will do. It's a risk, and I make sure to point this out to her.

Minty had argued this exact point with Tatum the whole way back. She's livid with Tatum for putting her hand up and for not accepting the legit ink Zannah is offering.

Floss slumps, disappointed by my response, so I slip my hands around her waist and draw her to me for a hug. "There's no need for you to change," I assure her. "I like you the way you are."

"The problem is I don't like who I am." She pulls back to look me firmly in the eyes. "I hate being Magenta."

"Why?"

She launches into an explanation about middle-class syndrome and how she absolutely detests being the same colour as her parents. She also points out how she hates being the only Magenta warrior and that she's had to work twice as hard as the others to achieve the same results.

I want to argue her points, put my foot down, and tell her "No", I don't want her to change. But I know if I don't support her on this, she'll spend the rest of her life resenting me for holding her back.

"Okay," I say begrudgingly. "If it's what you really want to do, then I'll support you."

Her jaw drops. "Seriously? You're not going to continue fighting me on this?"

Zavier of the past would've been horrified by the idea, but my opinion of Purples has changed for the better. I no longer think of them all as evil. Heck, I no longer think of Vallons as all evil. *How different my mindset has become.*

"I'm worried, and I'd prefer you *not* to do it. But at the end of the day, I want you to be happy, and I will love you regardless of what colour you are."

Her hands slide up my shirt, tickling my skin, and she nibbles seductively on her lower lip. "Well… If we're not going to waste the next hour arguing like Tatum and Minty, I can think of a much better way to spend our time."

My brows bounce skyward. "You must have read my mind."

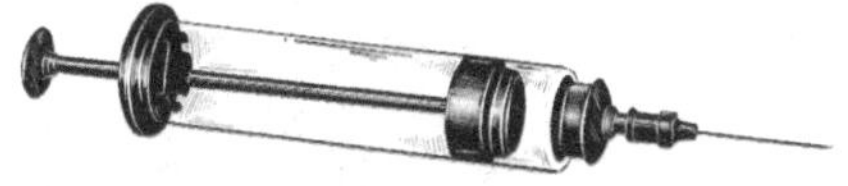

While Floss and I enjoyed killing time together, Minty and Tatum look far worse for the hour shared. We could hear them arguing in the room next to ours the whole time, but we'd tried not to let it ruin the mood. All I kept thinking was, *thank frost it isn't us for a change!*

By the time we get back to Harlow and Jax's hut, it's packed. Boshell has brought Luna and Koby, and Oscar and Destiny are standing with Woody and two Pastels I've never met before. The Pastels are both decrepit, so I'm guessing they're here to volunteer for the ink trial.

INK TRIAL

-JAX-

When Zannah and Slater arrive back at the hut, I pull Slater aside to speak with him. "The only way we're going to know—immediately—if these inks truly work, is if we inject the test subjects, right?"

"Right." Slater's posture is stiff, and his response is clipped, but he keeps himself in check.

"What do you think?" I probe further. "Do you believe either of the inks will be detrimental?"

His eyes slit. "Are you asking me this so that if shit goes down, you can turn around and pin the blame on me?"

Here we go.

"No." My voice rings firm. "I'm asking you because I'm interested in your opinion."

"I don't know what the purple ink will do, but I doubt that either of the inks are deadly. Like Harlow said, it's more likely they'll be less effective without the added ingredients of our ancestors than cause anyone harm."

His answer is conjecture, but he seems certain enough that the inks won't do the Pastels harm, which is the most reassurance I'm going to get. The Pastels who've volunteered for the injections have been told there are risks involved, yet they are still ready and willing to go ahead, so I swallow my doubts and prepare two syringes of purple ink, mixed with morphine.

"Are you sure you want to go through with this?" I double check with Beau, who's bravely offered to go first.

Beau nods, and I ask him to roll up his sleeve and hold still as I inject the needle's contents. His reaction is far more volatile than I'd anticipated, and I call for everyone watching to stand back. He throws himself on the floor and thrashes around wildly, screaming blue murder.

Quinn reaches for him, but I take hold of her hands, stopping her from getting too close. "It's not safe to touch him in this state," I say.

The worry in her eyes is agonising, but eventually Beau settles, slumping to the floor and I release her hands, allowing her to comfort him.

Multiple gasps fill the hut and Slater gives a low whistle at the dramatic change in Beau's body shape. His physique is fuller, no longer decrepit. His hair and shimmer remain pink, only a much deeper shade.

"It worked!" Zannah says and hoorahs. "I can't believe it."

"I thought he'd turn purple?" Oscar says, scratching his head in confusion.

"I'd presumed the same thing," Stavros replies.

"His physique has changed for the better," I say. "And that's what matters most."

After witnessing Beau's violent reaction, I remove the chairs and replace them with propped cushions instead, keeping the procedure to ground level. The last thing I want is for any of these test subjects to topple from their chair and break their neck. Quinn looks hesitant about being next up, however, Beau assures her he's fine and she will be too, so she keeps a brave face and holds still for the injection. Her reaction is just as violent and agonising to watch, but when she settles the results are akin, darker colouring and a stronger, fuller figure.

Stavros and Oscar help them up and escort them to their beds, making room for the next two decrepit Pastels. They've chosen to go with the purple ink as well, and the process is much the same with a similar outcome, only these two have resulted in a deeper colour, most likely because they were pinker than the other Pastels to begin with.

Stavros has kindly offered his bed for them to rest, so while they're being escorted away, I ask Tatum and Koby to step up to the plate.

Koby says he wants to go red like Will and Daisy. When Koby first arrived in Spring, he was keen to leave for Winter. He wanted *desperately* to see the ice caves his mother had always spoken about. But after spending some time with the twins, he's since changed his mind and has requested to stay. Boshell has taken him under his wing, treating him like an adopted son—similar to what Lexan did for Zavier.

Tatum says she doesn't mind what colour she goes, but as I fill a syringe with red ink, Minty rushes forward and tells me to wait.

"If you're not going to take the legit red ink, then you should probably use the purple," she says to Tatum. "You work with children, and some of them might find you too scary to be around as a Red."

"She raises a good point," I say in agreement, so Tatum heeds our advice and opts for the purple ink instead.

Boshell must've pushed aside all doubts about being a test subject and puts his hand up for the syringe of newly created red ink. "Don't waste it, I'll take it," he says. "This way you'll get to keep the ink you sourced for yourself," he tells Zannah, free of any mockery or contempt.

I notice Stavros roll his eyes and share a non-verbal look with Oscar that says it all.

Koby receives his injection and reacts as violently as we've come to expect, but Luna still panics, her motherly affection for him bringing out her protective side. I inject Boshell next, and while the immense agony he feels is written all over his face, he fights to say in control—probably more for Luna's sake than anything else. Their colouring deepens to a Pastel red, which is a shade lighter than Minty and Zavier's colouring. It seems the newly made red ink affects the pigments more prominently than the purple ink.

Harlow asks Oscar to help them to our room, and Luna assists without returning.

As I'm preparing a new syringe with the purple ink for Tatum, Floss pushes her way to the front.

"I want to be injected with the purple ink too."

I glance at Zavier before responding, asking him a silent question.

Zavier has a low opinion of Purples, and I can sympathise with his reasoning. What my brother did to his parents was despicable and cruel, and the way my mother and Electra tortured him, Floss, and Minty, was just as malicious.

Pastels have suffered greatly under my mother's rule, and I fully intend to make amends and fulfil my father's legacy. I'm grateful to Harlow for inspiring the idea of reconstructing the vertic switz ink, because this purple ink gives me hope. As Oscar said earlier, it will be easier to break down the colour system if Pastels are physically stronger and are capable of taking on the same tasks as Magentas and Purples. I can integrate them into the workplace without any restrictions.

"We've discussed it," Zavier says, making his way over. "And it's fine by me." He tugs Floss to him for a deep heartfelt kiss.

My eyes flick to Harlow, who is watching them kiss with a wistful expression, and I wonder, *is she thinking the same thing I am?* I can't wait for us to share a moment like this. I haven't initiated anything as yet, and neither has she. The timing hasn't been right, and the way I see it, her heart and body still need time to heal given all that she's been through. Besides, there's no need to rush things. My love for her runs deep, and I'm in this for the long haul. For now, I'm just happy to be able to hold her safely in my arms while we sleep.

Floss' reaction to the injection is just as I'd expected, ridiculously overdramatic with a lot of cursing and howling, whereas Tatum grits her teeth and strains to keep herself under control like Boshell.

"Tatum?" Minty's voice quavers. "Are you okay? Are you hurting?"

Tatum forces a toothy smile. "It's painful, but not nearly as bad as I'd expected it to be."

"Are you kidding me?" Floss balks.

Both girls seem much more with it than the others post-injection and interestingly, their colours have changed more dramatically. Tatum is now Magenta, and Floss is verging on Violet.

While Zavier and Minty take Floss and Tatum back home to rest, those of us remaining, congregate, discussing the possibility of taking the ink trials further if everyone wakes up feeling fine tomorrow, with no side effects.

A PLACE TO CALL HOME
-ZANNAH-

"The more rescues that we can inject before taking them back to the caves, the better," Stavros says. "Once the Pastels of the colony see how effective this ink is, and are assured it's safe to use, they'll all want to jump on board."

"Even if these test subjects do wake up feeling fine tomorrow, I'm still concerned about the long-term effects on their bodies." Jax says. "These inks are new to us; we can't guarantee they're completely safe."

"Nothing's completely safe," I butt in. "And even if there are some side effects down the road, being physically stronger and healthier beats being crippled and arthritic, and we all know it. What could be worse than living in constant pain all the time?"

Jax thinks this over and nods in agreement. "You're right, but the other problem is I have limited morphine left. I can get more nauclea latifolia roots from the forest—it's abundant with the trees—but they'll be less affective at keeping the pain at bay. Their reactions without the added morphine are likely to be more violent."

"It is what it is, and at least this way the Zeeks won't return home doped up," Stavros points out. "We'll head out into the forest at first light, and I'll help you dig up some more roots."

"I'll join you both," Woody offers.

Jax thanks them and tells the rest of us to meet back here at six tomorrow morning, adding, "We'll wait until we see the results of today's trial and then we can discuss our next move."

Once we've finished speaking as a group, Slater pulls Woody aside to discuss another matter. I'm curious what the "matter" is, but instead of prying, I use this free moment to tell Jax I won't be able to join him and the team on their mission to Summer tomorrow.

Afterwards, I peek into all the bedrooms to see how the test subjects are doing. I know I'll get the blame if this trial goes wrong, even though it was ultimately Harlow and Jax's idea to create the new ink.

Luna is keeping a sharp eye on Boshell and Koby, and says they're doing okay. However, I need to lean down closely to make sure the other four are still breathing.

When I get back to the common area, Stavros says that Slater told him—to tell me—he needs to do something with Woody, but he'll meet me back at my hut later on. I glance at my watch; it's already late. *Where could they possibly be going? Frost! I should've listened in.*

Jax and Oscar overhear, and Oscar casts me a judgy look. He opens his mouth to say something, and I thrust a palm out.

"Don't even think about it, Manwhore!"

Stavros sighs. "I know I've said it before, but please be careful."

I snort. "I'm fine. I know what I'm doing."

Even though I'm excited about where things are going with

Slater, my eyes linger on Jax, hoping to find a hint of jealousy. There's none. His face only shows concern—like I'm his little sister he cares for and is worried about. *That's it.*

I've always known where I stood with him, but I suppose deep down I'd secretly hoped he was a little attracted to me, even if he didn't fully realise it. *Nope. It's clear he has tunnel vision for Harlow.*

He must think I'm staring, waiting for his opinion, because he says, "If this is what you want, then I'm happy for you, but like Stavros says, be careful. Slater can be reckless and selfish."

"So can Zannah," Oscar points out.

"I'll see you all in the morning," I say, giving Oscar a hard shove, which knocks the wind out of him.

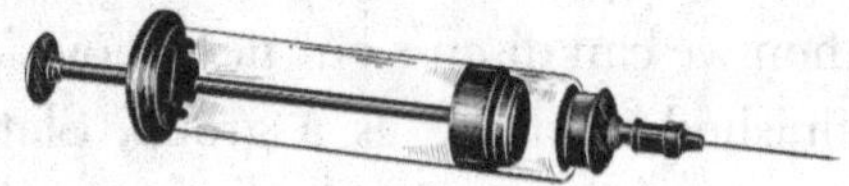

I'm lying on the hut floor, stretching, when Slater arrives an hour later, all smiles.

I sit up, frowning. "What's with the grin?"

He extends his hands out to me. "Come with me, I want to show you something."

Curious, I take his hand and allow him to pull me to my feet.

We walk for a while, passing several luminescent gardens along the way.

"Where are you taking me?" I ask, but he doesn't say.

Eventually, we stop in front of a medium sized hut, and Slater heads to the ladder. He stops mid climb to beckon me over. "Are you coming?"

"Whose place is it?"

"Mine. Ours, if you want?"

"What…?"

"I bought it with some of the jewels Kenneth gave me. I didn't want to spend the night sleeping in your ex's bed."

"Oscar is *not* my ex."

He reaches the deck, and spins to look down at me as I climb. "But you've been together, right?"

I hesitate long and hard before answering. I don't know how he's picked up on this when nobody else has. "It was only a onetime thing, and it was years ago. Tell anyone about it, and I'll deny it."

He offers his hand to pull me up the rest of the way, and even though I don't need it, I appreciate the gesture and take it.

"I'm not planning on telling anyone, I just wanted to hear you admit it. If we're going to start something, I want us to be honest with one another."

"I thought we'd already started something."

He grins in a way that makes his eyes glow brighter. "I'd kiss you right now if I wasn't so afraid of you stabbing me."

"Yet you're offering for me to move in with you. Do you think that's wise?" I raise a brow.

"Are you going to move in?" His expression falls dead serious. "I know it seems sudden, but we've been sharing a mattress for days now, and what's the difference between staying together here or anywhere else? We can still take things slow in other ways."

I really want this, but I'm nervous. I'm afraid he's never going to love me the same way he loved—maybe even still loves—Harlow. I'm not easily lovable; I've been told as much. And I've never had a real relationship, so I'm not used to letting others in. I'm afraid of falling for him and getting burnt. I've never been this vulnerable with anyone.

"Promise me I'm not just your rebound."

His brows crinkle. "We've already discussed this. You're not."

"I need you to promise me."

"I promise you're not my rebound. I'm still hurt over the way Harlow ended things, but like you've pointed out, it was Ruby I was in love with, not Harlow, and Alex is dead. It's time for me to move forward and start living as Slater." He steps closer and slides his hands over my hips. "I don't find myself constantly thinking about her like I used to. I find myself thinking about you. You're the one I want to move forward with. You're the one who's looked out for me and stood by me throughout this whole harrowing ordeal." A cheeky crooked smile curls his lips as he adds, "Even with all of your endless threats." He leans in, bringing his face to mine. "Not to mention, I think you're drop dead gorgeous."

"I do still have a knife on me," I warn.

"Screw it, I'll take my chances."

His lips meet mine, and I respond hot and hungrily. I've told him I want to take things slow because I want him to respect me, but slow isn't a speed I'm used to moving at, and restraint is certainly not my strong point.

Luckily, he's the one to break away. "I'll show you inside. It's pretty bare at the moment, but Woody helped me get a bed for tonight, and he said Sonja will help me round up some extra pieces of furniture tomorrow while you guys go on the next rescue mission."

"Actually, can I come and help choose?"

"Yeah, but I thought—"

"I told Jax I'm not coming. None of us know what the setup is going to be once we get to Summer or who's going to be present for the handover. I was worried if any of those same guards we fought outside the church saw me, it'd cause trouble."

"Good point. I'm glad you're not going, especially if I'm not. I'd much rather you come furniture shopping with me and Sonja."

He leads me through the candlelit hut, grinning excitedly. It's fairly average, but I make sure to act impressed. The fact that he bought it for us to live in together *as a couple* is what I find impressive, especially given we've literally only started dating today.

We park our butts on the bed when we're done, and he asks me if I'd like him to do my tattoo.

"I thought you were against me getting it."

"I don't mind so much now that I know how you feel about me. I'm hoping if we're dating, it means you're not going to keep threatening to kill me?" He says it like a question.

"For now, anyway," I tease.

His eyelids slant. "That's what I'm afraid of."

"Behave yourself, and I won't kill you."

He asks me what I want drawn and where, telling me no snowflakes or the letter J.

"I'm surprised you drew the J for her knowing what it represented."

"I don't actually know that the J is for Jax, although the idea did cross my mind at the time. My first thought was Josh, followed by Jax and then I decided it must be for her human sister Jade, but now I'm not so sure."

"And Josh is?"

"Her human boyfriend." His eyes flash with regret. "Anyway, let's not talk about it. I'd rather not know who she got the J for. It only makes me feel like more of an idiot."

I drop the subject, and after a long while of throwing tattoo ideas back and forth I say, "Draw flames licking up my arm. That way you'll know they represent you, and no one else."

"That's a bit more of a commitment than moving in together, wouldn't you say?"

"I'm committed to giving us a fair shot if you are."

He pulls out a needle he must've swiped from Jax, and by way of answer, he announces, "Flames it is."

CRUCIAL TIMES

-ZANNAH-

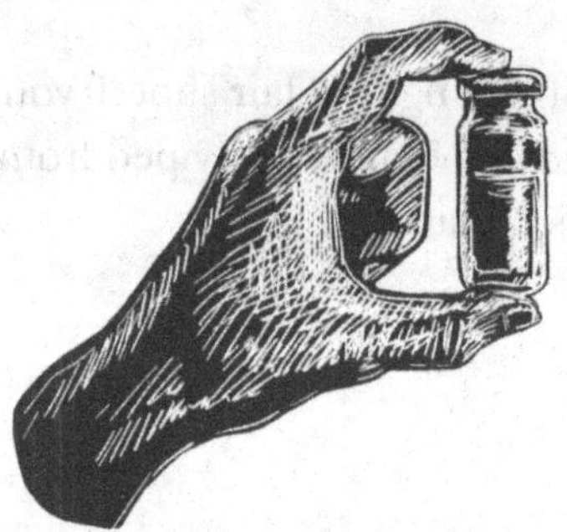

$\mathscr{I}$ wake up the next morning to Slater's arm slung across my waist and his warm body pressing into my back. I've never been snuggled all the way through the night before, and I've decided I rather like it.

I lift my arm to look at the tattoo he's given me. My skin burns like I've got real flames licking up my forearm—wrist to elbow—but I smile regardless, impressed by his mad skills.

The movement must wake him because he raises his arm too and twines his fingers around mine. "Does it hurt?"

"It feels a bit warm," I say, playing it down.

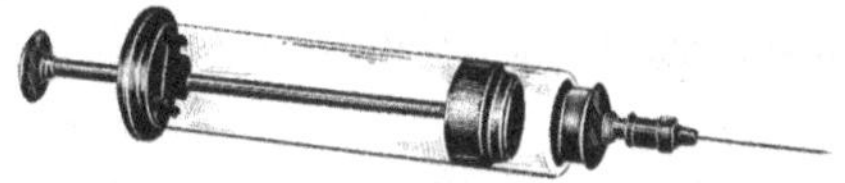

After freshening up, we leave for Jax's, stopping in at the village marketplace to get something to eat and drink along the way.

We're running late, so needless to say, everyone's already present when we arrive at the hut. The smile on Jax's face tells me that all test subjects have made it safely through the night.

"Thank the stars above," I utter in relief.

"It looks like someone's on fire this morning," Oscar says as I enter. His eyes trace over my forearm, and he sneers in disapproval.

Soon everyone is looking at my forearm, including Stavros, who shakes his head at me. I stick my tongue out in retaliation. I love my brother, but he's a self-righteous prick.

Jax looks at the tattoo too but gives no indication of how he feels about it before bringing up present matters. He doesn't look well. He's paler than usual, and when he points to the newly made batches of ink, I understand why. He's donated a lot of blood for this cause. Probably far more than he should've given he's heading to Summer later today.

"After a long discussion with Stavros and Woody, I've decided the best course of action would be to teach all of you how to correctly give an intravenous injection." He says, holding a needle out in front of him. "This way we can do injection rounds simultaneously in larger groups.

"I mean, let's face it," Stavros chimes in, "The more time these Pastels have to consider the idea, the more likely they are to pull out, especially when they see how violently their fellow Pastels react to the substance."

Jax runs us through a step-by-step example several times, using Stavros as his sample patient. He also verbally lists off the "dos" and "don'ts" and gets us to practice administrating fake injections on one another while he observes us.

Towards the end of his lesson, Sonja sticks her head in to say,

"Woody has rounded up all the Pastels and has them waiting on the field."

Jax gently places the pack filled with ink jars on his shoulders and tosses the other—much less delicate pack—to me.

I peek inside before swinging it on my back. It's filled to the brim with nauclea latifolia roots. "Wow, you really are a nauclea latifolia dealer these days," I tease.

Despite being tired, stressed and literally drained, this gets a laugh out of him. "That's only the half of it. You should see the secret stash in my closet."

A joke too? Wow. You can tell he's got Harlow back.

TAKING IT TO THE NEXT LEVEL

-JAX-

The field is abuzz when we arrive, full of curious Drakes and anxious Zeeks.

"Zannah," I call, commanding her attention. "Distribute the roots amongst the Pastels."

I'm glad when I overhear Slater offer to give her a hand.

Woody has the Pastels divided into two separate groups, those who are keen and eager for the injection, and those who are either red or peach already, scared, or not interested. There are only six pure Pastels in the opposed group, which changes to two after yesterday's test subjects speak with them, and they can see how strong and well they look. However, after witnessing the violent reactions of the first round of Pastels, one of them quickly returns.

Thankfully, Stavros' test subject recovers quickly and jumps to her feet, shouting to the other rescues with exhilaration, "That was nothing compared to what we've faced in Summer, and look at me now. Brave the injection for a brighter future!" She raises a fist in triumph and whoops, spurring on others to whoop with her.

Stavros was right. It's better that they've been given the roots in place of the morphine, for although their initial reactions are worse, they're recovering rapidly with renewed strength and energy.

Zannah hands me her used syringes to dispose of once we're finished. "You should rest for an hour or so before leaving for Summer. You look terrible."

I chuckle. "Thanks, Zoe, I can always rely on you for a compliment." The others hand me their used syringes too, and I place them all into a metal container which I seal with a lock. "I don't have time to rest now," I tell her. "I'll rest tonight when this is all over."

Her eyes slant. "At least eat something rich in iron before you go. You want to look strong and fearsome when you see the Queen, not half dead."

"I will."

She gives me a friendly punch to the arm and then takes off, telling me she's going furniture shopping with Slater. I work to keep my expression neutral, but I'm as shocked now as I was last night when she pulled me aside to inform me that she wouldn't be joining us on today's mission. Zannah isn't one to sit out on the action, but she'd given a valid reason as to why she shouldn't come along, and I'd thanked her for putting our team first.

She's made some really mature decisions lately, which have made me proud. While Slater is still one of my least favourite Zadonians, he seems to bring out the responsible side in Zannah.

Now that all the Pastels have recovered from the injection, there's excitement in the air. I watch as one of the males bench presses a young Drake girl, showing off his new strength.

Harlow is on her way back from speaking with the Red and

Peach rescues who hadn't needed the injection, so I meet her halfway and lend her my arm. Even with all the marks marring her face and body, the sight of her still takes my breath away.

"It's so nice to see these Pastels interacting with the Drake families who took them in last night," she says. "Even with the language barrier, they were still able to form a connection. Hopefully by the time the twins are eighteen this will be the norm and there'll be less segregation between the races and colours within the races."

I stop walking and gently tug her about to face me, wrapping my arms around her waist to pull her close. "I hope so too." I pause a beat before adding, "A lot is riding on the Queen's decision today."

Harlow's eyes are round with worry. "I'm afraid she'll say no to your terms, and things will turn ugly. I don't imagine she'll abdicate her throne without a fight."

"Then we negotiate until we come to an understanding. 'Always set the terms higher than you expect the other party to agree upon'. It's what my father always used to say. 'It gives you wriggle room to negotiate'. I'm not going there to start a war; I'm going with the purpose to end the ongoing conflict between our races.

Her grip tightens around me. "Promise me you'll be careful. I don't want to lose you."

I lean down and kiss her forehead. "I promise."

"I'm sorry to break this up," Oscar says, stepping over with Stavros, Woody, Floss and Zavier. "But we should leave. Zannah warned us that the queen doesn't like to be kept waiting."

My concern for Harlow must be evident on my face, because Zavier says, "Don't worry. I'll stay with Harlow while we wait for Sylvie and RJ to arrive."

Sylvie and RJ will be doing several round trips with the warrior sleds to get these rescues safely back to the caves.

"Thank you, Zavier. I appreciate it."

I'd like to give Harlow a proper kiss goodbye, but we have an audience, so I settle for another kiss on her forehead. "Don't overdo yourself," I warn.

"Heed your own advice," she replies.

It's a race against time to make it to the Summer border by nine given how late we left the village, but we intermittently jog and sprint to make it dead on the mark.

Oscar stands on one side of me panting, while Woody stands on my other side breathing evenly. Woody isn't as affected by the long jog here. His long legs and tall lean frame are built for speed and agility.

I keep an impassive face and concentrate on my breathing, trying my best not to let any weakness show. I'm struggling much more than I usually would. Today's blood donation has depleted a considerable amount of my strength—but it was a necessity. If I'd waited for the rescues to return to the caves before offering them the ink, their family members and friends may have talked them out of using it. This way around, their family members and friends will see how strong and healthy they are and will be more likely to accept an injection for themselves come the time I introduce it into the caves.

A line of guards on horsenback descend upon us as soon as we cross the border into Summer and demand we remove our weapons. I was expecting this, and that's precisely why I made all the warriors bring an extra canteen of water. If this meeting turns violent, we have a secret weapon. We can use the water to summon shards.

They lead us over waves of sand to a red dirt road, and eventually to the footbridge of the castle, which stretches above a filthy, stinking moat. There are two guards waiting for us at the open portcullis with their blades out and held at their sides.

"We'll take them from here," the taller of the two says to the horsen guards, and Woody interprets what he's said to the others.

I open my water canteen and pocket the lid as I cross over the bridge, and I watch as the others—except for Woody—follow my lead and do the same. Winter's magic is new to Floss, but Stavros had given her a brief lesson this morning on how to swiftly summon a shard from the moisture around her.

Beyond the opening is an outer court decorated with large Godly statues shooting flames up from their hands in intermittent blasts.

From here, the guards lead us through a large opulent foyer with a grand circular candle lit chandelier, to a set of sandstone passageways lit with tall burning torches. I was already sweating from the jog here, but I'm sweating even more profusely now with the intense heat of the closeup flames. The guards' foul-smelling odour emanates from them in the confined space, a mix of rotten cheese and sour fruit.

Eventually we are led into the throne room, where Queen Sjaan sits tall on a decorative throne, wearing a red gown and a jewel encrusted crown atop her head.

I've seen sketch drawings of Sjaan, but this is the first time I've met her in the flesh. Looking at her now, all I see is the image of Slater with long blood-red hair. Kenneth stands at her side, his face an impassive mask much like my own.

I capture the slightest hint of unease when Sjaan's gaze falls upon Woody, but she doesn't comment. Instead, she redirects her full focus on me.

"I hear Winter has a new Commander," she says, her voice like ice. "Let us hope you are nothing like your late mother, Gods bless her soul."

"We don't believe in Gods," I reply. "And even if we did, I doubt she'd be blessed." A trace of a smile curls Sjaan's lips.

"Azazel has done many evil things," I continue, "much like yourself."

Her lips snap back into a severe line and her face hardens once more. "My son says you have a trade deal proposal. Let us see it."

As I reach into my pocket, the two guards turn their blades on me.

"I'm just getting the scroll," I say, pulling it out slowly.

The shorter of the two guards snatches it from my fingers and takes it to Sjaan. "Your Majesty," he says, bobbing as he hands it to her.

Sjaan curtly dismisses him and unravels the scroll. Her glowing eyes blaze like the surrounding torches as she scans over the terms, and once she's done reading them, those raging eyes lift to meet mine.

"What is the meaning of this?"

Kenneth puts his hand out for the scroll, acting as though he's never seen it before.

I stand tall, unwavering, and with the harshest voice I can muster, I say, "You want a trade deal; those are my terms."

"Your terms are unreasonable," she spits. "Just as your mother's were, and all those ruling before her."

"I'm not asking for an exchange of voltz. I don't want them nor do I need them. I'm also not after your vertic switz ink or jewels. What I want is peace between our races."

She launches up from her throne. "What you want is for me to abdicate my crown!"

"My race has suffered greatly under your rule, just as it suffered under my mother's. I think it's time for the younger generations to take the thrones for a brighter future."

"How dare you come and insult me in my own castle? I'm not afraid of war, and I'm not going down without a fight." Her face whips to the guards. "Seize him!"

My reflexes immediately kick in, and I reach for the canteen, but before my team or the guards are able to react, Woody tosses a handful of seeds from his pocket, which instantly flourish into long vines, winding around the two guards like ropes, binding their hands to their body.

"This is supposed to be a peaceful trade deal! You harm the Zeek Commander, and you'll lose your existing trade deal with the Drakes," Woody declares.

58

TIME TO WORRY

-ZANNAH-

By late afternoon, our hut is fully furnished with an assortment of bright inviting colours. Slater is big on colour I'm learning. I'd planned on having more of an input on our purchases, but despite liking loud colours, the guy doesn't have bad taste. I'd love to sit down, relax together, and enjoy the moment, but I can't. I'm too anxious.

"I thought our team would have been well and truly back by now." My leg bounces on the spot as I glance out the window at the darkening sky. "It's almost time for the predators to come out of hiding. Woody and the warriors might stand a chance against the creatures of the forest, but if they have the rescues with them, they'll be doomed." I suck in an anxious breath as another alarming thought springs to mind. "You don't think your mother would have—"

He shrugs, shaking his head with a helpless look. "I don't know."

I growl in frustration. I feel like kicking myself. *I should have gone with them.*

Slater stares my way, quiet for a moment, and then picks up my sheathed blade and tosses it to me. "Come on. Let's head out and look for them."

Dakari is standing by a yellow guard at the village entrance, his face lined with worry. A glimmer of hope fills his eyes when he sees us coming. "Are you heading out to search for them?"

"We are," I confirm.

He stuffs a rock into my hand. "Good. Take this and let the spirits guide you."

I don't believe what he believes, but I accept the rock and stuff it into my pocket, knowing that it'll bring him some peace in mind.

Slater and I power walk through the trees with him leading the way. He says he has extra sensory perception that allows him to feel certain presences and detect their location. He admits it's not always one hundred percent accurate—especially when his emotions are heightened—but it gets him close enough to what he's looking for, that after a quick search, it can be found. It's a neat ability. *I wish I had it.*

After a long while of little conversation and rapid strides, we hear screams, and accelerate to a sprint.

We eventually stumble upon the group to find three dead fuegors, several other dead luminous creatures, and five wounded Pastels—but the battle isn't over. Woody and Jax are still wrestling with another two fuegors, while the rest are fighting off large luminescent predators I never even knew existed. They have hard, shiny skin with reflective eyes and killer fangs. When Slater jumps in, most of the luminescent creatures scatter, leaving only two remaining. He slices right through their middles in one swift hit, spraying green gooey liquid everywhere. *Gross.*

I head straight for Jax and Woody where they're putting up a solid fight against the ferocious fuegors, but going by the blood coating their skin, they've been badly clawed and bitten.

I charge behind the fuegor that has its teeth sunk into Woody's leg and plunge my blade into its back. The blow isn't deep enough to kill it, but it's painful enough to make it release Woody's leg to howl. Jax has since taken down the other fuegor and seizes this window of opportunity to fire a razor-sharp ice-shard through this fuegor's uptilted neck. Slater and Stavros jump to our aid while Floss and Oscar keep guard over the Pastels who are huddled together as one large shaking mass.

We stand at attention, blades raised and waiting. A moment passes with only small crackles in the distance. "They're still around," Slater says. "But they're retreating."

Jax lowers his blade momentarily to attend to the wounded. One of the Pastels is bleeding profusely from the spot where his arm used to be.

Jax pulls off his shirt and rips it into a long rag to tie around the guy's gushing wound.

Stavros offers to help, but Slater cuts in. "That's not going to save him, he'll still bleed out before we get to the village."

"I can't just leave him like this. I have to do something. I didn't save him from Summer to have him die in Spring."

"I know what to do," Slater says, "but it's going to hurt. Flip him to his side and give him one of those root thingies that you gave to the other rescues."

Without argument, Jax pulls out two nauclea latifolia roots and pops them into the Pastel's mouth, telling him to chew.

Slater passes me his blade. "Hold this tight." He places his hands on both flat sides, and within seconds they burn red, heating up the metal up to a glowing molten. The heat is immense and radiates to my face, but I hold still and grimace, aware of where this plan is leading. This is going to be absolutely horrendous.

Lines of strain mark Slater's face. "I'm going to let go in a second, and the side of this blade needs to be pressed against the

Pastel's open wound. Are you prepared to do this, or do you want Jax to do it? I'd do it myself, but I'd burn the blade's handle."

"I'll do it," I say firmly with a nod.

His eyes dart to Jax's momentarily. "You might want to hold him down securely."

Oscar, slow to the mark, clues on to what's happening, and his face turns green. He looks away and mutters, "*Awww,* Frost no!"

"You need to count to two before pulling back, got it?" Slater says.

I nod once more, and he lets go.

Gasps and cries fill the air as the rescues click on to what's happening. The Zeek with the missing arm quivers and whimpers under Jax's tight grip.

As I press the glowing metal to his raw flesh, a deafening shriek rings through my ears and echoes through the trees. I have killed without remorse, but I feel awful about this. I wish there was another way.

Even after I've pulled back, the Pastel continues to howl and thrash. Jax asks me to hold him while he checks over the others. As I support him against me, the smell of burnt flesh wafts through my nostrils making me feel queasy.

Jax ties scraps of his ripped shirt over the large open wounds of two others. "If we can get them back to the village soon, there's still a chance we can save them." He returns to where I'm holding the Zeek with the missing arm and lifts him up in a cradled position. The Pastel lets out another squeal and passes out, turning to dead weight. Their faces are both ashen. Jax still hasn't recovered from this morning's blood loss, and here he is, losing more from several puncture wounds across his body. He'd also have fuegor venom running through his system. He and Woody both. He can't afford to put his body under any more stress.

"You shouldn't carry him all the way back to the village in your state." I open my arms out. "I'll carry him."

"You're not carrying him," Slater interjects. "I'll carry him." He reaches for the Zeek in Jax's arms, but Jax swivels away rejecting his help.

"The problem is," Jax argues, "these rescues are in far worse condition than yesterday's rescues and most of them need to be carried. It's what's taken us so long to get this far. These Zeeks are too weak to travel the distance, and we don't have enough hands to carry them all. We males have been carrying two at a time and rotating, while Floss has carried one, but it's still not enough. They keep collapsing."

"Fine, but you're not in any condition to carry this one, he's a dead weight. Take one of the kids. Slater will take him."

Jax looks like he wants to argue, but he doesn't. He knows I'm right. He hands the wounded Pastel to Slater and picks up one of the kids instead. I help to lay another of the wounded over Slater's arms, before picking up one for myself.

Slater takes the lead of the group, while the rest of us flank the sides, and Jax guards the rear. It's not a perfect solution, but it'll have to do. Slater says that most things in the forest are afraid of Vallons and would usually stay away, but because there are so many Zeeks, all these creatures are seeing is a mega feast, and one Vallon is not going to be enough to scare them off from the entire group.

We've barely made it a matter of metres before Slater's head whips around, and he shouts, "JAX!"

A roar instantly follows, and I swing around just in time to see a fuegor pounce on Jax, its jaws are open wide exposing killer teeth. Jax immediately tosses the kid forward—into the group—and goes straight for his blade. But before he gets the chance to use it, the fuegor latches onto his shoulder and reefs him back.

My heart lurches. "JAX!"

59

BITING MY NAILS
-HARLOW-

$\mathcal{A}$s the hours pass by to the late afternoon, Zavier and I bite our nails down to the quicks. We haven't seen or heard from anyone regarding the mission, and we're beginning to fear the worst. If the team doesn't get back with the rescues before sundown, they'll be mauled by fuegors. *They might already be dead.* I quiver at this thought. *The Queen might have ordered her guards to kill them on sight.* Queen Sjaan is not like her sons. She has no compassion for us Zeeks.

Zavier voices similar concerns to mine, adding, "I wish Floss hadn't become a warrior. I don't know why she always feels like she's got to prove herself to everyone."

The answer is simple, I think. *Saul is the reason. He's burdened her with the hang-up of never being good enough.*

By the time the sun falls behind the trees I'm virtually hyperventilating. Unable to continue sitting and doing nothing, we ask Minty and Tatum if they'll mind the twins while we see if we can find out what's happening.

"Maybe they're at the fields already, and they've just forgotten to tell us they've returned," I say, grasping at some semblance of hope.

"Floss can be inconsiderate, and I wouldn't put it past her, but we both know Jax would never leave you at home with the kids, worrying. He's far too decent."

If I wasn't so choked up on fear, I'd tease Zavier about this comment. I'm not used to him praising Jax.

Before we get to the fence opening of the village, we hear a commotion of whimpers and cries, along with Dakari's voice and— I gulp—Kenneth's. *Why's Kenneth here? He's not meant to be in the Drake Village.*

I instantly look at Zavier, and our eyes clash wide with alarm. *We run.* When we round the corner we see Kenneth, Dakari and the Drakes on guard duty hauling Pastels out of a horsen cart. They're all in a dreadful state, scuffed and shaken, with a few gravely wounded.

"What's happened?" I glance about frantically. "Where are the warriors?"

Kenneth picks out another two Pastels and places them on the ground. "They're coming."

"But what about fuegors?"

"Slater and Jye are with Woody and your warriors," he says. "They'll be okay."

Dakari leans over the far side of the cart, tilting his ear downward, and as I listen in closely, I hear the rumble of a whisper rise from inside. *Jax?* I race over to see if it's him, but Dakari sees me coming and jumps over the cart to stop me in my tracks.

"You don't want to see him like this. Go home and get the left-over ink and pain killers. We are going to need them."

Tears fill my eyes, and forgetting my manners, I shove him away. "No! I want to see him."

"With all due respect, you should let her go," Zavier insists. "I'll get what you need."

I finish racing to the cart and look down to find Jax, pallid and lying in a pool of blood.

"Harlow." His voice is crackly, and a pained expression over-takes his face. "I didn't want you to see me like this."

I leap into the cart and cup his face. "Don't say that."

I overhear Dakari telling the guard on duty to fetch Roz. "Make sure she brings supplies."

There are three Pastels left in the cart with Jax. My stomach turns when I realise one of them is missing an arm.

Jax lifts his hand and places it over mine. "I'm sorry."

Warm tears streak down my face. "You have nothing to be sorry about. Just stay with me."

"Make sure you get all the critically injured Pastels injected right away and give them priority before attending to me. Promise."

I want to refuse, but I promise.

"I love you." Even through the pain, his eyes twinkle up at me as he says this. "I've always loved you."

"I love you too. Stay with me, please. You need to stay with me."

His eyes flutter closed, and I my heart squeezes into a ball. "Jax!" My voice is verging on hysterical.

Kenneth stands tensely by the cart. "He's not dead—yet. Look at his chest, it's rising and falling."

"What happened?" I ask. "Did your mother—"

"The meeting didn't start out as peacefully as I'd hoped, but an agreement was eventually made and settled upon, and my mother handed over the Pastel slaves without argument. I thought everyone would've already been back here celebrating freedom. It wasn't until I set out to go hunting that I heard the screams." His expression is earnest. "This wasn't a setup."

Eventually Zavier returns with Minty and hands me a pack with the ink, tourniquets, syringes, and nauclea latifolia roots.

Kenneth stares inquisitively at the purple jars of ink. "Is that what I think it is?" He asks.

"Yes." I pass him one of the jars, a tourniquet and a handful of syringes. "Now please, help us." I point to the Zeek with the missing arm. "Starting with him."

Zavier and Minty help too, tending to the other two in the cart, while I tend to Jax. He's lost so much blood. *I'm going to have to inject him too.*

It's lucky Jax taught us all how to give an intravenous injection this morning or I wouldn't have the faintest idea what to do. When the ink hits Jax's system, his body jolts once, but nothing more. He doesn't even rouse. Meanwhile, the Pastels being injected around me scream and thrash like they've been splashed with acid.

Their violent reactions scare the horsens who lurch forward and semi-buck, rocking the cart. The rescues standing outside the cart are sent into a wave of panic, and Dakari and the guards have a tough time trying to settle them down.

I tap Jax's face and then shake his shoulders, desperate for a reaction. After several minutes of seeing no results, I give him another dose, praying for a miracle. Again, it does little. My body shakes as the fear of losing him sets in.

The yellow guard returns with Roz, Sonja, and two Hazels, and together they assist us with the wounded. Roz jumps in the cart and starts with Jax. He would tell her to work on the Pastels first, but since he's passed out, he can't argue and I'm not about to object on his behalf. *He can't die on me! He can't. He can't.* The words repeat in my head in a loop.

By the time the others arrive, leading and carrying the remaining Pastels, I'm a sobbing mess. All the warriors are battered, and Woody's leg is a torn and bleeding mess. Slater is with them, and he, Oscar, and Floss are covered in a strange slime-like goop. I hadn't known Slater and Zannah were going on this mission. Last I'd heard, they were sitting it out.

Zannah lays down the Pastel she's carrying and rushes over. "Is Jax alive?"

"Yes, but only just." My voice quivers. "I've injected him with a double dose of the Purple ink, but it hasn't done much."

"Well inject him with the Red!" Zannah blasts.

"But I've already used the Purple, what happens if mixing the two has a bad reaction?"

"Worse than dying?" If looks could kill, I'd be dead. "Do nothing, and we'll lose him anyway. It's worth the risk. You should've injected him with Red in the first place. He's already a purple, and the ink's made from his blood, of course it'd do next to nothing. How stupid are you?"

Fear sparks inside me, drowning out Zannah's insult. I'm so terrified of making the wrong choice, I don't know what to do from here. Jax can't die.

Stavros is speaking with Roz, but he pauses mid conversation to tell Zannah to watch her mouth.

Slater steps across to referee and my eyes lift to meet his, pleading for assurance. "Will using both inks kill him?" I ask. I don't know why I'm looking to him for answers, especially when it comes to Jax's life, but I'm desperate.

He shrugs, his usual look of resentment—generally reserved for me and Jax—replaced with worry. "I honestly don't know."

My eyes flick to Kenneth next, "What do you think?"

"I've never seen Purple ink before. I have no idea how it works."

Stavros finishes speaking with Roz and then jumps into the cart beside me. He puts a blood smeared hand on my shoulder and squeezes compassionately. "Roz says his body is shutting down. He's lost too much blood. Zannah's right. We need to take the risk and inject him with the red ink before it's too late." He rummages through the pack, pulling out the jar of red glowing liquid. "Do you want to do it, or would you prefer me to?"

My hands are shaking too hard to do anything. "You do it," I reply.

There's only us and Jax in the cart. The other wounded have since been carried off to more comfortable locations. Stavros gets me to move to the other side of the cart before giving the injection, and it's a good thing he does, because this time Jax reacts ultra-violently, giving Stavros a few hard knocks before smashing a hole right through the cart.

The horsens get spooked and charge ahead, throwing Stavros on top of me.

Kenneth and Slater rush to stop and settle them, and as soon as the cart stops moving, Stavros and I right ourselves and leap to Jax's side.

I glance at his face first, then his chest. It's still, lifeless. "He's not breathing!"

"Quick, breathe into his mouth!" Stavros straddles him, and once I've given my breath, he commences with compressions.

We do three full rounds to no avail.

Sphinx releases a blood-curdling howl in the distance, furthering my state of panic.

"It's not working." Salty tears dribble into my mouth. "It's not… I can't… What do we do?" My mind's not firing right. I'm breaking into hysteria.

"Zap him," Slater shouts. "Use your power and zap his chest."

Panicked and desperate, I shove Stavros out of the way and slam my hands to Jax's chest while summoning the elements around me.

The electricity leaves them with a flash of light and Jax's body jolts upright, gasping in a breath.

His eyes meet mine, wide and unseeing, appearing like pools of purple and red swirling resin.

"Jax!"

His eyes flicker, and then he falls flat on his back again.

"No!" I throw myself on top of him, believing I've killed him, but then I feel the rise and fall of his chest. *He's alive.*

60

GETTING BY

-HARLOW-

It's been a rough few days of pain, exhaustion, and very little sleep as I juggle my time between tending to Jax and caring for the twins. Jax has been drifting in and out of consciousness. Each time he wakes, he's delirious. He calls out names and thrashes wildly, as though he's being injected with the ink all over again, and a couple of times he's projectile vomited.

It's a good thing I have friends now, because I need them. They've all kindly offered to chip in with the twins outside of their work hours. Acacia would do more for me during the day hours, if I let her, but I feel guilty dumping the twins on her when she already has a baby of her own to care for.

Surprisingly, Slater—as I've now been calling him—has pushed his resentment aside and taken the kids for a few hours each morning to give me time to rest. *Not that I've ever used the time to rest!*

I thanked him for his part in helping me to save Jax, and he'd accepted my gratitude without a snarky remark. He seems changed for the better since that awful day, or perhaps it's Zannah who's having a positive effect on him. He mentions her sometimes and smiles. Floss was right when she said they were better suited. Slater has a lot of love to give and there is plenty of good in him, but he needs a fierce woman like Zannah to keep his Hyde side in check.

I've seen a lot of Zavier, Floss, Minty, and Tatum during the evenings, and Floss seems changed for the better too. She's been much warmer to me, verging on friendly at times, and seems more content within herself and her relationship with Zavier. I think her new colouring has helped give her confidence. She's always had a hang-up about being a Magenta.

Slater arrives at seven to pick up the kids and after shouldering the pack, followed by the harness, I help to strap the kids to him. Lyla is a mini-me, pale skinned with red hair and a red shimmer. The only feature she inherited off Slater is his swirling irises. Axel, on the other hand, has a mix of both of us. He's dark skinned with irises like Slater, but his features are angelic, and he has a red shimmer.

"By the way," I say, keeping my eyes lowered. "I don't know what you've told Zannah about Axel being…well…um, Lucas, but I haven't told Jax anything. He knows what happened to me in my previous life, and I don't want him to have any preconceived hatred towards our son. I want him to love him."

"Do you love him?" He bristles and then adds, "Axel, I mean."

"I do. I've let my resentment go."

"That's good, I'm glad." His eyes meet mine. "And for the record, I haven't said anything. I've been trying to let go of the past and move forward. Axel's our son, and I love him as our son."

Slater's eyes are still on me, clearly thinking, so I change the subject to ease the awkwardness. "Stavros says Kenneth and Jye have swung by the village every evening since the incident, asking for an update on Jax, Woody, and the wounded rescues. Have you seen them? Apparently, Kenneth was asking after you too."

"We caught up last night. He told me that he and Dakari have formed a personal alliance, and there's a promise of a better relationship between our races once he comes into power. He also said he was hoping to get a chance to meet our kids at some stage. I think he's curious about them. They're the first of their kind as far as he's aware. I told him I'd talk to you about it."

"I'm fine with him meeting them."

I trust Kenneth. He's the Jax of Summer. He's working under the nose of his mother, striving for equality within his own race, while trying to form stronger relationships with both the Zeeks and Drakes for the future. I believe he's a good Vallon with good morals.

Slater leaves with the kids, and I head into the room to tend to Jax's wounds. As I'm redressing one of the deeper lacerations on his chest, his eyes flutter open and I jump back, waiting for him to start thrashing. He doesn't move. Instead, he just stares my way, wide eyed, seemingly confused.

The way Slater's irises swirled like fiery pools of molten lava had creeped me out to start with, but the way Jax's swirl metallic violet and red looks magical. His hair is different too. It used to be the colour of blackberries, but now there are highlights of cherry-black mixed through his dreads. It's a nice combination, and I'm looking forward to the time when I can run my hands through them. Even though we're together in theory, we haven't had any *proper* time together; we've still never even kissed. He's kissed my cheeks and my forehead, but never my lips. I was sore and sorry for myself after having the kids, and he's been slipping in and out of consciousness since the rescue mission.

His eyes leave mine to dart around the room, and he jolts up, wincing. "How long have I been out?"

My heart flutters. *He's coherent.* "A few days."

His eyes continue scanning his surroundings a moment longer

before taking in my position. "You're afraid." He swallows. "I'm sorry, have I—"

I peel myself away from the wall and move closer. "Please, don't apologise. You haven't been yourself. You've been hallucinating from the venom."

His brows dip. "Where are the others? Did they make it back?"

"Everyone's safe. All of the Pastels were injected and the unharmed Pastels have since been returned to the caves. As for the ones who were attacked by the fuegor, they're improving by the day."

"I feel responsible," he admits. "I should've brought the leftover ink with me, but I was worried we'd be searched by the guards on arrival. I was too busy worrying about the meeting and the handover itself to consider that I could've easily left a pack of supplies close by."

"None of us knew how weak those rescues would be. We all presumed they'd be in a similar condition to the others. Stavros told me what you did to save Alistair. He would've been dragged off and killed if you hadn't jumped in."

"He lost an arm."

"He would have lost his life." I step to the bed and wrap my arms around him. "You did it, Jax. You saved them. Most of them are back in the caves with their families right now."

He draws back. "I smell terrible."

"I don't care," I say, holding on. "I'm just glad you're alive and awake."

Jax doesn't let me hug him for long. He seems embarrassed and insists on having a wash. I try to help him up, but he doesn't let me, telling me that I'm not supposed to be doing anything strenuous after my surgery.

While he's gone, I freshen up the bedding and give everything a wipe over, as to make him feel more comfortable when he returns.

I'm just about to take the old bedding out to wash, when he steps back into the room, hair dripping, with knitted brows. "What happened to me? My eyes, they're strange."

I know he knows the answer, but still I place the bedding down and say, "Why don't you lay back down and I'll tell you exactly what happened."

"I can't, there are too many things I need to do. I want to see the kids and check up on the wounded rescues."

"Slater has the kids. Please, lie a moment. I'll lie with you."

He gives in at this, and lies back down, allowing me to curl up next to him. I'm careful not to touch any of his wounds. He asks me questions about what happened, and I tell him everything I know, as well as what I've been told by Floss, Stavros, and Slater.

He remembers Kenneth coming to his aid and me seeing him in the cart, but he says everything after that is hazy. I fill in the gaps, making sure to tell him about the positive shift regarding Dakari and Kenneth's relationship.

He winces as he rolls to his side to face me. "Are you upset?" he asks, lacing his fingers with mine.

"About what?"

"You told me once not to use the ink because I'd lose the 'beautiful colour' of my eyes."

"You haven't lost the beautiful colour; you've gained a colour. And I'll take the added red over losing you."

"I meant what I said that day in the cart." He lets out a pained breath. "I love you, and I feel like I haven't really had the chance—"

"I love you too." Not willing to waste another moment dreaming about it, I lean in and press my lips to his. My insides flutter nervously. I'm afraid he'll draw back on me, like he did the night of the mask festival, but he doesn't. His lips respond instantly to mine —warm, supple, and filled with desire. Pleasurable shivers run through me as our kiss intensifies, and I'm finally able to run my hand through his dreads.

He wraps his strong arm around me, attempting to pull me in closer, but the forced movement is all too much in our current states, and we both draw back wincing.

"I'm sorry." His face reddens "This isn't exactly how I imagined our first kiss would be."

"Don't be sorry. It was perfect."

"Perfectly painful." He chuckles and runs his finger softly along my cheek. "I can't wait for things to finally settle down so that I can spend more quality time with you."

"I can't wait for that either."

We continue to snuggle and chat until Slater returns with the twins. Jax is delighted to see them and devotes another few hours explicitly to the three of us, before slipping into Commander mode.

61

COMMANDER MODE

-JAX-

I force myself to leave an enjoyable afternoon with Harlow and the twins to check in with the Pastels who were attacked by the fuegor. My stomach turns when I see Alistair and I share my deepest sympathies with him for the loss of his arm. He tells me he would've willingly forgone both of his arms if it meant being away from Summer and the Queen's guards, but regardless, I feel as if I failed him. I was supposed to protect him and these other wounded Pastels, and escort them safely back to a better life. Instead, I put them in harm's way.

As the evening rolls around, I gather all the warriors and

together we make our way to Dakari's hut. I plan on holding a meeting which includes Kenneth. I've been told he's stopped in every evening since the fuegor incident to check on the wounded, and I feel we have a lot to discuss.

The meeting with his mother, Queen Sjaan, started out hostile, but we were finally able to come to an agreement. Sjaan refused to abdicate her throne—as I suspected she would—but agreed to put Kenneth in charge of all foreign affairs and trading, as well as agreeing to additional rules which had already been written into the trade deal agreement:

- *No Red guards are allowed to cross the Winter border under any circumstances.*
- *No Zeeks are to be captured and used for slaves.*
- *If any of these rules are violated, the trade deal becomes null and void.*

Kenneth is in charge of recruiting the fishermen and is to see to it no Zeeks are harmed by any fishermen or they'll face execution.

The outcome isn't perfect, but it's a start in the right direction. I believe when Kenneth comes into power, the relationship between our races will change dramatically for the better.

62

BACK TO THE CAVES

-HARLOW-

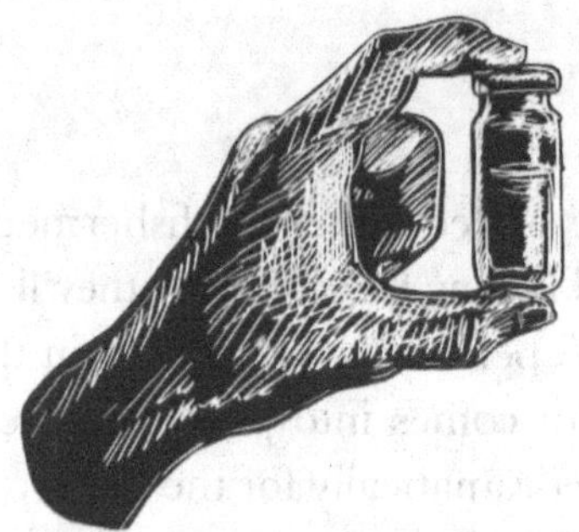

It's only been two days since Jax fully regained consciousness, yet, in that time a lot has happened, and a lot has been arranged.

Jax felt it was too risky to produce any more ink from his blood because of the two contrasting inks running through his system, so he and Oscar went back to the caves yesterday to ask Kieran if he'd be willing to donate his blood to the cause.

Jax asked that the twins and I stay and wait until lunchtime the next day before joining him—which is today. He said he'd prefer us to come out with Kenneth and Jacinta for the peaceful trade deal announcement, that way he could address all things Vallon, together.

I wonder what Zeeks are saying about his swirling irises.

Oscar and RJ arrive early to give me the low down on what's happened inside the caves so far and then help carry my bags to the sleds. Apparently, Lexan agreed to be a test subject for the new ink made from Kieran's blood, which turned out to be just as effective and efficient. *Yay!*

Slater, being a proud dad, helps me carry out the twins so he can be around for the introduction to their aunt and uncle.

When Kenneth and Jacinta arrive, my blood stills. I've never met Jacinta, but Slater said that she and Raven were 'the best of friends'. Thankfully, Jacinta mustn't hold me responsible for what happened to Raven, because her greeting is warm, and she gushes over the twins. She's nothing like Raven. She's shorter—although she still towers over me—and curvier with ringlet hair. Not to mention, she has a much better grasp on the Zeek language.

I hand her Axel and she rocks him gently. "Look at his sweet little features," she says and then looks up at me. "I can see a lot of you in him."

Kenneth runs the back of his finger along Lyla's cheek. "I'm so glad they survived the early delivery."

We stand around and chat. However, when Woody arrives, Oscar impatiently announces, "It's time to leave."

I hop into the front of the sled next to him, while Kenneth and Jacinta pile into the back with a twin in each arm.

"Keep them safe," Slater says, his eyes darting between all of us in warning.

Kenneth hands Lyla back to me. "We will."

Woody slips into the sled with RJ, taking the back bench seat and dangling his super long legs over the front seat. These sleds were not made for nine-foot-tall men.

"Back to the caves," Oscar calls out, sounding as unenthusiastic as I feel.

I'm not excited about returning to Winter's caves. The mere thought of it has me feeling nauseous. I'd much rather stay in

Spring where all my friends are, but I'd follow Jax into the pits of hell if that's where he needed to be.

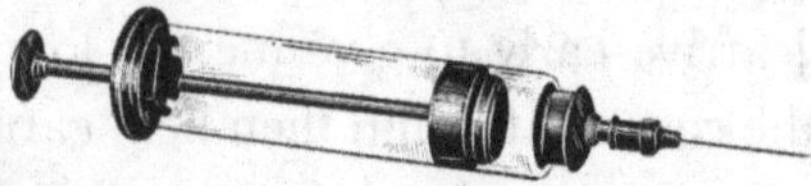

When we pull into the warrior cavern, we are met by a dozen armed warriors. They eye Kenneth and Jacinta with mistrust, and me and my babies with disgust. I quiver, terrified that Jax has made a huge mistake involving us all in his announcement.

Regardless of their obvious condemnation, the guards perform their duty and escort us all to the grand chamber where Jax and Kieran have Zeeks of all colours and status gathered and waiting. Whispers and gasps fill the space as we make our way to the front and take our positions next to them. I glance at Jacinta to make sure she has a secure grip on Axel.

Several of the injected rescues sit in the front row, clearly so Jax can call on them to show off the physical gains they've obtained by using the ink.

Jax steps forward and after spilling out a bunch of formalities and offering apologies for his long absence, he boldly makes the announcement about the new peaceful trade agreement he's made with the Vallons, then reads the signed document in full for everyone to hear. More gasps fill the chamber, and numerous questions and arguments are called out by members of the audience. Soon fingers point in my direction, with voices shouting, "What's her story? Why is *she* still alive?" and, "Show us the baby."

A few small objects are pegged at me, and they hit my skin with a sting. My throat closes, and I turn my back to the audience, holding Lyla tight to my chest and protecting her like a shield.

Jax throws himself in front of me. "Enough!" he shouts, the growl of his voice ricocheting loudly off the chamber walls. "The next Zeek to throw an object in this direction will be spending the night in the cell." The chamber falls quiet, and Jax continues. "As you can see by Harlow's colouring, she was never pregnant to me.

She was pregnant to a Vallon, a Vallon who died protecting her and their unborn children." Gasps and chatter start up again, but Jax raises his voice demanding their attention. "Harlow didn't let colour or race define who she loved and cared for. She loved Alex even though he was a Red and a Vallon, and he loved her even though she was a Pastel and a Zeek. Their indiscriminating natures have brought about a much-needed change we should all embrace. Because of their shared love, Harlow has given birth to a set of twins who are special, not only because they have unique special powers, but because they are the symbol of a new beginning for all races on Zadok. It's time we Zadonians unite and learn to love and accept each other no matter our colour or race."

Woody and Kenneth step up beside Jax as he says this, showing a sign of unity, while Kieran, Oscar, and RJ stand tall behind them, showing their support.

"The Drakes are not segregated by colour status. They live in harmony with one another, which is exactly what I want for our colony. I want peace and harmony between the colours." He pauses a moment and then adds, "This brings me to my next announcement. With the help of a Vallon, I have created a new ink, similar to the vertic switz ink, and I plan to make it available to all Pastels."

I glance over my shoulder and watch as Jax beckons the injected rescues from the front row to come and stand before everyone.

"Take a look at these Pastels. They have been injected with the new ink. They have gone from being weak and sickly to becoming strong and powerful, just like Magentas and Purples."

There's tension in the air with mixed reactions. Some Purples and Magentas scream and curse, while others "ooh" and "ahh" with piqued curiosity. One Pastel bravely stands to applaud, prompting others to follow, and soon the chamber becomes so noisy Lyla starts to cry.

"Shhh," I whisper. "It's okay." Although I'm sure she can feel the nervous tension emanating from my body.

Rae and her team fight their way to the front of the crowd.

"Don't buy into this nonsense," she shouts. "These Pastels might have been modified to appear stronger, but it's all a façade, they are still genetically flawed. They will continue to breed frail children and weaken our race!"

A few Purples and Magentas jump on board with this argument, causing some of the braver Pastels to retaliate. Several punches are thrown, followed by yelling and screaming. A group of warriors race to break it up and find themselves caught in an eruption of chaos.

"You and Jacinta should leave," Jax says to Kenneth while the crowd grows wild. "And take Harlow and the twins back with you for now. I want them safe until I can contain everyone."

I turn back as Jax says this, my heart pounding. "I don't want to leave you," I say.

Warriors charge through the crowd with their blades raised, warning everyone to quieten down, and Oscar and Kieran move to the front, blocking me and Jax from the boisterous audience.

"This is only temporary. I'll bring you back, I promise." Jax pulls me to him and kisses me so deeply, and passionately, that my knees grow weak. "I love you. Now please, go with Kenneth and Jacinta. I'll have my warriors escort you back to the sleds."

"I'm staying," Kenneth argues, "I'm not leaving you in the midst of a riot." His eyes flick to Jacinta's. "Help get Harlow and the twins safely back to the Drake village, and then when you get back to Summer, tell my mother I'm away handling foreign affairs and will be returning shortly."

Jax steps to the front and signals some guards across, asking them to escort Jacinta and me back to the warrior cavern. "RJ," he calls as an afterthought. "I want you to go with them and stay with Harlow and the twins until it's safe for you all to return."

A wave of panic passes over me as we are led away, and I consider turning back, but RJ puts his hand on my shoulder and says, "You must leave. Don't worry, Jax is going to be okay. This colony will learn to see reason."

LINKING CEREMONY

-HARLOW-

(A month later)

I hear Sphinx howl with excitement in the distance, and I'm out the door and down the ladder as fast as my legs will carry me. While Jax has sent me many letters this past month filling me in on the unruly goings on in the caves, I haven't seen him in the flesh since the day of his big announcements, and I've been missing him terribly. I wanted to go back to the caves and join him, but RJ warned me against the idea. He said the colony wasn't ready for me and the twins just yet, but in time they'd come to see us as a symbol of unity, and they'd look up to us.

RJ has stayed in Spring with me this whole time, helping me with the twins. His ongoing rambling has been quite effective at sending the babies to sleep of a night. It blows my mind how much knowledge he has, and how he manages to retain it all. I swear he has more facts inside that brain of his than an encyclopaedia.

"Jax!" I squeal, jumping into his arms. "I can't believe you're here."

"I've missed your pretty face." He swings me around in a circle, and that's when I notice my mum and Lexan trailing behind him, along with Oscar.

"What's going on?" I ask, frowning suddenly. "Why are my mum and Lexan here?"

Jax places me down and cups my face with his hands. "Things have finally settled down in the colony, so I thought we ought to celebrate with a linking ceremony."

"What?" I'm so stunned I nearly fall backwards. "W…where? When?"

"Here… This afternoon," Jax answers, and my insides light up with excitement. "I had Sonja and Woody prepare the field for tonight's festivities, and I put Acacia in charge of finding you a dress." His eyes flick to my mother and Lexan, and he gives me a "don't be mad," look. "I know you don't have a great relationship with your parents, especially your mum, but a lot has changed, and I thought you might like to have them here for the ceremony."

I was aware that my mother had left Saul and moved in with Lexan because Jax had written it in his last letter to me. He'd said as soon as he abolished the law of "no inter-colour relationships", Krista and Lexan made their relationship official.

I'd showed Floss the letter, and she'd elbowed me playfully, saying, "I'm sure that rose a few brows, especially with certain Zeeks who've remained sceptical of our heritage."

In that same letter, Jax had also mentioned that Rae was leading a pack of rebels to fight against the new integration laws, but after a sad attempt at a riot, which was squashed by the majority in favour of the new laws, she and her pack found themselves locked in the cells.

"I thought I was supposed to return to you…" I say in confusion. "That we'd be getting linked in the caves."

He arches a dubious brow. "Is that what you would have preferred?"

I shake my head. "No. I'd much prefer to stay and have the ceremony here…but you need to be—"

"I have some news," he says, taking my hands in his. "I've appointed Kieran as Second-in-Command. He will be in charge of all cave affairs, while I'll be primarily involved in all foreign affairs and trading."

My cheeks heat. "I'm sorry, but I'm not entirely sure what this means."

"It means you and I don't have to live in the caves. We can remain here where you're happy. We'll need to visit the caves on a regular basis to make sure everything is running smoothly, but this will be our permanent home."

Overwhelmed with excitement, I throw my arms around him and squeeze him tightly. "Thank you," I say. "I can't believe it. This is a dream come true."

Visions of Lyla and Axel attending school with Atohi and the Drake children of village flitter through my mind, and I'm filled with a sense of happiness and warmth.

"Hey, Baby Girl," my mother says as she and Lexan approach, and I detect an anxious undertone to her voice. I hate it when she refers to me endearingly, like we're close. It feels so superficial.

I draw back from Jax and acknowledge them both with a short and awkward, "Hello."

"I hear congratulations are in order," my mother adds, and then embraces me, making me tense up. "I'm sorry for not being there for you and Floss when you needed me most." Her voice wobbles and her arms start to shake. "I've made a lot of terrible mistakes as a parent."

"Make that both of us," Lexan chimes in, placing a warm hand on my back.

It's going to take more than a simple apology for them to earn my forgiveness, but I'm willing to make nice for the sake of the twins. I'd like them to have a relationship with their grandparents.

"Would you like to meet the twins?" I ask, extending an olive branch.

My mother nods eagerly and takes Lexan by the hand—*my dad by the hand.*

It's still too weird for me to think of Lexan as my dad.

"We would love to."

I lead them to our hut while Jax fetches Zavier and Floss so that they can be a part of this big "family" moment.

Once inside the hut, I lead them to the twins' nursery where I hand Axel to my mum and Lyla to Lexan.

"She's beautiful, Harlow," Lexan says, tears glistening in his eyes. "She looks just like you."

"You mean she looks just like me," Floss stirs as she enters. "Minus the colouring and freaky eyes, of course."

She greets our parents with much more warmth than I did, but in all fairness, they've done more for her than they've ever done for me.

Lexan uses his free arm to give Zavier a fatherly hug. "I've missed you, Kid. Life in the caves has been pretty dull without you."

Zavier's eyes are glistening too. "I've missed you too, Old Man."

Minty and Tatum come over to join us, so we move our little gathering to the common area.

It doesn't take long for word to pass around and soon, all of our neighbours are over, wanting to catch up on all the gossip from inside the caves.

Kiyra and Alistair are the only two rescues who've elected to remain in Spring. Woody took Kiyra in the night she was rescued from Summer, and right away she'd requested to stay on a permanent basis. She was supposed to move into our hut once all the rescued were returned to the caves, but when Woody came back from the final mission wounded, she'd chosen to stay put and look after him. The two have grown rather cosy ever since.

I'd wondered if Dakari would have a problem with his own son entering into an interracial relationship, but he seems to be accepting of the idea, which makes me respect him all the more. Times are certainly changing, that's for sure.

Boshell's twins and Koby arrive, bringing Alistair an arm they've made for him to wear to tonight's ceremony. They'd carved it from a fallen tree branch they'd found, telling him he can strap it to himself so he has two arms again. Will and Koby complain that it looked much cooler before Daisy ruined it by sticking the flowers on.

"I think it looks perfect, thank you," Alistair says.

"The kids got a little over excited after they'd finished helping me make the arch for Jax and Harlow's linking ceremony," Boshell tells him.

"Did everyone here know about the ceremony, bar me?" I ask, surprised.

Their bright eyed, tight-lipped responses say it all.

I sit and chat with everyone for an hour before Acacia whisks me away to get me dressed and ready for tonight's linking ceremony.

"How could you keep this from me?" I ask, as she weaves a colourful array of luminescent flowers through my dreads.

She chuckles and lowers her face next to mine, meeting my gaze in the reflection of the mirror. "If I'd told you, it wouldn't be a surprise now, would it?"

As the sun sets, casting an array of pinks and oranges in the sky, Sienna and Sylus lead me and Zavier to the field on horseback. Jax really did let everyone in on his big secret. He's gone all out.

The hippy style dress Acacia chose for me is a beautiful jade colour that perfectly matches the leaf earrings she and Daisy designed to go with it.

Acacia had said, "I chose jade in honour of your human sister Jade. This way, you'll have a piece of her with you during the ceremony."

Zavier glances across at me and smiles. "You look stunning," he says. "I'm so happy for you, Harlow."

Jax had sent Zavier a letter asking if he'd do the honour of giving me away. I'm so glad he did. It's exactly what I would've chosen.

My breath hitches when we get to the field. All the firepits are lit and burning brightly, and a path of luminous flower petals have been scattered between two long rows of moss-covered logs. The sky above glimmers with glow flies, and all attending Drakes have painted themselves with multi-coloured luminescent paint made from the glowing flora of the village.

My eyes go straight to Jax standing in front of the wooden twined arch Boshell and the kids made. My cheeks heat at the sight of him. He looks so handsome dressed bohemian formal. I can tell Acacia chose his outfit. It's different to what I'm used to seeing him in, but I like it. Sphinx stands at his side with a purple glowing symbol on his head, which I'm guessing would've been drawn by Daisy. Stavros and Oscar stand on the right side of the arch with Rebel and Lucy at their sides, and to the left stand Acacia, Floss, and Daisy. All three girls are dressed in yellow, Acacia's favourite colour, with yellow and purple flowers woven in their hair.

The beat of music fills the air as Sienna and Sylus help Zavier and I to dismount. Drakes from all over tap on their drums and pluck the strings of their handmade instruments, creating a festive and joyful sound.

While Zavier leads me down the aisle between the moss-covered logs, the flower petals around us lift and swirl and my dreadlocks flow softly behind me in the breeze. My eyes snap to Acacia's, and she winks. She's using her air magic to create a mystical atmosphere.

We pass Slater and Zannah, sitting with Kenneth and Jacinta towards the back. Our twins have helped break down the barriers between the brothers, just as they have with me and Floss.

Zannah's hair is a deeper shade of red than mine these days; it's blood-red like Raven's was. I'm glad they came. I wasn't sure if I'd see them here or not.

I smile and wave to all my friends and neighbours as I pass.

Everyone has put in so much effort for tonight's surprise celebration; it's hard to believe how much they've all achieved without my knowledge.

Minty and Tatum sit in the front row with Axel and Lyla, and they hold them up as I pass, allowing me to blow them a kiss each.

When we get to where Jax is standing, Zavier gives me a kiss on the cheek and then offers me over. Jax takes my hands, gives them a light squeeze and smiles. "You look beautiful."

Standing behind Jax beneath the wooden twined arch is Dakari in his colourful headdress and full tribal gear.

The music quietens as Dakari addresses the guests. He gives a speech in Zeek followed by Drake, about the union of two people who love one another and the obstacles they can overcome. Jax and I have written our own vows, and Dakari asks us to read them to one another. My hands shake as I share my inner feelings and promises. Jax's vows are more poetic than mine, but he's had much more time to prepare. When we're done offering our commitment to one another, Dakari pulls a handful of seeds from his pocket and sprinkles them at our feet. They instantly sprout into long vines and wrap around us, binding us together.

"May the Zeek stars shine over you, and may the Drake spirits bless you," Dakari says followed by, "You are bound for life by the power of the vines. Hulle is gebind!"

The Drakes roar and cheer, and leaves fly everywhere as the trees alongside the field sway under their power. Jax presses his warm lips against mine and a swirl of heat stirs in my belly. *We're linked.*

When the ceremony finishes, the true Drake festivities begin. Some carry the logs over to the firepits to sit on and watch the performances, while others opt for picnic blankets.

I spot Sylus, Sienna, and Jye sitting on a blanket with a peach male Zeek I've never met before, so I stop to introduce myself.

"I'm Evan, Sienna's partner," he says, catching me off guard.

"Evan's been living with me since the Vallon ink trials," Sienna explains. "He says he's happy to remain hidden away with me in Summer, but I don't think it's fair. I've spoken to Dakari about accepting us into his village until such time as Kenneth gets his mother to come around, or she dies, and he comes into power. I'd like to be able to go out and do things together, like other couples do."

"Will you miss the open-air circus and trick riding?" I ask.

"The circus, no, the trick riding, yes, but I've also asked if I can keep my horsen Blaze with me. Dakari is considering it."

"Thank you for leading me to the ceremony on Blaze," I say. "It was a wonderful experience. I'm sure you'll be very popular with the Drake children if Dakari allows him to stay."

I leave their blanket to chat with Zavier, Floss, Minty, and Tatum before settling on a blanket beside Jax—next to Stavros and Acacia.

Slater has the twins laid out on a blanket he's sharing with Zannah, Kenneth, and Jacinta, so I leave them be.

The Drakes entertain us with their performances, keeping everyone captivated. At one stage they invite Jax and me to join in, and it's both exciting and nerve-wracking all at once. Their songs and stories, mixed with Spring magic, are absolutely breathtaking. Drake culture is much more festive than Zeek culture. The way they can move nature's objects and make plants grow spontaneously out of nowhere still completely astounds me.

Jax interprets for me just like last time, bringing meaning to their words and actions. I can't wait until I have a better grasp of the Drake language.

When the festivities wind up, I stand to fetch the twins from Slater, but Jax tugs my hand bringing me down on his lap.

"Leave them," he says, grinning at me like he's got another secret up his sleeve. "I've spoken to Zannah. She and Slater are keeping the twins tonight. You and I have somewhere else to be."

"We do?"

"We do."

My eyes dart in Zannah's direction. "And Zannah's honestly okay with this?"

"It'll do her a world of good," Stavros cuts in.

After giving Acacia a big hug and thank you, Jax takes my hand

and leads me back to the village, heading in the opposite direction of our hut. He stops at a ladder which connects to one of the many suspension bridges that span above us like an intricate web.

My heart leaps excitedly. "Where are we going?"

I've never walked along the suspension bridges or seen inside any of the tree houses, although I've always wanted to.

"Somewhere special, just for the two of us."

The suspension bridges are rockier under foot than I'd imagined, but Jax wraps his arm around me, steadying me, as he points out different landmarks along the way. The view from up here is stunning. Natural fairy lights glimmer around us, and the luminous gardens below glow brightly with colour.

We cross several bridges before Jax points to a small tree house emitting a soft yellow glow from its windows. "That one there is ours for tonight."

"Really?"

"Really."

My whole face lights up as I step inside the quaint treehouse to find a beautiful handmade wooden bed surrounded by greenery, flowers, and soft glowing candles.

Jax slides his warm and loving arms around me, and my skin sparks with heat. "Do you hear that?"

I cock my head to listen. "Hear what?"

"Precisely." He smiles in a way that makes my insides gooey. "No chaos, no fighting, and no crying babies. Tonight's just about you and me."

His soft lips press against mine, and I melt into them, breathing in the scent of woodfire on his skin. I've been dreaming about this very moment for months, and now that it's finally happening, I'm quivering with nerves. I've never felt so loved. Jax treats me and the twins like we're the centre of his universe.

He draws back to scoop me up and carry me to the bed where our lips meet again, hungry and full of passion. I slide my hands up his shirt, trailing my fingers over his ripped abs, as I work my way up to his chest. He levers up, tugging his shirt fully off to reveal a rock-hard torso which shimmers magically in the flickering candlelight. *God damn he's magnificent.* I raise my arms, and he slides my dress up and over my head, tossing it to the floor.

His eyes roam over me, drinking me in, and I blush. "You're so beautiful," he says, lowering his body back to mine—bringing us skin to skin.

His hands skim from my shoulder down my sides seeking and caressing places that have me jolting with pleasure. His lips graze my neck and then trail leisurely down my body tracing every curve and scar. I shiver involuntarily with delight.

"I feel so lucky." My words come out huskily. "You could've had anyone, yet you've chosen me."

His lips ascend my body to my face. "I'm the lucky one."

I duck my head and run my tongue along the dip of his collar bone. He tastes of salt and smoke.

His fingers twine around my dreadlocks and he gently tugs me back to meet his loving gaze. "Never underestimate yourself," he says tenderly sweeping a stray dreadlock from my face. "If it wasn't for your open-mindedness, we wouldn't be celebrating with mixed colours and races. You made this happen."

"We made this happen."

His lips claim mine again, gentle and teasing at first, before pressing deeper with a sense of urgency and passion.

I wrap my legs around his waist and together we find our rhythm, making it impossible to tell where my body ends and his begins. Pleasure consumes every piece of me and washes away any worries and insecurities lurking in the back of my mind.

"I really love you, Jax", I whisper, gasping.

"I really love you, too", he says before silencing me with another kiss.

THE END

Thank you for reading The Zadok Series.
If you enjoyed this series please consider leaving a rating and/or review on Goodreads, Amazon, social media, or any of the retailers websites. A simple review goes a long way, and I enjoy receiving feedback.

ABOUT THE AUTHOR

Born in Queensland, Australia, 1984, Nikki Minty rose into this
world with a wild imagination. As a young girl, she would lay in bed
with her family of a night, co-telling stories about the big bad wolf
and his turbulent adventures.

9 780064 505626